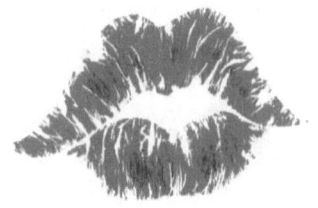

EVERNIGHT PUBLISHING ®

www.evernightpublishing.com

Copyright© 2022

Allegra Grey and Emily Sloan

Editor: Audrey Bobak

Cover Art: Jay Aheer

ISBN: 978-0-3695-0605-4

INTO THE STORM

DEDICATION

For everyone who has struggled the last couple years, and hasn't always managed to be kind or nice when they're tired, scared, or grieving.

INTO THE STORM

INTO THE STORM

Storm Crows MC, 2

Allegra Grey and Emily Sloan

Copyright © 2022

Prologue
Jenna

"One last fight, mi *cielito*." The honey-soft whisper melted her resolve. So did the gentle kiss that followed, and the next. Auggie held her tight, like he knew the exact amount of pressure to keep her from falling apart. She inhaled his scent: detergent, soap, a hint of sweat from his warm-ups—much better than the stale air around them. Her head rested on his shoulder, and she shifted her weight to straddle his hips despite the awkward chair they occupied. One more half-broken relic in a forgotten mansion full of them.

"Just this one. Then it's done." She repeated the phrase she'd turned into a mantra the last two weeks. He stroked her hair and chuckled, the sound reverberating in her ear and the still basement. Despite the old studio's soundproofing, the sounds of a gathering party above crept through the open door and sped up her heartbeat. Her fingers curled into his arm.

"It's done," he echoed in a velvet whisper. "Take the money, get the gym set up. Let Carlos run it a few weeks while you and I head to some islands where they don't care too much 'bout clothes and got a shitload of booze..." His hand slid down her back, cradling her waist. "See 'bout getting a family started, yeah?"

She laughed, the sounds above forgotten. "Maybe in a year or two, caveman. I'm not having your kids 'til I'm out of school."

"Then we practice." He nuzzled her hair, tightening his grip. "So much practice, I may have to carry you to your classes next fall."

"That's what online is for." She put her lips to his, moaning as he slid one hand up her torso, almost but not quite touching her breast. *Damn it*. "Auggie, please..."

"After. Nympho." He tugged her hair, pulled her head back until she met his cognac-and-sunlight eyes. "We're almost there."

And then they were. The fight blurring past, the win. The elation. Auggie's lips on hers at the edge of the ring before his coach dragged him off, the music soaring and nothing mattering.

Laughter rang down the walls as they rushed to the basement. Jenna in the lead, a magnum of champagne held aloft, Ash and Carlos at her heels. Carz gave a *Lobos* howl and parkour-leaped ahead of her, landing at the base of the stairs like Batman himself. "Come out, *mano*!" He ran into the semi-darkness across the dusty granite floor, leaving Ash and Jenna to trail along. They'd abandoned their heels upstairs, but drunken sliding across the polished stone was almost as much fun as keeping up with Carz would have been.

"Come on! We got the good stuff!" Jenna yelled, bumping into Carz's shoulder. He'd stopped at the door of the old recording studio. "Hey, come on—"

"Back, Jen. Back." The snarled order caught her off guard as much as the bruising grip he laid on her arm. "Ash, get the medic."

"The…?" Jenna stared dumbly at her soon-to-be brother-in-law while her best friend turned and ran, sliding and cursing back toward the stairs, yelling names of the medic crew into her phone.

And then Carz turned.

She hit her knees on the gritty floor, a silent wail shearing through her soul, taking all the air from her lungs, even as her lips sealed shut.

Go back.

Go back, go back, go back.

To when this wasn't reality. To Auggie's big hand holding hers. Promising forever. To when there wasn't blood on his lips, and a red-black halo surrounding his perfect face.

Go back.

She turned away from the void where Auggie had been in time to see Bennett Fitzgerald, organizer extraordinaire, in full Crisis Management mode, standing at the door, triumph in his eyes. He put a proprietary hand on Ashlyn's waist. His lips almost smiled. And time dragged her forward, the scream in her head never stopping.

The Louisiana mud was thick and pungent. Dead leaves, old dirt. Swamp. Carz sobbed as he pushed the weighted bag out of the boat. He could barely walk, crying so hard his hands shook, and Ash gently took the rope from him to tie them to the docks.

Jenna's gaze stayed locked on the lake's rippled surface. Waiting for the miracle. Praying.

The Russian loomed out of the shadows, reaching for her as she got out of the boat. "Time for an apology,

Blue Eyes…"

****

Jenna woke with the scream trapped in her throat. She inhaled sharply, swallowed, closed her eyes, counted. Six months without incident. Zero without nightmares. *Three years, seven months, two weeks since my life ended.*

Her shrink always asked about the night Ben almost murdered Ash. The night Jenna put a steak knife in his side. She seemed to think Jenna's nightmares would fixate there. They never did. Jenna grabbed the pill bottle off the nightstand and dry swallowed two of its contents before sipping the zero-cal Gatorade she'd left for herself last night. Relaxing into the pillows, she picked up her bullet journal and checked the day's goals.

Get Ash the Hell Out of There.

She groaned and tossed the book away. A road trip to bumfuck nowhere to get Ashlyn out of yet another bad-idea relationship. She traced the eternity symbol tattooed on her wrist. *Guess I should pack. What do I even take to Redneck Land?*

Chapter One
Case

July 20

"You son of a bitch!"

Metal legs screeched against the sticky concrete floor. A scream accompanied shattering beer bottles as the Silver Spur's patrons thundered toward the exit. Case Kelly didn't even have time to shout "Fight!" before a body crashed into the bar six inches from his elbow. His booted feet hit the ground as Spider's head cracked back from Ice's fist.

So much for a quiet night with the Storm Crows. Even on a Wednesday, his club brothers couldn't put their fucking fists down.

He'd told Frog, "One drink." Case needed a shower and a good night's sleep, but Frog begged. *Just an hour.* One hour became two. One drink became four. A game of darts turned into a whole fucking tournament. *I'm a goddamn pushover.*

"Move!" He bumped into Frog, who hadn't budged. Kicking the stool to force Frog into action, Case glanced to the side for an easier escape...

Wham!

Case fell, his back slamming into the bar's edge. He clamped his eyes shut, white-hot pain searing behind them. Warmth dripped down his left cheek, and something wet and cold seeped through his t-shirt. *Shit.* Case clapped one hand over his face. His aching jaw tightened. Panicked shouts splintered the smoky air, hard to hear over the ringing in his ear. And the urge to maim someone. His free hand curled into a fist.

Always in the wrong place at the wrong time.

Ice had Spider trapped against the bar within arm's reach, controlling the fight like a goddamn professional. Spider flailed like a fucking idiot. Panicking. Making stupid mistakes. Hitting the wrong people. Another wide swing barely missed Case's nose. *Fuck this, I'm out.*

Backing up, his foot slipped in beer. Somebody caught his arm, dragging him from the scuffle. Or trying. He spotted the distinctive oiled dark hair in his peripheral: Blackie. "Thanks, bro—"

Spider's bony shoulder flew into Case's. "Fuck!" They both went sideways, and a bar stool's hard back wedged under Case's rib cage. Blackie sprinted away. *Jackass.* Frog at least stayed put, but further out of range finally, motioning for Case to hurry up. Bastard hadn't even put his beer down. A few other people inside stood, watching with their mouths open, but nobody moved.

Case shoved the stool away and staggered to Frog. "Feel free to step in." Frog didn't answer but held Case upright to watch the fight from a safer distance.

Won't be long.

Spider knew how to hold his own in a fight: you didn't become a Storm Crow without that skill. But against the national charter's junior Enforcer, who weighed forty pounds more in pure muscle and stood half a head taller? *So much for Spider being smart.*

What the hell happened? Not one minute before hell broke loose, Ice was cracking jokes and flirting with Karli, the sexy bartender. He'd slung his arm around Spider at one point. It didn't make any damn sense. Until Case's gaze fell on the cute platinum blonde standing in front of the hall to the bathroom, trembling and crying in her friend's arms.

All this over Sophia? Since when does Ice brawl over Crow Eaters?

"Get off him!" Karli's yell rattled the windows. She stormed in from the back room, five-feet, eight inches of voluptuous rage and hairspray, hefting a baseball bat like a rolled-up newspaper. It would be about as effective.

What the fuck? No way in hell is she getting in the middle of—

She was. Tall, sexy, badass, and a veteran of countless Storm Crow brawls, she wasn't afraid of this one. She married a Crow, a long time ago before cancer widowed her, but she still worked the clubhouse bar. Not a job for the weak. The Silver Spur was her second gig, one the guys had happily supported. Might be a lot harder if his idiot brothers won a lifetime ban for this shit.

"Karli, keep back!" Frog waved her off.

Ice's head shot up, freezing when he saw Karli. Spider took the opening, bruised knuckles catching Ice's face hard enough the big man staggered back, raising a hand to his busted lip. The vein at his temple throbbed. Blind rage. Case recognized it, though he'd only seen it once before on Ice: the day the Crows raided the Heathens' clubhouse last month. When Ice dropped half a dozen men and emptied a clip into their president.

Shit. Spider's a dead man.

Case launched forward, catching Ice around his midsection, winning the tackle on surprise rather than skill. They fell together, limbs askew, except for Case's arm still locked over Ice.

Spider straightened, shaking his head hard. Blood from his swelling nose spattered around his cheeks and chest. He squared up again, and Case's stomach clenched. "Don't!" Not that Spider listened. *As if he ever would.*

He advanced on both of them.

A mountain-sized shadow in leather and denim materialized as Spider's fist drew back. *Dragon. Thank fuck.* The senior Enforcer hooked his arms beneath Spider's and threw the smaller man to the side. He crashed to the floor at Frog's feet. "Stay!" Dragon barked, just as Ice snarled, his attention fixed on a new target.

"Fuck." Case raised his hands in a hopeless block as Ice got hold of his collar and let his eyes shut. *This is gonna hurt.*

He held his breath, waiting. Waiting.

He cracked one eye open, revealing a single, large hand across Ice's forearm. *White-knuckled grip, silver and black ring...* Case's breath escaped. Ice's body still trembled, either with adrenaline or rage or both, but his frosty, blue stare locked on his vice president. Anybody else would shrink, but Joker's dark, unblinking glare stayed still and empty as a grave. A chill rolled down Case's spine. *Some shit you didn't get in the middle of.*

Ice almost growled. "Joker, I swear to God, I'll—"

"Go outside. Cool off." Joker's tone left no room for argument. Ice looked like he wanted to protest anyway, but he stumbled upright and stalked past.

Dragon stood behind Joker's right shoulder, his thick arms crossed, a dangerous smile on his face. "I'll go sit with him."

They left, brushing past Blackie, who slumped in his stool, breathing fast. *Guess I should thank him later.* Getting Dragon off his latest conquest couldn't have been easy. Frog stepped up, offering Spider a napkin for his nose. He slapped it away, using his sleeve instead. "You stupid asshole," he said to Case, his voice thicker than usual. "The fuck you getting in the way for?"

"Sorry. Next time I'll let him keep skull-fucking you."

"If you hadn't jumped in, I would have—"

"Died?"

"Fuck you, Case. You're lucky I don't—"

"Shut up." Joker's voice hit like a whip. "Let's go for a walk."

Spider looked sheepish for a nanosecond before the usual scowl settled over his jagged features. He didn't argue. You could be pissed at the VP, but you didn't talk back to him. Especially not in public. Not if you wanted to eat solid foods this month. The only thing scarier than Ice going berserk was Joker making a point.

Case turned to the bar where Karli waited. Closer than he expected.

"Thanks." Karli crossed her arms, looking a little too much like Dragon. Somehow.

"No problem." *Liar*. He squinted. "You … weren't really gonna try to break them up, were you?"

"None of you big, strong men were doing shit."

"Not doing—" Blackie protested. "I got Dragon."

"Yeah. Real brave." She sighed at the glittering glass shards and puddles now decorating the floor. "I gotta get this mopped up before everyone comes back in." Spinning on her heel, she headed to the storeroom. "I'll get the kit for that cheek, Case."

"You okay, man?" Frog put a steadying hand on Case's back. "You might want to get some ice on that. It don't look so good."

Case prodded his throbbing face. It hurt like hell now. It'd be worse tomorrow. *As if Thursdays aren't bad enough. Now I gotta deal with this shit, too.*

"Do me a favor. Next payday, before you ask me to drink with you, fucking don't."

"Aw, come on. Ain't like this shit happens every time."

"Coulda been worse." Blackie wiped the rejected

napkin over spilled beer. "You coulda been Spider. Not only did he get his ass handed to him, he ain't getting laid tonight either."

"From where I'm sitting, that's the same goddamn boat I'm in."

"Huh. Guess it ain't your fucking night, is it?"

"Fuck off, Blackie."

"Tell you what." Frog righted his stool and sat down. "I'll buy you a beer to say sorry for *forcing* you to be social. How's that sound?"

"Like a trick. I gotta get home."

"Beauty rest ain't gonna fix that face tonight, son. You wake up miserable either way."

"Frog, I'm gonna hit you."

He laughed. "So long as you don't hit my face. That's my moneymaker."

"Business must be rough."

A throat cleared behind them. "Hey. You gonna move, or do I have to mop your shoes?" Case checked over his shoulder. Karli held a mop in one hand, the other on her hip.

"Sorry," he murmured, taking a big step to the left.

"Sophia good?" Blackie asked.

"She's in the bathroom fixing her makeup. Think most of it's for show."

Case nodded. *She's seen plenty of fights. Pretty, young, and a good fuck. Life must be hard for her. Maybe I should offer my sympathy...*

"You heading out?" Karli thankfully knocked him out of that dumbass thought.

"Yeah. Gotta get an early start tomorrow."

Reaching into his pocket for his keys, he waved good-bye, his shoulders loosening with each step closer to the exit. Until the door opened. Joker stood on the other side with a face like thunder, and Spider was nowhere to be seen. Case wondered for half a second if there was a body in the trunk of somebody's car. *Nah. Less trouble to get someone to haul his drunk ass home. Probably.*

"Hey." Case stopped, jamming his hands in his pockets. Only six years younger than Joker, and damn if he didn't feel like a fucking child. "Don't know what happened. One moment I was talking with Frog and Blackie, the next—"

"It don't fucking matter," Joker snapped. "Shouldn't have gotten in the middle of it in the first place."

"I thought—"

"You'd stop their punches with your face? Didn't look all that successful."

"But Karli was about…"

"Safe to assume nothing broke?"

Case shook his head instead of trying another explanation.

"Good. Next time, use your head. And I don't mean fucking literally."

Case nodded. Waited. When Joker didn't start talking, he went ahead.

"Is everything—?"

"All right?" Joker glowered. "Seriously? You're asking that?"

Case flinched, standing frozen as Joker stepped around him, back to the patio. *Follow and risk the wrath, or let it all wait 'til tomorrow?* Case rocked back and forth on his feet. *Nah, leave it for now.* Besides, the VP's wife could probably calm him down. *Eventually.*

"You gonna stand there like a dumbshit post all night?" Frog shouted from the bar. "Either go the fuck home or get your ass back here and drink!"

Case's cheeks flushed, and he spun on his heel toward the door. "Fuck off, Frog!"

Chapter Two
Case

July 21

Case loved the roads outside Oak Grove. Few cars ventured off I-39 these days, meaning he got time and space to enjoy the scenery. *And fuck if it ain't worth enjoying.* For the first few miles, a rolling, green horizon met with an aggressively blue sky as gentle breezes bent oceans of soybeans and grass to their whims. Further on, tall emerald and gold cornfields blocked out the world. Even through the visor, the fresh-cut roadside grass filled his nostrils. Better than sand any day. Better than where he'd come from, too.

Thursdays. Never can get the hang of fucking Thursdays.

The back of his head pounded with its own personal drum, urging his spine to snap between his shoulder blades, while a knot the size of Baghdad twisted in his stomach. Only the vibrations of his 2015 Electra Glide Ultra Limited offered relief. The fresh air in his lungs eased the tension, overpowering the smell of antiseptic and soiled adult diapers. The roaring wind and purring engine smoothed down the frustration with the last bed change, the guilty promises, his own bitter dreams. Better this than letting it out on his stepmom, Helen. Or Liam.

Or anyone else. His kid brother couldn't fix Helen's spine or her deteriorating health with better grades. Nobody could fix the anger and guilt eating through Case every single day. Especially not on Thursdays, when it was just him and Liam handling Helen's care until the night-time aide came in, and there was nobody to cheerfully buffer the truth for them, hide the little things that were getting steadily worse.

We need more money, get her to better doctors...

The road blurred, and he lifted a hand to wipe his burning eyes, slapping the visor. *Fuck.* He slowed down, blinking fast, breathing deep as he flipped it up. Not that it helped. *Would anybody notice if I don't turn around? Would they care?*

If I could do that, I wouldn't have ended up here in the first place.

His grip tightened on the handle, his jaw clamping painfully tight. The ride always did the trick before. *Why not today? Fucking why?* Fear swirled inside him. *What happens when nothing helps?* He screamed at that because nobody else could hear him. When he finished, his cheeks were wet and his forearms ached so bad he could barely hold the handlebars.

He turned on the next Y-intersection. The cornfield fell away, revealing another open expanse of sorghum, grass, and trees framing Wellge's filling station. The gods and Tree Wronski alone knew how it survived, a gently rusting relic fifty years behind the times. Case suspected it had something to do with the ancient, cash-only pumps and suspiciously cheap cigarettes Old Man Wellge always had in stock. And because of the latter, he loyally visited every week to buy a drink and a pack of cigs. He wasn't the only visitor today—a white Lexus SUV with Kansas plates sat at the pumps. *They gotta be lost as hell.*

Pulling his bike in, he killed the engine and took the helmet off, taking a full breath and wiping his face of sweat and tears. Slowly, he stood, arching his back and twisting, sighing at the satisfying pop above his tail bone. He patted his back pocket for his wallet, glancing at the woman by the pump as he started toward the entrance. *Wait.*

He did a double-take and froze three feet from the door. She stood, silhouetted in the fading light, dressed in shorts showing off legs men would kill to have wrapped around them, and a flowy top that hugged her curves in all the right places, especially her breasts. They weren't large, but enough to … heave. Definitely. *Aw, shit.* Her wide, glassy eyes shone with fresh tears, her lips parted to suck in the air, her face flushed.

"Hey," he said softly, taking a step toward her. "What's wrong? You okay?"

She jumped at his approach, straightening up like he wouldn't notice she'd been half-collapsed against her SUV's fender. "Yes. I'm fine. Sorry, I—" She lifted her phone, her bright gaze—damn near the same color as the sky—flicked to the screen, and he'd have sworn in court they actually dimmed. "I'm not? I'm such… I'm so sorry. I can't believe this is real life. Do you, um, have a phone that works here? I'm out of service, I think? And gas. And I don't have cash, and I—I think I've stumbled back to 1975…"

He bit his lip to keep from chuckling. "Yeah. I can see how you get that vibe." He stepped around the pump since she didn't seem like she'd take off running, but he kept his approach slow just in case. "Service is shitty out here, but I can help you with some of those other things. I have some cash. How much do you need?"

Her already big eyes somehow expanded. "I … have no idea? How do you even put it in?"

He grimaced. *So many ways to answer that, and yet…* "How do you—?" He looked between her and the pump. *City girl, country gadget.* "Not from around here, huh?" He grinned and reached for the nozzle. "Let me help. How much money do you want to put into it? Keep in mind, Carson only takes gold coins. Or fur in the winter months."

Her full lips parted, a model-perfect expression caught between confusion and horror. "You aren't—" The hint of a smile lit her face up once more. *Bet those lips taste as sweet as she looks.* "Listen, this day has been so many levels of crappy that I'm not sure I can detect sarcasm right now." Yet her soft voice was almost laughing.

"I think you did a pretty good job. But that ain't an answer."

"Because that leads us to the other problem. No cash or coins. And mom's furs are in storage in Kansas."

Despite the amount of crap in his day, he *didn't* detect sarcasm. He lifted a brow. Maybe she didn't like accepting money from strangers? It made sense. He didn't either. "I'll put twenty in. That should safely get you to a gas station with card readers." He moved around her so he could reach the tank, trying to ignore the whiff of flowery perfume under the station's usual gas and grease scent.

"Oh, no. I couldn't. I—" She stopped with a groan. "I don't even have another option here, do I? Wow. Worst bridesmaid trip ever." Her flawless forehead creased. "I can't take cash from a stranger, no matter how kind. I'll pay you back. I'm heading to like, uh, Elm Wood? Or Oak Stall? Something. Google knows. If you're from around here, I can drop it by your office?"

What part of my raggedy ass on a Harley screams 'office guy,' sweetheart? He couldn't keep the laughter back. "I'm from Oak Grove. Slightly south of Oak Stall," he said, hiding his smile with a shrugged shoulder.

"Right. Grove." Her cheeks flared pink, and she ducked her head before pushing her dark hair over her shoulder. *Does she know how fucking beautiful that makes her? She has to, right?*

"But don't worry about paying me back. You aren't technically taking my money if I never hand it to you."

"Thank you, Mister…?"

He caught himself smiling again. "Case. Just Case. And it's no trouble at all, ma'am."

"Jenna." Her worried gaze met his. "I'm sure it's plenty of trouble, Case. Though maybe not by your usual measurements." She touched her cheek, mirroring where his own day-old cut still stung. An unfamiliar pang hit his chest.

The day I meet the hottest girl in the goddamn world, I look like a hobo after Fleet Week. His lips formed a tight line, and he rubbed his stubble with a gentle hand. "Used to it." When he caught the question in her eyes, he quickly added, "Work at a garage. It's hands-on, and bruises ain't easy to avoid. This was me just being in the wrong place at the wrong time." Not a lie. *Ice and a falling sledgehammer probably have about the same outcome.*

"Heck of a wrong time." Jenna glanced at the gas pump's scrolling numbers. "Maybe we'll both get a redo on this week." Her teeth caught her lower lip. "I've got some bottled water in the car, if you need a drink?"

Yes. But water ain't it. "If you wouldn't mind?" It might make her feel less guilty about him paying for her gas. And maybe it would get his mind out of the gutter. "About done here." He waited a few more seconds and then released the pump, pulling it from the tank. "I'll go in and pay. I hope the rest of your day gets better. And hey, if you're sticking around Oak Grove for a bit, maybe I'll see you. Ain't exactly hard to run into people there. I think our population might be up to forty-two or something now."

"That many?" She opened the SUV door,

revealing spotless leather interiors and the kind of purse Helen used to drool over on TV shows. A moment later, she pressed a still-cold bottle of Voss water into his hand. "Guess you might see me then. I'll be there for a few days. Fixin' for a weddin' up at City Hall, I hear." She touched her bottle to his in a mock salute. "To better weeks."

"I'll drink to that," he said, taking a sip. "Take care, Jenna." He hesitated. Normally, he'd ask for a number. Or give his. But would she feel like she *had* to because he helped her? He might kick himself later, but he needed to let this one go. *A good deed. Mom would be so fucking proud.* With a wave, he walked away, his feet heavy, his body aching more now than before.

Fucking Thursdays.

****

Case didn't want to get out of the shower. Hot water ran down his face, his body, easing tense muscles and washing away the day's grime, sweat, and dust. Soap suds lingered over his chest and shoulders, Irish Spring a better smell than the urine-soaked sheets he changed earlier. Steam clung to the glass pane, a Titanic-like handprint dragged down the center. His fingers curled, pressing hard while his other hand pumped his thick, throbbing shaft. Visions of large blue eyes, soft lips, and sweet thighs swam through his head, and as he stroked himself, he imagined it was her pussy taking him.

It didn't take long. He bowed his head, watching water and semen mingling in streams over his leg and down the drain. He breathed hard, his forehead touching the cool tile, and waited for the relief to follow. And waited.

By the time he dressed and left his apartment, he gave up. The ride didn't help. The shower didn't do crap, and neither did jerking off. The only option left? Liquor.

A fuck ton of it. Maybe shit at the clubhouse relaxed enough by now for him to get wasted without having to worry about an explosion or drive-by. Who knew? So far, this year was a non-stop three-ring methadone circus.

The sky's radiant summer blue finally disappeared with the setting sun, replaced now with purples, pinks, and orange. Ravenwood rush hour meant about five more cars on Main Street than usual, but Case didn't think anybody could call it traffic. He navigated through it quickly, riding closer to the edge of town, smiling when he saw the clubhouse's familiar silhouette in the distance, a handful of bikes in the yard. *Thank gods*. He pulled into the driveway, the crunch of tires on gravel loud enough to rival his engine as he rolled past the half dozen bikes. Any Crow worth their salt knew who each belonged to. Their owners all had seats at the table even if they didn't get to vote on every issue.

He eased his ride in beside a black Dyna, brand new and gleaming chrome: Joker's. The thing exuded power and beauty, and everyone thought so except the bastard who owned it. Case couldn't blame him. He loved his own lady: a 2015 blue and chrome Harley Electra Glide Ultra, customized with care over the course of many, many months. Hell, she still had a few upgrades in store for her, and with each tweak, he loved her more. If he lost her in an accident, even a Dyna as slick and sweet as the one next to him wouldn't cheer him up.

Grease—the Road Captain—and Jingle walked out the clubhouse's side door, their shoulders almost touching, heads bowed toward one another in quiet conversation. Case killed his engine, the toe of his boot catching the kickstand. His hand dug into his pocket for the fresh pack of cigs, and he hopped over the parking bumper.

"Holy shit, Case." Grease whistled and rubbed his own cheek. "You look fucking terrible."

"Thanks." *That's exactly the shit I need to hear today.* "Feels worse than it looks."

"Least it was Spider's fist and not Ice's," Jingle said. "Bright sides to everything, kid."

"They here?"

"Ice is somewhere in the back," Jingle replied. "You missed Spider. Probably a good thing. You heading inside?"

"Nah. Rode up here to chill with you old farts in the parking lot."

Grease laughed. "And they say the youngsters don't respect their elders anymore." He clapped Case on the arm and took another drag. "Fair warning. Joker's in one of those moods. Bad enough what happened with Spider, but seems like he's pissy about some shit with his wife? I don't know. I don't pretend to understand that goddamn marriage."

"Don't think they do either." Jingle's brow quirked, but he didn't comment. Joker's ol' lady, Ashlyn, had shown up three months ago, the night a rival club ran him off the road. He decided she was gonna be his wife about the second his casts came off. Then they'd had a war with the Heathens that left everyone in the charter fucked up some way or another.

"Anyway." Another cloud passed Grease's lips. "Thought I'd let you know so you don't walk in with that shit-eating grin that pisses him off."

Jingle nodded. "Don't take it to heart, kid. That's the Wronski way. When they're pissed off, ain't nobody else can be happy."

"Thanks for the heads up." Case pulled a cigarette from the pack, and Grease offered his cig. He pressed the tip to the orange end of the road captain's, puffing on it a few times to get it going. "Well, if I fuck up, I'll see you two in a bit. Probably with a new bruise."

"Give it ten minutes."

"Five. Max," Jingle countered.

"You two should take that act on tour. Why not start now?"

"And miss this new crop of Prospects? They're dumber than the last. Can't buy entertainment that good."

The knot in Case's stomach tightened. He didn't know the new round well yet on account of most being brand-fucking-new. They were hang-arounds that latched onto the club while he still wore the Prospect patch, too busy running members' errands to make nice. He liked most of them, though. Except one. He peeked back at the row of bikes. *Good.* If justice existed in the damn world, Ripper or Bullet or Travis or whatever the fuck he called himself this week would never be a Storm Crow.

Without another word, Case moved to the front door, stepped inside, and took the much-needed deep breath he'd struggled to get since his stepmom's place. He felt the smile creeping on his face. He couldn't help it. He'd fucking loved the Storm Crow clubhouse since he first set foot inside. Walls hung with old license plates and club trophies, memorials and photos. It was a haven meant to remind you of good times. There was even a selection of bras and panties over the 1910s-era mahogany bar to remind you of damn good times ahead.

Karli caught his eye, did a bit of a once-over, then beckoned with a flick of her head. "Wondered when you'd show up." She leaned against the counter, giving him a clear eye line down her cleavage. Karli's body was beautiful, all curves and softness, her skin a canvas of vibrant colors and images. If he didn't respect her so much, he'd have begged her—weekly—for a night or ten to explore her ink, and everything else, with his tongue.

But she was not to be touched. For one, Dragon and Tree would slice off his balls. For another, *she* would. Karli's single status was Karli's choice, and only the dimmest bulbs dared push that button.

"What's up?" he asked, meeting her eyes. She smirked, leaning forward to test his attention. He managed to keep his eyes on hers. Barely.

"Not sure. Thought you could tell me." She nodded toward the opposite side of the room. He saw what she meant. Joker sat at his usual table, clutching his drink, one leg stretched over the chair next to him. "Not like him to brood this long over a fight."

He grunted and closed his eyes. *Fuck.* "This about Spider or Ashlyn?"

"Hell if I know."

He chuckled. "Guess I'll start with just a beer then. What's he drinking?"

"Rum and Coke. Think she's rubbing off on him." Karli hurried to get the drinks.

Case talked himself up for it, still raw from yesterday's encounter. He didn't want to be Joker's chew toy today, but Karli wouldn't send him if she expected that result. *Right?* He glanced back at her as she handed over the drinks with a good-luck wink. "Thanks." He got a deep breath and made a beeline for the table. If he went fast, he wouldn't have time to chicken out.

"Brought you a refill." Case put it down next to the nearly empty glass. Joker's midnight gaze fixed on him. On a good day, that glare could freeze Everclear. Today was not a good day. Case tensed. *What's one more fight this week?*

Instead, Joker slid his leg back to the floor before draining his first glass. He motioned for Case to sit. "Karli's been trying to get someone to come over since we opened. You're the only idiot who's been brave enough. Put that out," he ordered absently.

Case looked down at his cigarette and extinguished it in the ashtray. Sometimes he forgot Joker quit smoking after his accident. Cold turkey was a hell of a thing to do. He'd done it once but fell back into the habit. The cravings sucked.

"Figured my day can't get worse. Everything good, VP?"

"Depends on your perspective." He grabbed the ashtray, pushing it across the table. Case swallowed hard, his nerves still on edge. It had to be for show, right? The whole damn clubhouse smelled like cigarettes. "Nobody's getting shot at. There's that."

Case rubbed his nose and took a drink. "Nice change, ain't it? Think I dodge more lead here than in the Corps."

Joker's eyes lit up with the first flicker of warmth, and he chuckled. He paused after, almost as if the sound surprised him. "Hard to believe."

"Okay. Maybe about equal."

"Fair. But yeah, everything's fine. Just thinking."

"About?"

"Your mom," Joker said drily.

"She's not your type." The answer came without hesitation. "Unless you mean my stepmom. And if you do, uh, Helen ain't your type either. But I get it. Not my business. Guess it makes sense you got a lot on your mind with Sturgis coming up and all the shit going down."

"Sturgis *is* gonna be a shitshow." Joker groaned. "But we expected that after the Heathens fuckup. I ain't too worried. Gotta play nice. Smooth some feathers. Nothing the club ain't done before."

"I can't wait to go. Itching for a change." Anything to take his mind off bedsores and medical bills.

"Yeah. I may have had too many of those lately." Joker took a drink. A long one.

"What do you mean?"

"It don't matter," he said, twisting the glass on the table while his gaze darted toward the back door. A solid hunk of t-shirt and leather loomed in Case's peripheral vision. He tilted his head up as Ice's heavy, callused hand landed on the back of his neck, cold as hell and not at all gentle.

"What the fuck?" Case hissed as his head was forcibly turned. He glared up at Ice.

"God damn Spider did good work. The girls of Pharaoh County are gonna have open spots in their beds all week!"

He let out a humorless laugh. "Thanks."

Ice fell into the seat next to Joker without invitation. But then, he was about one of two people who could do that. Joker and Ice went way back. Before either of them wore a Prospect patch.

Ice stretched, his back popping, and propped his right leg out in front of him with a grimace. "Fucking knee," he muttered. He cleared his throat, but whatever he planned on saying never came out. Instead, his brow furrowed, and his expression sharpened. "What's wrong with you?"

Case glanced down at his body as if he might find the answer. "Huh? Nothing."

"Bullshit. Somebody steal a chick from you? Only thing I know of can put a look like that on your face is blue balls."

Nobody stole her. My stupid ass walked away.

"Guess you're pretending the fight never happened?" Anything to avoid explaining the surreal encounter. No way in hell that ended in anything but ribbing and sarcasm.

Ice rolled his eyes. "Ain't like I'm the one who did that to you," he said, tapping his own cheek.

"Leave him alone," Joker said. "Not in the mood to babysit him when you piss him off."

"Just teasing."

"I'm tired," Case admitted, glowering at Ice.

"Of what? Getting pussy thrown at you wherever you go?"

Joker frowned. "*There's* an image."

"It is exhausting. I know it was a long time ago, Ice, but remember what it's like."

Ice gave him a level stare before laughing. "Nice."

"This is why people drink alone," Joker muttered.

"People drink alone because they're alcoholics. Or because they're being emo as fuck." Ice settled his elbow on Joker's shoulder. "And you ain't an alcoholic, so that means—"

"When's the last time I punched your face?"

"About three hours ago? Point is, friends don't let friends drink alone. Even emo friends. Right, Case?"

Case shook his head. "You're on your own here, buddy."

"Told you. Smarter than he looks," Joker said, smirking.

"Hey!"

"That still leaves a whole lotta range between dumb as shit and average," Ice teased.

"Better hope you're wrong. Case'll be going with your crew to KC soon as we get back from Sturgis."

"Wait. What?" Ice and Case said together.

Case felt invisible. He hated when they got like this. "What's going on in Kansas City?"

Ice ignored him. "You made it sound like you were comin' when we were planning shit out in Church."

"Guys!" Case snapped. They both turned to him. "Yeah, still here. What's going on in KC?"

Ice licked the front of his teeth and stared down at his Budweiser, measuring how much he had left before turning it straight up to empty it. "Some recon. Their club's been seeing some strange shit, and they want extra eyes on it. Nothing huge. Not like the Heathens."

"That don't really answer my question."

Joker made an impatient noise. "Girls are going missing in Crow territory. Somebody's selling flesh, and you know how Tree gets about shit like that."

The last time they'd dealt with human traffickers was before Case's time, but from the way Dragon and Ice told it, Tree had gone scorched earth. Literally. At the time, it got reported as a meth lab explosion. Several of them.

"It ain't gonna come to that." Ice's eyes narrowed at Joker. "And we don't know if that's what's going on. We're just doing recon."

"Which is why you guys are fine to do it without me." Something in Joker's tone still sounded off. Ice set his empty bottle down and leaned against the table.

"This have something to do with the phone call you made?" Ice's expression relaxed like he realized the answer on his own. "She chew you out for being gone so much?"

Joker scowled. "Not exactly."

"When you say, not exactly…"

"You know Ash." Joker shrugged. "Sometimes she takes a lot of words to say something completely opposite. Besides, Bullet can't pull babysitting duty full-time. Kid's gotta do actual Prospect things. Can't do that if he's at my place all the time."

"That's true," Ice said, nodding sagely.

Case took a drink to hide his own sigh. He hated

that Joker relied on Bullet to look after Ash lately. Sure, he understood it. The Prospect was one of about three people Ash felt fully comfortable with, not counting her husband, and given what they went through at the Heathen clubhouse and how the bastard nearly died trying to protect her? Didn't mean Case liked it.

"That mean he's coming to Sturgis?" Case asked. It wouldn't be so bad. Easy to avoid somebody there. Or get so drunk you didn't recognize them.

"I'm hoping. But shit's complicated. She's got this so-called best friend coming into town. Her old roommate. I don't know. I can't explain what the fuck I'm thinking, but—"

Ice cut in, "You're wondering where the fuck Best Friend's been up to now?"

"Yeah. The way Ash talked about how things were before, and meeting her bitch mother… Don't know what to make of her friends suddenly appearing at my doorstep."

"Suddenly?"

"My wife has a way of forgetting to mention when she's invited people over. She swears she told me, but I know she didn't."

Case's head tilted. "So you think she's lying?"

Joker cast a sharp scowl at him. "No," he said firmly. "She probably meant to tell me and forgot she didn't. Didn't change that I found out this morning, and this chick's showing up tonight."

Case went rigid. That girl… *No. Couldn't be.*

"I can't skip Sturgis," Joker continued. "And I don't want to leave her with some asshole I don't trust. Thinking Bullet may have to miss out one more time. Maybe I can make it up with a few strip club errands or some shit."

Case's hand balled into a fist on his knee.

Leaving Bullet to watch Ash and this friend of hers meant Joker trusted him. And more than a little. He swallowed, the beer's aftertaste mixing with a jaw-clenching bitterness. He masked it with another drink, surprised to see the bottom of the cup.

"I'll stay." He all but spat the words.

"What?" Ice sat up. "Kid, weren't you saying—"

"Joker's right. Bullet needs to be put through the paces, and who else can do it? I don't mind. I've crashed on your couch enough times, boss. At this point, probably easier to fall asleep on that than my own bed."

"You don't have to do this, Case."

"I know." He released his hand, flexed the fingers against his leg. The plan felt good. Solid. "But Helen's getting over some shit, and Liam's a fucking mess most days. It's probably better if I'm close by anyway." It wasn't entirely a lie. Helen was always getting over something. It became her permanent state of existence after the wreck that shattered all their lives. And Liam, his youngest brother, could barely take care of himself let alone his ailing mom.

"That's … okay." Ice stood up. "I'm gonna go get you water. I'll be back." He cast an unreadable look toward Joker. One of their non-language moments.

When he was out of earshot, Joker leaned forward. "You've been talking about Sturgis for weeks now. And you ain't said shit about your stepmom. You gonna tell me what this is about?"

"It's kinda petty," he said slowly. "The shit you guys put me through when I was trying to earn my colors, I think he should have to do it, too. And the other guys might start thinking he's getting off easy. You know, for the club and all that." He got the empty cup halfway to his lips before remembering he'd already finished it. *Fuck.*

He sat back, ignoring Joker's disbelieving grunt until the VP shrugged. "If that's what you want to do, then I appreciate it. It's been, uh, *complicated* with Ashlyn. It's—"

"I get it, Joker. You don't gotta explain."

Joker relaxed at that. He was as uncomfortable talking about his feelings as Case was watching him try.

"But hey, if you really want to thank me, maybe the next few rounds can be on you? My asshole boss don't pay me again 'til next week."

"Lucky he don't fire you. Don't think *my* boss would mind all that much if I did."

Case's answering quip fizzled with Ice's return. Joker took the bottle of water, untwisting the cap slowly. Ice drew a breath between his teeth.

"You said New Girl is showing up tonight, right? Gonna face the music alone, or you wanting reinforcements?"

Joker cast a suspicious glare at him. "Don't matter. If you're aching for an excuse to meet her, you're always welcome. But if you crash on the couch, try to keep your pants on. At least until we know how she'll react."

"She hangs around Oak Grove long enough, she's bound to see Ice's dick." Case stood up. "Mind if I tag along?" The question came out so casually, Case almost fooled himself.

"Always. But you do it anyway."

He made himself laugh. Easier to do that than admit it stung. *He is kidding, right?* He followed after Joker, his smile transforming into a nervous frown. He'd earned his place. Earned his patch. Earned Joker's trust enough that the VP himself sponsored Case as a Prospect. *Unless...*

Maybe it's all in my head. What if...?

"Told you. Five minutes!" Jingle's braying laugh echoed from the picnic tables right outside the doors.

Another fake smile.

What if I'm just the butt of everyone's joke?

****

Jenna

Her chest ached less with each passing mile, but she checked the gas gauge every few seconds lest it detonate and reveal Brigadoon II: Gas Station Surprise was all a dream. It might well have been, if not for the missing Voss in the travel cooler. *Case*, she reminded herself. *Probably short for Casey? I need to find Casey who works at a garage. Shouldn't be hard, considering he's built like a Hemsworth and has a face to match, under the bruises. There can't be many of those in this hellscape...*

How can Ash even stand to be here?

Jenna gazed through tinted windows at the Stepford horror of Oak Grove. Actual white picket fences and teenagers mowing grass. There was even a church with a steeple fronting onto a pristine little village park with a damn picturesque fountain. You could practically see a wedding party waiting to happen. *God, please don't let that be the church. I'll die of a saccharine overdose.*

A few more turns revealed her destination: a tiny saltbox house freshly painted with a construction crew taking over the back yard. Ash had opted to remodel while planning a wedding. *The girl has no sense of self-preservation.* Huffing, Jenna checked her phone and sent a text to her best friend. *No way am I going in there alone.* However 1950s-sitcom-perfect the town appeared, the place was crawling with biker gangs and redneck criminals. Not that she hadn't been in her share of terrifying spots, but something about the kind of crime that hid behind fresh paint and Mayberry set pieces irked her already shaky nerves.

"Jenna!" Ashlyn appeared at the front door and raced down the gently sloping yard toward the car in a tiny blonde blur.

"Hey!" Jenna hopped out and met her in an over-enthusiastic hug, tears stinging her eyes. Ash looked good—healthy even, despite the fact some psycho literally shot her a month ago. All the Skype sessions, Snaps, and IG tags in the world hadn't *quite* convinced Jenna as much as this moment. She put a kiss on Ash's rosy cheek. "You're trying that new line from Etude, aren't you? Your skin is amazing!"

"You never steer me wrong." Ash kept hold of her hand, pulling Jenna toward the house, green eyes glittering. "Come on, get inside before you melt."

"Whatever. I'm usually in Pennsic for this heat."

"Pennsylvania heat is not the same and you know it."

Jenna followed without argument, pausing inside to adjust to the wave of cool, paint-scented air and take in the interior. "You worked fast," she admitted, mentally comparing the pics Ash had sent days before. New barnwood floors replaced carpeting, and the walls definitely hadn't been blue. A massive gray sectional and chairs provided enough seating for a football team to watch themselves on a television almost ready for its big break in a theater. Calming colors, muted tones: magazine-ready. If you ignored the TARDIS throw blanket, abandoned motorcycle boots by the door, and some errant sample invitations and menus scattered in piles across the white coffee table.

"Once I knew what I wanted, there was plenty of labor for installing it." Ash shrugged, walking on toward the kitchen. "I'm thinking of doing this with other houses. If it makes money, that's nice, but it could give some people a job, and I feel better about this than constantly shopping for wedding stuff... Here. Water. Hydrate." She reappeared with a bottle and shoved it into Jenna's hand. "You always forget when you're driving."

Jenna settled on the overstuffed sofa, taking a dutiful sip while eying the white crown molding above. "What does your husband think?"

Ashlyn laughed, dropping beside Jenna with her own bottle. "His only request is no lace and no potpourri. I didn't even know he knew that word. Otherwise, it's whatever I want. I'm here more than he is right now anyway, and I think the theory is if I stay on a project, I won't be..." she trailed off, her mirth vanishing. Jenna nodded. They both endured trauma in the past. Now Ash had a kidnapping on top of it. And with Ash's history, that could get tricky.

"Are you, um, you know? Doing okay? For real?"

"Most days." Ash's pink lips thinned, and she pulled her ponytail out to redo it. "Joker's pretty much a hardass about making it to all the therapy appointments, but it hasn't been that bad. Not like ... before. If it's a bad day and he's gone, I've got Megan or Bullet. A lot of people, actually."

Jenna grimaced. "You could have stayed with me."

"You were out of the country. And you've pasted me back together once already." Ash patted Jenna's arm. "I love you too much to put that kind of pressure all on you. Not when you're still healing, too."

"I'm fine."

Jenna waved off Ash's dismissive sniff.

"I mean it!"

"Name five people you've talked to lately. Even

online. And likes and Snaps don't count. I mean actual verbal communication."

"You. Mom. Seena…"

"Seena works with you."

"Thierry, Dean, Ethan—"

"I'll let you have Thierry. Your mom, Dean, and Ethan live in the same house."

"I'm in the guest cottage now, so technically I have to go visit them. And Ethan's seventeen, so he's almost a real human. If humans can live on pizza pockets, caffeine, and acne pills."

"Aw, poor kid. Still struggling, huh?" Ash's expression softened. "I wondered why he wasn't in any of your pics."

"He hates cameras." Jenna shook her head sadly and pulled up her phone, flipping to an album before handing it over. "He keeps preaching about superficiality and the end of meaning. But you can tell once his skin clears, he's gonna have better things to do than modern philosophy."

"Hm." Ash frowned. She turned the Galaxy, an old photo bright and frozen on the screen. "Funny all your starred pics are from another phone."

Jenna barely heard, staring at the open-armed ghosts. She swallowed, made herself shrug, and swiped the screen to another shot, ignoring her bestie's piercing stare.

"Have you talked to Carlos lately?" she asked once her vocal cords could move.

"He's been out of the country."

Jenna tilted her head, leaning in. "What's he got to say about biker man?" Ash's shoulder twitched, and Jenna laughed. "You haven't told him. Holy. Shit. He's gonna flip. Are you even inviting him to the wedding?"

Ash's eyes flared. "Of course, I am! Jesus, Jenna.

Carz is family for fuck's sake. I … have to figure out the right way to explain Nathan. That's all."

"You didn't bother finding the right way to explain him to *me*."

"Your disapproval is slightly less incisive than his."

Jenna coughed and wiped her face. "This place is rubbing off on you, babe. Incisive? I am at least seventy percent less likely to shank people who annoy me, you're not wrong."

"He liked Matt." Ashlyn's fiancé of the previous winter—a blameless saint, future surgeon, and every mother's dream. "Everyone liked Matt. Except me."

"You like him too," Jenna corrected. *I know that feeling: he's everything you're supposed to want, but you might as well take the ring and a divorce decree in the same trip to save some time.* "You just didn't love him."

"I love Joker with all my heart." Ash's green gaze fixed on Jenna. "So please try not to hate him?"

Jenna put her hands up then put the right to her chest. "Cross my heart, I'll do my best."

Ash nodded, biting her lip, and glanced out the window. The deserted street outside might as well have been a film set, and in profile with the sunlight slanting across her cheekbones, Ash looked every inch the glassy-eyed ingenue waiting for the hero, or for …

"Good, because I need your help." *Damn it, I knew that angsty pose was leading somewhere. And* I'm *the model?*

"I'm not doing a threesome with you."

Ash giggled, her nose wrinkling. "Ew. No. I meant I need your permission."

"For a threesome? Girl, that's between you and—"

"For me to tell him about everything."

Jenna's smile died. "No." She set the water bottle on the table to keep from throwing it. "Fuck no, Ash. That's not happening. The more people know, the worse it gets. And some gangbanger redneck fuckstick with motor oil for brains—"

"You haven't even met him!"

"And when I do, and he's some paragon of perfection, do you think that will make it better?" The question came out more like a snarl. "Nobody knows. Why the fuck would we risk—"

"Because Bennett is out next May."

The announcement slammed into Jenna's stomach like a lead weight. The air vanished from her lungs. *So soon?* How had she forgotten? Ash kept talking, the words running together like the endless ripples in a fountain. *Or a bayou lake.* "You know there's no chance he won't parole for good behavior. The Fitzgeralds will make sure of it. I want Joker to know everything before then. So we—um, so he will maybe be calmed down by the release date, and he won't do something stupid."

"Afraid this tadpole-sized pond's gonna delude him into thinking he can match the Fitzgeralds' friends?"

Ash pursed her lips and gave a tired shrug. "Something like that."

Jenna rolled her shoulders, then her neck, and took a deep, centering breath. "I'll think about it, okay? I'm gonna be here for a couple of weeks anyway. If Monkey Wrench seems cool, maybe…" She trailed off as Ash grabbed her hand.

"Promise?" Her heart-shaped face was so full of hope it hurt.

"You really think he's awesome, don't you?"

"He is."

Jenna wrapped her hand around Ash's and pulled her into a hug. "What happens when he disappoints you, chica?" she whispered into Ash's ear. "We tell him everything... That might not work for some guys." Ash's arms encircled Jenna in painful silence. This close, Ash smelled like Prada Candy and lavender soap. *Familiar.* Jenna closed her eyes, letting the tension fade, holding tight to her best friend. They'd made it through blood and fire and terror. Another broken heart wasn't so scary. Ash's head stayed on Jenna's shoulder, but her uneven breaths told how close the tears were. Jenna stroked her golden hair. "It's okay. If he breaks your heart, it'll be the last thing he ever does."

Ash sniffled. "I'm more afraid I'll break his. He loves me, but there was so much I couldn't talk about."

"Does he explain every part of Outlaw World?" Jenna shook her head. They both knew the answer. "No. And he was a soldier, right? He's not telling you every second of that either."

"He knows I had an abusive boyfriend who tried to kill us. I told him Ben threw parties, typical rich boy stuff..."

"In all fairness, I don't think anyone sane would lead off with 'my ex-fiancé arranged illegal fights as a hobby, including liaising for half the criminal underworld of the Midwest.' Especially if you're telling it to another criminal. He might get starstruck."

Ash's elbow nudged Jenna's side. "He thinks I'm a good person, Jenna."

"You are, idiot."

"Now."

"Then too." Jenna let out a breath. "We were barely twenty. What the fuck did we know about anything? You didn't arrange the fights."

"Just planned the parties. Spent the blood money.

Kept the secrets."

"Every debutante in the nation could say the same."

"None of them buried—"

"Stop." Jenna squeezed again. "Not today."

"Sorry. You're right." They both relaxed, content to stick together a little longer. Jenna counted heartbeats, waiting for her nerves to settle until the roaring, rumbling growl of several thousand cylinders split the ensuing silence.

"The boys are back!" Ash announced with far too much cheer. They disentangled themselves from the couch, Ash bouncing toward the door, Jenna glaring at her back.

Onward, valkyries, to battle...

Ash threw open the front door, leaving Jenna to smooth her shorts down and prepare to face the enemy. "Nathan!" Ash stepped out of sight, onto the porch, heavy footsteps came closer, and a moment later, a six-foot-four monster swathed in denim and a leather vest carried her back through the door. Nathan Wronski, aka Joker. Jenna folded her arms and forced a smile. *All right, I get it. A blend of Tarzan and Ragnar Lothbrok with sin-dark eyes, wrapped in ink and outlaw allure? Might as well blame a kitten for rolling in catnip.* Ash's pictures had prepared her for this. But then Tweedle Dee and Tweedle Dum rolled in behind him.

Jesus, Aslan, and the Tenth Doctor. Is there a breeding ground for hot guys in leather? Jenna couldn't turn away. Tweedle One was Thor's long-lost cousin, complete with a sexy beard and hammer-ready arms. Tweedle Two...

Tweedle Two was...

Her heavily bruised rescuer stood in the doorway, large as life—though shorter than Nathan and Tweedle.

Broad shoulders, intense gray eyes, and the kind of lips that inspired impure thoughts, framed by enough careless stubble along his chiseled jaw to signal he would absolutely be okay getting out of bed late. Not that she'd considered any such scenarios five or ten times in the last twenty miles to Oak Grove. Jenna's heart fell. *He's one of them. There goes that fantasy.*

"Jenna, this is Nathan." She tore her attention from the best and worst moment of the week to renew her half-hearted grin. *A promise is a promise. I should try.* Nathan appeared even less enthusiastic than she felt. His brown gaze swept over her before he granted a bare nod and extended one hand once he'd lowered Ash's feet to the floor. He stood a full foot taller than Ash. *If only I'd thought to wear heels...* Jenna had three inches on her best friend—not nearly enough to feel equal to something Nathan's size.

"Nice to meet you." He had a deep, pleasant voice, rougher than Case's, and his hand was damn well huge. *Ash's hormones definitely won this marriage. Maybe that means they'll wear off in six months?*

"Same. Nice to meet the subject of so many emojis." But her attention slid from him to the others. Joker noticed. He nodded to Tweedle. "This is Ice."

Tweedle nodded and shook her hand.

"Pleased to meet you, Jenna." He had a firm grip and a few calluses, scars and fresh bruises across his knuckles. *Fighter,* old instincts hissed. *A real one.* But his smile was sweet, somehow, and sad. *God, not more kryptonite. I can't do this right now.*

Joker motioned to the other one. "And this is—"

"Case," she finished for him, her smile tightening, and a treacherous heat touching her cheeks. "I, uh, haven't hit the ATM yet. But I guess you know where to find me."

"You've met?" Joker asked.

"You could say that," Case said, grinning. "You still worried about paying me back? I'm pretty sure the water you gave me makes us square."

"Oh. No way. Those are sponsor freebies from last week's shoot. I wouldn't feel right counting it."

"Jenna's a model." A wicked familiar half-smile threatened on Ash's lips. "She just got back from Italy."

"Only part of that was working." She'd partnered with an Italian shoe brand and done pictures on locations along with some general travel videos. It wasn't a passion project so much as taking anything to get her away from Mom's spring charity fashion show in Kansas City, then a few weeks chasing a friend's band around on tour. Until she'd gone from worried to frantic about Ashlyn's full-media silence and flown home right in time for Ash to re-emerge and announce she'd had a quickie marriage in Vegas and would Jenna please come help plan a real wedding. The memory made her glare at Ash.

Now here we fucking are, girlie. It's a good thing you're cute or I'd have already strangled you.

"What kind of modeling?" Ice's brow quirked.

"The boring kinds. Travel posts, Instagram ads."

"I don't know, some Instagrams get pretty interesting." As he spoke, Ice lumbered toward the sofa and flopped onto a seat. "Case, grab us some beers, would you?"

She expected him to argue, but Case merely nodded and moved toward the kitchen. "You want anything, girls?"

"We've got waters," Jenna answered, right as Ash said the opposite: "If you can mix us some rum and Coke, you're officially the best!"

"Okay, she wins. That would be awesome." Jenna held up her hands in surrender.

Nathan cleared his throat, his voice lower as if hoping she wouldn't notice the sidebar as he leaned closer to Ash. "Speaking of traveling, Case offered to stay here while we go to Sturgis."

Jenna's ears perked at that. "Sturgis?"

"Biker Coachella," Ash explained. All three guys winced but didn't argue.

"Doesn't sound skippable?"

"It's not." Ash focused on Case as he reappeared to hand Ice a Bud Light. "And you know I love you, Case, but you've been dying to go since the patch party. Don't fall on a grenade when you don't have to."

"It's what I was trained to do." He pulled Ash into a one-armed hug. Joker's eyes rolled, but he didn't act weird about the casual embrace. *Maybe he's not a jealous psycho?* "Bullet's gotta leave the nest. We'll see if he's learned how to fly yet."

Ash's lips twitched, and Jenna practically heard her brain change tactics.

"Is Helen doing okay?" This question must have been a big one because Ice got to his feet, Bud Light in hand, and waved to Jenna.

"Come on, I'll get those drinks set up for you if you'll show me how strong to make it."

She followed him into the kitchen, glancing over her shoulder at the remaining trio. Case stood close to Ash, talking softly while Joker listened. *Still no jealous madman vibes.*

The remodeling fairy hadn't hit the kitchen full speed yet, granting the familiar slip-slide sensation of stepping between centuries as her feet hit vintage linoleum. "Not too strong, I want to survive past sunset."

Ice laughed and pulled down a bottle of spiced rum and directed her to the fridge for the Coke Zero. "Half a shot to test the waters? Yours'll be on the left.

Don't get it mixed up—Ash's is a lot stronger." He did a fancy bartender flourish as he poured to make her laugh, and ended by flipping the bottle into the air and catching it behind his back. She'd noticed a slight limp on his left leg, but the cat-quick reflexes hinted at another story. Despite her better judgment, Jenna found herself leaning against the counter, telling him about clubbing in the tombs around Rome for *Carnevale*. Ice was an easy audience, seeming eager for the tale and genuinely interested. He followed by asking about a story Ash had told about Paris, which Jenna corrected—the boys they'd been flirting with were in a band, not actors—when Nathan walked in.

Jenna's jaws snapped shut, her back straightened. Reflex. "Hey, how about another drink, please?" she said, instead of finishing her own story.

"I'll take Ashlyn's," Joker said.

"I'll make her a new one." Ice handed it off, and Joker settled at the small kitchen table. He sat straight, hands folded, thumbs bouncing against each other. He looked everywhere but at her. She opened her mouth to ask Ice something—anything— to end the awkward quiet when: "The drive okay?"

"Um." Caught off guard, the answer spilled out with more truth than she meant. "Sure. Aside from Maps dying on me, and what seemed like eight hundred miles with no service and no gas stations. I wasn't murdered by banjo-toting hillbillies, so there's that."

"We keep them penned into Georgia now," Ice said, mixing a new drink. Nathan let a smirk slip, a dimple showing through his light scruff. *Okay, he's stupid hot and not crazy in an instantly noticeable way. But I don't have to like him.*

"Need any help bringing your bags in?"

He wants an excuse to get out of here too? "I

wouldn't mind." She'd tried to pack light but going to a new place with uncertain resources, vague plans, and no set departure date required more planning—and more potential outfits—than one might think. Plus, she hadn't fully unpacked from three-ish months overseas, so why re-pack?

"Is it unlocked?" He stood up, and Jenna tried not to wince at being hemmed in with his towering form on one side and Ice on the other. Maybe the discomfort showed because Ice pushed away from the counter. "I can do it."

No, I like you! Let him do it! It would be rude to say out loud, but damn. *On the other hand, maybe this is a good time to needle King Monkey Wrench?* "It's open." Jenna pulled the key fob from her pocket and tossed it to Ice. If he stole the car or the luggage, maybe it would get Ash out of here. "Thank you so much. I'll get you a drink if there's a bar here somewhere... I guess that place Ash's working at?"

"That works." Ice smiled.

Joker slowly returned to his seat and crossed one leg over his knee. His brown gaze swept over her slowly this time. Jenna stood still, letting him judge, keeping her expression dull and disinterested. *I bet he's used to women drooling. Maybe I should try that?*

"You can sit if you want."

"Not yet. I've been sitting for five hours." But she did edge closer to the table so he couldn't say she was totally avoiding him. "Are you here to lodge any last-second pleas against pink wedding invitations?" She could hear Ash and Case in the other room, talking in low murmurs, presumably about the unfortunate Helen, whoever she was. Case's wife? Girlfriend? Kid?

He actually laughed. "Don't care what color they are. Whatever she wants." His head tipped to one side.

"As long as she doesn't put *me* in pink."

"You're safely in black, as far as I know. The tie might be TARDIS blue at some point, but those negotiations are your problem." Jenna grabbed the rum and fixed a drink for herself, grateful for an excuse to avoid looking at him. "So, did Case really want to skip the festival, or are you worried I'm a bad influence?"

"Nah, it's his call."

Thanks for that helpful answer, asshole. His foot returned to the floor.

"Are *you* worried I'm a bad influence?"

"Worried? No." She took a drink. "You are quite an influence though." *Two of us can roll an enigmatic vibe. Hah.*

"So is she. But I don't have to tell you that. You already know." A single finger drummed the table's worn surface like he was trying to tick off all the boxes full of things Jenna already knew.

"Mm." Jenna let her shoulders sag against the tired wallpaper. "She'd be fine if he wasn't here. She has her grandparents and cousins. Me. Plenty of projects." Jenna waved at the room in general. "It's sweet that y'all are worrying."

Joker met her gaze. "I know she'll be fine. That ain't what I'm worried about."

Liar.

"So why's someone have to stick behind when Bullet's gone?" She knew all about that particular biker—almost as much as Nathan. And that one she wanted to hug. Bullet, also known as Travis, had nearly lost his own life saving Ash's. A debt their found-family took seriously. All four of them—three now—knew how rare that gift was.

"It's complicated. Nothing you need to worry about."

"I'll take your word for what it's worth." *Which is nothing.* Jenna grabbed the rum and set it on the table next to him. "So, what's a biker fest like? Do you all brag about the size of your motors and compare paint swatches? Drunken orgies? All of the above?"

"Something like that." The small smirk returned. "I'd rather stay home, but it ain't so much an option for me." He stopped sharp, almost like he was surprised. Maybe he didn't mean to admit it.

"Yeah, I heard you're, like, a manager or something. Sucks being in charge." She grabbed him a fresh pop too, this time, launching into an old routine: Act friendly, give a guy stuff he wants. Lean in a little, keep your eyes wide and a trifle dazed. "But at least you get to have some fun at the parties."

He lifted a brow, eyeing the can but not reaching for it. The front door's rattle and the thump of objects on the floor caught her attention, and she turned in that direction, but Ice didn't walk into view. Instead, Joker kept talking.

"I'm a regular party animal. Everybody says so."

"Especially Ash." Jenna laughed, tossing her hair with an airy shrug. "We were discussing threesome options earlier." The words stopped his cup halfway to his mouth. His brow twitched before he set the drink down.

"You come to any conclusions?"

"Well, I opted out. No offense, but I think married couples are such drama about it. She suggested Karli, and someone named … Jessalyn, I think? My vote's on our friend Audra. She is super into that throuple vibe."

"Jenna, stop teasing Nathan," Ash said from the doorway, not quite hiding a giggle. "And Audra's a stage-five clinger."

Jenna pouted. "You're ruining the game."

"I'll eventually get a vote, right?" Joker finally picked up the Coke can.

"Should you?" Jenna countered while Ash laughed. He focused on the drink.

Ash shrugged. "Karli ain't exactly a stranger to threesomes either."

Jenna couldn't tell for sure, but Nathan's face seemed to be a few shades redder. He poured with far less flare than Ice and handed the cup to Ashlyn.

Case coughed, leaning against the door frame with a look of bemused wonder. "Thought we weren't supposed to talk about *that*."

"*You* aren't," Joker hissed. His wife kissed his stubbled jaw.

"Don't worry, Nathan. I already know your vote's gonna be *no* 'til five pm on doomsday. But it's fun to shop."

"First marriage, now monogamy. Kids these days are hopeless." Jenna sighed, draining her cup. "Z or millennials or whoever we are, are killing the swinger industry."

Ash flashed her emerald wedding ring. "Don't forget the diamonds."

"Nobody's missing that one except warlords and arms dealers."

"Back up, ladies. You saying monogamy ain't for you?" Case asked, the corner of his lip tilting.

"Case," Joker warned.

"It ain't like I asked outta the blue!"

The two men exchanged a stare, but Nathan lost interest and got to his feet, wrapping his arm around Ashlyn's waist. He whispered something in her ear.

"I'm gonna steal Ash for a moment. Be good," he announced, straightening to his full height, pointing at his disciple. Maybe more like a puppy. Case seemed awfully eager to follow directions from the man. Case saluted, then leaned against the wall, tilting the Corona to his lips. He didn't say anything until the bedroom door closed.

"Courthouse wedding, huh? Think you're about a month late. Unless it's for that make-up game Mrs. Tilden's planning. Then you're early as hell."

"Compared to what she should have had, it might as well be a courthouse affair. We've got five months!" She poured herself more rum. Ash's family was old money, her mother a feared corporate lawyer, and her stepfather had run a pharmaceutical empire for decades. People like that didn't throw a backyard barbecue and call it a reception. "For a Tilden heiress's wedding, that's like planning a moon mission in two weeks."

"How is Ash still an heiress? Her mom cut her off."

Jenna laughed and waved a dismissive hand. "Bella changes her mind. Especially when her mother starts screaming at her." *Who does he think is paying for the renovations? Nathan?* Jenna's attention caught on Case again. His bruised face creased in a frown.

"Bonnie got to see the wedding. I say throw a party, toast the happy couple, and save money."

Jenna surveyed him more critically, noting the ink visible below his t-shirt sleeves: dark whorling feathers, crow wings, wolves in combat.

"You get to see bikes every day. What's the big deal about Sturgis? Throw a party, admire your friends' bikes, and toast some beer."

His gleaming smile faded. "I ain't going to Sturgis. So, maybe I agree with you." The words came out harsher now. "I get your point, but I think you missed mine."

Is it that hard to imagine I'm ignoring it? Jenna levered herself onto the counter, knowing full well it put her closer to his height but might distract him with her shorts and her legs dangling as she leaned back and took a drink. "But you want to go to Sturgis. So why aren't you?"

"Something came up." His eyes strayed to her legs. She tried not to imagine him on his knees between them, but the image stayed somewhere in the back of her head. *Stupid hormones.* "Life don't always go the way you want it to. There are worse things than missing parties."

"Is there?" Jenna blinked and smiled, wide-eyed naivete prepped for a camera that wasn't there.

"Wouldn't feel right to have fun when I'm leaving a sick mom back here."

So that's Helen. And he expects me to believe him? Like I wasn't right there when Ash questioned his choices. "You really do have a rescue complex, huh?"

Case froze. But his reply—if he had one—remained unspoken, as Ice reappeared in the doorway and tapped his shoulder. "Sorry, had a call. I need some help with this big one... Girl." He gaped at Jenna. "How the ever-lovin' hell did you get those bags in there?"

"Me?" Jenna chuckled. "I didn't. Manuel did. Our gardener. He's amazing with stuff like that." She hopped off the counter. "But I don't even know what room I'm in here."

"Oh, I know it well. Grim's. Come on." He didn't seem to wonder where Ash and Joker vanished to. "I'll show you when we drag that big son of a bitch in." The two bikers walked out and Jenna lifted her phone. *Okay, Google, how do I convince my best friend to ditch a biker club full of demigods?*

Chapter Three
Jenna

July 25

Packing for a two-week biker vacay appeared to be a lot like packing for any other festival, assuming you were also camping for said festival. *Maybe a leather-themed festival*, Jenna reflected, toeing aside a pile of riding gear to push open the bedroom door. Inside, Ashlyn stood by an antique dresser auditioning different bracelets. Her long hair fell down her back in loose curls, painstaking makeup accentuated her delicate features, and her outfit was…

"Lady, I say this as someone who is a professional model, it's only lunch. Unless you forgot to tell me we're lunching at Elaia."

Ash's wrap dress and espadrilles sure as hell wouldn't be out of place at the uber-trendy restaurant.

"Says the one dressed to kill already." Ash's nose wrinkled.

Jenna checked her shorts and draped silk top. She hadn't meant to dress up, but she'd made it to Oak Grove with mostly festival wear and designer shit from Milan. *Maybe I should go shopping to blend with the locals better after all.* "It's fun and games 'til you decide we have to take photos on the way. And then I'm going to obsess about what I should've been wearing. Or my makeup."

"You're disgustingly hot without makeup. Some of us have to use it." Jenna settled on the edge of the king-size bed and aimed her phone at her best friend. "Now, wear the blue bead one. I'm starving."

"You're bored," Ash corrected with a huff.

"You're melting down about this because we

have to go over the catering lists."

"You're mean."

"I'm right. Blue bracelet. Matches the earrings. Come on." She snapped a pic as Ash stuck her tongue out. "I'm sending that one to the group."

"Have I mentioned you're the meanest? I—" Ash cut off as the front door opened, and male voices carried from the hallway. Jenna watched her best friend's breath stop, then resume as she recognized the owners. Jenna didn't want to, but somehow she did anyway. Travis and Case. *Oh, good, the babysitters are home.* Four days with Ash, they'd had all of a couple hours alone. If it wasn't Nathan—aka Joker, aka High Prince of Hell—it was Ice, Case, Bullet, Megan, Jessica, Karli, or a hundred other people whose names and faces Jenna opted not to recall.

In the front room, the Tweedles sprawled on oversize chairs like a pair of overly stubbled Levis models, debating some fine point of Harley lore. Or something. Jenna ignored them and grabbed her purse. Ash smiled and dropped onto the bigger chair—Joker's throne—ignoring Jenna's glare in turn. "Hey, Case. We're all heading for lunch. You want to come?"

God, why? Isn't Bullet bad enough?

Case's glittering gray gaze swept toward Jenna. She fought to keep her expression neutral. Even if she'd rather have bitten his bruise-bedecked face off. *Honestly, someone should congratulate my self-restraint.* He knew exactly how good he looked in the white t-shirt and faded jeans, the edge of a wolf's snout visible beneath his right sleeve. *So much fucking ink on these Neanderthals, you'd think they'd spare some cash for a life plan that didn't involve being hired thugs.* She didn't reproach herself for the ugly thought: if she couldn't speak her mind, she could at least be bitchy inside. Jenna concentrated on her phone but she could almost feel his smirk. "Nah. One shadow's probably more'n enough crowd."

"You're not..." But even Ash trailed off with a glance at Jenna. "Well, maybe next time."

Jenna blinked fast, avoiding anything but the app on her phone. Ash wanted Case to come because she liked him. He was her friend. Just like that. *A few weeks here in the back end of fucking nowhere, and Ash adopts these assholes like some long-lost family.* Jenna swallowed the anxious scream that constantly threatened to tear itself out of her throat when forced to stand near any of them. "Yeah," she added with something like enthusiasm. "It's fine, there's plenty of room in the car."

"Next time," Case said with a half-smile. "Stopped by to see if Joker's around."

"Should be on his way back." Bullet turned to Ash.

"So anywhere from an hour to a month." Jenna laughed. The best thing that could be said for her best friend's husband—aside from his gorgeous exterior—was that he didn't burden anyone with his presence often. He'd been gone more than home in the last four days—and well before, from what Ash admitted.

A car pulling up the driveway drew the Tweedles' interest, but Ash popped to her feet and rushed for the door. "That sounds like Grandma. Jenna, clean!"

She surveyed the already spotless front room and shrugged. "Sorry, don't think you've got time for a vacuum." The idiots chuckled, but at least Bullet had the grace to tuck a book back onto its shelf. Case didn't stir from his seat. Not that it mattered. Ash swung open the door with a smile. But it wasn't Bonnie Tilden on the front porch.

"Hello, Ashlyn. Jenna." Darren Hartwell's easy voice and kind brown eyes froze Jenna's breath in her lungs, and the irritated scream mutated into a wall of terror.

"Detective," Ash said without missing a beat. She even sounded happy to see him. "You're a long way from St. Vincent … and this is your partner?" A lady stood beside Hartwell—just as tall, but darker hair and skin. She shook Ash's offered hand with a bemused smile.

"Detective Marissa Carter."

"Come on in. We've got lemonade or water. Or tea. Are you working? We have beer too. If you're off the clock."

"We can't stay long, but water would be great," Darren answered.

"How about cookies? Brownies? I made them last night."

The Tweedles awkwardly shuffled to the farther-middle of the room like allergic kids confronting a cat as Ash ushered the newcomers inside. "Oh, um. These are some friends. Case, Bullet… Detectives Hartwell and Carter. Darren here helped me and Jenna out a, uh, while ago. Rather a lot, actually."

Somehow, Jenna found herself in the kitchen, grabbing bottles of water and the brownie tray, plates, and extra napkins while Ash made everyone as comfortable as possible. Her own throat hadn't come unglued yet, so she concentrated on handing Detective Carter a brownie, whether or not the lady had asked for one, then Darren. Only as she drew back, his gaze captured hers. She froze, locked somewhere between now and the night she'd met him, her hands slicked with blood, her throat raw and throbbing where Ben's fingers tried to silence her.

"Jenna, it's going to be all right." He'd said the same thing three years ago.

"You wouldn't be here if that was true." The voice that came from her was low, broken. The voice of the girl who'd stabbed her best friend's fiancé in a fight for her life. A life she wasn't even sure she wanted to keep at that point.

"Hey, maybe … maybe you should sit down?" Case sounded strange, but so did everything else. The world spun at eldritch angles. Ash's hands found her shoulders, edged her back into a chair.

"Jenna, don't panic. It's been three years. There's always stuff like parole or … routine things…"

"Not, ah, not this time." Detective Carter cleared her throat. "We are here to notify you—"

"Don't," Ash snapped, standing up to her full height—even if that was only five-foot-five—she got between Jenna and the detectives. "Don't you dare start this early. He's due out in *May*. I'm not going to sit here panicking for ten months because you wanted to get ahead on paperwork, Darren."

"He's getting out next week, Ash. I'm so sorry. I know how difficult this may be. The paperwork got jumbled or I'd have been here—"

"Difficult?" Jenna found her voice. "No. Testifying was difficult. Almost dying was difficult. And you're… You can't say they're…" All the words tangled on her tongue, and she covered her mouth, afraid it would end in screaming. Or sobbing.

"How did this happen?" Case again, his voice level and calm. So normal. Like he handled monsters coming out of their cages every day. Maybe he did. Maybe he was one of them. *I should throw the brownie tray at his stupid head. At all their heads. Stop. Talking.*

"There was a fight. And a credible threat to Mr. Fitzgerald's life. He's being released early on parole for his recovery. He'll be expected to check-in and won't be allowed to approach either of you."

"You know him, Darren." Ash's voice was soft where Jenna's had been harsh. "Is there nothing to postpone it? Even a few weeks. I'm … I had a bad turn last month. The timing of this isn't great."

Darren sighed. "Great would be never having to let that asshole on the streets. There's no such thing as a good time to release a violent offender."

"Well then." Ash settled onto the sofa. "You've had a long drive and crying won't fix it. How's your family? And your old partner? Marcus Crowley, right?"

"Excuse me," Jenna muttered, making a mad, clumsy dash for the kitchen where an emergency bottle of Xanax sat hidden behind the sugar jar in the farthest cabinet. Better yet: a fifth of Grey Goose on the counter. She got down one pill and half a screwdriver before Case strode in.

"That went better than I expected."

She sneered. "They're still here."

Case's brow furrowed.

Hah. Not so Ash-Smart now, are you? "She's going to melt down when they leave. She can't be upset in front of them. I don't have that particular fucking problem." She shoved the pill bottle into his giant hand. "Maybe get her to take one as they're leaving. Pro-tip."

"And you?"

"Already taken. I'm launching myself to Mars on a rocket ship of vodka." She pulled out an actual rocket-shaped cup and tipped it toward Case.

He set the pills aside, putting a warm, solid hand on her shoulder. *Bastard.* "Before you lift off, Cosmo, let's step outside for a minute. Catch some air."

Jenna's hard glare fixed on him. "You don't need to play concerned, cowboy. I'll be fine."

"I know you will."

What if I hit him? It wouldn't help. She didn't even want to, particularly. *I wanted to punch Ben. And Auggie. And even Carz some days. Shit... He's still incommunicado. What the hell are we going to do?* The panic unfurled slithering tentacles through her, and Jenna barely got the vodka over the counter before it slipped from her fingers. "Fuck." She shoved away and ran for the back door. It didn't count as taking his advice if she ignored him while she did it.

The idiot followed her, that same big, careful hand catching her above the elbow, tugging her back as she tripped over an abandoned shovel on the concrete patio. One arm circled her waist, steadying her. Jenna tensed, an insult on her lips. She turned, intending to spit it in his face. Their gazes met. Held. And she looked away. Prayed he was too dumb to see the truth.

"I've got you, sweetheart." For a split second, staring down at the pavement, his voice transfigured, and the fear snapped her last brain cell in half.

Time, space, everything fell away, leaving her in a gray vacuum, crying into his white t-shirt, the ghost of a girl she'd buried three years ago in a Missouri courtroom. In May, she could have left the country. Stayed in Carz's apartment until she felt safe. Planned, at least. They had planned, ages ago, what would happen when the time came. They might even have managed to find a lawyer to push him staying in for another two years, the full term. Might. Could. Should. Broken hopes, forgotten fears slashed away with each sob.

He cupped the back of her head, but her brain couldn't process the touch or the softly whispered words. When he spoke louder, it felt like watching a movie where the audio and the lips didn't match up. "I'm sorry."

Sorry? For what?

"It's not fair. It's bullshit. I wish there was something I could do."

"Shut up." For the barest second, it almost felt right. Safe. But he'd spoken. The voice was wrong, and so was everything else. Jenna breathed in, straightened up, and pulled herself away from his warmth. "Unless you can convince Ash to get the fuck out of the country. All that ... everything we went through ... and they won't even hold him five fucking years. After all he did—" She cut herself off.

Nobody knew. Not soft-spoken Darren or his old partner, not the lawyers or the judge. Secret sins, buried deep enough that the rest of them could almost live with the pain. "I wish I'd stabbed him lower," she admitted. "I should have." *I hoped I did.* She dared to meet Case's gaze, challenging him. *Tell me otherwise, asshole.*

"Ash is safe." His deep voice sounded like he meant it. But how could anybody promise something like that? "You are, too. I don't know what he did to her, but I know he won't come here. We won't let him. And if he does? You'll never have to worry about him again."

"You think he needs to be here to hurt someone?" A sound too flat and bitter to be a laugh escaped. "You don't know anything about him. Or Ash. Or me." *I bet you don't even know how much I want to collapse onto this cement and scream until I can't move.* She bit her cheek, willing the pain to keep her on balance. "Big, tough, badass rednecks. You guys do what? Run around beating up old-timey shopkeepers? Scaring people with your bikes. You don't have any idea how this feels."

"I won't try to convince you that I get it." His expression was far kinder than hers. "But I don't need to understand it to know I want to help. Believe it or not, Jenna, Ashlyn means a lot to us. And you mean a lot to her. I'm here for both of you."

"Liar," she hissed, her vision blurred with tears. "We were nothing to you six months ago, we'll be nothing six months from now." But her voice shook when she said it. "You weren't there and you won't be there." Whether she'd addressed that to Case or the ghosts in her head, she didn't care. Most of all, she hated that she wanted to hug him again and that it felt right, for one horrid moment. "Go away, Case."

"No. You shouldn't be alone. Mostly because that would prove you right, and I can't allow that."

"Did you just—" She gave a startled laugh. "Asshole. You would be nice just to be a dick." Jenna wiped at her face. "Fine. I'm going back in for more vodka." But instead of turning, she reached out for his hand, twining her fingers around his. He glanced down, then at her. *Waiting for a punchline?* "Thanks."

A tiny smile kindled on his full lips. "You're welcome." His thumb moved against hers. "Damn... You make it hard for me to tell you this, but that bottle you dropped didn't make it."

"You're lying. I'd have noticed the smell of that much vodka."

"Worth a shot."

Jenna let go of his hand, hating that she wanted to hold on. *It's only your emotions. You're in a clingy goddamn mood, and he's tall and hot. It's a pheromone-based illusion you're too weak to see through, like at the Gas Station Before Time. Go in, drink, get ready in case Ash has an episode when Darren leaves, then...*

And then...

Party irresponsibly but with epic style until some better solution comes along?

"We're going to need more vodka," she told Case and pushed the door open. "Like an actual metric fuckton of booze. Can I send you with my card?"

"You could. Or I can text Joker." He patted the phone-shaped bulge in his left pocket. "Think he planned on doing a beer run." He frowned, watching the door. "Should probably call him anyway."

"You want to freak him out while he's driving?" Jenna countered. Her head cocked as she glanced up, considering. "Unless he won't be that worried. It's basically Travis's job to handle any meltdowns, right?"

He stopped mid-step, turning back to face her "It's not like that. Joker... He'll want to know."

"Just saying."

"You ain't walking into a typical situation, Jenna. Joker *wants* to be here. I get how it looks." He stared her in the face, and his shoulders fell ever so slightly. "And I get the feeling I can talk myself ragged, and it won't change your mind."

She almost smiled. "Seems like Travis is the one with Ash when bad days hit. Him or some other poor puppy who doesn't have a shiny badge-y piece."

"Hey—" He obviously stopped himself short of asking her to give Joker a chance. *Good boy.* "I don't think I'm too much of a poor puppy," he said quietly, smiling as her eyes rolled.

"You are the absolute poorest puppy. But you have a badge, so I guess they took pity." Jenna leaned against the brick wall, giving him a playful smirk. "So why are you here, anyway? Nursing a secret crush on Ash? Or ... Nathan?"

He chuckled. "I don't do secret crushes all that well. Joker was one of the first people who helped me get settled when I got back. It ain't easy getting back into civilian life. He got me work and helped me figure a lot of shit out. A long way of saying he's like a brother. Unless you're asking what I'm doing in Oak Grove at all. That's ... different."

"Secret bro-crush on Joker. Got it." She started for the kitchen. Darren's voice filtered in from the front room alongside Ash's occasional laugh, and murmurs of the other, less familiar voices. "So why are you here? Bromances aside."

He settled back against the counter, his arms crossing. Whatever humor he still had behind his eyes vanished. "My stepmother, mostly. And my brother. They live a few blocks over."

"Oh." Jenna's expression softened. She'd dismissed it as some half-assed excuse for Case to be around before, not like his reason for residing in the town at all. "Ash said she's, like, kinda sick?"

"She was in a bad car accident when I was thirteen. Hasn't been able to go back to work since. Then Dad died…" He rubbed his cheek, clearly uncomfortable. "Somebody had to be here. Liam was too young, and my sister offered, but that meant dropping out of college, and I'll be damned if—" He cleared his throat. "Sorry. You don't want to hear all this."

"No, it's … it's totally a thing I want to hear. It sounds like a way better story than this one." She gestured toward the front room. "And anyway, I get it. My dad got on a dumbass private plane when I was ten and flew it into a mountain."

"Shit. A plane crash?" He let out a low whistle. "I'm sorry."

"It's a long time ago. But my stepdad's been here." She wanted to ask if he'd put his mom in a nursing home but thought better. Ash was always reminding her people here didn't have money—like any money—and on reflection, that was probably expensive. "What about your dad?"

"Heart attack. Can't even say he really was living up to that point anyway. He was a hard worker, though.

And he never stopped trying to make shit better. And he loved us." He focused on a distant point, his features smoothing for the barest second before he pulled his attention back to the living and fixed that hypnotic gray stare on Jenna.

"What did your mom say about you rescuing your stepmom?"

"Mom's a whole 'nother level of batshit. I think that's the sort of conversation requiring a couch and a trained professional."

"Moms are difficult at the best of times." Jenna poured vodka into her rocket cup and held up the bottle for him. He hesitated but took it. "I only discuss mine in therapy, and she seems to be fairly normal. I can't imagine having anything more complicated." Like Ash's mom. The cool calculation of Bella Tilden-Marlow's gaze across a blood-smeared emergency room still made Jenna shudder. *I hope Case's mom isn't like that.*

"Difficult doesn't even begin to describe mine. I'd try, but nobody ever believes me anyway." He examined the bottle and grabbed a cup out of the cabinet. Jenna wasn't surprised. According to Ash, he spent almost as much time here as Ice, who appeared to be an unofficial roommate. "I'm glad nobody here will ever have to meet her. She hates Oak Grove. Probably more than you do," he added with a smirk.

"I don't hate it." She mixed in enough orange juice to pretend she wasn't drinking straight alcohol. "I just don't like it." *Especially not for my best friend who needs familiar stuff and better doctors.* Having to drive an hour for a psychiatrist or doing vid conferences didn't seem like the better choice. But here they stood all the same. "I hate that my best friend is hanging out with a gang. No offense."

Case drank straight from his cup, ignoring the

orange juice. "That's fair," he conceded. "Don't know if that's what I'd call us, but I understand why you think so."

"Yeah, the tattoos, bikes, one-percent rockers, general secrecy, all of y'all carrying burner phones, easy access to pot and recreationals in a rural area, locals being super careful and respectful... I do wonder how I got to that conclusion."

"Yeah. Makes no sense." He grinned, taking another sip.

"What about that epic shiner you were sporting when we met? I was meaning to ask if you're an amateur fighter or something. Cause I'm no longer buying the wrench story."

"Uh, honest mistake. See, I walked into a fist. Wasn't even fighting."

"Sure. Totally a thing I believe from a biker."

"All I'm saying is I don't like labels."

Her brow quirked. "Says the man who literally tattooed a Marine corps label on his arm."

"Unless you count all the labels I'm wearing. But aside from those specific ones, I resent them."

She lifted her right arm, flashing the compass and infinity symbols she bore. "Some of us avoid labels for real. Poser."

"I was young and dumb," he said playfully. "As opposed to now. A little bit older and dumb." He tilted his head, slowly eying the ink. "Not bad. Cute. Bet you have a dreamcatcher somewhere, too, right?"

"Oh, for sure. Right on my lower back," she lied easily. He was hardly the first person to think her ink generic—but she'd chosen them deliberately, so the real meanings were her own, and not something idiots would ask her about online. "And a butterfly on my pelvis. I wanted to get something on my thigh, but I couldn't think what would look hottest, you know?"

"Seriously, though, your artist did an amazing job on the compass." His heavy gaze shifted from her wrist to her face.

Jenna turned away.

"Guess you're somebody who finds their own way?"

She laughed. "More like I have a terrible sense of direction and hoped if I tattooed it on me, it would rub off. So far, no luck." But her fingers brushed over the infinity loop, an old habit now. She'd thought her compass led her to the guy she'd be with forever. "I ought to give up and get it lasered or covered. But I've been lazy." She took a drink. "Plus, it makes my Insta photos easier to recognize."

"I wouldn't worry. Looks good on you." He took another sip but quickly lowered the cup as the garage door creaked open. Two bikers filled the frame. "Hey, Boss," Case said, setting the cup down. Joker nodded at both of them before stalking past, right into the living room.

Jenna groaned. "Is this where he pisses off two detectives and gets sent to prison?" She muttered the question into her cup, barely loud enough for Case to hear. He laughed but didn't answer. Instead, he pushed off the counter and shadowed the others, hovering by the arched entrance to the front room, out of everyone's eyeline. She hesitated, then moved to his side and peeked around his shoulder.

Poor, unfortunate Bullet stood at the far side, trying to make himself as small as possible against the wall, and Ice seemed to be fighting a laugh. He nudged the Prospect, whispering. Bullet's face relaxed like he'd been let out of a firing squad. He rushed toward Case and Jenna's position.

"Beer run," he mouthed as he brushed past them.

Jenna sniffed at the Tweedles' antics— the fact there were now four oversize lumps of muscle and ink instead of two did not affect their collective identification. But her attention caught on Joker's dark expression, and the way Darren eyed him in return. *Oh, please be an asshole to the cop. Please. Solve so many problems...* But Hartwell played the even-keeled, aw-shucks cop, and Ash was in sunny debutante mode. Like two characters from a Hallmark movie crossed into an HBO drama.

"It really is so sweet of you to come out in person. I should call Grandpa. He'd love to catch up and get dinner for y'all. He might chew your ear off about some cases though."

Jenna's gaze caught Ash's for the fleeting moment, and she had to grab Case's muscled arm for support. Ash was *fine*. Ash was pissed off. *Oh, no way I'm sitting on the bench for this.*

Jenna grinned, stepping into the room fully, both feet planted on the twenty-first-century hardwood floor.

Ash continued her hostess pitch without missing a bet. "Seriously, Detectives. It's a long drive, and the deer are getting ridiculous. Tomorrow's a weekend, right? Why don't you let me and Grandpa Amos take you to dinner?"

"The Tildens have about fifty spare bedrooms," Jenna added. "It'll be no problem."

"Oh, it's all right," Hartwell said, his attention drifting back to Joker. "We really should start heading back. Good to see you both again, though I do wish it were under better circumstances." He gave a sad sort of smile and then stepped closer to Joker. "Congratulations on the wedding, Mr. Wronski." He held his hand out.

Case coughed like something caught in his throat.

Joker's dark eyes flashed Case's direction before he took the offered hand. "Thank you." It almost sounded cordial. Almost.

"I'll walk you out," Ice said.

"There's no need." Hartwell waved him off. "We'll see ourselves out."

"Don't forget you're invited!" Ash said, following him to the door anyway. "And if you ever get dragged this way on one of those antiquing trips, the door is always open."

Joker stood very still, his glare aimed in Case's direction. *Why's he the one in trouble?* Jenna looked between them, hardly registering the ten-minute ritual of Midwestern goodbyes even though she was participating in it. Then the front door shut, and the cops were gone.

As the car drove off down the block, Joker turned to Ashlyn. His expression finally softened. "I take it he wasn't dropping in to say hello."

"Of course not." Jenna scoffed.

Ash met her husband's gaze without missing a beat. "He was here to let us know Bennett is getting released. Apparently, he qualified for early processing or whatever. Something about fights or threats to his life. The usual. Not like Missouri is known for keeping prisoners five seconds longer than it can get away with. So, Ben's due out in a couple weeks."

Jenna watched her, waiting for signs of the prophesized panic attack. All she read now was calm. *Oh, dear.* Somebody's *in trouble and it's not Case.* She almost sang it out loud but settled for sipping her orange-tinted vodka. "Drink, Ash?"

"Hell yes. I'd like to toast the end of civilization properly."

"Can we talk about this first?" Joker asked. "Alone?"

"I'll take a drink," Ice said, turning to go to the kitchen.

Case glanced at Ashlyn and Joker before turning. Slowly, he started toward Jenna, his steps careful as if he was afraid Joker would notice the movement. "Told you," he whispered, trying to pull her back toward the kitchen. Jenna let him win. There was no door to shut, and open archways, so the actual privacy granted to Joker and Ash was mostly "out of the line of sight." Even so, she slowed her pace to be sure to hear the next reply.

"Alone?" Ash echoed. "No. I think there's been enough handling of things *alone*."

"Drinks all around," Jenna announced with an enthusiastic hand clap, giggling manically at the men. Ben would be out, the world upside down and on fire. Might as well drink good vodka while it burned. "We may be low on OJ. But there are plenty of shades of pop and rum and whiskey…"

Jenna plucked her phone from the counter and swiped a message to Ash. Not that she'd see it before the implosion, but that wasn't the point. "Hope your boy knows how to handle a nuke," she said softly to Ice as she stepped around him to inspect the rum supply.

"Wouldn't be surprised." Ice popped the cap off a beer bottle. "Unless the nuke's name is Ashlyn? Then, no. He's hopeless at that."

Case leaned back against the counter and grabbed his cup. "I must have missed something. Why's she pissed now? Or … is it better I don't know?"

"Probably better not to say anything the rest of the night." Ice's tone changed so quickly. He wasn't happy with Case either. *What did I miss?*

"Oh, that sounds sinister." Jenna wagged a finger at the sullen Tweedle. "Careful, or they'll demote you back to puppy. I—"

"Jenn!" Ash yelled. "Forget the drinks. Grab your purse." The blonde stood in the archway, ignoring her looming husband. Joker looked ready to crash through a wall. Or six. Maybe flattening a few tank divisions on his way. This had no effect on Ashlyn whatsoever as she whirled to snarl up at him. "We're going out. If I see one single god-forsaken Crow in the next four hours, I'll set this fucking house on fire, Nathan. You want me to act like a take-no-prisoners biker babe? Wish goddamn granted."

Jenna eyed her best friend, then Joker, and laughed. "Fuck yeah, let's do girls' night. Past due anyway." Phone in hand, she skipped past the guys to link arms with Ash.

"Do what you want, Ashlyn," Joker seethed. "Hear what you want. Think what you want." His focus flicked to Case. "Call Bullet. Tell him to cancel the beer run."

"O-okay." Case reached for his phone.

"I'd tell you to be careful, *babe*, but you'll probably hear that wrong, too," Joker snapped, stalking toward the small hallway and slamming the bedroom door behind him.

Ice sniffed. "That went better than I thought. Guess we're riding for the clubhouse? Fuck. I was planning on getting shit-faced."

Ash tossed her golden hair over her shoulder. "Why? You guys can stay here and get shit-faced. Not like he's coming out of his den anyway. If you still want to party at ten, the four hours will be up, and I'll tag the bar on Insta. But don't cancel the beer run. Nathan's too busy playing pissy panda to remember the case in the fridge is almost empty." She dropped a fifty on the counter and sauntered out the door, Jenna beside her.

"Have fun, boys!" Jenna waved from the door.

Ice followed them out. "Hey, Trouble. Know you don't wanna hear from me right now, but try not to burn any buildings down tonight."

"How mad are you?" Jenna hissed under her breath once Ash shut the front door behind them.

"Oh, I'll probably be able to speak in coherent sentences by midnight. Maybe he'll have remembered that I'm not an idiot by then … but we'll see."

****

Case

"Do I, er, text him or not?" Case stared at the fifty. It felt dangerous to go against Joker's order, especially with his mood being dark as burned dog shit, but somehow pissing off Ash didn't feel any safer tonight. He checked the screen, the text written but not sent.

"Give me your phone." Ice snatched it without waiting for an answer. His thumbs flew across the screen, and a second later, Ice's phone pinged in his pocket. "There. Sent it to the wrong guy. Now you just look like an idiot."

"Smart play, jackass. Except for the fact that you got the text and would tell me."

"You really don't know me at all, do you?"

"Christ. That was…" Case shook his head. The only couple he'd seen in that kind of meltdown was the week Blackie's ol' lady served him divorce papers. *Granted, that was probably more about Blackie fuckin' around.* He searched his memories of his parents, but even they'd never sounded that hard on one another. Including their poisonous howling outside the courtroom.

"That? It's nothing. She's pissed because he didn't tell her he put a hit out on Bennett. And now it's gone all sideways, and he's too fucking guilty to notice she's not pissed that he did it, just that he's not being upfront about it."

"How the hell d'you know that?"

"How the hell'd you miss it?" Ice snorted. "Goddamn amateurs. Ash ain't that hard to figure out, brother. Not like that spiky friend of hers. That girl…"

"You gonna tell Joker your findings?" He really didn't want to hear Ice's analysis on Jenna.

"Nah. Ain't my business. Besides, it's more fun this way."

Case's brow creased. "You really are a dick."

"I know. And speaking of…" The bedroom door opened at the far end of the house. Joker slouched down the hall. "Hey, man. Thought you'd be brooding a little longer. Here. Drink." Ice pushed the vodka toward Joker. He grunted and drank straight from the bottle.

"Home sweet fucking home."

"Is that what this is? Thought it was a hotel." Ice chuckled. "Had to kick a homeless guy out the other day."

"I keep telling Ash we gotta stop taking strays. This ain't a foster home for delinquents."

Case bit his cheek. *When did we move on to this track?* "Hold on. Everyone, pause. What's happening with this? Are we not gonna talk about the girls leaving right now, or…?"

Joker propped himself up against the counter, a single brow raised. "You okay, man?"

"He's frazzled. Doesn't like it when mommy and daddy fight."

Joker swore and swigged another shot of vodka. "Me either. Thought the next time we heard about that bastard it'd be a funeral announcement."

"I'll make some calls. See what went wrong." Ice

reached for the bottle. "And these four hours? Got somebody tailing her?"

"No. Not that stupid."

"Good. She'd kill you, and I ain't good with funerals."

"But after that…" Joker nodded to Case. "Spider and Grim dug up as much dirt as they could find on Fitzgerald, but I ain't comfortable going to Sturgis anymore."

"You can't exactly back out at this point, brother," Ice reminded him.

"I fucking know that." The anger radiated off him as he rolled his right shoulder like he wanted to warm up, throw some punches. "Damned if I do, damned if I don't. I'm gonna have to leave them both, Ice. They might say I'm playin' favorites, but I don't give a shit. I can't leave anyone else. Not now."

"You know I would if I could."

"What are you talking about?" Case inched closer.

"Bullet has to stay behind," Joker answered.

His stomach jolted. "What? I'm already gonna be here. You—"

"I want both of you here."

"Fucking why?" *Why not just kick me in the nuts? Why* that *fucking Prospect?* He slammed a fist down onto the counter. Ice's eyes narrowed.

"Really? Now's not the time to wonder if your dick's better than his. If you can't see why— "

"I can," Case said, accidentally interrupting. He held up an apologetic hand. "Sorry. I didn't mean… Fuck." Case swallowed hard, bowing his head. Ashlyn trusted Bullet with her life. Hell, she'd be dead and buried if he hadn't turned on the Heathens' president to save her after being kidnapped. Joker owed him. But seeing a Heathen getting a golden ticket to the fucking inner circle…

"You keep digging holes you can't get out of, don't you?" Ice snorted and tilted his beer bottle at Case's chest. "Here's a pro-tip, genius. Next time a couple of cops show up, give us a fucking warning."

"I couldn't!"

"And why the hell not?" Joker's voice was sharp.

"Jenna lost her fucking shit, and if I didn't stop her, she'd be halfway to St. Louis. I thought it was gonna be Ashlyn who panicked, not Jenna. But she just took the fuck off." He pictured her pale face, the tremor in her shoulders. The relief he felt when she didn't fight his hold on her… And when she relaxed enough to talk to him. "By the time we came back in and she wasn't high tailing it anywhere, you two were already here. I was doing what you told me to do." *Keep an eye on her. That's my job, right? Not my fault she's hot and easy to talk to sometimes.*

Ice sat at the table, propping his feet on the wooden top. "So that's why you two were so fucking chummy when we walked in. Quick work, cowboy. She say anything?"

Plenty. Stuff he didn't think she'd say to them under normal circumstances. He didn't know why, but it felt wrong to tell them. Like a betrayal. "Mostly that she stabbed him." *They already know that.* "She wishes she killed him. More or less." *Or more. A lot more.* But they didn't ask what it meant. Only what she said.

"That makes two of us." Joker stepped around the counter and pushed Ice's feet back onto the ground. "People eat there."

"Who eats here?" Ice asked. "Not a single fucking person. We eat in the living room like civilized assholes, and you know it."

Joker ignored him.

Again: "How did we fuck this up?"

"Don't worry." Ice's feet thumped onto the other chair instead of the table. "We'll get Spider on it. I'll make calls to the inside guys. Make sure someone feels our displeasure. How much damage can Fitzgerald do now?"

Joker stretched back, rubbing his neck with a pained scowl. "Please don't ask. The universe may decide to answer the question."

Chapter Four
Case

August 4

His hangover woke him up at four in the morning. After an hour of dying in the shower with the taste of bitter bile and rancid whiskey seared into his mouth, the chance of going back to sleep sat somewhere between *fat chance* and *never gonna happen*, so he accepted sleep deprivation. Putting on fresh clothes and driving to Joker's seemed logical at some point, though through the haze of dawning sobriety, he wasn't sure when.

You did this to yourself. Nobody challenges Dragon and lives. This is what happens when you let Jack Daniels do the thinking.

Once there, he tried helping the guys with their bags, but after two rounds in the bathroom, Joker shoved a Dasani at him and told him to stay put. So he sat, sipping mindlessly, glaring from the couch as the Prospects walked out, duffel bags in each hand. *I'm hungover. Not useless.* Except for the painful knots in his stomach and the jackhammer in his head, he was at one hundred percent.

Case grimaced when the back door slammed, and Ice walked into the room, trailing a Marlboro cloud behind him. Normally, a comforting smell. Today, he held his breath, trying not to gag.

"Finished?" Ice asked as Bullet kicked the front door closed behind him.

"All loaded up." The kid threw himself onto the armchair, sinking into the soft cushions and making himself at home. *This ain't your place!* Case imagined Bullet's head exploding and felt slightly better.

"Well, shit. I think we're ready to go." Ice looked around the room like they missed something. "We may be leaving on time! That's a record."

"Almost ready." Joker peered through the screen door, inspecting Bullet's work. Satisfied, he crossed the room, out of Case's sight. Ice followed him as far as the bathroom.

Then there were two.

Bullet's head tilted back, his legs straightening in front of him. Acting like he hauled the whole damn house outside. *Fucking pussy.* Case squeezed the empty Dasani bottle like a stress ball. Every time the plastic crackled, Bullet's jaw twitched. Weird how pissing him off improved a hangover.

"Case—"

"Knock that shit off." Joker stood at the end of the short hallway, his arm around Ashlyn's shoulders.

"Fine." Case balled the bottle up and threw it at Bullet. He aimed for his shoulder, but it hit Bullet's face. "Ten points! Put that in the recycle, Prospect."

"Hush! You'll wake Jenna up." Ashlyn hadn't been out of bed long. Her heavy eyes blinked slowly, and her long hair was down, finger-brushed and almost presentable. Still cute as hell. *Maybe I'd hate traveling too if I was leaving that kind of wake-up behind.* He couldn't help picturing Jenna in bed, pulling him back under a warm blanket. *Damn it.*

The next few minutes passed in a blur. Case didn't move. He wanted to vomit again, and his legs felt like Jell-O when he tried to stand. Ice came over, flicking his forehead and laughing at his pain. Joker said his goodbye from the front door. Case lifted his head to wave but stopped short of saying anything when he saw Joker had Ash's feet off the ground, kissing her like he wanted to fuck her. Ash didn't appear to mind. A week ago, they were biting each other's heads off. Now they were five seconds from stripping down on the porch. *They need to make up their damn minds.*

Case groaned, letting his head fall back, his arm covering his face as the bikes roared to life outside. His body clenched. *I should be going with them.*

The growling engines faded. *Definitely too late now.* The door opened again. The couch sank, and he glanced beneath his arm to find Ashlyn sitting by his feet. He moved to give her more room, but she leaned back on his shins and patted his knee. So she wanted to talk. Shit. "What's up?"

"Rough night?"

"Don't remember most of it." He told Frog he'd drop by for a couple of beers. Instead, they emptied his bar. Somehow, he wound up back in his own apartment, smelling like Jack Daniels and splayed on the floor. Didn't even make it to the couch. "Morning's been shit."

"That why you aren't at Helen's?"

He smirked. Even Ashlyn knew what Thursdays meant. *That's how you know you're hanging around too much.* "Liam's there. And one of her friends is in town, too. Said she'd help him take care of her today."

Ashlyn nodded. "You drinking enough water?"

"He's had a bottle."

Fuck. When'd Bullet come back in?

"You need to drink more," Ash said, altogether too sweetly. "And then get some sleep. It's going to be a long night."

I don't like the sound of that. "Why? What're we doing?"

"Going to Belleville. I thought I told you."

"Oh, right." She mentioned it a few days ago, but it sounded more like an idea instead of an actual plan. "That's tonight? Can't we do it another night? I thought we could—"

"Stay in?" Ashlyn lifted an irritated brow. "We haven't gone out in a week." She stood and walked over to Bullet, saying something too quietly for Case to hear. The Prospect nodded and turned toward the kitchen.

Guess that's the end of the conversation.

Bullet came back with another water, tossing it onto Case's stomach. "Take it easy, man. You got time to take a nap. I'll try to convince them to go tomorrow."

Sleep didn't come easy. His thoughts stuck on the road, with his brothers. He'd hoped the regrets would ease up once they rolled out. *So much for that.* Could be worse, though. Ash could be freaking out about Bennett, and Jenna could be giving him hell for existing. But since the detectives showed up a week ago, she almost treated him like a human. Sometimes. But progress was progress. Maybe he'd have some actual intel for Joker by the time the others got to Sturgis. Finally, he drifted off with images of strippers and biker parties spinning around him. He was halfway to fucking a hot brunette with mile-long legs when she grabbed his shoulder and shook him. Hard.

"Fuck!" He jerked back from her, bounced off the cushions, and she was suddenly a very definite he, with shaggy hair and too much stubble "Asshole!" Case grabbed the back of the couch so he wouldn't fall.

"Sorry," Bullet said. "Been trying to wake you up."

"Why?"

"The girls are almost ready."

Case groaned. "I just put my head down."

Bullet held his phone so Case could see the time. *8:00 PM.* Case shoved his arm away.

"Let you sleep as long as I could. Trust me. You *don't* want Ash or Jenna waking you up. It's not as gentle."

If Case could kill Bullet with a look alone, this would be the day he died. "I hate you." But he sat up.

"It ain't gonna be that bad."

He ignored him. Because if he didn't, Bullet would get a fresh bullet hole in his torso. Of course, the girls wanted to drink and have fun. But why couldn't they do that in the house? He knew the house. Knew the sounds it made. The people around. A bar outside of Oak Grove? One Case had never set foot inside, full of drunks and strangers, a solid hour from other Storm Crows? He didn't like it. He was pretty sure Joker would veto the fuck out of it too, but Joker's phone was off tonight. So was Tree's…

He watched Jenna bounce out of her borrowed bedroom and down the hall. Boppy pop music streamed from under Ash's door, presumably signaling her rituals were going well, but Jenna wore a frown when she stopped in front of Bullet and Case. She wore a tiny skirt and a complicated top that managed to suggest a lot of material while hiding absolutely nothing. She held up two pairs of high-heeled shoes. "Which would you stare at, boys?" The left was all straps, almost as complicated as her top, and the other a solid almost-shoe-shaped assembly. Her heavily lined eyes fixed first on Bullet but lingered on Case. "I can't go out in flats, so don't even try."

Breathe, idiot! Why did his throat feel constricted all of a sudden? *Does she have any idea what happens to that shirt when she breathes?* The thin material clung to her every movement, and her nipples were right there. Eye-level. *Fucking hell.* He sat straighter, scooting to the edge of the cushion, trying to focus on the shoes. Bullet's voice registered somewhere in the fog of his mind, but whatever answer he gave was lost.

Against his will, Case's gaze drifted downward. Were her legs always that distracting? Did his fingers *always* itch to touch them? "Um…" *Answer the question!* "I, uh, think … the strappy ones." It didn't matter. She could go out in combat boots and oversize Carhartts and draw just as many stares.

"Thanks!" Jenna dropped onto the couch next to him, getting the shoes on without hesitation. Her long, dark hair fell forward, revealing bare skin and lace across her back. Case's fingers dug into his palm.

"Megan said she'd come with us after all!" Ash called, emerging from her bedroom. The shorter blonde wore a swingy dress and heels almost equal to Jenna's. Marriage did not appear to hinder either fashion or makeup usage. *What if I send a Snap of this to Joker?* But then again, he'd never seen Joker argue over Ash's clothes. "I'd started to think she was allergic to any bars outside the county. But it's not like it's actually in St. Louis."

"That's good," Bullet said. Case's attention snapped from Jenna's slender ankles to him. "I think she'll have a lot of fun." Bullet sat down on the other side of Jenna. *Too close.* "Ignore that one," he said, nodding in Case's direction. "Bills came due this week."

Case opened his mouth to argue. Then closed it. *An excuse for acting so weird. Fucking hell.* "No point bringin' it up, asshole." He cracked a small smile. "You look great, by the way," he said to Jenna. Great didn't cover it, but saying she was a walking wet dream wasn't gonna go over well. Probably.

"Thank you. So, unscheduled STD testing?" Jenna raised a brow. "Or paternity test?" She smoothed the skirt and adjusted a strap on her shoulder as she sat up. Despite her cool words, she sounded more teasing than insulting. For a change.

"Nah. Those ain't that expensive." He smiled, but let it falter a little. "They told me Helen's new bed would be covered, then slapped me with a bill barely south of a grand." It wasn't a lie. But the problem was a week old now. "She needs it, though, so if I have to pay for it, it is what it is…" He shrugged.

"Don't they have payment plans for that stuff? Or like … people who fix it with Medicaid? I mean, it's a thousand? That's not a big—"

"Jenna," Ash hissed, too late. Her expression was somewhere short of mortified but only just.

Jenna blinked, obviously lost. "Oh. Sorry," she said hurriedly. "I've never had to deal with that stuff."

Case stood up and patted his pockets to make sure his wallet was there, and when he didn't feel it, he checked to see if it dropped out of his pocket and paused for a moment. The way the girls dressed, he wondered, for the first time, if he looked … *poor? Is that the word?* His jeans were black but faded and frayed at the bottom. His boots were newer but scuffed because he wore them everywhere. His dark blue button-down was open, revealing a black undershirt. Now he wondered if he should button it or at least roll down the sleeves. "Anybody seen my wallet?"

"You left it in the bathroom," Bullet said.

"I'll grab it," Jenna volunteered. "I gotta finish my makeup anyway. I'll only be a second." She fled that direction without waiting for an answer. Ash's stare swung to Case.

"Sorry." Her voice was quiet enough to avoid carrying. "But you know if you're having problems, it's not like I wasn't skating by on Joker and Grim's good graces for half the summer. We can always figure something out."

"I'm not having problems. Besides, you weren't

skating by on shit. We all pretty much adopted you the instant we saw you, Trouble." He grinned, stealing Ice's name for her. "I'm okay."

"He's too busy checking out Jenna's legs to be worried." Bullet was smart enough to whisper but stupid enough to say it.

"They're nice legs." He shrugged, giving a roguish smile.

"Who doesn't stare at Jenna's legs?" Ash sniffed. "I lived with her, and *I* stare at them."

"Are you talking about my very expensive legs?" Jenna popped her head out of the bathroom before strolling out with an exaggerated model strut, freakishly at ease on the sky-high platforms. "You should see the tags when I post pics."

"Just one of them." At least he had an excuse. "The left, if you really want to know."

"Your lost wallet." She stopped close to him with the worn leather in her manicured hand. Her fingers brushed his wrist as she relinquished it. Case gripped it harder than he meant to. Yeah, she was hot, but something so simple as touching his arm shouldn't have made his cock twitch the way it did.

"I am in your debt, milady," he said, attempting one of the accents he heard on that medieval show Ashlyn made them watch.

"But however would you pay?" Jenna's brows rose like she'd recognized the reference, and her gaze lingered on his.

With my tongue on your clit.

"So, uh, where exactly are we going?" he asked, not trusting himself with the answer.

"Just a place we know. You'll like it."

"No rockers or cuts." Ash aimed the order at Bullet. "It's in Belleville, so almost to St. Louis."

A college town. *Great. Frat boys and idiots who think their tenth-grade karate medal's gonna help in a bar fight. And just far enough from the St. Louis charter that we'd have to wait for backup.* "Luna Mara," she added. "A friend of ours took it over a couple years ago. And I know the band playing tonight, so don't antagonize anyone."

"Figures," Case said. Bullet was more deflated than him at least. But it made sense. Going so far out of the way meant the girls wanted a fun, uncomplicated night. In his experience, walking into a new place wearing his cut wasn't conducive for at least one of those things.

"We following you, or...?" It made sense if at least one of them rode with the girls. "Bullet's already volunteered to be the designated driver."

"I what?"

Case coughed a warning and Bullet shut his mouth. Jenna tossed her keys to the Prospect.

"Should be room enough in mine. And if we hit a freaking deer, at least we'll all survive."

"Hey. The deer would survive my Miata." Ash pouted. "Anyway, it's not my fault I didn't pick my car to fit a bunch of people. I had no intention of living where Uber doesn't happen."

"You need a second car. For group nights." Jenna shut her clutch and tucked it under her arm. "I keep telling you."

"After the wedding. I'm already planning on buying another house. Any other major expenses, Nathan's gonna freak."

Case tried not to fixate on Ash's words, but they stuck in his head. *Does Joker know about the house?* He headed onto the porch and stopped, while Ash and the others walked out, and waited while she locked up. He pulled out the phone and texted Joker.

Case: **heading to Belleville. Luna Marra?**

Is that right? Fuck it. Ain't a spelling bee. He pocketed the phone. "All set?" He offered his elbow to Ashlyn in case she needed help getting down the steps. Because if he took Jenna's arm, he'd have to fight himself to let go.

****

The band wasn't half bad. A few more drinks and he might even admit he liked them. *Too bad about the rest of the place.* The clubhouse spoiled him. He liked the familiarity of it. Luna Mara's gleaming stone bar, LED lights, and polished floor made him feel like an intruder. At least an unwelcome guest. Everybody, aside from Bullet, dressed like they walked straight out of a designer shop, and gulped down twenty-dollar drinks like they were freebies. Not one of the hair-sprayed girls wiggling to a recycled Paramore song worried about making rent next month.

"You gonna stand there all night?" Bullet asked, elbows on the bar, a beer hanging from his fingers. "Or are you gonna try to get a few numbers?"

"I'm good where I am." He felt the gazes, but not the urge to go investigate. He nodded at Bullet's beer. "That your first one?"

"Yep. Nursing the shit out of it. Don't worry. I won't get another. Not aiming for an ass beating." He tilted it so Case could see the label—Blue Moon— and chuckled. "Felt like a fucking douchebag ordering it." At least it wasn't one of those places that sold craft brews only. "Sure you're okay?" Bullet asked.

"The fuck do you mean?"

"You keep looking like somebody nailed you in the balls."

About how I feel.

He wanted Ashlyn to enjoy herself and watching her dancing and goofing off with Jenna and Megan felt great. Not so many weeks ago they'd all wondered if she'd ever be able to do normal stuff like this again. But he could do without asshole college boys slipping in, trying to steal dances. At least Ashlyn either moved away or made it clear she already had a dance partner, but Jenna...? Maybe she was just being nice, but every once in a while, she humored some dick and let him dance with her. *And why the hell does dancing with her look like fucking?*

"Guess dinner ain't sitting too well."

"Oh..." Bullet smirked and lifted the bottle. "I'm sure if you asked her to dance, she'd say yes."

If I break his nose, does it still count as picking a fight? "Who?"

Bullet chuckled. "Forget I said anything."

"You two never dance." Ashlyn bounded the last couple of feet toward them and grabbed Bullet's hand. "I know you can. Come on. This isn't Clubworld, Travis. We're dancing. You too, Case. Or are you afraid?"

Bullet grinned from ear to ear, and Case's hand curled into a fist. "I'm down to dance." Bullet followed Ashlyn out to the dance floor, leaving Case standing alone with Jenna. Well, alone if you didn't count every other dickhead standing at the bar staring at her.

"I ain't much of a dancer, but I can try." Not that he couldn't, he just hated it.

Jenna's gaze swept over him, thoughtful and enigmatic. "But would you enjoy the attempt?"

"I'd enjoy the company," he said, stepping closer to her. "Maybe you could teach me a few moves?"

"Not to be cliché, but I really don't teach. I like when my partner already knows their way around."

"That's probably for the best. I was never a great

student."

"So, let's see what you know." Her soft, slender fingers wrapped around his wrist, and she pulled him toward the dance floor. Jenna's hips moved with the rhythm, but her free hand came up, sliding along his shoulder as she drew him closer. The song's beat hit slower, not the frenzied bump-and-grind pace the band had kept so far in the set.

He grasped her hips, finally getting to feel her body the way he'd been wanting to for weeks. He focused on the heat radiating off her, the sweet scent of her perfume mingled with sweat. His hands tugged her closer until their bodies pressed together. He suddenly remembered why he'd been so interested in slow dances back in high school.

"Told you. I'm terrible," he said, bending his head so she could hear him. His voice sounded rougher than he'd meant it to.

Jenna's back arched and her thigh brushed his as she edged closer. His leg was between hers, and her skirt was so fucking short.

Fuck don't think about that.

"You're better than I expected. Not as great as you want to think." She traced a wicked line along his collarbone before her palm pressed flat to his chest, over his heart. He startled and Jenna's sapphire gaze shone with amusement. "Too bad."

"From you? I'll take it." He trailed one hand along her back, keeping eye contact. She leaned in. An inch hung between them. The crowd erupted into cheers as the last, soaring note of the song rang out.

"Set break,' Jenna said, so close her pink lips and lemon-drop breath were almost a kiss. And pushed away. "I need to run to the car. Get us a round of shots. You can use my tab."

"Hold on. What did you leave in the car?" He searched for the others. They'd already wandered back to the bar where Ash was being handed a glass of water and wasn't happy about it, while Megan downed a shot, slumping against Bullet. "I'll go with you. I know it ain't the city, but you still shouldn't be going out into parking lots by yourself." Especially not with the KC charter's problems still fresh in his mind.

Jenna's expression refroze into the annoyed near-snarl she'd worn for most of their early conversations. "I'm not one of your crow-hoppers or bed bunnies or whatever. If I want you shadowing me, I'll ask." She stepped back. "Ash may put up with stalkers, but I am not under contract with any of you." And slipped further back, using a migrating group in the crowd to escape his reach. She was slender and quick, and hot as hell—a fleeting smile and an apologetic squeak let her slide through groups and toward the door far easier than Case's larger frame.

Fuck you too, then.

But that didn't change the facts. She was a woman, it was dark, and something didn't feel right about letting her go off alone.

"Fuck." He shoved his way through, paying no attention to the names people called him as he pushed them out of his way. By the time he cleared the crowd and had a path to the door, Jenna had vanished.

He threw it open and strode past the bouncer. The street outside was crowded with those fleeing the club for the set break, getting a smoke or a breath of air or trying to talk where they could hear themselves think. He made his way through milling bystanders, taking the corner and then another—they'd had to park over a block away. The crowd thinned out within a few yards, and by the second turn, he hit the deserted side street. The Mercedes was dead ahead, between a Ford truck and a Honda, but Jenna... *Where the fuck is she?* He stopped, turned. Listened.

Voices echoed from a small alley a couple of yards ahead. Clean—like most of Belleville—but darker. "Stop it!"

Jenna. He rounded into the alley at a dead run. Two yards in, a bulky form pinned Jenna to the wall.

Instinct took over, and he reached for a gun that wasn't there. *Fuck it. Do this old school.* Too close to stop, he launched himself. The stranger jumped back but not fast enough. Both men crashed to the ground, concrete ripping denim and skin. He didn't feel it. The sound of flesh against flesh was as deafening as the drums inside the club, but he didn't stop. He threw punch after punch. The other guy got his hits in, too. Swinging wherever he could, landing on Case's side, his arms.

Somebody screamed as the man's bony hands gripped Case's shoulders, shoving him back and off. Case rolled, braced for the counterattack, but the guy scrambled up and took off down the alley. Case surged to his feet before movement caught the corner of his eye. *Shit.* He turned, the stranger forgotten as he reached for Jenna.

"Jenna? Are you hurt? Did he— Fuck, I'm sorry. I should have..." He swallowed hard, almost touching her face until he saw the blood running over his knuckles. He let the hand drop. "I'll call Ash." He fumbled with his phone, fingers still trembling from the adrenaline.

Jenna's breath came in gasps more ragged than his, but her hand shot out to his forearm, steady as a rock. "Stop." Her fingers tightened. "Stop, you need a ... you need someone. I'll call Ash, but we need to get you checked out. Your head. Did you hit it? I c-couldn't see if…"

"No. Don't think so." Of all the parts of him that were throbbing, his head was not one of them.

She got close, attention focused on his scalp "We gotta get to the car. I have a first-aid kit."

"I'm okay," he assured her, taking her hand. She was shaking. *Shit.*

"You're not. You're bleeding."

"I'm fine, Jen. I'm just… I'm glad he didn't…"

She took a shuddering breath and pulled at his arm, gentle but insistent. "We need to get to the car. I can't tell what's wrong in this light."

"Are you sure he didn't hurt you?" She'd never actually answered that question, he realized. "Jenna, tell me if you're hurt."

"Me?" She blinked. "It wasn't… He just wanted my purse, maybe? It was confusing. His accent got in the way. I don't know. My card's in the bar, and I'd put my ID in my bra, so he can have the lipstick and twenty bucks. Come on."

She didn't sound sure. He wasn't either. Guys who wanted to make off with purses didn't stick around or bother pinning their target to a wall. They ran. Less chance of getting caught or stopped. No, the asshole wanted something else. But Case let her pull him to the car. While she popped the hatchback and dragged out a big white box, he settled against the Mercedes's rear fender, checking out his legs. And the new rips in his jeans. "Fuck. I liked these." He brushed at the dirt, his knuckles stinging with each movement. "Jenna, *this* is why I wanted to come with you," he said without facing her, lest her big, sad eyes distract him. "I didn't want you to be out here alone."

"First off, just because your stalking worked out this time doesn't make it less annoying. Second, stop moving your hand." She grabbed his forearm. "Stand in the light." Jenna opened a water bottle and dumped it across his torn knuckles. "I had mace. I'd have been fine. But thank you for the rescue." Her attention fixed on his hand, she tilted it for examination as if the rest of him was only attached by chance. "I can get these cleaned up and sanitized. Your ribs okay?"

"They're fine." He tried and failed to make her look at him. "I'm about to sound like one of *those* guys, but you're a girl. I don't gotta tell you why walking out alone at night is bad. I know that's mansplaining or whatever, but I gotta say it."

"I'm not letting fear rule my life, Case. I'm prepared, I'm educated. But I'm not hiding from every passing threat." She said it softly, but with the hard steel edge of an argument already settled.

He grabbed an antiseptic packet from the kit and ripped it open with his teeth. *Deep breath. Don't squeal.* He wiped off the left hand—the less bloody one—but the pad turned pink before he finished. He tossed it into the plastic bag she'd left open. "Ribs are fine. Bruised. Not broken. I can still breathe."

"Uh-huh." Jenna ripped the next packet open and took over cleaning his right hand. "You want me to wrap these? I'm checking your ribs either way. You're on too much adrenaline to trust your assessments."

"Jenna, I swear, I'm okay. I've been in way worse fights than—" He hissed when the new wipe caught some skin, and he pinched it between two fingers to rip it off. She flinched for him, and as he surveyed the damage, he grimaced. "Okay, maybe I wouldn't say no to the wrapping."

She stayed quiet as she got the gauze strips out and began winding the tape around his knuckles, her movements sure and practiced. *Like she does this every day. Since when are modeling shoots that intense?* "Tell me if it's too tight." She breathed in, moving closer. He watched her, holding his hand as still as he could, wondering. She didn't fuss with the tape or try to wrap six different ways. *When'd she learn this? Back when Ash's ex was beating the shit out of her? A brother into boxing? A boyfriend?* Her dark hair was so close to his face, he imagined moving in the last couple of inches and kissing her temple.

"Do you know how reckless that was, Case? What if he'd had a knife? Or a gun? What if I'd had the mace out and hit you instead when you tackled him?"

Her questions made him smirk. *Fuck it.* "That would have sucked. But it worked out. Nobody got stabbed, shot, or maced. Let's agree to call it a win, eh?"

"Idiot," she hissed. It might have sounded more insulting if the second syllable hadn't broken into a sob before her right hand touched his hip. Catching herself? Or giving him the faintest hug imaginable?

Not knowing what else to do, Case draped his left arm over her, easing her into an actual hug. "I know," he said quietly, staring back toward the alley. Case shuddered with the what-ifs and let out a shaky breath. "I'm sorry, Jenna."

The only answer was a sniffle, a muffled sob, and Jenna's head pressed to his shoulder. Her hand swept along his left side, maybe checking his ribs. Maybe not. Either way, she didn't shove him away for once. "You can't go around jumping into fights for any damn thing."

"You aren't *any damn thing*," he corrected.

"It's dangerous!"

"Like walking around by yourself at night?" He held his smile to show he was teasing. "Don't hit me. At least not until I figure out where I'm not bruised."

Jenna frowned through her tears. "You're the one

who's bleeding. And probably concussed. Not to mention…" She brought her left hand down and laid it on his ribs with considerably more weight than she'd used before. Black dots swallowed the edge of his vision.

"Jesus, Jenna!"

"You've probably cracked at least one rib. And I can't imagine what Urgent Care might say about those knuckles. It's a good thing you're pretty because I don't think you'll win any prizes on wisdom."

"I've gotten into worse fights for stupider shit. Even if he kicked my ass, it would have given you time to get away."

"And leave you to get beat up?" She grabbed the edge of his shirt and yanked, revealing an impressive patch of red, raw skin. "Watch you have rolled on a broken bottle and not noticed?"

"I would have noticed that," he said, his hand going to the Mercedes for balance. "Probably."

"Case *is* short for Headcase, isn't it? Fucking hell."

"Didn't pick the name myself, so I don't actually know."

"They didn't even tell you? How do you not…? Oh, that's right. Macho dudes don't believe in talking." Jenna huffed and opened another antiseptic wipe, pressing it to a scrape on his side. Not deep, only pavement impact, but enough to sting. "Anyway, if you were thinking this would get you a blowjob…" Jenna glared. The streetlamp caught on the shimmery black mascara smeared across her cheek.

Case stared at her. "Is that what you think I was gunning for?" He caught her wrist, forcing her to stop tending the scratches. "Don't pretend you know what I feel or what I think. You may not like me, that doesn't mean the feeling's entirely mutual."

"I—" She stopped short, blinking back more tears. "I don't ... not like you. I don't like that you're a reckless, crazy, self-destructive lunatic. Or that you think a gang is a career plan."

He rolled his eyes. "I'm a mechanic. That's my career, not the club. Would it be better if I did something more worthwhile? Like a career in Instagram?"

"Why not? You're gorgeous, and people love pics of bikes. And you wouldn't be almost dying or hurting people. Or whatever it is you guys totally don't do all the time." Her arms crossed defensively. "But that's not the point, is it?"

"You're the one who brought it up." He blew out a frustrated breath. "I don't want to argue. Can we call a truce or something?"

"Why would I call a truce with someone I don't like?" She snapped the medical kit shut and started shoving packets and bandage scraps into the plastic trash bag.

"That's, um, how truces work?" He let himself smile. "Besides, you don't not like me. And I don't not like you." He shifted aside, giving her room, and pulled his shirt back down with a groan. Bandaged or not, it still hurt like hell to move his fingers.

"Get in the car. You're getting X-rays." Jenna pointed toward the passenger side. "As a mechanic, you should be worried about those hands."

"You're overreacting. They aren't broken," he insisted. "Look." He held one up and wiggled his fingers.

"You're an idiot. Car. Now. Or I call Ash out and the pair of us will stun gun you and drag you in."

"Jenna, I can't afford X-rays." His expression sobered. "Drag me in if you want, but they won't do it if I tell them not to."

"They'll do any damn thing you ask when I hand

them my card. You got hurt saving me. You're not paying the cost for being a decent person." Jenna's arms crossed again. "You can bitch, but my photo gigs pay well enough to cover stuff."

Especially since your trust fund covers everything else.

"Can you please let this go?" He hated hospitals and doctors and X-rays. The only thing he hated more was borrowing money. "I'll ice them, and they'll be fine. I promise."

"What if they're not? What if you're risking your actual income letting that go untreated? You can barely close your fist!" Jenna's hostility had fallen away, and she sounded ... frantic. Hurt.

Case stared at her. Was it wrong to miss the bitchy attitude? *It was a lot easier to argue with for damn sure.* "So, you're allowed to throw yourself in the way to help me, but I can't throw some money down to help you? You're fine letting me panic for the next week that I fucked up your life?"

"You're not gonna let this go, are you?"

"Say you're doing this for me. Will that help?"

If Joker found out, what would that say? *That I'm a pussy.* At the same time, she was right about mechanics needing unbroken hands. "Fine. I'll go." He almost choked on the words.

She clapped her hands together, bouncing once on her toes. "Thank you. Thank you!"

Grumbling, he walked around the car to the passenger's seat. "I gotta text Bullet."

Jenna climbed into the car without another word. She ordered the GPS to find the nearest urgent care, and in moments, they were on their way.

It took the better part of two hours before the X-rays were taken, analyzed, and they were released. Bullet and the girls were partying at a different bar, sending snaps and misspelled words of sympathy, and somehow Ash had two other possible rides. He had no idea if they were area Crows or passing fucking hippies. Case wasn't sure he wanted to ask, but he did.

"It's probably Ian or Paisley," was Jenna's airy answer. "They both go here. Paiz'll just crash on the sofa for a week and cry about some new shitty boyfriend. Ian only stays the night and vanishes on another spirit quest at dawn. His Insta is fucking amazing though." She smiled at Case, the expression somehow sunnier now she'd wiped the smeared makeup away. "You look so serious. You really do hate hospitals, huh?"

"Fun story?" He glanced over at her as they got into the Mercedes. "I went twelve years without going to a doctor or hospital." *Thanks, Mom.*

Jenna patted his arm. "But it's over. You have a script and better bandages, and we can get ice cream on the way. I think Sonic's still open."

"I would fucking love an ice cream," he said, letting his head fall back. "Guess if the couch is gonna be crowded, you should drop me off at my place."

"First, ice cream. Then I'll grab my other card at Luna, then we head back to your house."

"Sounds like a plan." He closed his eyes. The next time he opened them, Jenna was nudging him for the apartment number. He directed her to his unit, and when she parked, he cleared his throat, trying to talk past the embarrassment. "Didn't mean to pass out on you. Guess I was more tired than I thought."

"No worries." Jenna paused. "Do you need help getting up those steps or anything?" She bit her lip and eyed the building. "Sorry, I haven't been an ambulance driver lately. Not totally sure about the process."

"No, I—" Before he could tell her he lived on the

first floor, his phone pinged. He unlocked the screen to find a picture of Ash, Megan, and a few other people lounging in Joker's living room with an uncomfortable Bullet lurking in the background. "Looks like a party at Ash's place."

"Yeah, she called while you were sleeping. Ian drove them back, and some other people were headed over from the Silver Spur." She seemed as interested in that as Case felt.

"If you want to come in and use the restroom or just chill for a minute, you're more than welcome." *Hope it's not as dusty as I think it is.* He was hardly home, so at least his place wouldn't be messy. But the furniture was basic, and the chance of laundry piled in the front room…

Jenna groaned and slumped into the driver's seat. "I shouldn't." She pushed her already messy hair over her shoulder. "You need to get some sleep. It's fine. Let's get you settled, and then I'll get out of your hair." She unbuckled her belt and leaned over. "Can you handle yours? Did they numb your fingers or anything?"

"Yeah, I got it." He expected more pain when he stepped out of the car, but it didn't feel too bad. Sore, but he could ignore it. "I may need help with the keys," he said as they approached his door. The bandages kept him from being able to dig into his pocket. The phone was one thing, but his keys took less space, so they went straight to the bottom. He pointed to the slight bulge. "Mind reaching in and grabbing them? They're on the left."

"That sounds like a trap." Jenna's hand hovered at the edge of the denim. "Promise you tuck to the right? 'Cause I grab anything other than a key, I'm kneeing you."

"If you grab anything other than a key, it'll be a

shock to me too."

Jenna laughed at that, and her hand slid down. He kept his thoughts on license numbers—just to be safe—for the next two seconds as she drew the keys out. She didn't assault him, only opened the door and hesitated on the step. "I should, um... I can go. I know you're beat. Literally."

"I feel pretty well-rested now. You're more than welcome to hide out here. I don't mind." He stepped in and turned on the lights. It wouldn't compare to anything Jenna knew, but he had what he needed. A couch, a small coffee table, a flat-screen mounted on the wall closest to them, and a toy-sized kitchenette. But it was all clean and the plug-in ensured it smelled like fresh laundry when they walked in, rather than the pile of forgotten laundry sitting in a basket by the far wall.

"Make yourself comfortable," he said, trying to gracefully shed the button-up shirt, only for the buttons to slide out of his clumsy grip. The numbing shot must've done more than he'd thought. *Or seeing Jenna in my apartment has side effects.* "Uh, actually, could you help me with this first? Sorry. I don't mean to..."

"It's fine. Feels less like I'm a lost puppy that followed you home if I'm actually helping." She started on the buttons, keeping her head turned down. "Nice place, by the way. I wasn't sure you were the sort who'd own furniture. Kinda expected a bed and a pile of books about anarchism and minimalist lifestyles."

"You're confusing me with my mother." He chuckled, taking the shirt from her once it was finally off. He draped it across one of the two kitchen stools and glanced down the hall to make sure the bedroom door was closed before letting his gaze rest on Jenna. "Want anything to drink? I got water, Pepsi, or beer."

"Pepsi." She hung back, staying in the front room

as if unsure where to put her feet. She eyed his movements but was oddly still herself.

Did her confidence vanish with the makeup? Or is she more tired than she's admitting?

"I'm glad your hands are okay. You have enough ibuprofen and stuff? The doctor said about … taking it easy this week. Doesn't that screw up your work schedule?"

Case toed off his boots and kicked them toward the front door. "Should be fine. Even if I can't work too much with my hands, there's plenty to do at the garage." He opened the fridge and pulled out two cans, testing his grip before handing one to her. He set the other against his knuckles and sighed. Even through the bandages, it felt good.

"Oh. 'Cause, um, if you need to make it up, I could use an extra model for a shoot this week."

"What would that entail?" he asked, moving toward the couch. "Staring at the sunset looking pensive? Or would I have to sit in makeup for a few hours?"

"Oh, pensive sunset shot for sure. Look grumpy on a bike. Tasteful shot of rebandaging…" She laughed. "And you wouldn't need that much makeup. Filters cover a lot." Jenna settled onto the edge of the couch. Her head tilted. "Let me guess, your mom didn't like models any more than doctors?"

"Probably likes them more than Marines." He took one more drink before putting the can on the table. He lifted his hand to comb his fingers through his hair but stopped short. "Think I can take the bandages off now?" He didn't wait for the answer to start unwrapping his left hand. She might say no, and he really didn't want to be stuck wearing them the whole night.

"Stop! You don't take off a bandage after an hour! The wrap's to keep the swelling down, genius."

She glared and swatted at his wrist. Hard. "You're worse than an actual puppy, oh, my God ... do you need a shame cone?"

"Shit, sorry!" He returned the wrap to its position, though not as tight. "Ever think about going into nursing? Damn."

"I'd get fired for telling patients they're stupid too often."

He glared at the bandages. "They're itchy. And I'm gonna have to take a shower at some point, so these will have to come off anyway."

"You smell fine. Shower in the morning. And then you'll *re*wrap them." Jenna's jaw set. "You'll have to show up at Ash's sooner or later, and I'll do it for you if you haven't."

It did not sound like a promise he'd enjoy making her keep. She sat back, taking a sip of the pop. "I've felt guilty enough about people getting fucked over by helping me. I don't want anyone else on that list."

Interesting. He almost asked her to elaborate, but her expression warned him off. "A downside of being Ash's stalker is you can't hide from us either. I guess that's going to be a useful irony for a day or two."

"Mm." The sound dripped with skepticism. "Or you could skip stalker duty. Sleep in."

He frowned. "I know it don't make sense, but I really like Ashlyn. That ain't got nothing to do with the club. She's a good friend, and I want to be that for her too. Don't usually get the chance." *Not with chicks, anyway.* He could count his female friends on one hand and still have a couple of fingers left over.

"So you aren't shadowing her just to keep tabs for her over-controlling, paranoid, shady fucking husband?" Jenna huffed. "Ash loves you, and Bullet. She trusts you two like she does Nathan. But there's a fine line between protection and control. And with Ben coming out..." she trailed off. "I feel like we've landed back in some kind of cycle. And you're going to tell me you're different, this time is different ... but all I think is: How long? When do the fists fly, or the strings tighten?"

The tiny quaver in her voice slashed at his heart. He fell back against the cushion, rubbing his face like it would make his thoughts land in order.

"I ain't gonna tell you it'll be different." The words came out slow. Each one felt like a step out onto uncertain ice. "You won't believe me. But I can tell you that the club don't put up with that shit. Guys hitting chicks, especially their ol' ladies? That's one of the quickest ways to get your ass beat and booted out. Don't care what his last name is or what patch he's wearing, it's shade the club doesn't need or want. But Joker? He ain't ever gonna lay a hand on her."

Jenna looked down, her dark hair falling between them like a curtain. "I'm sorry, Case. I'm trying. You seem like a good guy. I think you are. But this all changed so fast. God... I left Ash alone for four months to do a tour, and I come back and she's got this whole life here? This whole giant story. A marriage, for fuck's sake. Now Ben. And tonight. And I—" Her voice caught. "It's so easy for her."

Holy shit. Jenna's got emotions again. Maybe I shouldn't have let her drive. He stared at her, waiting for the joke to drop, but she only sniffled and slumped against the arm rest.

"Don't know about easy. I won't lie to you. When she and Joker first got together, I didn't think it'd last. The club is a hard pill to swallow even to people who lived here their whole lives. But the more we got to know her, the more she came around... I mean, you know Ashlyn. It's hard not to like her. And when we realized that this wasn't a fling for them, it wasn't hard to keep rolling with it." He scooted closer, daring to put one hand on her shoulder. Her skin was too cool. He wondered if she'd bite his head off for throwing a blanket over her. "It's okay, Jenna. I get it. It's weird as shit. She's your best friend, and you want her to be safe. At first glance, I see how we don't give off that vibe."

Jenna's face scrunched, and the tears started. "Y-you don't—" The sentence broke off in a sniffle and she shook her head. "I hate it here. Nothing I do is r-right, everything's upside-down backward logic. W-who fucking gets mugged in some backwater college town the size of a postage stamp?"

His jaw almost detached as her head flopped onto his shoulder, and her arm looped around his side. *Oh, shit. She's ... is she hugging me?*

"Tell me to stop being stupid and go home."

"You're not being stupid," he managed once he could talk around the shock. He waited one heartbeat, then three, and finally put his arm around her. She did not slap him. "I hated it here, too. After I enlisted, I swore to myself I was never gonna come back here. And when I wound up landing back here again, I couldn't look at Helen or Liam without..." He stopped, the shame becoming a knot in his throat. "For what it's worth, you're doing plenty right, Jenna."

"What if I kissed you?" she whispered.

He froze. *Did they give me narcotics after all? This has to be a hallucination. She's about to turn into a Gila monster, right?*

"Would that be stupid?" Her head lifted from his shoulders so their gazes met. Hers were so blue it was like falling into the sky. Real, non-photoshopped humans weren't meant to have eyes like that. "It feels like it would be the wrong thing. But I want to. I keep wanting to. Maybe if we kiss, I'll be able to think straight again."

He stared into those twin summer skies, waiting for the punchline. The insult. He couldn't find it. *This has to be a trap.* "I keep wanting that, too."

"Is that why you keep annoying me?" Her lips found his. Her hand slid into his hair. Her tongue touched his. Somehow, her leg swung over his, and she straddled his lap, her skirt riding up so far it was barely more than a belt. "What do you want, Case?"

Excellent question. He let his palm glide along her bare, smooth calf. *Depends on if I'm dreaming.* Maybe he was still asleep in the car? But his dreams had never been so vivid. Jenna's weight, her warmth, the honey scent of her perfume... His hand moved up to her ass, the bandages forgotten, and he held her still as he lifted his hips, a soft sigh escaping. No way to dream of that intense heat between her legs. "I want you," he said before he recaptured her mouth. No more waiting. This time he took control, exploring her. Demanding more.

She rubbed herself against him, encouraging his wandering hands. Hers swept through his hair and along his shoulders. "I want you too," she whispered between kisses. "If you're not too hurt."

I could be on death's doorstep and still make this work.

Fingertips traced the waist of his jeans. "Small-town boys do know how to get a girl off, don't they?"

His fingers mirrored her movements, grazing along her skirt. "They do their best," he said, grabbing her shirt and lifting the flimsy material over her head, grinning as she raised her arms to accommodate him. He threw it aside, his hands returning to her skin, exploring the planes and curves of her stomach and sides. Days of staring at her photos and seeing her in half a dozen skimpy tops didn't prepare him to touch her. The real

Jenna shivered and moved with him in a way her imagined counterpart never did. "Gods, you're so hot," he whispered, his lips brushing along her jaw and down her throat.

"So are you." She bent back, letting him explore her breasts. His jeans unfastened, and she stroked his abdomen but didn't quite touch his aching dick. "Would it be a bad idea to fuck?" she whispered.

Never. Never, never.

"Probably." He traced light kisses along her collarbone. "But bad ideas can be fun." He cupped her breast, and damn it if he didn't want to rip off the bandages. *Finally, get my wish and I'm stuck with fucking gauze between us?* His thumb circled her left nipple, teasing it to a peak. "Can I confess something?" He nuzzled the gentle rise of her breast. "I wanted to fuck you the second you walked out of your room tonight."

"It's the miniskirt." Jenna nipped his earlobe. "I was hoping it made you think X-rated things."

"It ain't just the miniskirt. I wanted you before that." He flicked his tongue over her nipple, grinning when she cried out. His gaze locked with hers, and then he closed his lips around it. His hands moved down her back, fingers curving around her ass, squeezing as he lifted his hips again to grind his erection against her while his teeth worried gently at her peaked nipple. Jenna whimpered and clung to him, and he felt her thong dampen.

"You want to fuck everyone, Case. Isn't that your whole rep?" She teased the back of his neck. "Not that I blame you. You are so … so very … hot."

"A gross exaggeration." He grinned and squeezed her ass again, but this time he moved, turning to lay her on the couch, her legs still around his waist. He lifted his undershirt up and off, then covered her body with his. *Finally.* He had Jenna, satin-soft and moaning under him.

His hand brushed her side, over her skirt, slowly caressing her thigh. "Do you want me to touch you, Jenna? To make you come for me?" Before she could answer, he stroked her through her wet silk thong.

"Mmm. But your cock would be nice too." Jenna raised her hips to his hand. "Or those pretty lips." She raked gentle nails across his shoulders. "What gets you off, Case? I want to know exactly how kinky you are when nobody's looking."

"I'm more of a show-not-tell kind of guy." He got onto his knees so he could drag her skirt and thong off before he stood, unzipping his jeans. He didn't push them down. "Turn." His voice was quiet but rough. He waited for her to move, bending to grip her knees, pushing her legs apart so he could kneel between them. "My pretty lips, huh?" He ran his palm along her stomach, hip, thigh, then paused at her pussy. "I like the way you think." He used his thumb to tease her clit until her head fell back. Those gorgeous legs shivered on either side of him as he sank down to show her exactly what he'd been thinking about all night.

She fisted her hand on his hair but didn't pull. "Yes. There…"

He ran his tongue over her entrance, circled her clit, then moved down to lick her dripping pussy while his thumb kept her clit at attention. It didn't take long. Her reactions were visceral and absolute. Like she'd been ready to explode long before he got her skirt off. She whimpered with the first climax and finally tugged his hair. "Case. I'm… Please…" Another soft cry and heat slicked her thighs. He lapped at the cream, ignoring her plea to draw out her climax while he delved his tongue into her, already imagining what her velvet body would do to his cock. "If you fuck ... like you lick... I'm gonna scream. Fuck."

He didn't want to stop. Wanted to lick her until she came again and again. But he didn't think he'd be able to control himself much longer, and if he came before he even— No. Not an option. Case lifted his head and let go of her to push his jeans down along with his boxer briefs. "It's all right. These walls are thick." He reached for her waist, dragging her off the couch and into his lap. He almost kissed her, but hesitated. Some girls didn't like that after. "Come here," he said, his voice thick, husky. Lowering her onto his cock, his breath caught in his throat. Gods, he couldn't breathe. She felt so fucking good. Tight and hot and perfect. "Fuck," he groaned once he remembered how his lungs worked.

Jenna put her mouth on his and bit his lower lip— not hard enough to draw blood but getting his attention. "No coming yet, gorgeous." She grinned and her body tightened. "You gotta fuck me like you need me first." She began moving, slow but steady. Her hands roamed his shoulders, careful of his bruised ribs and injuries, so gentle his heart thumped.

He pushed her back against the couch, getting the leverage to snap his hips forward. He kept the slow pace, but with each thrust, he pushed harder, deeper. Reaching down between them, he stroked her swollen clit. Her nails dug into his shoulders and she arched.

"Case. Babe, you're..." She trailed off in a sharp, needy sound that became a muffled scream. Her body clenched hard, shuddering around him. Her legs flexed at his waist, locking him in place. "Don't stop."

He grunted, the sound slightly muffled by her shoulder, and he thrust again, slower, harder. His body shook, his thrusts erratic. The pressure built too fast. He pitched forward, buried deep inside her as he came.

"Fuck, Jenna ... I... Fuck." His arms went around her again, holding her as he tried to catch his breath.

Jenna laughed, breathless and husky, her expression soft and unguarded. "Shit. That was ... irresponsible. But so fun."

"Um." He couldn't talk. His cock had all the brains. And it was keeping them. Shit. He was still hard. Case watched her glowing smile, her gorgeous breasts.

"Feels like you might be up for round two. You always this resilient?"

He laughed. "Usually takes me a couple minutes." Then again, he didn't normally come so goddamn fast, either. He was about to say so until he actually looked at his cock. "Fuck." *Well, that explains the speed.* He couldn't remember the last time he'd taken a woman bareback. Slowly, he pulled out of her, their gazes meeting as his cum rolled down her thigh. "I didn't even think about getting a condom. I'm..." *Gods, this is awkward. Do high school shit, act like high school shit.* "I swear, I'm clean."

"I figured you might have said something to the nurse if you weren't." Jenna shrugged. "But I'm clean too. And on the pill. So no worries. But you should be better at this if you're gonna bring home random girls."

"Yeah, I never—" He didn't want to talk about random girls to Jenna. Not here. Maybe not ever. Sure as hell not when she had his cum inside her. *Fuck, why is that turning me on?* "It's not something I forget. Like ever."

"Maybe we're both really tired. Might be a good idea to get to the bedroom for round two."

He smiled to answer hers. "Oh, so now we're going with *good* ideas? Wonderful." He steadied her as she slid back onto the couch, and he got unsteadily to his feet. "I'd carry you, but my hands are fucked up apparently." He held one out to her and tried not to react as she put his palm to her cheek. Her eyes locked on his. Those soft petal lips touched his thumb. He felt the caress all the way to his dick. *If I wasn't already hard...*

"Don't worry. You look amazingly fuckable with wounded paws, puppy." She pulled him toward the bedroom. "I bet there are plenty of things you can do without hands."

"That's a safe bet." A strange warmth spread into his chest. He stopped at the door, dragging her close, his lips claiming hers. "I'm feeling especially creative." Then he bent and swept her into his arms, laughing at her curses as he carried her to the bed. Calming her back down was going to be half the fun.

****

During the night—before sunrise to be more accurate—his ribs tore him awake for rolling onto his side. Putting his head back on the pillow, he flipped it to find a cooler spot, one arm holding Jenna to his side. He woke again to a brighter, warmer room.

Must be after seven. He needed to get up and shower, check in with Joker, make sure Bullet hadn't chewed his own leg off, and get some food. Hell of a lot for a day better spent in bed with Jenna. He yawned and stretched out, groaning with the bruises and aches lighting up, and reached his arm over to ... empty cotton sheets.

He shot up, clutching his throbbing side. "Jenna?" Her name hung in the air. No answer.

Case tossed the blanket off and stumbled toward the bathroom, halfway hoping she was in there, applying makeup. Getting dressed. Something. But the lights were off. Overwhelming silence from the main room told him she wasn't in there either. *Did she ... leave?*

He seized his phone from the nightstand. He

didn't remember putting it on the charger, so she must have. He opened the messages.

Jenna: **Hey I went ahead and showed myself out. Door's unlocked.**

Jenna: **Had a great time. Thx.**

"Holy shit…" He collapsed onto the edge of the bed, reading the texts again before dragging his gaze to the window. He couldn't be angry with her. They weren't together. They didn't make any promises. She was right to leave. It meant nothing. It was supposed to mean nothing.

Nothing is good. Right?

Chapter Five
Jenna

August 5

The dream ended as it always had, in blood and choking screams. Jenna slid across the slick crimson, pleading, reaching, and finding only the dark. She tried to call for help, but the words stuck in her throat until it choked the wind from her lungs and she woke gasping.

The mattress bounced and something big and warm and body-shaped landed across Jenna's chest. "Unf!" She groaned and slapped at the thing, only to get vanilla-scented hair flopped across her face and a peal of laughter.

"Up!"

"Fuck off, Ashlyn."

"It's afternoon."

"And?"

"You didn't get in until after five this morning."

"So?" Jenna rolled onto her side, dislodging her friend enough to drag the cover over her head, though the layers of cotton and batting did nothing to muffle the chatter. Her body ached from the night before, bruised on the shoulders from being slammed into a wall, but much more sweetly sore in her thighs. God, that had been a blast. Almost worth getting mugged... Though that was a weird mugging.

"Hello?" Ash broke into her thoughts. "Jenna! You weren't answering."

"I was asleep."

"Liar." Ash dragged the cover off again. "Was it Case?"

"Does it matter?"

"It was Case." The bed rocked as Ash dropped

onto it again. "Guess you're exhausted, huh?"

"Mmhm." Jenna cracked one eye open to glare. "Are you here to lecture me?"

"No. I like Case, and he's at least mostly self-reliant, so I figure he's got about a seventy-thirty shot of surviving Hurricane Jenna. Significantly better than most boys."

Both Jenna's eyes opened at that. "It was sex! We didn't start dating."

"As if relationships never start after a successful one-night-stand."

Jenna sat up, tossing a pillow at Ash's head. "I'm not … interested. My vagina may appreciate his tricks, but all interest stops at the waist."

"Guess that's technically true if your head's lodged up your a—*ow!*" The second pillow slapped Ash square in the face.

"Shut. Up."

Screaming, tangled pillows and howling laughter ensued until Megan stormed through the door. "What the actual fuck are you two…" The tall brunette's face went slack as she took in the scene. "If you break that computer, Grim may actually shoot one of you."

"Whoops." Ash edged six inches away from her defensive position in front of the monitor. Jenna shot the interloper a dark glower. Who invited her, anyway?

"Sorry," Ash continued. "I meant to get her up for lunch but, uh, we got distracted."

"Well, get ready. Both of you. I've got the day off but if you want to get any of the wedding shit done today, we need to move." Megan's stare hit Jenna's without flinching. "And I'm not taking in that Paizlee girl. So, sort that out, Ash."

"Paiz is fine." Jenna waved her hand. "She's due at a festival next week anyway. With any luck, she'll latch onto one of the Crow dudes 'til then."

"Hm. Introduce her to Dragon. That ought to keep her occupied." Ash beamed. "He might even know some sex stuff she hasn't tried yet!" When Megan's brows rose, she added, "Paiz is a camgirl on off-seasons. Onlyfans and the whole deal."

Megan's deep-green gaze blanked, and she shook her head. "You live in an alternate dimension. I swear it's the only explanation. Because I think you just said you brought home a callgirl."

"Yeah? I mean she does other stuff but that too." Ash shrugged. "You mean you don't know any others?"

"Not … that I'm aware of. Not professionals for sure."

"God, this place is weird." Jenna sighed. "Run by bikers, yet totally fucking vanilla? I can't even... How?"

"I take it last night was vanilla too?" Ash's brows waggled. "She stayed with Case," she added for Megan's benefit. The revelation was the first time Megan showed anything but disapproval or confusion. Instead, she only nodded, as if this was to be expected.

"It was…" Jenna trailed off. "Not boring-vanilla. More like … French vanilla. *Crème brûlée?*"

"Good with his mouth, huh?" Megan chuckled.

"And other things." Jenna felt her cheeks heating, so she shoved the covers off and got up, turning away from the other two to sort out her clothes for the day.

"So, are you going to be trying a lot of French desserts now?" Ash pressed.

"No." She grabbed a sundress and set it on the bed before rifling through her bag for a bralette and panties. "This was a one-time indulgence."

"Why? If he's fun in bed, and he's not seeing anybody…?" Megan sounded confused again, so Jenna deigned to show her exasperation in a huff.

"Because there's no point, and if he gets attached, I'll only have to be a bitch to him. He's nice, he's fun, and I would rather go hiking in Manolos than live here. Not to mention he's … affiliated with, you know. No offense. But I want to work in a museum someday. If they did background checks for some reason?" She shook her head. "No way."

"Oh." Megan's shoulders straightened, and she rubbed her arm. "Guess that makes sense. Didn't know being friends is such a risk for you." Ash, however, had narrowed her eyes. Jenna grabbed the clothes and fled before her best friend could speak.

The retreat didn't help. Ash shoved into the bathroom behind her. "Get out, for the thousandth time," Jenna snapped.

"You should've locked it." Ash sat on the tub and watched Jenna yanking on the clothes. "So what the hell was that little display about?"

She wanted to be mad and rail at the invasion of privacy. But they'd shared bathrooms at school, parties, and traveling. Getting dressed together in tents and hotel rooms, even huddled behind trees on occasion. *And once you've tried to bandage one another's gaping wounds more than once, what's there left to be shy about? Ash may literally have seen my bones. No boyfriend's likely to get that bingo box.* That thought circled her head as she stared at Ash's upturned, delicate features.

"I know you don't like Megan. I think I've got some idea why."

"Ash…"

"No. Don't 'Ash' me right now. Megan is my cousin, my best friend, and I love her. But you're also my best friend, my chosen sister. We *chose* one another, Jen. That doesn't stop being true, now or ever. So please stop taking your worries about the club out on Megan?

You don't need to worry about them either. They're my new family, but you're family too."

"Not just me," Jenna whispered. Ash winced.

"No, not just you."

"And what are you going to do about that? When they find out about…" She hated the thrill of triumph she felt when Ash's posture fell.

"I'm not sure. It probably won't matter."

"You don't get to call someone family and not claim them when it's inconvenient."

"I will always claim them both." Ash grimaced. "I know I messed up. I get that. But when was the last time you ever talked to anyone else about Auggie?"

"Don't."

Ash stood up. Three inches separated their heights, but at that moment, Jenna was the one to shrink back. "You can drop Case and pretend you don't like him. You've done that plenty before. But you need to talk to someone about *why*, Jenna. Before it eats you alive."

"So, Joker? He knows?"

"No. I'm still waiting for your decision on most of it." Ash hugged her, and Jenna didn't pull away. "It scared the hell out of me, but I've started. Even a few steps down feels so much better. The secrets burn holes in your heart. Let them out. A few? Please, Jen. I don't care with who. Anyone. I found Nathan. But anyone…"

"What if we go to the Burn?" The words fell out of Jenna's lips like a tidal wave. "I could talk to someone there. One of the far-away friends. Someone we only see at festivals. Maybe … maybe that would help. Like you said. Things look different out on the playa."

Ash's mouth opened and shut. "I—"

"Please? We always go. You're right, I've been a bitch about stuff because you, you're so at home here. I feel like I'm ten steps behind, and it's got me off balance. We need more than a girls' night, Ash. We need—"

"An adventure." Her smile returned. "All right. You'll tell a secret to the Burning One. We'll have our adventure. And maybe we can consult with Carz, if he shows. About Ben. And the rest."

"I like this plan." Jenna threw her arms around Ash. "We're going to be awesome."

"We're going to set shit on fire at least."

"Oh, for sure." Jenna stood back and reached for her makeup case. "Also, I want to talk about last night. Before the sex and stuff. That mugging thing?"

Ash nodded and hopped up onto the counter beside the case. She opened it for Jenna and handed her cleanser. The beginning of an old ritual. The recognition helped ease some tension from Jenna's chest. "Why didn't you call the cops?"

"For one, I figured Case probably wouldn't be super into that. And the guy had an accent."

Ash froze, a mascara tube clattering into the sink, but Jenna continued, "Russian, maybe? East Europe for sure."

"You don't think…"

"I don't know what to think. He caught me right at the alley, dragged me in. Pinned me. Before he could say anything much, Case was beating the crap out of him."

"Fuck." Ash picked up the mascara and dropped it into the bag. "Fuck," she repeated. Then said it several more times. "I paid everyone, Jen. And Carz handled any favors required. They'd have no reason to partner with— no! He's not even stable enough! Hired? Could he have hired—"

"Ivan always liked Ben, even if none of the others did. We have no idea where he's at these days."

Ash rubbed her face, curling into a crisis-safe ball against the bathtub. "Did you fuck Case so he'd be more useful?"

"Did you marry Joker for free bodyguards?"

"I wish I was that smart." Ash managed to laugh. "I'd have married someone I didn't like if that was the goal. No sense putting people you care about in danger."

"Good point." Jenna sank to the floor next to her. "Carlos will be there, right? Message him. You know he'll want to talk too. If I'm not totally paranoid, this might affect him even more than it does us." Ash nodded and pulled out her phone, but instead of swiping, she stared at the screen.

"Jenna, I already caused drama because of my mom's bullshit. If I'm attracting this? Tree is going to drag me into divorce court on Joker's behalf. Hell, I might not even fight him. I mean, damn it, I thought this was done. Ben's bridges were burned, for fuck's sake."

"And maybe I'm overreacting. Meth heads come in Russian makes and models."

"Yeah. I know. That's totally possible. We're only being cautious right? It's all going to seem silly in a week." She leaned her head on Jenna's arm. "Worst comes to worst, we'll have each other."

"And Carlos probably knows how to get new identities if we completely fuck up." Jenna's cheerful announcement earned a laugh.

"Come on." Ash hauled herself to her feet and pulled Jenna after her. "If we don't get out of here, Megan's going to choose my wedding accessories out of spite, and I am not walking down the aisle wearing rhinestones or fishnet."

Chapter Six
Case

August 17

Case pulled his Electra in front of the house, booted feet anchoring on the concrete. He didn't want to go in, but he couldn't keep avoiding it, especially since his club brothers rolled in from Sturgis an hour earlier. They'd be at the clubhouse for a while, but if Joker thought Case skipped out on duty... *Have to debrief soon, anyway.*

A few days before, Bullet asked about sorting out the fallout from Jenna's attack with the St. Louis charter. *Fuckin' Prospect. Too smart for his own good.* Case didn't argue. But he did take advantage, riding out that morning without a backward glance. He knew that made him an asshole. And a coward.

Case slowly walked up the path, pulling his phone from his pocket and firing a quick text to Bullet. No point waking Ash or Jenna when the Prospect was available to open the door. The breeze rustled the trees in the neighbor's yard, carrying cigarette smoke toward him. "Son of a bitch." Case stopped on the top step. "Didn't see you there."

Bullet sat quietly at the small, black table, one foot propped up on the rail, hidden in the diamond-patterned shadows of the new trellis, puffing a Camel down to the filter. Case glanced at the ashtray. Fresh butts were still smoldering. *Guess I'm not the only one having a shit morning.* "Was gonna say something, but figured I'd see how long it took you."

Case lowered himself into the empty chair, adjusting his cut and the Beretta at his back. "Bum a smoke? I'm down to my last two."

Bullet pushed the pack over, extinguishing his own cig.

"Hear anything yet?"

Case didn't answer until the cigarette caught the flame from his lighter. He let the cig hang from his lips, clasped his hands behind his head, and tipped back onto the chair's rear legs. "It's a shit show."

Bullet grabbed his pack, pulling out a new stick. "Making sure we're on the same page. I was asking about St. Louis. Not Jenna."

"I fucking know that." The chair's front legs hit the porch with a dull thump. *Too many brains under that shaggy hair.* "She say anything?"

"About you or the mugging?"

"Either."

"Like it never happened."

"That was my experience." When he tried talking to Jenna the day after they hooked up, she gave him excuses, like answering texts or notifications or whatever the fuck Instagram called it was too fucking urgent. He got the hint. *Loud and fucking clear.* "Guess they didn't go out?" Bullet said he'd call Case if the girls planned another wild night.

"Nope. Tree wound up calling Ashlyn. She's brave, but daddy-in-law's fucking scary." Bullet grinned, lighting the cig. "And St. Louis? What'd Griff say?"

"He's got some Crows looking close at it. There are a few shops around that area that got cameras. But not to get our hopes up. Shit like that happens."

"Sounds like you ain't sure."

Case shrugged and took a long drag. Before he could answer, they both got a text from Joker: Bossman was on his way. Bullet settled into his chair, and so did Case. Neither felt the urge to talk or risk entering the house. *Better out here than in there.* Voices drifted to them through the windowpane, but he didn't turn around. If Ash or Jenna wanted to see either of them, they'd come out.

He stood when Joker's Dyna roared around the corner. Sticking his hands in his pockets, he ambled back down the steps, stopping halfway up the path with Bullet on his heels as Joker parked. "Ain't you a sight for sore eyes?"

Case smiled at Joker, moving to grab the duffle from the rack. Joker pulled his helmet off and shrugged out of his cut with a dull nod by way of greeting.

Great to see you too, boss...

"Ashlyn home?"

"Yeah." Bullet looked green around the gills.

Joker pulled cash from his back pocket and handed it off to the Prospect. "Pick up some pizzas for tonight. Ice will be here, so make sure to get enough."

Bullet took the money, practically running for his bike.

"You." Joker pointed Case toward the porch. "Follow me."

Fuck.

Joker stopped on the porch and glared at the ashtray before sitting. *Great. Another thing to piss him off.* Case put the duffel by the door, then took the other seat—the one he'd just vacated. He tried to keep his foot from tapping the decking. He'd wanted silence earlier, but now it stretched too long. Joker's sharp stare fixed on Case's hands. The bandages Jenna insisted on were gone along with most of the swelling, but his knuckles still ranged from red to purple. He fidgeted.

"Anything broken?" Joker asked, as Case's last nerve was giving out.

"Just bruised. Same with the ribs."

"Tell me again what happened."

He'd given a quick debriefing over the phone the morning after the Belleville incident, leaving out the part where he learned how to make Jenna come, but this time without the background noise and shit reception, he gave more details on the attacker, the street layout, and the club. Joker listened, focusing on the trellis. "Accent?" Joker asked after a heartbeat. "What kind?"

"Not sure. Eastern Europe, maybe?" He'd never been good with accents. The Prez— Joker's dad—could pinpoint people on a global map based on how they talked right down to the region and their mama's maiden name. All Case could do was conjure the vague impression that someone in a movie set in the old USSR sounded like the man in the alley. "Think this Fitzgerald fuck sent him?"

"Don't know." Joker's hands curled into fists, and he drew his legs in. "Could be bleed over from St. Louis. Random fucking mugging. Hard to say without the asshole in question pinned down."

Case felt sick. "It didn't feel that random to me." He had to force the words out, fighting the urge to gag on them. *Maybe I'm reading too much into shit. Maybe I should've been more focused on catching the fucker than licking Jenna's pussy. Clearly she's about as vulnerable as a wolverine.* Joker sat back, tapping the table.

"Then maybe Burning Man ain't such a bad idea."

What the fuck?

The shock on his face must have shown. Joker's brow arched. "You didn't know?" Joker pointed toward the door. "Ashlyn and Jenna been planning it for a few days now."

"I, uh, I wasn't..." His face felt like somebody lit it on fire. "Tree told me to take care of the mess with Griff. So, I—"

"Didn't check in here for the rest of the week?" Joker smirked. "Don't see how following up a whole lot of nothing takes up so much of your goddamn time, brother. Griff get a hotter set of hang-arounds?"

"Fuck no. It's…"

"Jenna?"

Her name was a slap. *Why do you ask me questions when you already know the fucking answers?*

Joker's head tilted. As if sensing weakness, he continued, "She tell you anything?"

An icy chill filled Case's chest. "Not yet."

Joker let out a long exhale and stood up. "Thinking maybe you should've come to Sturgis after all. Maybe I can find someone else to do the—"

"No!" He got to his feet fast but took a step back when Joker's frosty gaze snapped toward him. "It won't work." Having to step aside and watch Ice or Blaze wheedle into Jenna's good graces? His gut knotted at the thought. They'd fuck it up. Take too long. And he'd be in prison for attempted murder if either one put so much as a hand on her bare skin. *Fuck.* "She hates the club, but I finally got some credit with her. I'm making progress, Joker. I swear. It's gonna take time."

"We're fuckin' short on that right now." Joker glanced at the door, probably worried about the girls jumping out any second. "I offered to go, but Ash says it ain't a good idea. I didn't want to pull Bullet again, but I don't see a way around it."

"You're gonna send *Bullet* to Burning Man?" *Does that asshole shit gold? Why in the hell would Joker trust any Prospect this much—especially one who wore Heathen colors not two months ago?* Case swallowed the lump of guilt in his throat. He understood all the shit the kid had done. *But he's still a fucking Prospect.*

"Don't think he can handle it?"

"The playa will eat that man alive, Joker. He'll come back in a patchouli-scented bodybag." Case couldn't keep the bitterness out of his tone. It didn't help when Joker laughed.

"Guess he'll need a guide, huh? Somebody who's been there and knows the lay of it."

"Fuck." *You asshole.*

Joker's wide grin was worse than a smirk. "You said you were making progress, brother. What better way to get ahead than a long road trip?"

Anything for the club. Anything but that.

"You can't buy tickets last minute. And I don't got the money for..."

"If you want an expense account, that's an option."

If I sign on as an Aegis contractor. That's how he's sending Bullet on this—as an employee.

Case kept his employment simple so far, only working the garage. The club's private security arm paid better, but he'd avoided it because being gone for long stretches got tricky with Helen and Liam.

"Joker, I..." *Some things weigh heavier than wanting to be useful to the goddamn club.* He shut his mouth rather than say that out loud. "I can't do it, brother. You know I can't be seen back there."

Joker's brows rose. "You know what camp she's gonna be in. Avoid it."

"Sure. And then somebody recognizes me and she finds out I'm avoiding her. That'll go over well."

"Come on. You haven't seen your mom in, what? Five years? So, you might be forced to say hi to her for a second. It ain't the end of the world."

He clenched his jaw on his real answer to that. "Does Ashlyn even know you're sending us? She might get pissed off that you—"

"Already taken care of. How do you think you're getting tickets?"

Case raked a hand through his hair and groaned. "Fuck. Fine. But I've got to get Helen covered. Thursdays—"

"Won't be a problem," Joker cut him off. "Karli will handle that, and we'll call in an extra aide to help her. I'll catch your brother at the garage tomorrow and fill him in, too. I know it ain't the vacation you wanted, brother, but you *can* get out of town for a few days without the world falling to shit. We'll make sure you're covered."

His throat felt tight, cutting off his speech. Guilt and relief warred together. The idea of weeks with only himself and the girls to worry about. *No pill regimen, bedsores, injections, or awkward conversations with Liam.* Case managed a nod. "Better get you in before Ash kills me for keepin' you out here."

Chapter Seven
Case

August 25

He hated Burning Man and they weren't even there. Yet.

They left early in the morning, the route planned down to the minute, including stops along the way and check-in points because someone—Ashlyn—had let Tree see the map, and it turned out the Prez felt almost as itchy about the whole damn thing as Case.

The itch only intensified as they rolled through Missouri. *At least it ain't raining.* The sunny, clear skies were the one saving grace. Traffic through Columbia always sucked, but riding it in rush hour was rough as shit on a bike with only one other rider at your side. And since they were leading a Mercedes SUV, they couldn't weave or jump ahead of blind spots. By the time they reached Concordia for their second stop, Case was five seconds away from snapping. And that was when Ash announced they needed to stop in Kansas City.

"Jenna didn't pack for Burning Man. She needs to grab a few things. It won't take long."

"Joker know?"

"I texted him."

Case glared at her but couldn't argue. She'd just turn off the route and drag them off-schedule anyway. He spent half of the three hours to Kansas City composing an impassioned argument against allowing women to drive on road trips. This shit wouldn't be happening if a Prospect was driving the Mercedes. Then again, that would mean another Prospect to put up with. And a man alone in that car with Jenna... Scratch the argument.

He spent the last hour and a half trying not to

think about Burning Man. Eight years of avoiding the festival and all its fucking fan club since the last time his mother dragged him to the desert, and now he got to experience a National Lampoon road trip before returning to hell. *Fuck this. My joke of a life. Babysitting a goddamn Prospect and two dumbass chicks who'll be in the ER for sunburns by day two.*

"It isn't too late to load up your bikes into the trailer and ride with us," Ash said when they stopped for gas a few miles south of the city.

Fucking tempting. With the late summer heat and strong wind gusts that caught the side of the Electra, setting his front wheel wavering, it didn't sound like a terrible idea. Until he looked up and saw Jenna against the side of the SUV, designer sunglasses covering half her face, head bowed toward her phone screen. *Fucking gilded cage.* "We're good."

Once they got into Kansas City, traffic picked up again, and Bullet almost got sideswiped by a dipshit motorist who didn't know how lane merges worked. It seemed like the least Jenna could do was live somewhere convenient. But no. Of course the princess would live near the Plaza Estates. He could almost feel money in the air as they turned off I-35. He didn't even want to think about how much the mansions stretching out along the shady avenues cost. More than he'd make in a lifetime.

The Mercedes led them down a maze of picturesque streets into a world of massive homes behind towering trees. Most didn't even bother with high fences, they sat there in their splendor, daring you to put so much as a toe on their immaculate green lawn and give the butler and trained attack dogs something to maul.

Finally, the SUV signaled, and they turned into a sweeping curved driveway. Freshly paved, of course. Case gunned his engine once just to piss off the whole neighborhood before shutting it down.

"Can you imagine growing up here?" Bullet called as he dragged his helmet off, cheeks pink from the wind, hair pressed flat from sweat and the helmet. Case shook his head.

"Can't imagine knocking at the front door," Case scoffed. "Far cry from the group homes, huh?"

The house was a masterpiece: a mass of red brick and elegant lines, complete with white Corinthian columns and bay windows. From the front, it looked like four, maybe five balconies and a porch that he imagined nobody sat on. *You don't sweat where the neighbors can see when you live in a house like this.* The trees that mirrored one another on each side of the red front door were perfectly rounded, and the shrubs and hedges outlining a cobblestone knee-high wall were the deepest emerald he'd ever seen. Jenna hurried up the path without admiring it or speaking to anyone.

Ashlyn alighted from the SUV and came over to Case and Bullet, smiling apologetically. Handing them two Fiji waters, she rested at Case's side, facing the house. "Her stuff's already packed. She's double-checking it real quick. You guys good?"

"Be better if we were still on the road." Case took a swig.

"Aside from that?"

"Yeah, we're good." Bullet turned his bottle upright to chug half of it in one go. Ashlyn patted Case's back before following Jenna into the house. The Prospect ambled over. "Think she'll actually let us in to help her with her bags?"

"What? And risk scuffing her floors with poor? I doubt it." He wrinkled his nose and spun around to sit down on the curb. *Hooking up with Jenna was a one-off. Time to move on. Doesn't matter how many bedrooms she's got, she's not letting you into any of them.*

A few minutes later, Jenna and Ashlyn were walking back, a man and a woman behind them carrying bags under their arms. *They've got a fucking staff? Of course. Barbie dream homes don't come without them.*

Popping the trunk open, Jenna pulled out a couple of the bags she brought back from Oak Grove and stepped away to let the newcomers start loading. *Must be nice.*

Ashlyn stood on the curb, balancing on the arches of her feet while digging around in her purse for lip balm. Case headed to her side.

"Think we can take them with us?"

She laughed. "I wish. Eric and Amelia are awesome. But I think the house would catch fire without them. Jenna's mom's never operated a washing machine successfully, let alone a power tool."

Case didn't bother answering. He stayed put while Ashlyn went to say goodbye. What shocked him was Jenna's farewell. She hugged them. *She touched the help? Is she feeling well?* They embraced her easily, too, wishing her a fun trip and safe travels.

"Are we in the goddamn Twilight Zone?" Case asked no one in particular as he fastened his helmet.

Bullet shrugged. "I think I'd like the Twilight Zone more."

At least the stop was over. They sped out of the neighborhood and back to the interstate, where Case finally felt at ease. With traffic thinning out after Kansas City and the wind dying down, the ride didn't suck. For about an hour. Then the breeze picked up like it wanted a fight. The crosswinds forced him to the front of his seat, his elbows cocked. Bullet slowed to get directly behind him, both riding in the middle of the lane. *Maybe being blown into oncoming traffic ain't so bad. It'd end this shitshow.*

In his rearview mirror, he saw the turn signal on the Mercedes flicker. *Guess Ash noticed we're getting battered out here.* He glimpsed the off-ramp sign. Junction City. He slowed, swerving toward the shoulder and motioning for Bullet to go on ahead. The feeder lane didn't have any traffic, which made the roundabout less of an issue—thank the gods—because, in his experience, nobody knew how those fucking worked. Turning off the road and into the gas station, he pulled in next to a pump. He checked the surroundings before he switched off the engine. *No graffiti on the walls or bars on the window. Off to a good start.*

Good enough to get off the bike and let his arms relax.

"Fuck," he groaned, slowly swinging one aching leg over the seat. He pulled his helmet off, grimacing as he wiped his forehead. The heat on his cheeks turned to an instant chill when the wind hit his skin, but he welcomed it, rolling his shoulders until he was sure he had full range of motion. Bullet was on the opposite side of the pump, making similar noises and postures as he convinced his own limbs to move.

The girls' SUV pulled up at the next line of pumps, and they hopped out like they'd come straight from a spa. Case gritted his teeth and forced a smile when Ash waved. The wicked Kansas breeze took hold of Jenna's floaty sundress, and he didn't dare open his mouth. He was too tired to fight, and too interested in bending her over the bike to talk.

Instead, out of habit, he re-checked the storefront and catalogued the cars in front of it. A maroon Camry parked crookedly across a white line, angling into the handicapped space. Next to it, a silver Impala gleamed. A newer model recently purchased based on the paper plate. A few spaces away sat a black Ford F-150 extended cab. A monster of a truck, almost as new as the Impala. Easy to feel like a king sitting in that. If you didn't mind being in a cage.

A man in dingy clothes was resting against the tan brick building, one foot propped up beneath him, a cigarette in hand, and a baseball cap pulled down over his eyes. Three high school boys poured out of the door, laughing way too loud, energy drinks and hot Cheetos clutched in their fists. Case eyed them as the girls walked past. Teenage heads turned, and Case's teeth ground. *Don't fucking do it, idiots.* Case knew what the smiles they gave one another meant, but as long as they got into the fucking Impala and drove off, he didn't give a shit what fantasies they made up.

"We there yet?" Bullet asked, stepping up beside Case's bike.

He barely heard him over the wind and speeding cars on the interstate. Case pulled his attention back. If the boys got stupid, Jenna could just mace the little fuckers.

"Not even close, kid."

Bullet raised his eyebrow, but he didn't say anything. He didn't need to. There couldn't have been more than a couple of years separating the two of them— Case didn't care enough to ask—but damn if it didn't feel like a decade. Bullet looked more like one of the hot Cheeto idiots than Case ever had. "I need to take a piss."

"I ain't stopping you."

"Just letting you know so you can keep your eye on the girls."

Bullet nodded, his arms crossing. "Been playing bodyguard for a while now. I think I got it down."

"If you did, I wouldn't fucking be here."

Bullet bowed his head, avoiding making eye

contact. "I'm gonna grab a drink. Maybe a pack of smokes. You want anything?"

Oh, fuck off, Travis. He almost said it. Until over five years of Marine Corps conditioning reminded him that free shit was free shit. *If he's offering?* "I'll take a Gatorade. Don't care what flavor."

He checked on the girls. Ashlyn held the pump, giggling at Jenna. He watched Jenna's hands as she dragged her glossy hair up, loose strands flying in the wind. Some odd, magic maneuver with an elastic left most of it up in a wild, messy bun he wanted to undo. Her smile was as wide as he'd ever seen it, her cheeks pink, half her face hidden behind sunglasses that probably cost more than his apartment. She was fucking gorgeous. *And happy*. When was the last time she looked like that? His memory replayed her sweet, soulful smile in his apartment. In his bed. Her cheeks were almost that color when she came.

It was one night, not a goddamn wedding ceremony. Get your shit together. It's almost a month, asshole.

He turned on his heel and headed into the store. Ads for ice, Coca-Cola, and those printouts of missing people covered the windows. *Mostly women*, he realized a second later. *Mostly young*. And they were close to Kansas City. He didn't review the dates, but he wondered if they were tied to the missing girls the club was hunting. *What's the saying? Correlation and causation or some crap like that not meaning shit?*

After he pissed, he checked the mirror. His face was red—windburn—and his hair was damp and dark from sweat. Turning on the cold water, he rinsed his hands and arms before splashing his face, letting the water run down his neck and into his shirt. He didn't bother drying off.

"You took long enough," Jenna said when he met the girls at the front door. Their arms were filled with drinks and snacks. Before he could respond, Jenna shoved a Gatorade at him. "Drink. You look dehydrated as hell."

"Thanks. You look great too." It was the most they'd spoken since their one-night stand. And she kept talking.

"Sure you don't want to load your bike into the trailer and ride in the, uh, what do you guys call them again?"

"You can call it a car." He smirked, twisting the Gatorade's cap off instead of touching her cheek. "But *cage* is the word."

"Don't bother, Jenna." Ashlyn laughed. "For these guys, riding in a cage is worse than death."

"Sounds more like a control problem."

Case shrugged. "Or maybe we don't want to intrude on girl time."

"Offer still stands," Ash said. "You both look like you could use a nap." Bullet shuffled up beside them from the registers, eyeing the SUV with a little too much longing.

"We need a few more minutes to stretch our legs," Case said a little too firmly for the Prospect's benefit, "but we'll be fine."

Bullet pushed the door open, holding it for the girls. Case waited for them to go first, but as Ash's foot crossed the threshold, Bullet's back straightened and his shoulders turned. Like a coon hound going on alert. "Wait."

Case didn't need a second warning. He grabbed Ash, pulling her back and stepping in front of her in one motion, leaving two confused females in his wake. He kept one arm outstretched, trapping the girls into the store, and followed Bullet's eyeline. The smoking stranger stood in the same place, ten feet from the door. No longer alone. Next to him loomed a barrel-shaped guy, bald and menacing, with massive Cyrillic ink-covered arms crossed over his chest. He was shorter than Case, but not by much. A third man stood near them, his head halfway in the icebox, moving bags around. *Fuckers can't even try to blend in?*

"You're blocking the door." Jenna nudged the back of his shoe with her toe.

Case's eyes caught Bullet's.

"Want me to get them to the car?" Bullet whispered, even as the shady trio started moving.

"Get who what?" Jenna peered around his shoulder. Case spared her a split-second glance before he reached for the Beretta hidden under his cut.

"Too late for fancy maneuvers, Prospect."

Case stared at the big guy. He wore a smile, like he wanted to ask them about their lord and savior Harley Davidson. His smoker buddy tailed him with a scowl the faded baseball cap couldn't hide. Both men's hands stayed deep in their pockets. Case didn't need a crystal ball to know they weren't holding gift cards and Bibles.

"Can we help you?" Case asked in a wooden voice, pushing Jenna back. She stumbled, and he tightened his grip to steady her.

"Girls." Bullet kept his attention trained on the men. "I think I left my wallet inside. Can you go check?"

Thank the stars Ash wasn't an idiot. She got hold of Jenna's wrist, hauling her backward. He all but heard a fake cheerful smile in her voice. "Yeah! On the counter, right?"

Case hoped there was a back way out. Maybe if the owner had sense enough to hide them.

"Don't go far, pretty girl," Baseball Cap called in

a voice as slippery as his greasy hair, a heavy accent rolling the syllables. "We gonna have a good time once you ain't with these Crow assholes."

Case glared. *This is a club thing? Exactly who the fuck are the targets?* "You ain't their type." He felt a hand on his elbow, and Bullet stepped up. His head tilted to the icebox as the third man slammed the door and straightened up. If Case had blinked, he might've missed the man shoving something in the back of his waistband. *This place was a fucking weapons drop?*

Shit.

"We don't want any trouble." Bullet lifted his arms, hands out.

"Your types are all trouble," Big Guy said. "And Crow whores never mind whose cock they're riding. That dark-haired one looks like she knows how to have a good—"

Case's fist struck his jaw, laying him out on the concrete. Icebox growled and lunged for Case, tackling him into the brick wall, knocking his breath out in a wheezing gasp.

"Fuck off!" Bullet sprung. He snagged Icebox by the collar, fighting to drag him down to the concrete.

"Back the fuck off," Baseball Cap snarled. He pointed a 9 mm at Bullet's chest.

Case pulled his Beretta, leveling it at Big Guy as the asshole sat up. He froze, twitching like he wanted to go for his own weapon. *Try it, asshole.* The screech of peeling tires and a few shouts reminded Case they had an audience, but he didn't care. If they streamed all over the KCK news tonight, so fucking be it.

"Put your gun down now. Or I kill your friend." Baseball's aim didn't waver. Neither did Case's.

Icebox groaned, touching the back of his head where it hit the pavement. His palm came back stained red.

"Think I give a shit about a Prospect?" Case kept his voice flat, calm. Emotion came after a fight. If you wanted to see the other side of it. "We'll get another. Don't think you'll feel the same way when I put a bullet between his eyes." He moved the barrel a fraction of an inch toward Big Guy. "Move again, and I'll make good on that threat."

Icebox made a quick try for his side arm, and Case rushed forward until the Beretta was flush against Big Guy's forehead.

"Stop." Icebox's arm shot up again, hand empty.

"Just shoot him," Bullet said, his face red with anger. "Or stop talking and shoot me, asshole. Come on, pussy. Do it!" He stepped up on Baseball Cap, arms outstretched in a dare. Caught off guard, Baseball hesitated, the muzzle lifting a hair's breadth. Bullet leaped. His hands closed around the barrel, and the gun arced upward. Bullet crashed into Baseball, and both men tumbled, rolling and scrabbling like wrestlers. Icebox sat up slowly, swearing in a language Case didn't understand. His hand went to his belt.

"I said, don't move, motherfucker!" Case nudged Big Guy's head again. The man was sweating harder.

Fuck. This is going to hell.

Icebox and Big Guy exchanged a look. He heard a crunch. Baseball screamed. Bullet staggered up, Baseball's gun in his hand.

Baseball bellowed something, then, "One of you fucking shoot them!"

Icebox's hand moved.

"Strike three, dumbass." Case swung the gun to Icebox and fired. The shot echoed, and Icebox yowled, blood streaming from his elbow across the concrete and Case's jeans.

Big Guy screamed at him in what sounded like Russian. Baseball Cap sat motionless, his own gun still trained on him. Case stepped closer to Icebox and threw the asshole's overshirt open. A Glock sat in a worn harness. The guy was half a step from shock, clutching desperately at his arm to stop the blood. Case grabbed the Glock in one fluid motion and trained his Beretta on Icebox. "Want to keep pressing your luck?" Case asked.

Sirens wailed in the distance. Not close. Not yet. But the town wasn't big enough for them to be that far off. *Fucking Thursdays.*

"Go," he spat at Icebox. "Get the fuck out of here before I change my mind."

"We ain't gonna kill them?" Bullet sounded disappointed. Like shit wasn't complicated enough without adding a public triple homicide.

"Not today. Hurry." Case kicked Icebox's leg.

Baseball Cap crawled to Icebox, his face a ruin of blood and bruising, and the cap itself forgotten a couple of yards away. Bullet had taken a chunk out of the guy's ear, but Baseball grabbed his friend by the uninjured arm and hoisted him up. Case lowered the Glock but kept the Beretta aimed at their backs. Big Guy stumbled to his feet, watching Bullet, who pointed the stolen gun straight at him. Slowly, he raised both hands and backed up, following his friends to the Black F-150.

It became a mad scramble once they cleared the F-150. Big Guy raced for the driver's door, yanking it open and diving inside. Baseball Cap threw Ice Box into the back seat and leaped in after him. Backing up fast enough for the tires to squeal, the window lowered, and Baseball Cap poked his head out. Case didn't wait to see if he had a curse or a bullet prepared for them. He fired twice. One shot soared a couple of inches above Baseball Cap's head, forcing him back into the truck to take cover.

The other was meant for the back tire. The metal hubcap scraped the pavement, but Big Guy didn't slow down.

Only once they hit the road and raced out of sight did Case holster his gun. Checking the Glock's safety, he stuck it in the back of his jeans until he could get to the bike's saddle bags. "Get the girls. Hurry!" he yelled, already heading for his bike.

Bullet ran to the door. "Let's go!"

The sirens sounded closer. Maybe about a minute out. Two at most. Jenna and Ashlyn tumbled into the parking lot, Ash stopping next to Case.

"Are you hurt?"

He shook his head and pushed her toward the Mercedes. "Get in the car and drive. Don't stop. We'll be right behind you."

"Okay."

"Hold on." Case shrugged his cut off and handed it to her. "Yours too, Prospect!"

Bullet didn't ask questions and did the same. "Put them under the seat."

She tossed the cuts into Jenna's lap before she climbed in. Bullet's engine roared to life a second before Case's. Ash drove off and, catching the kickstand with his foot, Case rode after her, Bullet hot on his heels.

****

About thirty miles from Junction City, Ashlyn pulled off to a rest area. The second the car parked, Jenna hurtled into the restrooms. Case watched her disappear behind the corner of the faded masonry, his helmet in his hands, clutching hard enough his knuckles turned white. Ashlyn spared a quick glance over her shoulder as she came around the SUV's front, keys in her hand, pushing hair away from her face.

"Joker told you to come here?" Case got off the Electra and set the helmet down on the seat.

"Eventually."

"I want to know what that means."

She bit her lip and pointed at the covered picnic area. "Over there."

Case and Bullet followed Ash to the nearest of the cheerful red tables. She folded onto the wooden bench with a heavy sigh. Bullet sat across from her, with a full view of the incoming traffic. Case stayed on his feet. Bullet produced a fresh pack of Marlboros, slid a cig out, then set the pack on the table. Case took one for himself, glad he'd kept his lighter in his jeans. As he held the light up, he studied Ash over his glowing cigarette. She propped one elbow on the table, her breaths even, staring at the main building. Way too calm for a chick with raging PTSD, barely two months out of a major firefight and gunshot wound. *Maybe she took a Xanax in the car?*

"He wanted us to head for Manhattan. Said there was a clubhouse along the way. This was the compromise. But he wants you to call him."

"Fuck." *He trusts you with his wife, now you're running from the cops. Way to wear the patch.* Setting the lighter down, he grabbed his phone and stepped off the concrete slab, away from Ash and the Prospect. Leaning against a tree, he scrolled through his contacts, hit dial, and waited for Joker to answer. His heart thudded in his ears, louder with each ring. The VP picked up on the third.

"Everyone safe?" Calm. Cool Not even yelling.

Case exhaled. "Yeah. We're at the Rest Area in Solomon."

"Tell me everything that happened."

Case crouched down, starting from when he first saw Baseball Cap, closing his eyes to conjure the details. Clothes. Accents. Ink. Cyrillic. The truck, though he didn't catch the plate number. The things they said, the weapons. "Couldn't tell if it was 'cause of the cuts or... Don't think they were bikers."

"Recognize the language?"

"Sounded like Russian, but shit, I don't know. All those Iron Curtain ones sound alike to me. The big one had an accent but not an in-your-face kind." Case froze. Could it be the same thing as Belleville? "We at war with the Russians?"

"If we were, you wouldn't have to ask. They'd have mowed your asses down along with the whole damn gas station."

"So what is it?"

"Wish I fucking knew."

Case rubbed his face, kicking listlessly at a twig by his foot "What now?" Maybe they should turn around. Second attack in as many outings? The Kansas City shit might be bad, but this couldn't be coincidence.

"Toad's swearing whoever did it ain't local. Says they've got a pretty good handle on Junction City territory, and nobody's challenged it in a while. He's gonna deal with clean-up. But I don't recommend going back through Junction any time soon."

Thank the gods. Case's shoulders relaxed. He knew the Crows had safe houses along I-70, and Joker had him memorize the clubhouse locations in case shit went sideways. But that didn't always mean the cops were in their pocket. "So how do we play this?"

"Ash said you got the cuts off. Good call. Keep 'em off. Stow the bikes in the trailer. Want you riding cage to Burning Man. And keep your heads low in case Toad can't clear this as fast as he thinks. The hotel ain't far. How's Ash?"

Case checked his six. Ashlyn and Bullet sat where he'd left them, heads together, voices too low to hear over the interstate and wind. Jenna wasn't there. *Must be scrolling her Insta on the toilet.* "Actually, pretty okay."

Joker stayed silent too long. "You drive. I know Jenna's taken something, but—"

"Got it." *And I'll have to drag Jenna's unconscious ass out of the bathroom.* "Oh, hey! Before you go. In the fight, Bullet ran up on that asshole with a goddamn death wish. I know Prospects are meant to prove their balls, but shit was weird."

"Fuck. Try talking to him tonight. Make sure he's squared away. I can send someone out to replace him if you need to, but it'll be a pain in the ass."

Wonderful. I get to play Dr. Phil.

"You okay?"

"Pissed. But I'm solid, VP. I'll let you go so we can put road behind us." *Wish you'd just order us home.* He hung up and snapped the twig in half. The pieces fell. He gave himself three deep breaths before dusting his jeans off and heading back to the others. "Ash? Check on Jenna. She's been in there a while."

"No problem." She rose, touching his arm as she passed. He watched her open the restroom door, then turned to Bullet.

"Joker wants us to load up. No cuts and no bikes."

"Figured. Am I driving?"

"I'll do it. Give me something to focus on. Ash good?"

"Worried about Jenna." Bullet snatched his pack of smokes and stretched. "I'll get shit started."

"Cool. I'll be right there." Case tossed his cigarette down, stomping it with his boot. "Gonna wash up." He followed Ash's path to the main facility. The door swung at him before he grabbed it. He jumped back to let Ash and a freakishly pale Jenna through. "Hey, ladies. We'll be heading out in a few." Jenna didn't look at him.

Is she even awake? Her eyes were open but blank, and not lined black like they'd been before, and her hair was dripping water down her arms and onto Ash's where her friend held her up.

He put one hand on her shoulder. She blinked like she just noticed she wasn't alone. "You still got time to stretch your legs. Get some fresh air."

"Thanks, Case," Ash said with a sigh. She led Jenna away. He watched them, his jaw clenching. He wanted to pull her into his arms. Tell her everything was okay. That she was safe. *She wouldn't believe me. I don't even believe me.*

****

The hotel wasn't a large one, and far from five stars, but it had a bed and a shower. That was all Case cared about. Ash checked them in, and they filed down the narrow hall in exhausted silence, shuffling under the weight of bags that hadn't been this heavy ten hours ago. Case remembered tossing them into the SUV that morning. Now he could barely keep his own duffel on his shoulder. He and Bullet got to their room and broke off, not bothering with verbal goodnights to the girls. Inside, Case dropped onto the nearest bed, letting Bullet slog the terrible four feet to the other one. Case surveyed the room by turning his head and nothing else. A solid fifteen minutes passed before he stirred a single muscle, and only thirst drove him that far.

"Gonna grab a drink. You deal with the air conditioning. And call Joker. Let him know we're here."

"I'll give that a few more minutes. Ash is on the phone with him. She texted."

"Just don't forget."

He followed the hotel's tired beige signs in search of the vending machines. The adrenaline burned off at least an hour ago, but his hands still itched for the weight of the gun, for one more punch. *Maybe this place has a workout room?* He wandered the halls, passing the vending machines a few times until he'd assured himself that no gym existed—and because walking felt better than lying around doing nothing but obsessing about the things he should have done differently—but eventually, he stood in front of the machines. *How bad of an idea is caffeine tonight?* Hell, part of him kept shouting they ought to set a watch. *Thanks, Corps.*

"Hey." He recognized her voice without needing to turn. He almost didn't. If she still had the same expression that she wore at the gas station. But he forced himself.

Jenna stood a yard away, even more ghostly in the fluorescent light, her eyes red-rimmed. And his hands ached for something other than guns or right hooks. For a treacherous second, he imagined closing the distance between them, hugging her, kissing her worried lips until she relaxed against him the way she had in his apartment.

"Hey," he said quietly without moving an inch. "You all right?"

Jenna nodded, avoiding his gaze but not running in the opposite direction. *Progress?*

"I was worried about you. It's barely been long enough for you to heal up, and…"

Case didn't dare say anything, fearing it might remind her that she'd spent the last two weeks running instead of speaking.

"Do you do this? All the time? You and Travis, you're so … calm about it. And it's not normal. What if you're hurt? We haven't even gotten to a hospital, and

Ash said Travis won't go and—" She choked a little, wiping her cheeks, but the tears didn't quite roll.

If she starts crying...

"Ain't nothing normal about any of it, Jenna." He risked a couple of steps toward her, keeping his voice quiet, like Dragon talking to a spooked horse. Or Joker, when Ash was having a bad turn, come to think of it. He wanted to grab her and pull her close. To hug her until her eyes shone with something other than tears. He settled for touching her arm. Lightly. Cautiously. "I'm not hurt," he said, trying to make her look at him. "I promise, I'm not."

"You could be bleeding internally or have a brain bleed. What if you've got a concussion? A fracture, you—" Jenna broke off, hand over her mouth as if she could stop herself talking. "And your so-called brethren? A-aren't you supposed to h-have backup or something?"

He almost told her he'd hunt down the nearest urgent care if it'd make her feel better before he realized what he was about to do. Case exhaled, trying to get his brain focused. "Travis and I are fine. We've both survived way worse. Tomorrow, we're back on the road, and it'll be normal again."

"They hurt you! How can it be normal tomorrow? Y-you're just … letting it happen. It keeps happening!" Jenna sniffled and reached out, only for her hand to falter and stop before she touched him. "Why am I caring? You don't, do you? Was that night— Was it really about helping me? Or just the fun of one more brawl?"

The words slammed him right back to that gas station wall. *Fuck*. His face burning, he retreated, letting go of her rather than risk letting his hand clench on her arm. "You think that was fun for me? Do you know what keeps going through my mind since that night? The what-ifs, Jenna. What if I hadn't followed you? What if I hadn't been there in time? I was fucking terrified, babe. I still am. I don't even want to think what would have happened to you and Ashlyn if things went differently today."

"If you hadn't been there today? Ever think that's why anything happened at all?" She wiped her cheek, glaring. "Those assholes were picking a fight with the pictures on your jackets, but it's somehow about our vaginas? Typical. You're so deep in your little bird cult you can't even tell that it might be the problem."

"Oh, damn. My irony senses are tingling," he said drily. "If I tried that argument on you? That you were attacked because of what you were wearing? That'd make me a jackass."

"Plenty makes you a jackass. That only helps the case, Case."

He turned to put the dollar into the machine, pressing the Coke button and listening to it drop through empty air to crash at the bottom. He could relate. "I didn't blame either of you for this shit today, Jenna. Stop putting words in my mouth. All I said was I was scared. Losing that fight wasn't an option. But that don't mean I loved being in it." He put the next dollar in to get a second one.

"You could've run. Let us call the cops. You could have done a lot. But none of that was an option either. Because of that stupid bird. That's all that's really important to you." She turned around and stomped off down the hall.

Case bit his lip. Nothing good would come from the words on the tip of his tongue. He forced himself to head the opposite direction.

He threw their door open as Bullet hung up with someone. The stupid asshole even smiled. That expression fell away as he stared at Case.

"The vending machine eat your change or something?"

"Or something." Case tossed a bottle at him and fell onto the bed, head propped up on the pillows. "Bullet. Do me a favor. Fuck off." He twisted the cap off his Coke, wishing it was someone's neck.

Bullet chuckled. "You should have grabbed some ice. You ain't moving so good."

"Because I got pushed into a wall, fuck face," Case replied, taking a sip.

"Okay. Since you ain't taking the hint, I'll come out and ask." He leaned forward in the chair, gesturing at Case. "You sure nothing's broken? I don't mind swinging you by the ER or a local vet. Whatever passes for sawbones around here."

"You're starting to sound like Jenna." He looked away, the heat still on his cheeks.

"She's scared," Bullet said. "She ain't used to all this shit. Don't—"

"If you tell me not to worry, I'll kick your ass."

"I was gonna say don't take it personally, but okay."

Case opened his eyes, so he could glare at him. Then he propped himself up on his elbows and tilted his head. "Speaking of okay, what the fuck was that about back there?"

Bullet's brow scrunched. "What do you mean?"

"I'm all for taking one for the team, kid, but asking to be shot? That was fucking weird, even for me. I, uh, I just want to ask if…"

"That? Figured it'd throw him off. It worked." The Prospect was selling it hard, but Case wasn't buying. Bullet sat too straight, breathed too hard. His fingers drummed impatiently on the chair's arm. "I swear I'm okay."

He didn't have the sort of bond with Bullet to press the point. But he was almost a Crow, and Case's only present backup for the rest of this fucked-up trip. *Bullshit that I have to be out here with a Prospect. Now it's a Prospect with a death wish? Fuck me.*

As if sensing some of that, Bullet stared into the blank TV screen on the wall. "Hey, man. I'm just, uh, on the wrong foot. What am I wandering into? This whole Burning Man thing. Jenna told me to Google it, but the internet don't clear that shit up."

Case rolled onto his back, relieved at the subject change. Anything was better than fucking around with all that headspace babble. "I ain't been since I was seventeen. Shit's probably changed, but from what I remember? Think of it like drugged-out hippies and hipster assholes pretending that they're living in some alternate universe. Kinda like if *Star Trek*, *Dune*, and *Fast Times and Ridgemont High* got mixed in a blender. With some peyote for shits and giggles."

"I've only seen one of those."

"You're shitting me," Case chuckled. "Which one?"

"The Star Track one... With that guy from that one show Ash forced us to watch. *Heroes*, maybe?"

"It's Trek! Not Track!" *And now I sound like Grim.* "Kid, we're gonna have to educate you when we get back home." He tried to think of more recent movies, but his gauge was off from living around vintage film nerds and too many deployments spent with hard drives full of random-ass films and pirated DVDs of anything from Bollywood to Charlie Chaplin. "How about *Barbarella*, *Fury Road*, and, uh, *American Pie*?"

Case frowned. "Shit. I can't even think of any half-decent new movie about horny dumbass college kids. But that's definitely a vibe."

"This sounds fucking awful."

"Pretty much." Case set the Coke on the nightstand and sat up long enough to pull his shirt off before shutting his eyes and hoping for a dreamless sleep. "Make sure the alarm's set," he muttered, yanking the other pillow over his head.

Chapter Eight
Case

August 28

Case had never heard Bullet swear so much. Ash, Jenna, and even Case tried to explain to him that the traffic was part of the Burning Man experience, but he didn't want to hear it. Especially since when he offered to drive as a favor, nobody warned him. He hated it, even more when the speed limit dropped to ten miles per hour. It took a couple of hours to get through, mostly because they had to help the guys at the gate search their shit, which involved pulling the motorcycles out of the trailer and letting them go through everything. Luckily, they weren't half as dedicated to finding as Case was to hiding his Beretta. Their other guns were safely stashed with a Crow nomad who'd met them fifty miles out.

Jenna directed Bullet where to park, and when Case and Bullet moved to get the bags, Ash pulled them away. "Don't worry about it. Someone will get that later."

Case and Bullet exchanged glances. Much as Case suppressed his memories of this place, he distinctly remembered having to help set up the camp.

"You may want to grab your goggles if you can reach them, though." Jenna pulled her hair up into a ponytail, tucked it beneath a wide-brimmed hat, and, linking her arm with Ashlyn's, started toward the camp, goggles dangling from her hand.

"Just grab your bag," Case told Bullet, shouldering his and following the girls with slower steps.

"Expecting your mom to jump out from a tent?"

Case rolled his eyes. He already checked before leaving the hotel. Thankfully Trish and her group nearly were on the other side of Black Rock City. "Her camp's at four o'clock. We're safe here."

"I don't even know what the fuck that means."

"You'll learn." Case shrugged, picking up the pace to close the distance between them and the girls, especially now that more people were trickling from their cars as well. Losing them on the playa was a real danger. One he didn't think Joker or Bullet really appreciated. *This is gonna be a pain in the ass.*

Like most of the camps, the one the girls belonged in was surrounded by a wall of trucks and RVs, but even over them, he could see the white, canvas tops of massive tents. "Hey, Trouble. Stay close, huh?"

Ashlyn grinned and stopped, holding her other arm out so she could wrap it around Case's elbow as he came up next to her. "Afraid we'll leave you behind?"

"Something like that."

The girls led them past a line of storage containers, all painted with vibrant colors and abstract faces. Jenna greeted one of the men leaning against the corner where the containers made an entrance to the camp. Case let go of Ashlyn to step through the entrance with Bullet. His mouth fell open as he took in the other side.

"Definitely ain't in Kansas anymore." Bullet's shoulders slumped.

"No shit," Case said, tearing off his sunglasses. *Burning Man ain't what it used to be.* There was one giant tent in the center. Probably the communal area for the entire camp, surrounded by similar sprawling structures. Gleaming double-decker RVs straight off a Hollywood lot lined the perimeter, while tents in shapes and styles from Renaissance Faire to *Star Wars* dotted the rest of the area.

"So is this the *Star Trek* part?" Bullet asked,

staring at a massive tent-like thing that could probably fit Case's apartment twice with a little bit of space left over. "This the Enterprise?"

"A few hits of whatever they're smoking, and I'll bet it'll even take off." Case nodded toward a group passing around a bong so flashy he could probably pawn it and cover rent for a year. They looked like college students, but considering the amount of plastic surgery happening these days, who knew? *And considering the modeling world...* For the first time, he wondered if Jenna had gotten work done. Or Ash. *Great. I'm stuck on the Isle of Plastics.*

"Hey, guys! We're over there," Ashlyn called from behind them, getting on her toes and pointing wildly toward the back corner of the camp. "It should be set up already."

"Behind the big, white circus tent?" Case tried to keep his tone calm.

"It's called a yurt," Jenna corrected. "Thought you'd been here before." *Her* tone sat somewhere between teasing and accusatory. "And it's ours, by the way. Thierry says to go ahead and get comfy, everybody's out for a few hours at a pop-up concert—" She stopped to check her phone and let out a piercing squeak. "Ohmigod, it's Island of Misfit Sex Toys? They're gonna be doing another show. He says we can meet them? Ash! Didn't you party with their drummer? Do you have his Snap? I want to get pics. Kyla will die of jealousy..."

And like that, the girls were off in their world.

Another reminder. He never noticed it before with Ashlyn. He knew she came from money, but hell, when she first rolled into Oak Grove, she was job hunting and crashing at Joker's and Megan's places. It made her seem human. One of them. *Not so much now.*

Every day outside of PhaCo, Ashlyn changed, shapeshifting like she was coming out of a shell. Today, she walked beside Jenna in an embroidered lace shift and heavy boots he'd never seen before, full-face makeup with her blonde hair braided under a wild steampunk hat. She looked like one of the girls on Jenna's Instagram. *Like Jenna.* For the first time, he could see how they'd ended up friends.

"Gods, give me strength," Case whispered.

"Not like you remembered it?" Bullet readjusted the bag on his shoulder, waiting for Ash to pass them so he could follow her. Jenna was too busy checking her phone for new updates every three seconds, her excited bouncy steps kicking up white playa dirt. Her long, tanned legs showed in glimpses through slashed harem pants. It should have been stupid. Instead, he knew already he'd be dreaming about dragging those pants off.

"Not even slightly," Case answered once the girls were out of earshot.

As a kid at the Burn, he'd been lucky to get a sleeping bag underneath an RV's canopy. His mother never brought a tent. She always found somewhere to stay. Yet here he was, trailing two models toward a fucking desert palace. Their tents, or yurts, whatever the fuck they called them, had to cost almost as much as Jenna's Kansas City mansion. Three massive, white canvas dome-like structures connected to give the illusion of rooms really did occupy twice the floor space in his actual apartment. The center tent's arched doors were propped open, revealing area rugs scattered on the ground and cushioned benches arranged around a small table. He glanced into the tent to his right. The room was smaller—a relative term. Two twin beds greeted him, with a shelf between.

He shifted back from the tent floor. *Do I wipe my feet?* The carpets alone had to cost a grand.

"That one's yours," Ashlyn said, pointing to the room he'd just surveyed. "We'll be on the left." She kicked her boots lightly against a small post outside the tent's doorway and walked off to join Jenna behind their room's already-closed flap.

He followed her example to shake the dust off, then pushed Bullet out of the way to get to their room. Anything to get his bag off his shoulder. Only halfway there, he stopped. Stared around the tent. Maybe it was the sandalwood incense already lit, or the fluffy comforter turned down in both beds. Or the cool air washing over his sweaty face.

Motherfucking rich people.

"What's wrong?" Ashlyn asked by her own door.

"Is that air conditioning?"

"Yes?" She sounded so confused, he turned on her, ready to start yelling.

What is the fucking point of coming to Burning Man if you're going to set up luxury villages and not actually deal with the desert? Just build a giant five-story resort! If they strung a few of these yurts together, they wouldn't be that far off. But glaring into Ash's wide green eyes, his fury burned out under the air conditioner's frigid breeze. *Shit. I sound like Mom.*

"And here I thought we'd be roughing it." He shrugged and walked away, dropping his bag on the floor and himself into the bed. Only to groan. He stroked one hand along the top sheet, imagining the bliss his ten-year-old self would have felt to have this instead of a broken sleeping bag with his clothes for a pillow. *Probably three thousand count Egyptian silk spun by the rarest of spiders from the great pyramids or some shit.*

"You okay?" Bullet asked, walking through the

flap and sitting on the other bed. He seemed lost.

"Fucking annoyed. We drive all this way so they can fucking glamp…"

"Weren't you complaining last night about sleeping in cramped tents and dealing with the goddamn heat? Isn't this, um, better?"

"This is stupid," he said, his voice a little louder. Bullet held his hand up to remind him to keep it down, but based on the volume of the girls' laughter, they weren't paying any attention. "You know that Jenna don't exactly bring out the best in Ashlyn. It's fine when we're in Oak Grove. Here? We're surrounded by *their* people. Rich bitches in Hollywood costumes pretending—"

"Ash ain't all that different," Bullet said. "Yeah, she's a bit more, uh…"

"Everything?"

"Sure. She's a bit more when Jenna's around, but you act different when Joker's around. Or around me. It's normal, I think."

Case glared. "Joker's my boss. Not just my vice president. Don't you act different around your boss?"

"That's my point." Bullet spoke to his faded black boots.

Case opened his mouth, and closed it, his mind drawing a perfect blank. Finally, he said, "It ain't personal."

"No?"

And I thought the heat was uncomfortable. "Still figuring you out. But that don't mean anything. What's my opinion matter, anyway? Joker and Tree are the ones you gotta worry about, and you know one of 'em likes you."

"It's—" Bullet cut himself off so sharply, Case's gaze shot back toward him. His lips were drawn in, his fingers drumming on his knee. *Yeah, whatever that is—it's a conversation I'd rather not have.* Sighing, Case sat up and grabbed his bag, loosening the drawstring to avoid looking at Bullet. He dug around the pockets until he found the goggles wrapped in a spare t-shirt. Ridiculous, rimmed with decorative studs and padded for comfort—they'd been an impulse purchase when he was thirteen, traded for extra water and a long massage for the lady who'd offered them. How the hell they'd stayed with him all these years, he'd never fathom. Case evaluated the Prospect one more time and blew out a sigh. *Fuck it.*

"I'm not happy about this gig. My mom's around somewhere. She had me and my sister over the summer, dragged us here every single year. We had to go along with her nomad, hippy crap until I was seventeen." He rested his forearms on his legs, feeling the weight of all those blistering hot summers. "Know what she did when she found out I enlisted?"

Bullet shook his head.

"Fuckin' called Dad and reamed him. Said it was all his fault that I had a 'murder-boner.' Her actual words. Accused him of corrupting me, turning me into a product of a corporatist society that mindlessly sends their peons to die for the almighty dollar."

"Damn. She must be a hit at parties."

"She is, actually." Case grimaced. "She has a way of making people like her. Works on everyone but her kids. So, yeah, I'm not exactly dying to run into her." He reached into his bag to pull out a fresh shirt. "The only person who really knows that story is Joker."

Bullet's brows knit together. "I won't tell anyone."

"If I thought I couldn't trust you, I wouldn't have told you." Case stood up and ripped off his sweat-drenched t-shirt before yanking on a black undershirt. "Come on. I don't know shit about this side of the tracks, but it shouldn't be too hard to find food. I'm fucking starving."

"I could eat." Bullet followed his example with a change of t-shirt, so Case left him to it and went to find their jailors.

"Hey, Ash!" he called out from the common area. The small blonde emerged from the other side, a smile still on her face. He grinned back and half turned, throwing an arm around Bullet's neck and dragging him forward in a half-assed headlock. "Bullet wants a tour. And I want food. Figured you'd know the drill."

"Give me a second." She ducked her head back into the other room. Case released Bullet and crossed to the back of the yurt, where a stocked mini-fridge, hotplate, and two cases of water waited. *Fucking rich people.* He grabbed a bottle and tossed it to Bullet.

"You're gonna want to drink a shit ton of this," he said. "Trust me. Keep a bottle or something on you. Ash, did you pack Bullet a flask?"

"Yeah!" a disembodied voice yelled back. A couple of minutes later, Ash emerged with a large, mostly-empty bag on her shoulder, her hair pulled back, and her outfit completely new—and skimpy. He didn't know that much about fashion, but he could tell it was custom. Nothing with that many laces and rivets came off a rack. *Wonder if Joker would send us home if I sent a shot of her right now?* "Where's the rest of your outfit, girl?"

Ash sniffed. "Very funny. But if you want to be fed, you'll play nice." She stuck her tongue out and sanity returned. *And is it really Ash's strappy get-up or Jenna's thighs in those harem pants that's got you pissed off?*

"You drive a hard bargain." Case nodded at the still-closed door behind her. "And Jen?"

"She'll meet up with us later. Let's go. I want to introduce you guys to Thierry. Bullet, where are your goggles? Go get them. You'll thank me later. Case…?"

"Right here, sunshine," he said, pulling them out of his back pocket. "Ain't my first rodeo."

She nodded, but the moment Bullet vanished behind the flap, her smile disappeared. She grasped Case's wrist. "Thank you. I know this isn't what you're used to, but—"

"It ain't about me, Ash," he said, patting her shoulder. "Don't worry. I still plan on having a good time."

Her grin returned. "Good. We're going to have so much fun!" Still holding his wrist, she turned, waving for Bullet to follow as she led them back into the sun and sand.

The heat felt even more oppressive now that they'd emerged from the comfort of air-conditioning. Fortunately, Ashlyn immediately doused them all in sunscreen. A gust of wind came through right after, gluing playa grit to their still-sticky bodies. Wiping it off only made it feel worse. While Bullet groaned and itched, Case laughed. All the money in the world wouldn't change the playa's sick sense of humor.

****

Okay. It might not be so bad.

The actual circuit rolled out the way he remembered. A wide arc of constant movement: hipsters on bikes and in art cars, people peddling their crafts, their help, or more stealthily, their drugs. Case fell into the rhythm after a few minutes. Maybe in part because Bullet didn't. Every time somebody scraped by or came up to them, he tensed like a cornered animal. If Ashlyn noticed, she didn't say anything. For his part, Case was more concerned about the people he knew than the strangers. He scanned the crowds ahead of them, hoping for a sea of faces he didn't know.

The only part that felt unfamiliar was the camp. If he thought the yurts counted as extravagant, that was only because he hadn't seen the more massive ones in other camps Ash dragged them through, introducing an endless herd of well-groomed magazine ads in human form. Some camps boasted entire buffet tables full of fancy restaurant fare, with dozens of wait staff.

And Ash spoke to many of the magazine ads like family. Feeling increasingly like an unannounced extra in a reality show, Case kept quiet and took advantage of the food, sharing amazed looks with Bullet. *No wonder Ash can't always tell what's fucking real. They live in a goddamn movie set.*

Jenna still hadn't met up with them. That thought drifted across his mind in the third camp, but Ash was giggling and exclaiming with a dark-skinned model, their words interspersed with Spanish. He cleared his throat to step in. "Hey, I forgot my mask. I'll be right back, okay?"

He ignored Bullet's silent plea and rushed back toward their actual camp. He reached the main enclosure right as Jenna stepped outside. He nearly stumbled backward, surprised at her sudden appearance. Like Ash, she'd undergone some wild alterations: blue and purple streaks now sparkled in her dark hair, and she wore an assembly of straps and a corset he'd be seeing in fantasies. "Sorry," he said, rubbing the back of his head. "I was looking for you."

"Oh?" Jenna edged away. "Is something up with your tent? I can talk to Thierry."

"No. Nothing's wrong. I just… Wanted to … um.

Fuck." He made a face. "No! Not fuck. That's not what I mean. Fuck as in … fuck, Case, learn to fucking talk. I'm sorry. Let me start over." He got a deep breath in. "I wanted to talk."

"You are. More or less." Jenna waved him toward the tent. "Maybe you're dehydrated. Come on. I've got some smart water." Their room was only steps away, and the flap opened to reveal a bedroom-turned-closet with another minifridge tucked in between two clothes racks. Jenna grabbed a bottle without waiting for Case's answer and tossed it to him.

He took a few sips just to have something to do. *Of course, this wouldn't be easy. Never is with her.*

"You know what I mean, Jenna," he said finally. "It's been weird since Junction City. I wanted to clear the air. Apologize."

She waved it away. "You shouldn't apologize for being yourself. I was expecting the wrong things, probably. It's okay. That's all the outside world."

Dismissal? Insult? Both? He put his hand on his hip, repeating her words in his head. "You can be so frustrating."

"That's the pot shaming the kettle." Jenna laughed. "Listen, Case. You keep getting in fights, and I think it's an unhealthy pattern. But it's *your* pattern to sort out."

"Well, we all have our unhealthy patterns, I guess." He took another sip of water instead of pointing out that two incidents didn't necessarily make a pattern. *But that'll start another fight. See? I can learn.*

"Exactly. Like I was in my feelings because the sex was awesome, but *I* can sort my own hormones." She shrugged and sat on one of the cream-colored puffy chairs. "Let's just forget the whole thing, okay?"

"Okay," he agreed. "Friends?" He doubted she

ever considered him a friend. *A booty call and a thorn in her side, sure.*

"Of course. You did probably save my skin twice now, and you're sweet when you're not knocking people's teeth out." She gave him that sunny, sweet smile he remembered from Wellge's station. It felt like a million years since he'd seen it. "You sure you want to be friends with me?"

Relief and confusion warred in his chest as he nodded. "Of course." *And more.*

"Glad to hear it." She closed the distance between them in two steps and went up on her toes. Her lips touched his cheek in the lightest caress. His skin burned from that point outward. The tug-of-war in his chest faded into a simple ache. His arms came up to embrace her, but he made the hug quick and friendly. Because they were just friends.

"Now, time to get your goggles and mask on. The parties begin soon."

Just friends. Just friends. Just friends. The new mantra was going to take a shitload of concentration. "Can't wait," he said, his voice strained.

She laughed and touched his arm. "Stick with us, pretty boy. We won't let the sharks eat you. Unless you want them to." Jenna paused. "So how is this all going to work, by the way? I know you're here to play bodyguard, but you and Trav have to sleep sometime."

"So do you," he pointed out, though Jenna only laughed again.

"Sleep? Maybe. It has happened. If it's raining."

"Good thing I brought some five-hour energies and a few syringes of speed." He matched her confident smile with one of his own and waited for hers to falter. "I'm kidding about the speed." *She really thinks the worst of us all. Damn.* "It's a day-by-day thing. If we have to, me and Bullet will sleep in shifts." The fact was they had free rein to call in the Nevada charter for extra guys if he smelled trouble, and a couple of friends of the club were local event staff in case of emergencies, but Jenna didn't need to know that.

Jenna's head tilted. "Are we going to have you guys around all week? What if I want to hit the orgy tent? You drawing straws?"

"Or joining. Depends on which one of us is with you." He turned away with a smirk and walked to his room rather than think about Jenna and orgies. *There's a thought no one needs in daylight.* He dragged a mask out of his bag—a simple cloth one, printed with a skeleton's jaw. With this and the goggles, along with his shorter hair, it might keep any old friends from recognizing him. *Please,* he added in a request to the universe in general as he pulled the band over his head.

"You don't think Travis would come in?" Jenna stood in the doorway, a pout on her full lips. He blinked, dragging himself back to the conversation. "Or are you all being dicks and making him behave like some kind of saint until he levels up?"

"We aren't assholes, babe. I'm pretty sure Travis would jump through fire to get in there with you." He scooped up his boots and settled on a bench, trying to get her away from their beds. And thoughts of Bullet in an orgy room. "By the way, what's your name out here?" Burner names were a tradition. Never chosen but given. He hadn't dared ask Ash, lest she turn the question back on him. Case had left his name in the dust with his last Burn and had no intention of digging it up.

"Firefly, usually." Jenna shrugged. "What about you? You said you were here all the time before the Marines."

He finished tying one boot and sat up, debating

how to answer. "Figured it's been long enough that it's not gonna work. Might as well see if another turns up." He bent to tie the other one and then bounded to his feet. "Ready?" Her gaze swept over his body, and she nodded.

"Careful. Take that shirt off too much, you might end up with Adonis."

The name caught him mid-step, and his boot hit the ground too fast. Case barely avoided a stumble and covered with a dry cough.

Too close. Gods, does she know? She can't. Can she? Ash doesn't, and Joker wouldn't say shit without warning me... "I, uh, don't think I like that one either." He kept his face as blank as possible.

"Not a mythology fan? I'm crushed." She slid her arm around his. "Someone will have an idea. But it would be funny if you had a mythical name. Ash got Pele somehow. I feel like Travis is in danger of being called Cupid if he keeps carrying her mugs and messages."

"I, um. It's complicated."

"Well, maybe you can show off a hidden talent. Wow us all into an acceptable name."

"I doubt it. What you see is what you get." Which sounded kind of sad, somehow. "Can't we go with something Egyptian or Norse? I wouldn't mind being Baldr or Horus. Emphasis on the Hor."

"Maybe you can fix something and be Tyr. Are you any good with knots?" She laughed.

"Actually—"

"Don't answer." Jenna stepped away, waving off his words before he could offer a demonstration. "Horus though... You'd have to do some epic orgy stunts for that."

Fuck, I don't want to think about you and orgies.

"I can carry a tune. And when I was a kid, Mom

forced me to learn piano. But it was one of those Casio keyboards and some of the keys didn't work, so..." He smiled at the memory. "Other than that, I guess I'll have to resort to stunts. That or dismemberment."

"I don't think the camp wars usually get that bad, but good to know." Jenna retreated to the other side of the main room, grabbing two glasses to fill with lemonade from a cooler, and handed one over to Case. "Sip, if you value your sobriety." And then downed half her cup. "Just don't start any fights tonight. I like you, but I don't want to have to put you or Trav on a leash."

"A leash, huh? Didn't know you were into that." *I have got to stop thinking this way.* He took a drink and grimaced at the bite of alcohol burning down his throat. She'd gulped hers like water. *What the hell?*

"I'm into anything that's fun for all involved." Jenna smirked. "Don't look shocked. That suitcase you helped me with wasn't all full of clothes."

Why did she have to say that? "Come on. Let's head out. I'm sure Ashlyn's wondering what's taking us so long, and Bullet may have died of heatstroke."

"Don't be silly. Ash never lets her pets die. Poor puppy's probably being dunked in sunscreen and forced into a post-apoc costume. But we should get out there and get you fed too. Maybe you can stop him being transformed into a model if you're quick." She didn't sound concerned. Nor did she rush her steps out into the sunlight as they crossed the camp's general common area, hailing two men who'd emerged from the yurt across the way. "Thierry! I want you to meet our guests!"

Case drained the vicious lemonade and set the cup aside before joining her. *This is going to be a long-ass day.*

Chapter Nine
Jenna

August 30

The blistering heat and sandy breeze had begun their annual war with Jenna's hair—not helped by the amount of hairspray the stylist plastered on for that morning's shoot. And the water pressure in the encampment's showers didn't seem to extricate the grime so much as polish it. She grimaced and twisted another damp lock up around an elastic headband, wishing she could air dry it, but then she'd be stuck in ponytails or wigs, and she needed options. With the number of pictures required today, she needed her own hair on display too, which was why heatless curls and braids were the bulk of her festival styles between shoots.

Her Insta was blowing up, Tiktok was solid, and she'd added a couple of other new apps to see how cross-platform translated with short vids. But she wasn't posting as much as normal. Somehow every time she touched the screen, all she could think of was Bennet's glacial stare and Ash's blood dripping on the carpet. Not the most chill of Burn visions. She'd taken an edible from Thierry a couple of hours earlier, but it mostly made her feel slow instead of calm. A fine line, but a line nonetheless.

She focused on her makeup and threading new laces through her favorite boots, waiting for familiar voices to pass by on the other side of the foam and canvas. But when she'd finished and stepped out into the sunlight, safe under a linen hood, mask, and goggles, only one figure reclined under the camp's public shade fly, his gold hair tousled and perfect, and his tattooed arms chiseled perfection. *Damn it.* "You seen Ash?"

"Hm?" Funny how she didn't think anything bad of his gray-slate eyes when they turned to her. The color wasn't so far away from Ben's, and neither was his build. But the similarities seemed so hollow and academic when the person behind it was … him. "Gone off on a quest," Case said with that heartbreaking, devilish smile.

So like someone else.

"Why aren't you questing too?" She sat in the chair next to him and grabbed a bottle of sunscreen off the table. Case was far more covered-up under loose linen pants and shirt. He'd almost have been a hippie, save the military-style belt and boots. With the dusty hair and henna trace-work across his hands—acquired the day before on a lost dare, he looked a galaxy away from the leather-and-denim biker she'd met in Illinois.

"Needed a damn nap." He slipped the goggles down like a knight preparing his armor. She couldn't see his expression behind the dark lenses but something about the tilt of his head communicated that his gaze followed her hands smearing the lotion across her arms and legs. *I should tell him off.* The thought didn't keep her from bending forward an extra few inches to reach her calf and rubbing the lotion in a bit slower.

"So, you've napped, and my next shoot's tomorrow. That gives us hours to ourselves before the sun goes down. We need an adventure."

"Isn't this whole thing an adventure?"

"Hm." She settled into the chair and picked up her mug. "You practically grew up here. Aren't any of your friends around? You've gotten dragged all over creation hooking up with our friends and favorite art pieces, and haven't once asked to check in with anybody." She drank, watching him over the rim. "Not even your mom…"

His jaw clenched, his thumb rubbing circles on

his index finger. *He's nervous.* She'd seen the tic before, after the Junction City fight, and in the hospital waiting room. "She's practically on the other side."

"Oh, no! Not the other side of the festival. Such a vast distance and we have no— Oh wait! We do have transport. Carts! Rolling cafes. Food and art to see along the way. It's only Mordor, Samwise."

She felt his glare, even though she couldn't see it.

"Please all the Burner gods, do *not* let that be my next name." He fidgeted, and Jenna stayed quiet. Waiting. "I guess I do need to see her. When Ash and Bullet get back from their thing, I'll head off."

"That could be three days from now. Playa time is real and does not conform to the rest of the universe. You know this. Or you did." Jenna smirked and stood up. "On your feet, soldier. I'm going out there." She grabbed a bottle of water from the cooler, slipping it into the sling attached to her belt, and made sure her collapsible cup was in its pouch on the side of her bag. "Get your gear, or I'll find your mom on my own."

He didn't get up. This time, he lifted his goggles so she could see his expression. The exasperation only made her laugh, clearly not his desired effect. "Why does this mean so much to you?" he asked when she waved him up again before finally getting to his feet and replacing the goggles.

"Dunno. Maybe I'm curious." She watched him bend to pick up water, taking a moment to appreciate his form.

"I still know how it works, Jenna. Bullet on the other hand? He's still operating in real-time. So, Ash will be back." Half true. The poor guy walked around like a lost kid in a mall trying to find an adult. But he also didn't argue well with Ash.

"Eventually," Jenna agreed.

"Um. I should warn you. My mom. She's, uh, a lot to take in. Especially for the first time meeting her."

Jenna's eyes rolled. *Such drama.* "Have you looked around recently? We are *all* a lot here. My best friend has an adoring train of whackadoo artists and that dancer guy with the honey farm. We're camped with a guy whose pet crocodile has an Instagram and will talk for three hours about his theory of soulmates while texting his accountant. And Thierry is a former MMA fighter with an organic beauty line and serious views on the world-saving values of seaweed. You are in an entire festival-city of people who are aggressively eccentric enough to qualify as living artworks."

"And yet none of those people are your mother. Otherwise, you'd understand." They walked toward the camp's entrance, despite his hesitation.

"My mother is terrifyingly, oppressively normal. I can introduce you on the way home if it will make you feel better." She regretted the words the second they fell out of her mouth. *Hi, Mom! This is the outlaw biker I slept with last month! Isn't he hot? No, I don't need therapy again. Why are you screaming?*

Case rolled his shoulder in what she assumed was a shrug and looked around them as they stopped outside the entrance, at the edge of the thoroughfare. "Cart." He pointed out an oncoming vehicle and raised his hand to hail it. A rickshaw-esque golf cart sporting red velvet seats and a wildly fringed canopy buzzed into Jenna's eye line around a lumbering café truck. The driver flashed a hundred-watt smile as he pulled up next to them.

"Hey, Firefly. Need a ride?" But his attention was on Case, lingering appreciatively on his narrow waist. If her travel companion noticed, he didn't show it. Then again, why should he? People stared at Case all the time.

"We do, Kickstart." Jenna grinned. "You need anything to drink while you're here?" She didn't wait for an answer but ran back to the shade fly and grabbed a Gatorade from the cooler. She carried snacks as well as stone beads and bracelets in her pack for payments and tokens, but she knew Kickstart from past years. Returning to the scooter, she tucked the bottle into a small cooler on the floorboard by his feet.

"No dehydrating this year because you get high and forget liquids exist. Case, you want to sit up front?" *Might as well let Kick have the extra scenery.*

Case glanced at her, his lips twitching. But he got in next to Kickstart. She slid into the back seat, her messenger bag on her lap. "He's afraid I'm gonna name him Samwise," she stage-whispered. "But he doesn't seem to like Soldier either. Maybe you should try naming him?"

"A few words come to mind," Kickstart said, not hiding his appreciative stare sweeping the length of Case's body. They spent the next few minutes catching up, but then he turned his attention back to Case with a flirty wink. "This your first Burn?"

"I've been to a few."

"And still no nickname?" He lifted a brow.

"Might have, but it was a long time—"

"Hype?" A strange voice yelled loud enough that Kick's foot slid off the pedal, and the cart slowed. Case's head shot in the same direction.

No fucking way!

"Yo, Hype! Thought I recognized those goggles!"

"Someone you know?"

Kick eased the cart to a stop, and Case stood up, disembarking and taking slow steps toward the broad, deeply tanned man in a fluffy pink tutu waving him down. "Guess that answers that." He laughed, turning to

Jenna.

Jenna stared at Kickstart. "Hype?" she mouthed, laughing. "God, I feel like I should stay out of the blast zone..." But she reached in her bag and pulled out silver foil Pop-Tart packages, pressing the stack into his hand. "I want to see you at the party tonight. So please, eat something. And drink the Gatorade. You can't live on edibles."

"I am somewhat aware of that concept. But it sounds suspicious." Kickstart grinned. "Go make sure Hot Stuff doesn't punch the old dude. I'll be around tonight. Promise. Message me!"

"You're the best." Jenna hopped out and approached Case and Mr. Tutu. Kickstart's cart whooshed off down the row.

While Case stared at the guy like an alien unsure how to make first contact, Tutu didn't have the same hang-ups, and swept him into a mighty hug, so tight Case coughed and wriggled in his grip. *Like a kid.* The thought stopped Jenna's steps. "So, Hype? This one of your old camp?" Her question drew a hearty chuckle from Tutu.

"You could say that," the man said happily. "You going to introduce us, kiddo?"

Case smoothed out his shirt, a muscle in his jaw twitching. Jenna was almost glad she couldn't see behind his goggles. "Dio, this is Firefly. Dio's, er, an old family friend."

"That's putting it mildly. How close did I come to being your stepdad?"

"You and half of St. Paul," Case mumbled under his breath. Jenna heard it, but she wasn't sure if Dio did.

"And you finally bring home a friend!" He pushed Case aside and hugged Jenna by way of greeting, his massive arms sticky against her bare midriff. She returned the embrace casually, laughing a little at his overwhelming scent: weed, patchouli, and antiperspirant. A common Burn mix.

"Sounds like you dodged a headache, Dio. Can't imagine he was easy to handle as a teenager."

"Gods, you have no idea." He laughed and clapped her shoulder before glancing at Case. "How'd you get him here? Last time I saw him, he was swearing up down and sideways that he'd never step foot back here or in Minnesota again."

"He's playing bodyguard these days."

"Sounds glamorous."

"It's not," Case snipped before Jenna gently kicked at his ankle.

"But I found out he kinda grew up here, and I can't just let him skip out on seeing his family."

Dio's smile melted so fast Jenna almost backpedaled. The look he turned on Case was pure outrage. "After all these years, you need to be forced to see her? Really, Ap—"

"Spare me." Case's voice was frosty. He'd never sounded like that, even when they'd argued. "She dumped me on whatever porch would take me. This is a courtesy call, not a reunion."

Dio crossed his arms. His eyes had a few extra creases at the corners, his smile thinner. "Well, whatever it is, you're both welcome. Camp's this way."

"Family," Jenna murmured as she grabbed Case's arm. It felt like holding a statue. He was all coiled tension and stony anger. But he followed Dio, even if his steps were stiff. "Remember: no maiming, Hype. If you don't draw blood, we can get high after. Or go visit a masseuse?"

"Why 'or'? Why not 'and'?" He made a poor attempt at a laugh. Jenna rubbed his forearm, over the tattoo of fighting wolves. They trailed his almost-stepdad in near silence, Dio hailing other friends and pointing out interesting people or displays. He knew everything about this section of the festival—maybe all of it—and Jenna found it easier to encourage his tour-guide routine.

Eventually, they turned off the main paths and reached a campsite spread around an old, yellowing RV surrounded by branching awnings and canopies, small pup tents, and sleeping bags in a semi-circle around a fire pit. Pot smoke hung heavy in the air, along with tea and fresh-baked brownies. A thin, older man sat under one of the RV's spangled awnings, swaying as he blew a mournful tune on an ocarina. A half dozen others sat in various poses around him, all dressed in tan and beige linens. Two of them got up to tend a portable stove, from whence drifted an appealing melange of spices.

"Look who I found wandering the desert." Dio turned, his arm outstretched in a stage man's presentation. "The prodigal returns!"

A blonde woman sitting in front of the stove screamed so loud Jenna stopped short, expecting danger, but the woman scrambled to her feet and threw herself at Case, her thin arms flung around his neck. Case gasped, feet slipping a couple of inches before he regained his balance and patted her shoulders more like someone trying to steady a drunk friend than welcome them. Finally, the woman stepped back, and Jenna's breath caught.

No DNA test required here. The woman's eyes were a dead match for Case's: slate ringed in smoke, framed by thick lashes. Her blonde hair was the same wheat-and-gold, though hers fell down her back in waves. High cheekbones and a sharp chin framed full, red-stained lips. She could have been a picture from the golden Hollywood era. If not for the hippie outfit. A shapeless linen bag dress, which didn't quite hide the fact she had an hourglass figure, showcased her elegant shoulders and an ornate Celtic pendant at her cleavage. *So not exactly as modest as she wants to pretend*, Jenna thought with a smile. *But the mystery of Case's good looks is solved.*

"Hi, Mom." Case cleared his throat.

"Hi, Mom? That's all I get. After half a decade?" She stepped back, raising her hands like she was about to conduct an orchestra. "You're letting your hair grow out. That's good. I hated that the Army made you cut it."

"Marines."

"Such beautiful hair." She looked at Jenna as if noticing her for the first time. "He was born with a full head of it, you know. I think that's why I had the absolute worst heartburn when I was pregnant with him."

"Mom, don't." Case's cheeks were a shade or three darker than normal.

"That's why I chose his name. He so reminded me of the sun, all beautiful and golden." *Casey is a sun name?* Jenna opened her mouth, but Case's mom continued, "Speaking of names, I'm Selene. Lady Fae while we're here, of course. What's yours?"

"This is Jenna," Case answered for her, then grimaced. "Firefly. Sorry."

"Lovely to meet you, Lady Fae." Jenna grinned at him to watch him cringe. "Sorry, I have to ask you now. What is his pretty, golden name? I've only ever known him as Case."

"Case? Case!" She literally huffed, her bare foot tapping impatiently on the sand. "An object? You'd rather be an object than—"

"Mom. I'm begging you—"

"Apollo Hyperion Kelly. Don't you dare interrupt your mother!"

Case recoiled from the name like a slap. Jenna

clapped her hand over her mouth, a giggly gasp escaping. Until Case's suspicious gaze found her. She edged away, trying to appear sober and unmoved.

"It is a lovely name," she said more to Lady Fae than him.

"Isn't it?" Lady Fae sighed. "I blame those wretched children at that public school your father forced you to. They taunted him, you know, the little monsters." She shook her head and gestured to the soup with a fully be-ringed hand. "I'm sorry, where are my manners? Would you like something to eat, dears? You aren't allergic to anything are you?"

"No allergies, and honestly I'd love a snack. I was nervous about this morning's shoot and I didn't eat." Jenna avoided Case as she moved toward the food. Dio had beaten them both there and was already eating from a wooden bowl, placidly ignoring both the dramatic reunion and the ocarina musician. "I can't believe he didn't introduce himself properly. I spent the last three months thinking someone named him Casey! Apollo works so much better. No wonder he grew up tall and pretty and fond of projectile weapons..."

Lady Fae sniffed. "The weapons part didn't come from *us*. We raised him to be a pacifist. When he told me, he was joining the Army—"

"The Corps! I'm a Marine for fuck's sake." Case was right behind Jenna, his scowl so deep she wondered if his eyebrows were in danger of freezing in that position.

"He spent two years with his dad and decided to shave his head and strap on a gun!" Lady Fae continued.

"That's not what happened."

"Come along, Firefly." She took Jenna by the hand, leading her toward the circle of onlookers, who'd gone back to watching the ocarina player's recital. "Have a seat, please," she urged, nudging the musician over to give Jenna room next to her. She lowered herself onto an embroidered cushion as Lady Fae retrieved a pitcher from a thin wood shelf rigged to the side of the RV. There were four pitchers in total, all filled with different colored liquids. Whatever Case's mom thought she should have, it was going to be red.

"Apollo, sweetie, do you want a drink?"

Case sat on one of the empty cushions across the circle, his knees bent in front of him. After a long moment, he pushed his goggles up over his forehead. "Nah, I'm all right." He sounded somber. Tired even.

"Nonsense. I'll make you something."

"Then why did you even ask?"

"I don't know." Lady Fae shrugged, pouring him a cup of red liquid from the same pitcher. "Dio, if you could serve them some chili?"

"On it." Dio set aside his empty bowl and grabbed a couple of spares and the soup ladle.

"It's vegetarian," Lady explained, handing Jenna one cup and sending Case's around the circle. "And it's not too heavy. I know, everybody thinks, I can't eat chili out here in the heat. But beans are a great source of protein, and we all need the extra energy with this weather."

"Oh, I am all for energy." Jenna nodded. "I never think I'm hungry on the playa, like it's too hot for food. Then someone hands me food, and it's two plates and a nap later..." She sipped the drink and smiled, grateful to encounter only the familiar taste of cherry Kool-Aid. "But we are supposed to be back at camp to meet up for the rave on the pirate ship tonight. Can't risk Hype fainting on me. I'd never be able to carry him." She accepted a bowl from Dio.

"Oh, he knows better," Lady Fae said, gazing at

him fondly. "He fainted here once. Tried time and again to get him to sit in the shade and drink something, but he was always a free and restless spirit. And that was the summer he discovered he hated clothes, too…"

"Mom!" Case's—Apollo's—expression was so perfectly outraged, Jenna almost laughed again.

"He pitched over mid-run, at the center of camp. Dio had to keep him in the RV with ice packs for hours. He's been much more careful since."

"I'm not hungry," Case said, glaring at the bowl Dio was holding. "I already ate. A hot dog. With all sorts of processed meat."

Lady's nostrils flared at that. "You can hardly call poisoning your body with that garbage 'eating.'"

"Tasted like food."

"Hm. He still hates clothes too. I think he looks for reasons to strip off his shirts," Jenna put in to defuse the situation, taking a bite of the chili with a pointed glance at Case. "Oh! It's really good, ma'am. Who needs hot dogs?"

"Nobody *needs* a hot dog. Nobody needs brownies or vodka, either. Or extravagant parties in the middle of the fucking desert." Case cracked his knuckle and lifted his chin to see into Jenna's bowl. "We can go as soon as you're done. I just wanted to come by and say hello."

"That's why I had to drag you here?" Dio chuckled, earning Case's glare.

"Why do you always remember shit the way *you* want to?"

"So, I guess a 'hi, Mom' really is all I'm worth to you now." Lady Fae's voice wavered on the last word. Jenna considered her, then Case and Dio, her own parental arguments playing in her head. Maybe nobody got along with absentee parents.

"He's running on lack of sleep. And nutrition," she said softly to Fae. Which wasn't strictly true, but the playa was a place meant for peaceful resolutions.

"Thank you." She focused on Jenna with a gentle expression. "But getting fussy because he needs a nap and proper food is something a child would do."

"Well, when you're raised by children..." Case stood up. "There was a tent over there with some walking sticks. Meet you there." Pulling down his goggles, he stalked off.

"Some things don't change," Dio said, watching his back. "He'll come around, Selene. He needs more time."

"It's been five years."

"In the scheme of things, it isn't that long."

She nodded at Jenna. "I'm sorry you had to see that. Sometimes you have to suck the poison out to treat the wound. And ... there's a lot of poison there."

"You should see the screaming matches with my mom. Y'all are practically a spa trip." Jenna licked her lips and risked continuing, "He showed up. He talked. Not pleasantly, but that's a good sign when you're starting over."

Fae's smile widened at that. "I'd like to make up for this display, all the same. I'm not sure if Apollo told you, but I do palmistry, runes, and tarot. I'd love to give you a session before you go. Anything of your choosing."

"That sounds great." She finished the chili and set the bowl aside before offering her hand. "I wouldn't mind some kind of guide going forward. Might as well be my own hand?" She'd always liked psychics. Whether or not it was "real," they were people who saw things from different perspectives, and that could be helpful when you had a problem. And Bennett was certainly a problem. Not to mention Ash's husband, the club, Case, her own feelings, seeing Carz tonight… *So many problems, and only one festival to solve them all.*

"True enough." Lady Fae moved forward on her cushion to get closer to Jenna and crossed her long legs. Taking in a deep breath, she released it with a loud, "Ohm!" She repeated it twice more, then opened her eyes and took Jenna's hand. Fae studied the lines and ridges carefully, tracing the one that curved around her thumb while Jenna tried not to wonder what lotion Fae used to keep her skin so soft.

"A very determined spirit. Some people call you stubborn, but you trust your mind. Perhaps more than your heart. Yes. Your heart is very … guarded. Hurt? No. It goes beyond that. I see a great loss. It changed you. But you'll find your heart open again. Soon, in fact. You have two great loves in your life. One is, hmm, in the past? The next is ahead of you. I see … one child. A daughter. And a very long life. Is there anything specific you'd like to know?"

Christ, I hope the kid isn't any time soon. Jenna's nose wrinkled. "My best friend's psycho ex is out of jail. Any hints of gigantic drama coming up? I'd really like it if he vanished into the wind."

Lady Fae's lips pursed and she fell silent, tracing a new line a few times. "Hm. I suspect he will vanish. Eventually. You will be confronted with a difficult choice: between what is easy and familiar and what is harder. Choose the path least traveled, dear. That's the path that leads to happiness and health."

"Why can't happiness be on the easy road for once? Just to surprise us." A nervous laugh escaped and she glanced off in the direction Case had vanished. Funny that she didn't think he was gone. Mad as he was, he wouldn't run off. *Irritating ability, that.*

"Oh, most times happiness is easy, but you still have to choose it." Fae leaned away to stir the chili pot. "Before you go, can I ask you to do something for me? Can you keep an eye on that one? He's always been so independent, so set on his own path. I worry that he's fallen in with the wrong crowd. Again. But I have a good feeling about you. You have a good soul. Good energy."

"I'll try," she promised, feeling a stabbing sadness at Lady Fae's words. If his mom ever saw the hard-eyed killers and snakes her son called brothers, she'd wish for the Marines to take him back. "Thank you. I hope the rest of your Burn is bright as always."

She left Lady Fae and Dio with a last round of hugs and set off after Case, pausing around a tent corner to pull an edible out of her pack. She'd been doing so good—almost no pills or party favors since she'd gone to Ash's house, if you didn't count the Junction City thing. *But this is intense. A little.* She broke it into quarters, popped one into her mouth, and put the rest back.

Starting along a row of open-fronted tents, she scanned for canes. Then the next row, and another... *He really wouldn't go too far. Right?* She stopped, transfixed by a place with crystals on display. No money, but they might take a couple of the necklaces. Or some of the other high-end candies stashed in her bag. *What if I ask them how to find happiness and offer to hang out for a day?*

Maybe I should have put that thing in eighths.

"You *would* get distracted by shiny stuff." Case's hand touched her back as he spoke, and Jenna jumped, letting a quartz crystal swing on its silk rope as she turned.

Speaking of shiny. His goggles glittered, and his skin gleamed in sunlight. "Hey, how much do I have to pay you to keep all of this between me and you? I'm willing to take out a predatory loan if necessary."

"You are the predator. Big, bad soldier." She giggled and patted his arm. Then forgot to move her hand. "No worries, Apollo." *Why don't I hate touching him? Why is he so ... touchable?* "I can probably keep it a secret."

"Don't call me that," he pleaded, lifting his goggles and flashing some very sad puppy eyes. "Jenna, please. Only one of the guys knows my name, and I'd like to keep it that way. And don't tell Ashlyn."

"I'll keep the secret. Even if it is a pretty name, Apollo." She let go of his arm. He did that nervous thing he did with his thumb and index finger, rubbing them together in a nervous tic. *Why do I know that? Damn it. Stop knowing things about him!* Jenna tried not to look. Mostly because she couldn't trust herself not to put his thumb in her mouth. Among other things.

"What did she say after I left?"

"She's worried about you. She wishes she'd done stuff differently and hopes someday you won't totally hate her. And then she read my palm." She held up her hand, palm out, and laughed.

"She read your—" He didn't finish the sentence. Somehow her hand had come up and touched his face, and he froze the second she made contact. She hadn't fully intended to touch his stubbled jawline, but she hadn't *not* intended to either. Certainly, this wasn't the response she'd predicted. *It's almost like he doesn't mind me touching him.*

"I really do like your name."

At those words, Case sighed. The spell broke. He caught her fingers in a gentle grip, tugging her hand away from his cheek. "Try growing up with it. When I was home taught, it wasn't a big deal, but public school in Chicago? Didn't work so great." But he hadn't let go of her hand, and the buzz in her ears was nothing to do with THC.

"But it does suit you."

His thumb stroked the center of her palm, and he stepped even closer. "How does it suit me?"

"Tall, blond, built for dreams. Badass. Likes weapons. And sex. Ego for days…"

"How can I not have an ego when you use all those nice adjectives to describe me?" he asked, his lips curling into a smirk, the tension falling away from his shoulders.

"Why would you care what other people thought of your name? You seem so above all that."

"Because I hate the reminder of why she really picked it."

"I don't understand."

He bit his lip. Another tell. He did it when he wanted to think about his words before he said them. *When did I learn that? Shitshitshit! This is why I can't take anxiety meds around him. I need all the anxiety right now. All of it. Come back, anxiety!*

"Mom loved the novelty of having a baby, and when we were born, she slapped stupid names on us and patted herself on the back for being so edgy and clever. But being a mother got boring." He blinked and cleared his throat, edging back. "Sorry. That got a little Dr. Phil."

"No. I get it." Jenna slid her arm around his, pulling him out into the lane to head back to camp. Or somewhere. Anywhere but standing still, where her not-so-anxious brain could process the hormones and happy chemicals from being around him. "My mom handed me off to nannies because she didn't know what else to do. Yours couldn't afford the nanny. For what it's worth, the lady I saw back there loves you. She wants to see you even if it only ends in a fight."

"The lady you saw back there is a master manipulator. She thinks Dad ruined me. Turned me away from her. I'm the brat who won't listen. The kid who's rebelling. She loves the fight. Because it'll give her more material to play her part."

Jenna sighed. "Maybe you're right. But I'll probably be a disaster if I have a kid too, so I don't feel safe about judging her lack of skills." That won a chuckle.

"Oh, I'd be a terrible father too. Why I'm not planning on spawning anytime soon."

She wished his goggles were off. *Well, might as well risk a proper fight. I'll stop thinking about his lips if we're yelling at each other. Mostly.* "She told me flat out she absolutely deserved you being pissed off. There was nothing about you being bratty or rebellious. Just that she's afraid you're angry and alone and she didn't help." Jenna fixed him with her most serious expression. "You don't need her approval. You don't need to like her. But think about someday when you've fucked up royally and you're facing your kid. Because, honey, you have too many one-night stands not to end up an accidental absentee dad. I should know."

"Damn, Jenna. You really know how to put a mind at ease." Case ran a hand through his hair.

"Just pointing out a fact of life."

His head moved to the side. They continued on a few yards, then he spoke. "You're the one who made it a one-night stand, you know."

"I made it a—" Jenna's jaw dropped. "That was clearly the game you were on!"

He bent lower, his lips almost touching her ear to whisper, "And if you ever want a second night, let me know. I'd be happy to help you out. As a friend."

She made a face and pushed his shoulder, starting

off down the next row of tents. "As a friend? It would be me helping you out, Puppy."

"Maybe I need a lot of help." He laughed, following after her but wisely staying one step back. "I gotta tell you … there are worse places to walk than behind you."

Jenna spun around to glare at him. He'd taken the damn goggles off again, and she tried not to meet his gaze. "That is not how you compliment a girl's ass." She stepped up to his chest, putting one hand on his shoulder. "I was going to drag you to the orgy tent, but your manners would get you kicked out." Unfortunately, she could see his eyes darken.

"And that would be a shame, wouldn't it?"

"If you can't even say something that makes me want to kiss you instead of kick your ass? Yes."

His big, warm hand found her hip and slid along her waistband, pulling her closer, right up against him. She'd realized his linen pants weren't leaving much to the imagination, but this close, her imagination found quite a lot to fasten on to. His breath tickled against her ear. "I'm starting to think my game ain't been so clear, sweetheart. 'Cause I've been thinking about kissing you and a hell of a lot more."

"How much more?" Jenna's arm wrapped around his waist. They stood off to one side of the path, almost in someone's camp, and she suspected they'd appear in a few photos. It didn't matter. All she cared about was the intense way he looked at her. "Are we saying friends with benefits? Orgy buddies? What do you want, Apollo?" she whispered the name against his throat.

Case shivered and his fingers tightened on her hip. She might have worried, if not for his erection pressing against her stomach through his pants. He caught her chin and turned her lips to his. The kiss deepened, became demanding and desperate.

"Friends," he answered in a husky whisper. "With all the benefits. I want to learn every single way there is to make you come, Jenna."

"Talk like that will definitely help." Jenna returned his kiss and ran her hand over his chest, down to his waist as her back arched just enough to push against him. "So why don't we get back to camp and figure out a deal?"

She could barely think straight on the trip across the playa. She wanted to recapture her boundaries, but instead of reaching for that, her hands found his arms, his body, his skin on their own accord. The hesitation to lean against his side evaporated as they rode in one of the roving café-buses, then another people-mover. By the time they reached Silver Sea's gates, she didn't want to pull her hand from his. Then they were in her tent, and his shirt came off, and she could touch him all she wanted. Days of eying him, weeks of fantasies washed away every last bit of resolve.

Jenna kissed him hard as she dared. "So, about these benefits?"

"Open to negotiations." He reached for the bottom of her shirt, tracing the seam of the fabric before pushing it up to her breasts. He stopped there, cupping them with a reverent sigh. She felt the mattress on the back of her legs and sat. Case joined her, and they scrambled and slipped, body over body, reveling in the feel of one another's skin. Her legs opened for him, and he settled his hips between her thighs, grinding his length against her. "What do you want out of this?" he asked, a single finger teasing her nipple.

"You." The answer came before she could stop herself. She grabbed for his drawstring and pulled it loose. "I want you." She put an unsteady hand on his bare chest. "I don't want to be scared anymore."

His finger stopped, his gaze flashing up to hers and holding steady. The moment stretched out and she tensed, excuses lining up in her head. Until he lowered his lips to hers again. The kiss was softer, and his hands were gentle. Taking hold of her waist, he switched positions, rolling onto his back. "Show me how you want this, Jen."

She didn't hesitate, pushing his pants further so she could rub against his cock, pressing down, moaning when she found the right angle. "I want lots of ways. I want you to pull my skirt up in an alley. Bend me over a pool table. I want it so hard I can barely scream, and so slow I'm begging … or maybe you are…" She moved down, barely letting the tip of him inside. "Would you beg for me, Apollo?"

His fingers gripped harder, his breaths heavier. "Yes," he breathed. "Jenna, please." His voice was soft, but the need was clear. "I want you so much. I could have fucked you right there … in front of everyone. I needed to be inside you. Feel you coming on my cock."

She eased up then pressed down, taking him inside gradually. She was almost writhing by the time he reached her limit. Even then, she moved her hips in a slow, soft rhythm just to watch his face. It felt so good to hear his voice without the anger or hurt. To feel pleasure from him, and with him. Why had she been scared of it? "You feel so good, Case. Will you come for me? Put all that cum in my pussy?"

He didn't answer. Not with words anyway. He let out a moan of pleasure and relief, his knees bending behind her, resting his heels against the steel frame of the bed "Don't stop, baby," he begged, hips rising to meet hers with each thrust. There was a stutter to them. Like he wanted her to go faster, but he didn't ask.

She shuddered, her body tightening as her pace began undoing her control. "Mm, maybe I needed you too. I'm so close…"

"Fuck, Jenna!" He moaned again, his eyes clenching shut. "I—" He cried out, his cock swelling even more. She whimpered his name, moving faster until he drove up in a rough thrust and spilled deep inside her, his pulses hitting her g-spot until she almost screamed. The orgasm hit like a wave: a moment to breathe, then sweeping through, leaving her breathless and shuddering on Case's chest. Sticky, damp, and completely spent, it took a full minute to gather her thoughts. Or to have any.

"That… was fun." Jenna laughed and rolled off, sprawling alongside Case with one arm still draped over his heaving chest. "I vote we do it again sometime."

He turned to face her, his hand stroking her back, obviously not bothered that his arm was pinned beneath her. "Sooner rather than later."

"Maybe after the party? Or at the party? Right before it?" Jenna swept his hair back from his face and let her hand linger on his stubbly cheek. "Is there a daily limit on benefits?"

His free hand settled on top of hers, rough and calloused, but so sweetly careful. "Hell no."

"I don't want to wear you out."

"I can handle it."

"Four more days of festival might overwhelm your systems as it is. How will I explain if we have to drag you back to Illinois in a coma?" Jenna let herself explore his body again. Case was all muscles, with surprisingly few scars considering his lifestyle. Not quite as many tattoos as his brethren either. *If only we could stay in the festival circuit and never go back.*

His smile grew. "What if I swear to go really, really slow?" he asked, kissing her between each word before easing her to her back, his body covering hers. "Gods, you're so fucking beautiful."

Jenna's cheeks warmed. She heard plenty of comments from strangers on a daily—hourly—basis, but they saw the full makeup, filtered, one-shot-in-fifty *@jennastar* in a sea of hashtags. Her sexual partners generally said it before the fucking, not after. Not that she generally gave them much chance to say anything at all after. Post-coital discussions were not in the rule book. "You're pretty hot yourself," she whispered. "And good with your hands. I told you to stop taking chances with those."

"I always thought I missed my calling as a surgeon." He was slow, as he promised, trailing feather-light kisses along her jaw. His path down her throat proved thorough, finding every spot that made her squirm. She moaned, head falling back in surrender, and grabbed his hair in case he had any thoughts of stopping.

This was usually the time she shoved a guy off the bed. Maybe it was the festival, the idea of spending the next few days in this otherworld, playing in the orgy dome or the sexy parties. Firefly didn't have Jenna's biases. Or history. *That has to be it.* And later…? *Later is someone else's problem. Tomorrow-me can fuck right off.* Case found a pulse point with his lips and any forethought sailed out of the tent. "Bad boys aren't supposed to be this quick on the uptake."

She felt rather than saw his smile. "Maybe I'm not as bad as you think." *A joke. Or a lie.* Her back arched beneath him as his hand moved over her leg, her knee already bending before he got to it. Lifting her hips, her eyes closed when she felt his cock, hard again, pressing against her. She reached down to wrap her hand around him, stroking once, unaware of the sound of people in the adjacent tent. The next sound, though, was much harder to ignore.

"Firefly!" The masculine voice yelled loud enough to be heard for a mile. "Quit playing and get your ass out here!"

Jenna's hand froze around Case's cock.

He raised a brow, caught somewhere between amusement and annoyance. He didn't know the speaker. *Couldn't.* Jenna let go of him.

"Fuck my life," she muttered, dropping her head to the pillow.

"Babe?" Case stirred, rolling off of her as he obviously sensed a possible invasion of privacy.

You have no idea, she wanted to say. But instead, she shook her head. *There's no good way to explain, is there? Not yet. Later, maybe.*

"Shh! You're interrupting!" Ash giggled, far closer to the door. "Sorry, Jen! You—"

"I'm on my way! God, can't a girl breathe?!" Jenna dropped a quick kiss on Case's lips before jumping to her feet, already grabbing for the nearest emergency slip dress. She slung it on, added a robe, and grabbed a pack of baby wipes. She used one on her hands, checked her thighs, then threw the package at Case. "Sorry! Gotta do this." She didn't wait for his answer, just shoved her feet in the nearest pair of boots and ran. "You absolute asshole! You said tomorrow!" she yelled before she'd even gotten through the door.

In the yurt's common room, Ash knelt by the minifridge, loading drinks onto a tray. Bullet stood by the other bedroom door, his expression hostile. A third person sprawled on the white beanbag chair, grinning like the Cheshire Cat. Jenna grabbed a support post to keep her balance. *Has it been a whole year?*

Carlos wore a steampunk-apocalypse ensemble involving straps, denim, and gears, but nothing hid the broad shoulders or careful way he moved—panthers were probably jealous as he got to his feet, arms opening. "I said maybe tomorrow. *Mas o menos*. You know how it is." His accent turned the words to music. Or maybe she was that damn glad to hear his voice. Jenna's gaze swept over him one more time, looking for signs of injuries and seeing none. *Thank God.*

"Jackass!" She threw herself into his arms, inhaling the familiar mix of expensive tobacco, sunblock, and Tom Ford cologne.

"True." He laughed and hugged her hard enough she couldn't breathe. "Get over here, Pele." By the time Case sauntered in from the bedroom, they were all three tangled on the cushion pile, laughing hysterically. Jenna saw Carz glance up at Case, then deliberately focus back on her and Ash. "So, we heading to a party? Thierry said there's a badass pirate ship to run on tonight."

"Depends." Jenna sat up. "You staying the whole time?"

The teasing smile faded and Carz's chocolate-and-whiskey stare pinned her in place. "The whole time, *churri*."

Jenna's nose wrinkled at the endearment, but she hugged him anyway.

"We can talk later," he said under his breath. Something in the words pricked her nerves and she pushed away. Bullet and Case had regrouped by their door, watching Carz. Like they'd found a lone wolf in the sheep pen.

Oh, hell.

****

Case

It wasn't jealousy. Case didn't get jealous. Not when it came to women. It was the protectiveness. The fact that the girls were all nice and cozy with this... *What is this bastard?* He squinted. The stranger was built, with that asshole swagger plenty of chicks liked. But Ash and Jenna weren't the kind to fall giggling into a stranger's lap. *Unless they're trying to pick his pockets?* The thought didn't seem as unlikely as it should have, but still. *No. They know this asshole.* He'd never heard Jenna yell that many insults so calmly or greet anyone with that much enthusiasm. Except Ash. But as the guy turned, finally far enough from the girls for Case to get a full view of his face and the tats across his throat, white-hot anger spiked up Case's spine.

He still couldn't name what he was feeling. But anger was part of it now. So much anger. And this time, he knew why. He forced a smile and kept his voice even. Casual. "Hey. Since the girls ain't doing intros, guess I'm takin' over. That's Bullet. I'm Case. You?"

"Weird names for the Burn." The stranger's eyes glinted as he walked over. Giving them a damn good view of the ink on his face. He was about Case's size, with tawny skin, glossy dark hair, and a smile like a knife. He extended a tattooed hand. "Carz works. Don't think the girls ever call me much else."

Case hesitated but accepted.

"Jerk, sometimes," Ash chipped in. "And Jenna calls you a lot of names."

"Only when he deserves them." Jenna wouldn't look at him. "Besides, your Burn name never fit anyway."

"You could give me a new one."

"I've been trying to name these two for days! I can't name stuff."

Case shifted his stance, trying to look like he wasn't aiming for a fight. "Used to be called Hype. That one"—he nodded toward Bullet—"probably won't be back anyway. Another week of this, that shell-shocked look's gonna be permanent."

Bullet stepped forward to shake Carz's hand, and Case glanced at Ashlyn. Reclining on the cushions, her long gold hair in elaborate braids and ribbons, her dress a pool of hand-dyed silks and lace, like a flower child's desert fantasy. And what a fucking lie that was, if you knew a goddamn thing about the bloody-mouthed wolf tattooed on her friend's arm. Not to mention the ink on his face. *Just how much has she been hiding from Joker?* As if sensing his hostility, she rose and padded across the room to retrieve the drinks tray from the table. She ignored Case.

"It ain't that bad," Bullet said. "It's mostly the sand. It's fucking everywhere."

"You get used to it." Carz shrugged. "By the second or third time, you figure it into the experience." He accepted a cup from Ash and handed one to Jenna, settling back onto the cushions next to her. Jenna didn't move away. In fact, she seemed fucking comfortable pressed along the guy's side. Like she hadn't been writhing on Case's cock minutes before. "You guys hitting backstage at the big concerts?"

"I think we were only gonna do the party. Who's even playing today?" Ash frowned. "I've lost all track of time."

"Maceo Plex is all night, with some others."

Jenna shrugged. "Thierry knows their manager. If you want in, we can definitely drop by. I think I'd rather dance my face off at the rave." She dropped her head on his shoulder, and Case's stomach roiled. "You won't ditch us for the music monsters?"

"Never. I wasn't even sure I'd bother showing up 'til I got your messages."

"Liar." Ash toed his leg aside with her boot and

walked over to shove water at Case and Bullet. "You always show up."

Case took the bottle and glared. Ash continued ignoring him.

"So do you," Carz said. "But then, you weren't married before…"

"What's that got to do with anything?" She turned back to him. "A wedding ring doesn't mean you drop your friends and live in a hut on a mountain top."

"Just a hut in the Illinois wilderness," Jenna sniffed.

"Some good ol' boys don't let their wives go places with orgy domes and stoplight parties." Carz wasn't looking at Ash as he spoke, but at Case and Bullet.

"Some good ol' boys are idiots then," she answered.

Are they? Case bit his tongue to keep his doubts silent. Suddenly, he wished Joker had put his foot down, and kept his ol' lady the fuck in line. *She shouldn't be here, arms around strangers. Hugging other people. Cuddling up to them on the cushions. Head on goddamn strangers' shoulders. Fuck. I'm jealous. Gods damn it.* More than that. The anger bubbled up with it. He reached in his pocket and grabbed his phone, knuckles white against the black plastic. "By the way," he said out loud, "since this is an every year thing for you guys, any advice about where I can go to get a goddam signal?"

"Out here in the wilderness?" Bullet's voice was flat. Case sympathized. He stared at his screen, counting half a dozen unsent messages. There were about to be several more if he didn't get a signal.

"Of all the luxuries the millionaire assholes can't live without, you'd think Wi-Fi would be right at the top."

"There's some personal Wi-Fi, but the extra population crashed the network a couple days in and they didn't get the temporary cell towers yet." Ash's expression was worried and so empathetic his chest hurt again. *Is this how Joker feels when he gets pissed at her? Like he just kicked a puppy?* "They said next year they'll handle it, but…"

"You gotta go out the gates and get back to the real town," Carz said. "Or carry a sat phone like a real billionaire."

"You can use my Wi-Fi if you need to," Jenna volunteered. "It won't work for texts but—"

"Nah, communications can wait another day. I have to get all nice and pretty for this party." *And find one of the club contacts.*

"I tossed some stuff in your tent earlier." Ash laughed. "I won't be offended if you opt out but it's Da Vinci theme, and we were going through the costume trailer."

Case grimaced. Their camp—or more specifically, the leader and millionaire photographer Thierry—had its own wardrobe department, run cooperatively among the idiot rich kids. He and Bullet had a bet about how much of its contents would end up traded for drugs, lost, or stolen by the end of the festival. Not that it mattered, since none of the campers seemed to care.

"I, for one, encourage all three of you to be the sexy apocalypse pirate crew. We will be the captains." Jenna beamed at her own concept. Case ignored her in favor of his phone.

"Only if I can wear my wolf." Carz took a drink. "I didn't haul that outfit here for nothing."

"You always wear your wolf." Ash tapped his arm, where the wolf tattoo showed through the mesh shirt. It was nothing like the one decorating Case's arm. And tied with the red drops inked along Carz's hand, it sent a very specific message.

He sipped his water and stayed quiet, his expression neutral, his thoughts racing. Fortunately, Bullet either didn't recognize the tattoos or knew better than to make it obvious that he did. A bloody wolf tattoo meant only one thing: *Lobos Sangrientos*. And those red drops didn't happen for no idle rich-kid dealer.

"I'll wear whatever you want me to wear," Case announced, sitting back on one of the benches, propping his legs up. "Unless it's heels. Last time I tried, I made it ten minutes before I tossed them in the trash."

"I don't remember that." Bullet smirked.

"Before your time. Lost a bet. Frog don't play."

"So, he made you wear heels?"

"A fucking dress, too. Actually, they're pretty convenient," he said with a grin.

Bullet rolled his eyes but laughed.

"Stick around long enough, you'll get your chance. I'll bet Ashlyn won't mind lending you a dress. I had to borrow mine from Megan. Her hips don't lie. Her tits don't either. Had to fill the thing out with Kleenex."

Bullet paled noticeably as if afraid Ash might stick him in a dress then and there. Or that Case would. The thought held some appeal.

"Travis, don't worry." Ash nudged his elbow. "At least not 'til you're back at the clubhouse. Tonight, you're both wearing whatever you want. As long as you sit still for makeup. This is a definite guy-liner kind of night."

"I never pass up the opportunity to dress like a pirate." Case saluted them with his bottle. But it was Jenna who got up and came over. He watched with mounting suspicion as her hand touched his wrist.

"Want some help with the makeup?"

He opened his mouth to tell her to worry about her own face. "I'd appreciate your help." *I'm an idiot.*

"Let's get that started. Then you can dress while Ash and I figure out last-second details."

And just like that, he followed her back into the girls' room. *Like a goddamn puppy. Fuck me.* He mentally kicked himself as she dropped the flap behind them. This part of the tent was as they'd left it: messy, strewn with costume pieces, and the faintest lingering scent of sex.

"Have a seat. I'll grab my kit." She dug through a small pile of discarded clothes, dragged out a pink and black case, and dropped it beside him before kneeling to rifle through the contents. "I only bring necessities and everything's waterproof, so I might have to give you something to get it off in the morning unless you're into raccoon aesthetics. Here!" She pulled out a black kohl stick and smiled. "You ready for this?"

"So, how do you know Carz?" he asked, tilting his face up so she could start applying the liner. It was that or ask her to pull her dress off again.

"Met him at a party forever ago. Freshman year spring break maybe?" Jenna smiled, her expression dreamy and distant. "Don't worry, he's not angling after Ash. No need to get Joker worried about competition."

Wasn't worried about Ash.

He was worried about both of them. Did they know who Carz was? What he was? Ash and Jenna might not even know what the tattoos meant. That, like Case's Storm Crow, you had to earn the right to the ink. And more. That you had to kill.

"I couldn't call him anyway. Still no signal."

"Like you don't have your mysterious crow ways. Send a bird signal." Jenna finished his left eye and considered it, then dropped a quick, soft kiss on his cheek. "Fifty percent done." She started on the right.

He smiled, reaching for her knee, fighting the urge to slide his hand up her thigh. "It's so hard to think when you're this close, I—" His head jerked to the side as someone outside the yurt yelled. *Idiot.* The liner stick caught his eye, and he recoiled, hissing and blinking away the discomfort. "Shit! My fault. Sorry, babe." He lifted his hand to rub but caught himself before wiping out her progress, and Jenna yanked his hand away, getting up in his face with a frantic, worried scowl.

"Case! You can't move like that. Do you need an eye doctor? Crap, you'll have to go into town. An eye patch will keep it clear if something's wrong."

"Jenna…" He grasped her wrist gently and drew her in for a kiss. "I don't need a doctor every time I get hurt. It barely got me. I'll drop in some eye drops and be fine. Maybe not even that."

"Are you sure? It's red. You should check. I bet the medic tent—"

He put a hand over her mouth and chuckled.

"Baby, stop. You fuss worse than my stepmom." He waited for her to nod before he let her go.

"Sorry." Her dark-blue gaze lowered, and color showed on her cheeks. "I just worry. People get hurt, and if they're not paying attention…" She exhaled and shook her head. "My therapist says I have to think before I jump into action. But you have really pretty eyes. And I'd hate to be the reason you have to hide one."

"And hands?" He leaned in to kiss her, hoping the arousal would short circuit some of her tension. "Better get this done, Jen. If we take much longer, they might think I've stripped you down again." He took another kiss from her, running a hand over her hip, dragging up that stupid scrap of silk she thought was a dress. "If we take much longer, I might."

"They're getting ready too. You can be quick."

He laughed at that until she climbed into his lap and straddled him. He felt like a wolf himself as he dragged her mouth back to his. Her lips were so soft, so ready to let him in.

"Don't know if it'll be quick enough, gorgeous. But the hottest chicks are allowed to show up late, right?" He untied his pants and shoved her dress up. "Start the timer."

****

Case tended to be the guy who got wasted fast, lost his shirt halfway through the night, and ended up doing stupid shit—pranking Ice came to mind—or else between some chick's legs. He didn't remember much of the Corps parties, but his squads told enough stories. He hoped some of them were true. *But not tonight.* He recognized that as the Silver Seas crew pressed into the flow of people along the festival street, toward a shrieking, crashing battleground everyone else seemed to think was a party.

A pair of buses-turned-tanks lumbered past, spouting fire from stovepipes while their builders capered and howled at the distant stars. Case reached for Jenna, wanting to drag her back to the tent and already knowing that wasn't an option. They both had goals tonight. Instead, he kept her at his side as they aimed for the rave's turbulent crush of bodies with the rest of their crew.

The crowd swallowed them without warning. Neon flashed into endless skies, pounding drums and throbbing bass rocked the air and ground beneath. The rave coalesced and pulsed—a group of people becoming one amoeba of music and writhing limbs with a thousand heartbeats.

Unfortunately, the music sounded awful. Nobody else cared. The DJ stood, elevated on a metal stage, multi-colored lights streaming around him while strobes flashed to the beat. He gripped his headset with one hand, staring at his turntables, pretending to do something with his hands because he kept missing the drops. *Too high to work? Or here because his parents are rich enough nobody tells him off?* Case recognized him as one of the Silver Sea members and dimly remembered Ash saying a friend was opening the concert. *Fuck. She ought to tell him to practice next time.*

Bullet stayed close for the first hour, but once the girls dove into their fourth round of shots, he hovered closer to Ashlyn who mostly seemed unaware of him. Or of Case. Her attention fixed on Carz, Thierry, or other there-and-gone friends Case didn't bother to remember. So many people were hugging Jenna, draping beads or tokens on both the girls, hanging on them for pictures. A galaxy of humans. Who could blame Ash for forgetting their presence? He replayed summer memories: Ash dancing with Megan, chasing Ice across the clubhouse, pulling Joker aside for a kiss. *How did I miss it? How am I surprised about all of this?* She was more like Jenna than Megan after all: A Society girl. Did Joker see it, too? That she wasn't happy back home? That she was different? He kept his distance, making sure he could see the girls but no longer wanting to interfere.

Another hour dragged on until the DJ changed. The music improved. People bounced together, the smell of sweat mingling with weed and shitty beer. Bullet looked more out of place than ever, dancing with a pretty purple-haired girl who Ash threw his way, but with an expression Case had last seen on a kid going into a firefight. Case didn't get close enough for pity dances to be offered and kept his expression at a scowl. He didn't know any of these people, didn't like any of them, and if they thought he was an asshole, he didn't give a shit.

He'd about decided to abandon the girls to Bullet's care when Carz slithered through the crowd and looped an arm around Jenna. The music added to the shouted, overlapped conversations and made it impossible to hear what the Lobo whispered in her ear. Whatever it was, she threw her head back, laughter ringing loud enough that he could pick it out over everything else. She turned, her arms draping Carz's tattooed neck. His hand curved around her waist, red-inked blood drops impossible to miss. They danced, grinding and swaying as if they'd done it a thousand times. *Maybe they have.* Case sneered and chased down bile with another shot of beer.

The beat slowed and Carz moved on to Ashlyn. She went with it, not missing a single step, smiling as their gazes met. So fucking easily. He'd seen her dancing with Joker at the clubhouse— never once with all these showy twirls and whispers. The paper cup he'd been drinking from crunched in his hand. He'd seen plenty of his brothers' wives get friendly with men who weren't their husbands, but he usually filed that under none-of-my-damn-business and moved on. *But Ash? Fucking really?*

I'm gonna be sick. Or kill him.

"I gotta piss," he called to Bullet who leaned closer, tapping his ear in the universal sign for *huh?*

"I said, I have to piss!"

Bullet nodded finally and Case beelined straight past the line to the latrines or porta-johns or whatever the rich dicks wanted to call them. *Probably traveling thrones. Fuckers.* He stopped several yards off, enough distance from the crowd that he could hear himself think.

Get his head straight.

He wanted to call Joker. Tell him this whole goddamned thing was a mistake. His mind was in a million different places with too many fucking ghosts from his past, and now he had to babysit two chicks who may or may not know they were dancing with a hitman. He didn't know which possibility felt worse.

Deep breath. It ain't that bad. Just need to get hold of the local guys, get a signal…

"Smoke?"

He recognized the deep, velvet voice before he saw the speaker. Carz was all menace and charm, even as he held out a lit joint. *How the fuck did he get out here so fast?* And why? Suddenly feeling exactly how isolated they were, Case reassessed the Lobo. He was Case's size, built a little thinner. But that didn't mean they were evenly matched. *Better challenge this one to a knife fight when you've got two guns in your belt.*

Case accepted the joint. The hit felt good, but he didn't take a second. Handing it back, he hooked a thumb in his pocket. He watched the crowd down the path: revelers abandoning or just reaching the rave, oblivious to Case and Carz's position. They might as well have been on Mars.

"Tense, *cabrón*?"

"Long fucking week."

"On the road with those two?" Carz chuckled, lifting the joint to his lips. The lit cherry reflected in his eyes like hellfire. "I believe it." He offered it again.

"Done it before?" Case asked before taking another hit. *If we're gonna kill each other, might as well enjoy the quality weed on the way out.*

"More times than I can count."

"So you go back a ways?" He passed the joint off, watching Carz. The man stayed blank.

"You can say that." Such a careless shrug had to be practiced, but Case couldn't call him out on it. Yet. The man was harder to read than Joker or even Ice. Fuck, he gave off *Tree* vibes, and that didn't feel good at all. No way Case ever wanted to face the Storm Crows' national prez as an opponent, let alone Tree thirty years younger with a cartel at his back. *Shit. Time to try throwing a curve.*

"Way back enough to know what the fuck happened to them?"

Carz lifted the joint but didn't quite put it to his lips. His opaque gaze darted back to the nucleus of the party, and he took a deep breath through his nostrils. "Have to be more specific, *Hype*. Lot of shit's happened in the world."

"With Bennett."

Something hot flashed beneath that poker face like a warning. Case didn't flinch. Backing down to a cartel hit boy wasn't in a Crow's DNA. "This ain't about dick measuring. All I give a shit about is keeping my family safe. The asshole's out now."

"Family, huh?" Carz's eyebrow twitched.

Case tensed. *Gods, if we throw down, Ash will lose her shit, Jenna will kill me, and Bullet's gonna have to figure out how to get a body back to Oak Grove...*

Then Carz stepped back, took a final hit, and motioned for Case to follow. "Let's talk."

Carz led him through a few too many turns to a mirror-walled yurt guarded by a hulk of muscle and menace acting a shade too chill. Carz waved the thug to the side and opened the door with a key card, stepping back to let Case in first. He hesitated at showing his back to a wolf, but right now, Case was in *his* territory surrounded by *his* pack. *I need the answers before I talk to Joker. If I survive to relay the intel.*

He walked into the yurt. A few low-watt night lights kept the room from total darkness and illuminated the plush cushions and an orgy-ready seating area. *Even the cartel's camping in style.*

Carz swiped a bottle of McCallum off the bar on the far side and poured two cups. "Drink?"

It sounded like an offer, but Case knew better than to refuse the hospitality. He watched his host over the rim as he took the first burning sip.

"Sit down," Carz ordered as he lounged on one of the chairs. "*Familia.* Is that what they are to you?" he asked once Case settled at the very edge of a seat, his boots firmly on the ground in case the thug outside attacked.

"Yes."

"Both of them?"

He pictured Ash as he knew her, in the clubhouse with the others. She was Joker's wife, and Case realized he'd spent more time with her in the last year than he'd spent with his actual sister since high school. But Jenna? Jenna was… "Yes." The word came out with more conviction than he'd meant it to. Was it true?

"Easy to say, Hype. But it ain't all easy. Your boys don't like when people ruffle their feathers. They're, uh, particular about their territory."

"You moving into Illinois?"

Carz's smirk answered before he did. "Not talkin' 'bout where we're going. Where I've been."

"Oh." Didn't have to be a master of fucking riddles to figure out what he meant. He'd need to weigh whether or not to tell Joker that Ashlyn hooked up with a *narco* hitman at some point. Maybe next time death felt like a good option. Case's brain refused to bring up Jenna's name in the same category. "Don't know that I would call Ashlyn territory."

Carz shrugged. "Not how I see it, but none of my girls have ever worn a property patch." The way his jaw set made Case wonder if Carz expected him to challenge that. Maybe he should. Sighing, he took a small sip and then sniffed, hating how fucking good the drink tasted. *Why do I only find good booze in shitty situations?*

"See it however you want. This isn't about a pissing match over pussy. I need to know what we're up against. Bennett wasn't some average abusive piece of shit who went on a power trip and beat his girl, was he? There's all sorts of weird fucking vibes with this mess. It don't smell right. I ain't the smartest guy, but I do notice shit."

"You notice shit? Well then, tell me, *cabrón*. What you see?"

Case sipped the whiskey before he answered. Where to start? Looking at Carz's inked hand, he weighed his options and pushed away the memory of Ice's hand planted on a casket's shining lid. They'd failed Hailey. He needed to do better for Ashlyn. And Jenna. *You can't out-play a master. Keep this shit simple.* "Pretty girl drives into town and lands herself in the middle of a biker war. Bullets flying. Shit exploding. She didn't bat one damn eyelash." He cleared this throat and prayed the next part wasn't a mistake. "But Ash has these funny moments, says weird fucking things. Breadcrumbs that don't lead fucking anywhere because the next moment, everything's okay again. And when you try to get either of them to explain what the fuck just happened, they look you in the goddamn eye and tell you it's nothing." Case slumped back in the chair. "If they ain't scared of us, and they ain't scared of *you*"—he pointed at Carz's blood drop tattoos—"makes me wonder what the fuck *did* scare them."

Carz's brows had risen a fraction of an inch.

"You a fresh patchie?"

"Yeah."

"Figured. Your big brothers wouldn't be askin' me for help so upfront."

"They would if they were backed in a corner with no other sources." That won a faint twitch of a smile.

"It isn't all my story. Best I can give is some direction."

"I'll take anything."

"Ever been to a frat party, *cabrón*?"

"Never did the college thing."

Carz relaxed, crossing his legs, seeming almost conversational as he lit up another joint. "I ain't talkin' no bullshit public school party here. The real deal." He blew out a low whistle. "Old money. Old schools. Parents let money raise them. Never hear the word *no*. All the cash in the world, given everything. Can you imagine? What would still excite people like that?"

"You tell me." *I don't want to know.*

"When kids who ain't had a hard moment in their lives get a whiff of blood, that adrenaline rush hits like motherfucking cocaine. They want more. And they want to watch. They'll pay anything for another hit." He drained the cup and set it on the ground. His cold stare fixed on Case.

"You hear about things like that. We joked about it. One of the guys in my unit always said he'd find a rich guy to sponsor him when we got back. Keep on busting skulls and get paid to do it." Case sighed. "We never believed him."

"You should've. Saw a lot of vets in the rings."

"You saying the girls were at these ... parties? You were?"

"We needed the money." Another elegant, too-calm shrug.

Case's jaw flexed. "The girls *have* money."

"Their parents have money," Carz corrected. "But I wasn't talking about them." He shifted, reaching into a pocket.

Case tensed for an attack, but only a phone emerged. He watched Carz swiping the screen and kept silent. And still. "Here." Carz held out the phone. Case stared at him for a full second before he took it. And saw the screen.

The floor rocked. Case collapsed back into his seat. Jenna grinned up from the hitman's phone, her shining dark hair shorter and streaked with blue, her arms wrapped around a boy with Carz's eyes but darker skin and bigger shoulders, and a crooked nose. She was incandescent with laughter. Beautiful. Flawless. Happy. And the boy stared down at Jenna like nothing else mattered.

If she ever looked like that in my arms, I'd never fucking let go...

"*Mi hermano.*"

"Where's he? Why isn't he here?" But he already knew. Jenna's fear of fights. The boy's broken nose, and the marks on his knuckles, just visible where he held Jenna...

"Dead."

"How?" The question came out before he could stop himself. He winced and shook his head. "You, uh, don't have to... I'm sorry."

Carz chuckled. "Sorry? We're past that, I think, *Caja.* You didn't kill him." He rose, returned to the bar, and poured another shot. "He died, and it wasn't fuckin' right." He swallowed the shot and measured another. "Sometimes, the past is best left where it is. When you go digging, you may end up with secrets you didn't ask for. Lots of shit buried out in those bayous, you know?

Like those caves your crew has."

Bayous? What the fuck? He could ignore the caves. That was a distraction—and an easy guess when the club held so much territory along rivers known for cave systems.

"Never been good with a shovel," Case said. He finished his drink, trying to swallow his curiosity as much as the whiskey. But he failed. He pointed at Carz's right hand. "The girls know what that means, don't they?"

Carz's grin returned as his fingers moved over the wolf, then traced a blood drop. "*Mis hermanitas*? Let me put it, how would a lawyer say? They are not unaware."

He crumpled the cup and tossed it into the recycle bin by the door. *So Jenna can pal it up with a fuckin' Lobos hitman but an MC is trash? Must depend on the bank balance.*

"That a problem?" Carz was smiling again.

"I ain't one to judge. But Jenna is. Just wondered."

Carz looked surprised for the first time. "A wolf is still a wolf," he said with a gesture at Case's tattoo.

"Don't think she minds wolves so much. Just Crows." Case wiped his hands on his jeans. "I gotta get back. But thanks for talking to me. You didn't have to, and I'm grateful."

"I didn't do it for you. Tell your boss that if anything happens to Ash— "

"I ain't doing that." Case laughed, holding up a hand in surrender. "But I'm sure he'll understand you."

"And Jenna? Do I warn *you*?"

He shook his head. "She's too smart to stick around. But I hear you all the same."

He expected his nerves to calm down when he stepped out of the yurt, but they didn't get the message.

His stomach twisted, his lungs felt tight—like he'd climbed six flights of stairs while holding his breath. He recognized the feeling, but it didn't make any goddamn sense. Ash had panic attacks. Case didn't. Not since he first came back to Oak Grove.

And fuck. He could *not* have one in front of a fucking Lobo.

He knew his trigger: Anger. With Carlos for not stopping the girls from getting hurt? Bennett for hurting them? Joker for forcing him to come here? Jenna for accepting a fucking *Lobos Sangrientos* runner and not him?

His lungs burned now, and he took the hint. But knowing didn't make it better. Nor did the realization that Carz had whipped out that picture and successfully derailed Case from asking anything else about the parties. He had no idea why the girls were involved with underground bloodsports, only that Jenna had been fucking glowing next to a hitman's fighter brother.

And he needed to get back to the rave.

This should be fucking fun.

As he moved back to the party, his gaze darted endlessly without seeing, taking in too much movement and too many people, too many sounds and flashing lights. *Shit.* The air felt thick, heavy, barely breathable. People bumped against him, rubbed, laughed, and called to him, each one more annoying than before. *Jenna. Find Jenna...* He saw Bullet first. No longer dancing. His hand rested on some man's elbow.

Case's brain finally went still. He focused. The stranger was dancing, grabbing at Ash's hip, shrugging off Bullet's restraint. Case pushed through the crowd toward them, almost shaking with rage as Jenna slipped between the stranger and Ash. And the asshole ground himself against her ass like he'd tried to with Ash.

Motherfucker.

"You need to back the hell off," Bullet warned, intervening again as Jenna turned sharply away from the unwanted attention, only for him to grab her.

"Who the fuck are you?" The asshole's fingers tightened on her waist.

"You don't want to find out."

Ashlyn reached under Jenna's arm and pushed the asshole off. "We aren't interested." She held up her hand, flashing her emerald wedding ring. *She really thinks that matters here?*

"Don't see a ring on *her* finger. I—" His half-shouted reply broke off sharp as Case stepped up. "You her fucking husband? You wanna go?" The man puffed his chest, holding his hands out wide: a peacock trying to look bigger. Even his hair was fanned and gelled upright like he could disguise the fact he was a couple inches shorter than Case or make up for the bony bare chest beneath his open leather vest. Case's eye caught on the row of glinting silver rings along his ear. *I could rip them all out right now.*

"No," Case answered. "You should."

"Come on, Jen," Ashlyn said, pulling her away from the guy. "Let's find somewhere else to dance."

Jenna's wide stare lingered on Case. She shook her head. "Don't."

"Honey, you don't have to leave because of them." Peacock's hand landed on her arm.

Case's patience snapped. His right hand shot out, snagging the asshole's vest. The guy stumbled, dropping Jenna's arm to keep his feet under him. Case swung again. Peacock landed flat on his ass, wailing, blood gushing from both nostrils.

"Case!"

"You said you wouldn't—"

He ignored the girls' protests, kept his focus on the enemy. A couple of dancers helped Peacock to his feet, and he staggered away, whimpering. Case snarled and started pursuit until someone gripped his wrist. He blinked down at Ashlyn without seeing her.

"Case?"

He breathed and blinked hard. "I'm okay." His gaze landed on Jenna. She turned her head, half-hiding behind Bullet. Ash didn't share her shyness. The blonde's fingers caught his chin, dragging his face around. Her bright green eyes bored into his.

"Liar."

Fuck... Am I?

****

Case

September 1?

How can I be hungover without getting drunk first? He vaguely remembered knocking out some fuckface for getting handsy with the girls. *Then...? Oh. Right.* Jenna refused to acknowledge him. Ashlyn barely paid attention to anybody else. And Bullet kept asking him if he needed to lie down. Eventually, Ashlyn took the choice away, telling Case she needed to sleep and dragging him with her. When they got to camp, she handed him a bottle of water and tried to get him to talk about what happened.

"I don't know." Honest words when he said them. *Now?* He rubbed his face and wished they were true. He couldn't tell her the truth. If she found out about him digging into the past...

"Why are you awake?" Bullet asked, his voice raspy. He coughed, his hand going to his neck, his face contorting with discomfort. "Fuck. My throat hurts."

"Dry air," Case explained. "Get some water."

"That don't answer my question."

"Stupid question." He swung his legs over the bed and rubbed his face. "I feel like shit."

"You look like shit."

"Not looking so fresh yourself, asshole."

Bullet gave a strained laugh. "I'm going back to sleep, man. The girls want to drag us to some stupid photo thing today and I, uh, I ain't loving this."

"Better than being shot, right?"

"I don't know anymore," he said miserably as Case got to his feet, laughing.

"I'm gonna go take a leak. Maybe walk around a bit. I'll be back later. You good?"

"Yeah. See you later, man."

He slipped his feet into his boots and pulled on whatever shirt sat near the top of his bag. Checking that his cigarettes were still in his pocket, he stretched quickly and headed out. The sun was barely an hour or so over the horizon, though he no longer had any idea what time it was. The air still felt cool, and the sky beyond the dusty playa held tinges of pink and purple. He breathed in and tossed his shirt over his shoulder, walking toward the latrines.

He made a point of being slow to return. A few faces he recognized now. People the girls knew, introduced him to, but fuck if he remembered their names. The same guy from earlier asked him if he needed a ride anywhere, and when Case said no, he acted so disappointed. Case almost apologized. Instead, he pulled out a cigarette and offered him one which the dude took happily before driving off. Case found a halted café-bus a ways from camp and settled into their impromptu shade fly as a girl in tattered silk and leather began a harpsichord concert. A couple of hours of weird music and anonymous strangers might get his head on straight. Or at least calm down his urge to punch everything in sight.

"Well, if it ain't Case-fucking-Kelly."

Or, I could accept I'll never get away from my friends.

He turned, bracing himself for this fresh hell, but then relaxed when he recognized a massive form clad in black leather and denim. "Flex?" The man greeted him with a grin and a one-armed hug that came with a clap on the back. He wore his hair down, long and black, falling south of his shoulder blades. "Shit. Didn't think I'd see a friendly face here."

"Couple of the guys like to ride up here at least once," he explained. "Reno ain't that far."

"Oh, good. And here I worried somebody sent you."

Flex's smile faltered.

Case groaned. "Did … somebody send you?"

"I was heading up anyway, but I do got a message for you."

"Shit."

Flex laughed. "You don't even know what it is, yet."

"If Joker's got the VP of the fucking Reno chapter playing messenger, it ain't a good message."

"It ain't from Joker."

"Then…?" It took Case a moment, then he closed his eyes. "Tree?"

"Called last night. Been trying to contact you, but Viper told him service is shitty out here. If it exists at all. Made me drag my ass out of bed at the ass crack of morning to give you this." He pulled a folded-up paper from his jeans pocket and slapped it into Case's hand.

Case unfolded it and held it close, squinting. "Fuck, Flex. Could he have written any more like a five-year-old? What the fuck?" He tilted his head, but it didn't help.

"I'll sum it up. This guy … Fitwell? Shitgibbon? Don't fucking remember—"

"Fitzgerald?"

"That's it. Dumb fuck sent Tree some chicks. To keep. Pissed him right the fuck off."

Case frowned, trying to make those words line up. "What do you mean? Sent chicks? To keep?"

"Think I fucking get it?" He coughed, scratching the back of his neck. "Well, I do. Just wish I didn't. Trafficker motherfuckers got some weird-ass priorities. Must'a sent some threats too, but Viper was keepin' pretty vague."

"Wait. Let me see if I got this straight. Bennett sent the girls as what?" *Collateral? Payment? Unless he wants Ash.* The thought hit him in the gut. *That would explain Tree's sudden interest in Ash's whereabouts.*

"Who fuckin' knows? Traffickers are always batshit crazy. Ain't my place to handle 'em, thank Christ. You got your orders. Don't see how much else matters."

"That's 'cause you don't know the girl. She ain't gonna go easy."

His brow furrowed. "She that little blonde one I met when you patched in? Joker's girl?"

Case nodded.

"Throw her in your bag and toss her in the trunk. Can't imagine she'd put up much of a fight."

"Sound plan, man. Why don't you show me how it's done? Let you explain the methodology to Joker back home, too."

Flex chuckled. "That's a *you* problem, brother. I'll be around a couple hours if you need any help. And if shit goes bad and you're still on this side of the map, you know who to call."

"Keep your phone close, then. Shit always goes bad lately." *Assuming I can even get signal to call.* He waved Flex off on the next people-carrier, and trudged back to Silver Seas, already dreading the fight.

Chapter Ten
Jenna

September 2

Thierry wanted another shoot with the pirate ship, then an interaction with a giant wild boar made of knives and farm equipment. He'd somehow decided that the Da Vinci theme meant a *Game of Thrones* aesthetic—by way of *Mad Max* and *Star Wars*—and if he ordered her into one more layer of pleather in this boiling heat, he was going to find out the hard way if the boar's knife-edge hooves really were sharp. Jenna didn't need to fake the scowling pout on her face as she stared into the camera. Wearing a massive Elizabethan neck ruff, corset, and a half-skirt of fake thorns and roses, at least looking murderous would fit the character. It wasn't all Thierry's fault. Rage and terror had been swinging wildly within her brain since she'd logged into her MyFi over breakfast. Messages she'd prayed never to see appeared like ancient curses.

Ash lounged nearby under a pop-up shade fly, sipping lemonade in a gown of silk and painted leather, her hair bound up in an ornate flower crown with spikes radiating at the back, attended by a hovering stylist and—as always—Bullet, who'd been pressed into service as a beleaguered, rags-and-leather Hades-turned-Cowboy figure.

Ingrates. Traitors. Why the hell am I the one out here doing extra takes?

"Five more minutes and then I feed you to the fucking boar, Thierry," she hissed at the bobbing photographer.

"Yes! Like that. Love this energy. Tell me about the execution, Your Majesty." His cheerful British accent and wide smile sharpened her annoyance.

If you weren't a genius, I'd already be feeding you that goddamn camera. Instead of speaking, she forced a vicious smile.

By the time he finished, and Jenna got back to the shade, it was being pulled down. Ash handed her a drink. Then Carz materialized from one of the nearby tents. He wore old jeans and a faded blue tee under a long-sleeved linen shirt. If not for the throat tats, he might have been a telenovela star, though the white parasol in his hand somewhat undermined his badass vibe.

"Firefly, I need a moment." He snapped the parasol up and held it over her, smiling. "Come with me?"

She nodded, some of her tension evaporating. If not for the corset, she might have hugged him.

"If you're leading me to sunscreen and water, how can I refuse?"

While the others got things packed up and selfie-ed with passersby, Carz guided Jenna to the other side of the statue. *Of course, he knows the sculptors*, she thought with a sigh as they continued into the lane of tents. *Probably their dealer for the event, if not their friendly neighborhood supplier. Or banker. Or backer?* She'd never questioned Carlos about his side gigs and this probably wasn't the time to start. They stopped by a strange, quasi-medieval canvas pavilion. He lowered the parasol as they got under the shade fly and grabbed a bottle from the cooler right inside the door. She raised a brow as she accepted the water.

"A friend's. They're out doing chores."

"Friend-friend, or hot-girl-you're-banging friend?"

"Are those mutually exclusive categories?" His smile vanished. "About the Crows with you. The one you're fucking?"

"Case." She frowned. "You don't like him?"

"Hell no. And don't give me that look. I don't care what dick you wanna ride, *churri*. But he's pushing into shit that don't concern him."

Jenna winced, wanting to deny it. But Carz never lied. They'd at least kept that pact sacred among them: lie to everyone but one another.

"Did you tell Ash?"

"Of course, I told Ash. She said you'd better talk to me yourself." Carz crossed his arms. "This asshole wants to hear 'bout the past. How I know you. Like I'm some *cholo model* with ink he don't earn, or you don't know what this is." He held up his hand where the tattooed blood ran from the *Lobos Sangrientos* wolf inked on his arm. "I get why Ash is married to her gangster motherfucker. I ain't never forgiving myself, but I see how it went down. She is taking care of her life, and she ain't got much choice with that family of hers. But you? What the hell are you doing, *cariña*?"

She avoided his gaze. "It's just a festival thing."

"No asshole thug is pushing that hard about a playa fuck. If he ain't half in love with you, he's hunting a payday. I promise you that."

Her stomach dropped, and she ran nervous fingers across her compass tattoo. "You think Ash's husband…"

"Put a pitbull on the scent of his new wife's history?" Carz snorted. "You don't get where that fucker is by trusting all the things falling out of pretty little mouths. I'd do the same."

"Did you tell him?" Her voice sounded rough, and she drank the water again, hoping he'd chalk it up to dust and heat.

"I told him 'bout Auggie." When her panicked

stare swept up to his, he gripped her shoulder. "Not all, but enough. Ain't gotta be a genius-level to fill in the details of the shit Ben was playin' with from there. And I sure as fuck ain't telling no Storm Crow that I been inside his wife."

Jenna made a face. "Do you have to put it like that?"

"I'd say made love to, but that wouldn't save the beatdown," Carz scoffed. "And it's a goddamn lie.'

Jenna shuddered, hating the memories in her own head. They all did what they had to on those nights that money and fights and drugs didn't pay the pipers well enough. They'd survived. Until the night Auggie didn't, and Ben didn't give a shit. So, they'd schemed and planned until Carz got his revenge on the old regional head of Los Lobos, and Ash paid off Ben's partners to get them free. But Ben hadn't wanted freedom. And he'd taken that tantrum out in Ash's blood. And Jenna's.

The messages. Jenna put the water aside, pressing a hand to her corseted stomach. "Ben DM'ed me this morning."

Carz froze. "What's he playing?"

"The videos. He, uh…" She swallowed and forced the question out. "You don't think he's got everything, do you?"

"He might. Could'a saved some shit back. Maybe he meant to build a case on Perez in the beginning. Or he's always been a disgusting scumbag. Both." Carz caught her elbow, pulling her closer, his voice lowering further. "What does he want?"

"Money." Jenna met his eyes, not hiding her fear. "Ash and I can get it. It's a lot, but—"

"You get it. I'll get some guys on the drop. Where's he want it?"

"Kansas City."

Carz nodded. "Figures. I plugged every hole he could crawl down in St. Louis." He leaned in and kissed her forehead. Jenna held on to his arm, waiting for the world to stop moving beneath her feet. Like waves on a midnight lake. "You pay him, and I promise he don't live to enjoy it."

"Ash thinks her husband tried to hit him in prison. It didn't work, obviously. What if this doesn't? What if he's gonna send vids to the Storm Crows? Like you said, she's got her reasons for this marriage. If Joker kicks her out, she's back under her mom, and they'll lock her in that fucking hospital again. We—"

"No. She'll come with me."

Jenna couldn't help staring at him. "Carlos, you know you can't."

"I spend six fuckin' months sorting out shit down south and come back to a shitstorm. Maybe it's better I keep you where I can see you after this, yeah?" His stare burned into hers. "*Mis hueras locas, 'mana.* You fuckin' think I'm losing either of you to some cunt mama or Bennie?"

"No." Jenna blinked fast to keep tears from falling and picked up the water.

He tweaked her nose. "I'd hug you, but that neckpiece is fuckin' scary."

"It's ugly." She pulled at it, uselessly. "Can't you cut me out of it? Why the hell do I let Thierry talk me into this nonsense?"

"Because he's a goddamn genius. Those photos are fuckin' art." Carz's knife winked into his hand from God knew where. "Turn around. Let's set you free. Then we get to camp, see about making some arrangements for your money drop."

****

The ride to camp took a part of the weight from

her shoulders. They joined others from Silver Seas encampment and stayed on less worrying topics like the road trip home and whether some of them could meet up in Kansas City or maybe fly from Nevada to LA first. Jenna joined in the debates over post-parties and DJs with all the enthusiasm her need for escape could muster.

By the time they got to camp, she almost forgot the looming disaster. Ash met them at the gates of Silver Seas, all hugs and smiles until they closed the tent behind them. "The guys are getting food, so talk fast y'all. Joker managed to get word in. He thinks we need to cut the trip short."

Carz swore. "Does he know about the blackmail already?"

"No." Ash bit her lip. "I don't think so. This is more about Ben fucking around with the Albanians again. And if he's gonna up security, I don't know how we're gonna get the cash and get to the drop."

"He's not going to be monitoring my bank accounts at least. So if all else fails, I'll handle the money," Jenna put in. "But the other stuff…"

Carz ran a hand over his face. "I'll put out some feelers in KC, and I'll head out this afternoon. All else fails, I can get Flaco or Trey to run some distraction for you."

Ash grimaced at that but nodded. "I hate it, but oh well. Backup plans are better than nothing, right?" She hugged Carz, leaving a shimmery pink kiss on his cheek. And with that, their best ally was gone. Jenna and Ash stared at one another in worried silence.

"I guess we should get back out there and, uh, look normal?" Jenna asked, already tired. "Or take a nap."

"I need to talk to Thierry. You go out and derail

anything they try to start 'til I get back."

She must've had some Storm Crow psychic connection, because Case met Jenna at the main shade fly with storms behind his eyes. His morning must have sucked too. "We gotta go. Now," Case said, each word sharp as gunfire in the summer air. His razor-edged gaze settled on Bullet. Who actually winced.

"That bad?" Bullet asked.

"Worse." His focus swept past Jenna. To Ash, who was sweeping out from Thierry's tent. Jenna frowned at her own costume. *I know it's weird, but invisible?* "It ain't safe here, Ash. Understand that I wouldn't ask you to do this for nothing. I can explain on the way, but we gotta get out of here."

"Such drama." Ashlyn smoothed the fluttering silk skirts and dropped onto a beanbag chair, facing Case with the laconic air of an aristocrat. Maybe it was the crown and perfectly tailored gown, or the rage simmering behind her cat-green glare, but for once, she looked like a Tilden. "Explain it now, so I know whether I'm paying someone to pack up for us, or if we can have an organized retreat. I'm not fucking over the camp logistics because Joker's in a mood."

The topic at hand finally sank in, and Jenna's jaw sank along with it. "You can't be serious about bailing today."

"It ain't just Joker. It's your father-in-law pulling the strings now. Something happened. And Joker thinks it has to do with the missing girls in Kansas City." Case took a deep breath, his gaze locking with Ash's. "Fitzgerald might be involved. If I thought the two of us alone could keep you safe, sure. But I don't think so."

"Because Ben is a supervillain now." Ash's nose wrinkled. Jenna bit her cheek, keeping her own face blank. *We have our parts to play.*

"I vote you pay to have somebody pack up." Case nodded as if he and Bullet had another shared brainwave. *Maybe if we knock their heads together...*

"I'll have to talk to Thierry again. But I don't see the connection, Case. Bennett's involvement in whatever has all your feathers ruffled has no bearing on our safety here. What's he going to do? Blow up the festival? This isn't a *Lifetime* movie." Ash shrugged. "If Thierry can handle us leaving early, fine. Or if I can find someone to handle our gear. But I'm making no promises this second. Jenna? Are you even up for leaving? I probably should, to keep the shouting down at home. But nothing says you have to."

Is it safe to let Ash go with them alone?

"Let me know what Thierry says. I can stay back and help if the extra hands keep things easier on him." Jenna glanced toward Case then back. "Not to be a bitch, but girls go missing in KC every day. I'm not wasting panic energy about a fact of life."

Case's jaw jutted forward, and he strode over to Ash, kneeling in front of her. "He sent girls to Tree," he said softly, barely loud enough for Jenna to hear. "As a gift. And a threat. Ash, I ain't saying he's gonna blow this up. I'm saying he could send somebody. I think he already has. The two of us don't have enough eyes. If something happened to you here, we're screwed."

Ash's shoulders straightened, and Jenna turned away. The girls they had been *before* still lived somewhere. She recognized Ashlyn's. And when Ash leaned in close to Case, the half-whispered words came out ever so slightly harder on the edges. "Just because none of you understand what breed of monster he is doesn't mean I don't. I lived with him. I fucked him. I wore his ring. Ben and I had an understanding. One my husband broke without my permission. So don't test my patience about Storm Crow concerns right now, *Apollo*. I love you all dearly, but I will not break *my* friends' trust to make your lives easier." She swept to her feet and into the sunlight in a whisper of silks, her gold hair and crown shining, leaving Case on his knees, staring after her.

Bullet hesitated by the yurt door, blank stare bouncing between Ash and Case.

Jenna sighed and forcibly remembered Carz's suspicion: Case had been assigned to get with her, not choosing to. "We are definitely heading to KC if we leave. Sorry. I need a spa day." Her voice must've broken Bullet's spell because he nodded at her and rushed after Ashlyn. Case, on the other hand, rose and dusted off his jeans, his breaths slow and deep.

"I can see how hard this is for you," he said in that same deathly quiet way he'd used on Ash. "Whatever you want, *princess*."

"Thanks." She gave him a camera-ready smile and tossed her expertly curled hair over her shoulder. "Is this freak-out honestly because of some boogeyman or because you're sick of being here?"

"Why would I be sick of this? It's been nothing but a pleasure." His face flushed. "Maybe she's right. Maybe we read it wrong. But if you ain't worried, why should I be? You both know more than we do."

"Wow. The concept of your cult being wrong really gets to you, huh?"

"You know what, Jenna? Go fuck yourself. You don't get to talk about my brothers—my club—when you grew up with a fucking silver spoon in some country club."

Jenna tilted her chin up. *Like hell you're going to intimidate me.* "You're so fucking mad that Ash isn't crying and falling into your arms begging to be saved. That's what women are supposed to do, right? Cry and hide behind their big strong savior."

"If you think we're all about damsels in distress, you obviously don't know the girls back home. You think Megan cowers in a corner? Karli? Ash isn't some charge Joker paid me to watch over. She's a friend."

A friend whose best friend you fucked on orders. The thought twisted in her chest until she turned on him. "You're not her fucking friend, you're the cute puppy her husband sent along as a spy. I think your pretty little crow-girls would be dead in a ditch if they spent five minutes with Bennett Fitzgerald. I think you hate being here, and you hate Ash, and you've been praying for dirt that would get you home. That's what convinced you to fall into bed with me again, isn't it?"

"Jenna, what—"

"Did you really think Carlos wouldn't tell me you were sticking your nose in?" She advanced on him, but his expression didn't change.

"You know what? I'm sorry." He smirked when she stopped short at that. "I shouldn't have gone digging. It's all lies and secrets, and I'm done." He turned away.

"You're a spy and a liar, and all you care about is that stupid fucking vest." Jenna stormed to the cooler to fill her cup. A heavy dose of Everclear might actually make her chest stop hurting. He stopped halfway to the yurt. She waved a hand at him. "Go on. Pack up and leave. That's all you're ever going to do anyway."

"Coming from you, Jen?" He stalked back to her, so close she could have touched him. "All you care about is your fucking social media bullshit. It ain't real, sweetheart. Those people don't like you. They don't give a shit about you. Yeah, you're pretty to look at, and you take great pictures, but if something happened to you, you think they'd care? No. You don't like to think about anything close to that. Because shit gets too real, you run straight for the liquor or the Xanax. But you know what? I do care. If something happened to you, I would care. And I wish I didn't."

"Good acting, soldier," she snarled. "I almost believe it. Except for the part where you're only here on one more job for your dear leader. And now you get to drag Ash back to the cave like a good boy. Always doing what you're told."

"You're right. I didn't want to come. I didn't want to see my mother, didn't ever want to step foot on the playa again. I left that part of my life behind for a reason... And this is too close to going back."

She watched him, wary. *He's being too calm. Too quick.* She set her cup down and drew back a step.

"I'm gonna go tell Thierry I'm staying. There's not a fucking way in hell I'm riding to Illinois with you and Buck Rogers in there. I've had enough impromptu MMA shit."

He stood up straighter. "You can do what you want, princess. I'd never force you to ride with the commoners."

"Good of you to accept the social order." She hated herself for saying it, but the anger was talking. She blinked fast, blaming her burning eyes on the playa grit and rising breeze, so she yanked a scarf up over her mouth. "Go on and tell your boss his wife's gonna be wherever he wants. I think I'd rather go fuck myself than deal with this so-called protection anymore."

He moved so fast. One moment, there was nothing, then he was in front of her. She reared back, preparing herself for his anger. Not for the agonized gray gaze searching her face for ... what?

"Jenna." His voice broke, and he shook his head, his hands falling to his sides. "I ... I can't do this."

"You should have come to that conclusion a week

ago." Jenna stepped around him and continued down the line of yurts and pavilions. She didn't look back. What was the point?

****

Case

"You decent? Or are all the clothes in your bag already?" Ash called through the tent flap half a second before popping her head through it. She'd exchanged her princess outfit for a sundress and boots, though her hair was still in soft waves and ringlets, like a post-apocalyptic Barbie. Case only nodded, not moving from his seat on the bed. Packing hadn't taken more than a few minutes: he and Bullet had kept everything in their bags in case they needed a quick exit.

"T says it's okay to bail," Ash continued as he swiped a hand over his cheek and hoisted his duffle bag on his shoulder. "I told him Ben made parole, and it's kinda a situation. Anything we forget, he can get it to his storage facility, and the yurt company takes care of the tents and trailers."

"Ready whenever you and Bullet are." He hesitated. *Waiting won't take the suck out of it.* He cleared his throat. "Ash, I need you to do me a favor. Jenna's not coming, and—"

"I know. She announced that fact to Thierry."

"Maybe if you ask?"

Ash shrugged. "I can try, but I don't see it happening. Whatever you said got under her skin bad, babes. I don't think Satan himself would pull her out of the rave now." She pushed a lock of hair behind her ear. "This whole situation is complicated. There are a lot of feelings running amok."

He bowed his head, staring at his scuffed, fading leather boots. *Fuck, I'm gonna cry again.* He hated that he let himself do it already. He was *not* about to do it in front of Ashlyn. "Think Satan would try? I, uh, don't want to leave her here." He ran a nervous hand through his hair and dropped the bag. "I know it's not my job to. I need to let it go." Then again, to himself, "Let it fucking go, Case."

Ash settled onto the bed and touched his arm, nudging him to join her. "You're looking at it wrong. You're seeing the threat out there, and you think she's ignoring it. She's not. But the threat in here? And here?" She tapped her chest, then her head. "Those are so much worse, Case. If she stays, Thierry's here. And tons of our friends. She *feels* safe. And you're asking her to leave somewhere that feels safe for somewhere that every part of her head says is dangerous."

Dropping his bag, he sat next to Ashlyn, sagging back to lie across the mattress. "How did this happen? I thought she was a bitch. I mean, she is, when she wants to be," he added with a sad laugh. "I didn't want this, Ash. I never meant to—" *To what? Like her? You know what orders are. You ain't been following them for fucking weeks...*

"Sometimes it just happens. You can't control it."

Case rubbed his fingers together, shaking his head. "I get why she doesn't trust me. But why do you? Joker and I, we're from the same world. But you, uh, you still love him, right?"

"Of course."

"I-I don't get it. How? Why? Why does it work for you two but not... Fuck." He grabbed the pillow, dragging it over his own face. "Kill me, Ash. Seriously."

Ashlyn's laughter was gentle as she politely tugged the pillow off him. "Think back to when I met you. Joker was laid up, and I got to know him and all of you while you were helping a brother heal, not just fighting or scheming. And it still took Joker *months* to get through to me."

"Okay. You've got a point, but—"

"It isn't not-working for you two, genius. It's that if you want it to work, you're going to have to take it slow. And work at it. I love Joker with every single beat of my heart, but that doesn't mean we never fight. It means I'm going to go be pissed at him in person, and we'll talk it out once we're finished shouting out the big feelings."

"He knows he fucked up, Ashlyn," he said, turning to study her again. "That man loves you."

Ash rolled her eyes. "I think I'm less pissed off about him doing it than not talking to me before he ordered the hit. And it's not like he's the one who messed up what happened. But if he'd tried talking to me, I could have at least explained better, so he'd have had a fuller set of intel…" She trailed off. *She's so close,* he realized, with a guilty twinge in his heart. He let out a deep breath and covered her hand with his.

"We want to understand, but we didn't want to force you to talk about it. Joker wanted to protect you. Because you were hurt, and he was scared. You know him. He's ashamed, Ashlyn. He won't say that out loud, but I know him well enough to see it. I ain't saying he shouldn't have talked to you first. But I think I would have done the same. No, I *know* I would have. That's the caveman in us." He groaned. "Never tell Jenna I said that."

"Talking about it is hard," she said after a long second. "There are things… I can't talk around them and sound coherent. But when I try to remember them straight on, I can't. It's part of why Jenna testified, and I gave a written statement. That and I'm certified crazy, so how much of what I say is real?" She smiled sadly, and

Case's heart sank. *She's right.* He'd seen Ash when Joker brought her back, too shattered and doped up on meds to form a sentence. It was so easy to forget how far she was from being healed mentally, when all the casts and stitches were long gone.

"You ain't crazy, Ash. It's the world that's fucked up. You're doing better than most people would if you ask me." He squeezed her hand, and Ash stretched out beside him, staring at the yurt's rounded ceiling.

"You said Bennett sent Tree a present. Some girls?"

When Case nodded, she exhaled and fidgeted with the hem of her dress. "Want to explain what you're thinking about that?"

Case weighed the options. Joker wouldn't want him discussing club business. But he didn't lie to Ash, either. And this concerned her directly. *I can't bitch about her not telling us shit if I don't extend the olive branch.*

"Before we came, Joker sent a bunch of guys to KC. The crew there's having a problem. Girls going missing. Like an uptick. Not the—fuck it sounds so weird to say the *normal* amount—but it stunk like traffickers. They've been chasing leads for weeks. Then these two girls showed up at the KC clubhouse. Mentioned Fitzgerald by name. Said they were gifts."

She didn't react. Her slender fingers rolled the dress fabric, unrolled, repeated.

Time to roll the dice too. "We ain't sure if it's a peace offering, or he's pulling Tree's tail. Like you said earlier, you know Fitzgerald. How would you read it?"

Ash turned her head, her jade stare focusing on Case. Calm, steady. Clear. *None of her foggy flashback look. That's good.* "Have any girls been taken from club families?"

"If they have, the guys didn't mention it."

"You're worried this is about me."

"Shouldn't I? You know Joker's gotta be thinking it."

Ash let out a soft laugh. "Ben wouldn't trade anything for me."

"How can you be sure?"

"Why trade for what's already yours?" She smiled. "Don't get all Property Patch about it, Case. I could tattoo Joker's name on my ass, it doesn't change that Ben was my first, um, everything. If he was sending a message about me at all, it would be direct: Give me back my stuff." She made a face, but Case was the one with indigestion.

The less I know about Fitz-motherfucker-gerald, the happier I am...

"So my guess is that he's letting Tree think one thing when it means something else. Maybe playing for a sit-down? Or for time. Letting Tree worry about contacting me when he should be checking another lead."

"Tree's not a guy to be fucking around with." He rubbed his face with his free hand and sat back, catching her shoulder gently. "What would you do?"

Ash focused on the ceiling. "Keep looking. They must be close to something if he's throwing girls at them. Try the underground fight scene. He loves backing fighters."

"Probably can get Grim on that," he said, making a mental note to ask about it when he checked in with Joker at their overnight stop. "We should probably still leave, though. If Ben is watching, hurrying off will make him think we took the bait."

"Faking Ben out might convince Jenna to come with us." Ash snickered and sat up. "But you may have to ride on the roof."

"Hell, shove me in the trailer or strap me to the grill. I don't give a shit so long as she comes with us. You could let me ride ahead, you know."

"Maybe for the first day, but we need to make good time, and that's easier in one car. A solid night's sleep should calm Jen."

"I hope so," Case said, his shoulders slumping again. "I do care about her, Ashlyn. Whatever happens after this, I … I want her to be… I don't know. Happy? Safe?" He breathed hard and then got to his feet before grabbing her arms and dragging her upright. "Come on. Been up in my feelings too much today."

She linked her arm with his as they crossed the threshold. "Go get stuff loaded. Leave Jen to me."

Smiling, he gave her a one-armed hug and kissed the top of her head. The ugly knot in his stomach remained, but it felt lighter. "Thanks, Trouble. I'll get the car loaded. Or Bullet will. I'll supervise." Pivoting on his heel, he fixed her with a serious stare. "One last thing: Don't call me Apollo."

She smiled. "Better get Bullet sworn to secrecy fast. Before you make him do all the loading."

"I'll tell him it was the Burner name you gave me," he called back, letting the flap close behind him.

****

Jenna

Jenna slumped across a mound of pillows, luxuriating in the freedom of Carlos's blue silk pajama pants and cotton t-shirt. She'd fled to his camp after a tearful episode with Thierry, hid ruined makeup behind goggles and a mask, faked happiness for half a dozen photos on the walk over, and broke down sobbing when Carlos's assistant stopped her at the tent door.

"Flaco ain't used to pretty girls cryin' all over him," Carz said as he walked in. His whiskey-gold gaze swept over her attire and the abandoned gown. "How'd you get out of that?"

"Flaco didn't mention he helped unlace me?"

"He didn't. I need to break any of his fingers?"

"Nah. He was a gentleman."

"And then the lady ransacked my clothes."

"I only stole five hundred dollars and half your cocaine while I was at it."

"Lying *gringa*. You'd grab the vikes first." He pulled a Gatorade from his mini-fridge and threw it onto her stomach, laughing at her protesting grunt. "What's going on?"

"Case is making Ash leave today. Or I should stay the 'Storm Crows' are." She put air quotes around the gang's name. "Blah blah, Ben's doing weird shit."

"They know about the vids?" Carz sat down beside her.

"No." Jenna opened the Gatorade and tried not to show any of the bitterness eating its way through her heart. Judging by the twitch of Carlos's lips, she wasn't succeeding. "He said something about—"

"Boss," Flaco called from outside. "The blonde is here."

"*The* blonde?" Ash laughed. "I don't know if I'm offended or flattered. Both?"

"Come on in." Carz rolled to his feet and pulled the tent door open, scowling out into the lean-to where Flaco and someone else were playing cards. "These two got names. Learn them." He stood aside to let Ash in. Jenna sat up as she dropped onto the nearest pouf.

"Relaying that spat with Case?" Ash took Jenna's Gatorade and gulped some down before handing it back.

"And that you're leaving."

"*We're* leaving, you mean."

"Like hell I'm riding with that asshole."

"Enough." Carz tossed Ash her own Gatorade and grabbed a couple of pillows to lounge in front of them. "Jen, you two need to get to KC together. You land back there on your own, you're askin' for trouble, and I can't be seen landing with you. None of my guys can."

She felt herself pouting. "Maybe I'll find my own guys."

"Here?" Carz laughed.

"Ben found his." Ash's solemn voice stopped the teasing. "He sent two girls to the Crows. Gifts, according to Case. They think it's a peace offering. Maybe a shot at me."

Jenna's nose wrinkled. "Why would he bother with them?"

"They've been hunting for those missing girls in KC. I'm guessing they got close to whatever new shit he's running. More of the old crew must've survived than we hoped."

Jenna's heart sank, and she hid her head under a cushion.

Carz whistled. "Two girls. That's a message all right. Ain't for no Crows, is it?" He took a vape from a nearby table and flipped it on. "Bet they was even blonde and brunette. Tacky motherfucker." He inhaled, and a fruity cereal scent rolled over the tent.

"He's going to ruin our entire fucking lives," Jenna muttered, still under the cushion. It didn't block out the memory of Case's blazing glares and angry words. "What happens if Ben drops a few videos to your scary-ass father-in-law next?" She peeked out in time to see Ashlyn's face pale. *I'm going to hell.* She took the pillow off her head and faced her best friend. "Or the whole goddamn club? What happens when Joker's wife's a camwhore?"

"Jenna." Carlos's golden stare narrowed. "That ain't funny."

"I don't intend to be." Her arms crossed, Jenna continued, "You already said he got embarrassed on your account when that other club took you. And your mom. If this drops, it's gonna be you or his standing in that club, Ash. You know who wins that war."

Tears glimmered in Ash's eyes. "He'd leave the club for me. He'd be miserable."

Delusional. But I can work with it. "If he left the club. Sure."

"You're never going to be okay with telling him … anything, are you?" Ash wiped her cheeks.

"If he chooses you over that club, I'll tell him our entire life story in song. In iambic pentameter." Jenna avoided Carz's glare. "But face it, if we don't get Ben paid off, you're going to find out the hard way which of us is right."

"And either way, I fuck him over. Again." Ash's voice caught in a sob. Carlos dropped the vape and got up, hugging Ash to his side.

"*Dios.* If he's not got *cojones* enough to handle Bennie, you never shoulda fucked him in the first place." This comforting wisdom didn't stop Ashlyn sobbing into his shirt. He rubbed her back, eying Jenna. "And you! Get off the fucking high horse. Stop being a bitch because your fuckbuddy's club loyalty went deeper than your pussy."

"This isn't about him."

"You think I don't see you playin' games, *mana*?"

"Screw you, Carlos." *We're in the wrong parts.* She stared across the carpet at her two best friends, a chill radiating through her bones. *It's supposed to be*

Carz saying reckless shit, me calling him names, Ash making peace. Carlos held Ash, whispering in Spanish while she sobbed. Too late, Jenna wondered if she'd overstepped. Ash wasn't okay—for all the ways she seemed fine, she'd been shot and traumatized all over again barely three months before. With Ben back, dragging all this up, ruining a life Ash had just begun building…

"Not 'til you put the claws away," Carz said over Ashlyn's sniffles. His arm tightened around her. Like she needed protection. *From me?* Jenna's head bowed.

"I'm sorry."

A scoffing sound from Carz informed her that wasn't enough. She grimaced. "Ash, I mean it. I'm in a shitty mood. I, um, I'm sure there's a way to work things out. Even if everything fucks up."

It took a solid ten minutes to calm Ash down. Carz had to change his shirt and mix her a drink. Jenna didn't ask if he'd slipped something into it.

"So we get the money and a drop to Ben." Ash spoke into a tissue. "We leave today. What about you, C?"

"I fly out tomorrow." He rolled his right shoulder, flexed his fist, and grinned. "Take a red-eye, beat you girls back. See what my trusted associates have let fester under their noses. Get ready to throw Bennie a welcome-back party." Hunger lit his face: a vampire scenting fresh blood. Jenna went to the kitchenette and opened boxes at random until she found a candy bar to throw at him.

"Stop being creepy." She still didn't like remembering Case with a gun in his hand and blood all over the pavement. Thinking of Carlos knee-deep in Ben's blood didn't feel any better.

Carz tore open the candy, grinning. "Gettin' squeamish?" He broke off a piece for Ash and bit into the remainder. "You know how this has to end."

"Same way it always does: a gigantic mess. And me trying to mop it up." She sighed, and the others chuckled. "I'll go pack. Ash, stay here in the shade. I'll send Bullet over when stuff's ready. If I'm handling both our shit, I won't have time to strangle Case."

She glanced back once before the flap fell behind her. Ash lay across the pillows, Carlos kicked back against a pouf, a tablet playing some viral video between them. She waved to Flaco, Carlos's associate, who nodded without getting up from behind a battery-operated fan in the shade. She didn't let the tears stinging her eyes start falling until she was well beyond the camp.

The life she'd barely begun to picture, one with Case as more than a festival fling, deserved to be mourned. At least for a few minutes. So did the stupid fantasy Ash had built in Oak Grove with Nathan. No outlaw VP would put up with being married to a wife with sex tapes flying over the internet.

By the time I get to camp, I have to be better. Case is a foot soldier, that's all. He's doing his best. It's my own fault I got closer than I should have. And his boss is about to break my best friend's heart into a million tiny pieces. So suck it up, Jenna. You have days stuck in a car with this mess. It's penance for being a soppy, stupid brat who knew better.

In Silver Seas, she found Bullet loading luggage on a cart, no sign of her once-and-former friend-with-benefits. "I'll drag our stuff out for you," she told Bullet. He nodded, his lean body propped against the cart, sweat glimmering on his tanned forehead. A floaty linen tunic shielded him from the sun. Jenna let herself stare. She'd mostly ignored him as a harmless puppy, but watching him toss Ash's bag into the cart drew the memories of

Junction City back. He'd walked straight toward a gun. Jumped a guy bigger than himself. Suffered through Burning Man. Got between Case's fists and unfortunate idiots.

"Travis?" Jenna called his real name quietly. He turned, shading his hazel eyes as he crossed the white sand. She beckoned him into the air-conditioned yurt. "I know things are going to hell. Back east. Home."

"You don't need to worry about it." His answer came so quickly. "Whatever that Fitzgerald guy's done, or doing, you're going to be okay."

"But will Ash?" She watched his face. Open, honest. Not a soldier's, like Case. Not a born predator, like Carz. He was meant to be honest in a better life.

"Of course." His gaze didn't even waver.

"Because of the club." She waited for him to nod. "But what if the club stops caring? If something goes down between her and Nathan?"

"Never gonna happen. She's his ol' lady."

I'm going to hell. I'm going to so many hells. They're going to have to invent a new one. Jenna let her sorrow show. "But how's that gonna last? She got the club embarrassed once already. Now her ex is causing problems. I'm not a biker chick, but I can do math. That's a lot of strikes."

"She got kidnapped. Nobody's blaming her. And this Fitzgerald thing's just shitty luck. Midwest ain't that big sometimes."

"And when Case reports to Joker about Carlos? That one of Ash's friends is a *Lobo*?" She put her hand on Bullet's arm. "When he tells them that Ash used to live with Carlos? What happens then?" The half-lie almost choked her, making her eyes water.

Bullet stiffened like she'd hit him. "He's an ex?"

Jenna shrugged the question off. Ash stayed with

Carz after the trial, when Ben was gone and she was spiraling, dropped from school, popping pills, and partying through their friends list. Whether it ever was a relationship, Jenna couldn't explain. The ties among them—born in hell, as deep as blood and broken hearts—had never fit in her vocabulary.

"I need to know what happens. How bad this will get." *Now that I made it worse.*

He stared into the distance, calculating. Finally, he shook his head. "Don't worry about it. I'll try to keep Case off that target 'til we're back. It'll come out sooner or later, but maybe in-person's better." He studied her, a new tension in his posture. "Joker's never gonna hurt Ash, no matter what. Is that what's scaring you?"

"No." She moved away, reaching for the nearest bag. Time to pack things up in more ways than one. "I don't think he's going to punch her or anything. But there are plenty of ways to hurt someone who loves you without using your fists." She shoved a few shoes into the tote, then upended a table full of hair tools on top. "And when he dumps her, she loses all those Crow friends she's been relying on. Not to mention you."

He stopped in the doorway, his expression stricken. "That's not true."

"Isn't it? You're really gonna care about her if her Crow hubby kicks her out?"

He ran a hand through his shaggy brown hair and adjusted the headband he'd used to keep it off his face. "Ash jumped that asshole Scratch. She knew she couldn't take him, she was just tryin' to keep him from killin' me. He shot her for it. And she's why the Crow medics scraped me off the ground. So don't think I care more about a patch than her."

Everybody loves Ash. Jenna sat down hard on the bed, staring at Bullet. It wasn't the disappointment of a miscalculation pricking her heart. Jealousy. She recognized it. Apparently, so did Bullet.

"You were hopin' I'd run and make sure Case knew about her and that Reyes prick, huh?" He crossed his arms with the same hard expression he wore in fights. "That's your game. You're scared and alone, so you want your friend back. But you're so fuckin' scared, you're clawing at people tryin' to help you. You're gonna fuck over your friend's relationship while you're at it?"

"Boyfriends come and go."

"Because you make sure they do." Bullet's expression softened, and he picked up a lone boot and tossed it into the open bag. "I have been in those shoes before. My feet are bigger, but..." He sat down on the bed next to her. "I bounced through so many foster homes, I can't even remember the faces anymore. They weren't all bad. Some of them were damn good people. But I didn't want their help anymore. I couldn't even remember what havin' parents felt like."

"I'm not a foster kid."

"I seen that house. You sit there and tell me you don't answer more to that maid than you do your mama. And when you needed help loadin' a car, it's the gardener, not your dad tellin' you to drive careful. It's that Reyes prick who checks up on you here, not no white-bread brother. And you're here for your sister. You found a family along the way. Same as me. And you're scared as hell of losing it. I'm sitting here tellin' you, it ain't a loss to let more people in. That's the math Ash done figured out. Been waiting on you to see it."

"And what if she miscalculated?" Jenna sniffled again, wiping her face and staring at the mascara smudges on her hand. "We thought Ben was one of us. Once. And it c-cost us ... everything. We're still fucking paying." *A hundred thousand. And probably a marriage.*

Jenna hoped he'd accept some diamond jewelry as part of it. Easier than cash and less traceable.

Bullet touched her shoulder, interrupting her thoughts. That annoying, soulful gaze met hers.

"So stop payments on the stuff you can control. He fucked you over. People can be assholes like that. But not everyone. You know that already, or you wouldn't hold on to Ash and Reyes. Try giving somebody else a chance, Jenna."

"Nobody asked you to make sense," she said with a groan, flopping back onto the bed. "I'll … think about it."

"Well, think while you pack. Case is about as pleasant as a bear with a sore paw right now, and he wants to be the hell out of here in a couple hours." Bullet stood up and tossed an empty suitcase onto the spot he'd vacated. "Or make up with him. That might—"

"Case Kelly can fuck himself."

"Okay. Then pack." Another suitcase hit the first. Bullet retreated as she growled and kicked both off the bed.

"This is why the Victorians invented valets," Jenna muttered, pushing herself upright and huffing a sigh. *Focus on this. Maybe it'll be Zen…?* She kicked the suitcase again to spoil her own false hopes.

Chapter Eleven
Case

September 4

Good of you to accept the social order.

He dreamed of the fight for the second night running. Both Jenna and Ashlyn loomed over him, reclining on golden thrones. Scepters in hand, they waved long, judging fingers, faces contorted in fury. Then the desert, sand lashing his body, the heat bearing down so hard he felt like his skin was melting. Then Joker walked in, holding Ashlyn in his arms, crumpled and small, blood everywhere. But when he approached the scene, his own face stared back at him, streaked in grime and tears. He held Jenna, her body limp, eyes open but filmy white. Empty.

Case's brain slammed into consciousness. Panting, his body covered in sweat. He bolted upright, trying to orient himself among strange furniture, beige walls... *Hotel.* He took a breath. *Not a tent. Not Joker's. I'm at the hotel. Wyoming. Cheyenne. That's right.* The last two days slotted back into place. Leaving Burning Man, they'd headed east and north, aiming for Iowa where the Crows were gathering at a rally. Good cover for sorting out how to handle Kansas City. He kept his thoughts on the logistics as he kicked off the covers and checked the window, where the first hints of sunrise cast a faint bluish hue through a gap in the curtains. Too damn early. Case groaned as he grabbed his phone from the bedside table. *No messages. Hallelujah.*

"Who needs sleep," he muttered, pushing himself up slowly.

Light snores came from the other bed. Bullet was still knocked the fuck out. At least they wouldn't be squabbling for the toilet. Standing on unsteady legs, he crossed the room, squinting when he flicked the bathroom light on. Getting his teeth brushed and splashing cold water on his face helped dispel the rest of the ugly dreams. Somewhat. When he stepped out, Bullet was propped up on pillows, swiping through his phone. Catching up on all his booty calls no doubt. Case waved for his attention.

"Yo, bathroom's open. I'm gonna go wake the girls up."

"You sure *you* should be doing it?"

"What's that, Prospect? You want to lick the clubhouse dishes clean for the next month?"

"Just saying, Case." He put his hands up. "It's early to start a fight."

She'd have to talk to me to fight. Case shrugged. "She's ignoring both of us. Doubt she answers the door either way." He wouldn't have believed it before the last twenty-four hours, but Jenna could in fact maintain a lethal silence. A full day's driving lay behind them, in which she responded only to the most necessary questions from them and spoke only to Ash otherwise. Thankfully, the torture would only last another two days.

Case dragged on jeans and a black undershirt before heading into the hallway. Making sure the room key was in his pocket, he padded toward the girls' room, skirting a cleaning woman and her overflowing cart. And stopped, checking the door numbers. *Did I pass the room?* He turned, scanned the numbers again. *Wait.* The housekeeper's cart was outside the girls' room. *Probably called for more towels.*

Stepping back behind the cart, he saw an empty bed. Empty closet. "Fucking incompetent Prospect..." He stomped back, jammed the key card in, and threw the door open. Bullet peered around the bathroom door, half-dressed, hair dripping.

"What the hell, man?"

"You told me the wrong fucking room number last night. Where are the girls?"

"No, I didn't." He yanked his gray t-shirt on and zipped his fly. "They're in 117. I checked on them last night. They'd just ordered a pizza."

"Nobody's in room 117. Except a fucking cleaning lady."

"What?" Bullet's eyes widened. "I'll go check."

Case crossed back to his bed to grab the boots he'd kicked off last night. He put on his cut instead of an overshirt to cut down on the layers. Wyoming's summer heat wasn't any less annoying than Nevada's, and he wouldn't be showing the colors on the road. And it would piss off Jenna. He swept the room one last time, pocketing his phone, wallet, and stuffing a stray sock into his bag before Bullet burst through the door. "They ain't here," he said, his face as white as the sheets. "I asked at the front desk. They checked out hours ago."

"What?" The words rolled around his head, refusing to compute. "What did you say?"

"They checked out," Bullet repeated. "The car's gone. But they left the fucking trailer. I've been calling Ash, but it goes straight to voicemail. Same for Jenna."

He didn't realize he was holding his breath until his lungs began burning. His gaze darted around the room as if something in there might give him a clue as to why this happened. *No. They wouldn't...*

"They ran?"

"Must have." Bullet's pale face took on a grayish tinge.

"Joker's gonna fucking kill us. You know that, right? Fuck. *Fuck!*" He spun, his foot lashing out at the drawers with a satisfying thunk, hard enough that the television on top wobbled and fell back against the wall. "Think they went back?"

Bullet's shaggy head shook side to side. Exactly like the lost puppy Jenna said he was. "Ash wouldn't..." *Let Joker kill us?* The kid had the brains not to end the sentence. "What's she always say? Look at it from the outside?"

"Is that what she always says?" Case asked, slumping onto the bed. "Guess you would know." The kid did spend more time with Ash than anyone but Joker. Case bit his cheek on a wave of insults. *No time for yelling. He's got a better shot of guessing what the fuck's happened.* "What are you thinking?"

Bullet put his hand on his left shoulder, where he'd taken a round from the Heathen President. "It's fucking weird that they'd leave the trailer if they were flat-out ditching us. Why not take it off somewhere safer to leave it? Not like they ain't got cash for a storage spot. We know Jenna wants to get the hell home. Maybe they forgot something?"

"Why wouldn't Ash tell you? Why would they fucking abandon us in the middle of fucking Wyoming?" He knew why Jenna would leave. Why would she stay? She owed them nothing. Felt nothing for them. It was a miracle she came this far with him—them—as it was. "Something don't smell right. But guess you'd know that better than me, too."

Bullet turned, expression hard and jaw set. "Fuck your attitude right now, Case. I've been busting my ass for you since I patched over, but I know I ain't never getting your vote. I get it."

"What the fuck are you talking about?" Case demanded, rising to his feet. "I ain't never asked you to bust your ass for me. And you don't know shit."

"I know this isn't about the goddamn club or your

need to be Joker's favorite attack dog. Ash and Jenna are out there. So if you'd rather compare dicks than focus, say the word. I'll head out there on my own."

Case's hand curled into a fist. He swept up his bag and swung it onto his shoulder so he couldn't punch anyone. "Lead the way, Fido. Gotta get your fucking bike out of the trailer." He held the door open, ignoring the heat in his cheeks. To be told off by a Prospect? *One who has a fucking point.* "I hate you," he muttered.

Bullet scowled and grabbed his bag. "Feeling's mutual," he snarled under his breath in the hall, barely loud enough for Case to hear.

Outside, he stalked toward the trailer while Case fell behind, waiting for the satisfying moment Bullet would remember who had the keys. Bullet had his phone out, still uselessly calling.

A few yards from the trailer, the kid broke into a run. "Case! Keys!" He hopped onto the back end, beating on the door. "Hey! Ash? Jenna? Answer!" Case closed the distance in seconds, hope and dread returning in a sickening wave. Inside, a tiny, mechanical tune sounded. *A cell phone? That why the girls aren't answering?*

His boots skidded on the asphalt as he hit the trailer at a dead run. He grabbed the lock, shoved in the key, and yanked it off. Bullet was already on his knees, dragging up the rolling door, the edge of it slipping along his fingers. Darkness and heat greeted them, but no movement.

"Ash? Jen?" Case called again.

Bullet fumbled with his phone. The ringing started. Case followed the noise. A bag tucked to the side, halfway zipped. *Jenna's.* He'd carried it for her.

"Move." He batted Bullet's arm away to drag it closer. A shiny, pink-encased tablet glowed up at him. "Please don't have a password." He hit the button on the side, and the home screen appeared. "Thank the fucking gods," he breathed. He scanned the information, seeing the missed calls. *And messages?* He tapped the icon. *Maybe she'd been texting somebody, telling them the plans?* "Get your bike and load our shit."

Bullet didn't wait. He moved away, grabbing his bike and wheeling it backward, flipping down the loading ramp and getting it in place before attending to Case's. "Can you use that to text Ash? She hasn't answered anything I sent."

Case bit back a snide answer. *Still not the time to hash that shit.* "Gimme a second." The top conversation, under Bullet, was a group chat: Ash, Jenna, and someone called DNC. He tapped it and read the last balloons. Read again. His stomach roiled.

"Oh, fuck." They didn't ditch to hit some Burner afterparty. This was so much worse. "Call Joker. Now."

"Case? He's probably on the—"

"Now, Prospect!" He met Bullet's blank-eyed stare. "Fitzgerald's got that *Lobos* fucker. Carlos Reyes. He's offering a ransom."

"Shit." Bullet dragged his phone out of his pocket while Case stared at the tablet. A few messages down was another threat. With a video.

DNC: **fuck around and everyone knows the truth**

Two hundred grand for their silence and Carz's life. Case hesitated, his finger ghosting over the video. Something in his gut told him not to hit *play*. He didn't want to see whatever it was. *We have to know.*

He hit *play*.

It started with the camera pointing right at a bed. Nobody was in the shot. Not at first. But he heard people talking in the background. Then somebody walked into frame. Stumbled, really. Turned their arm, revealing a compass tattoo. *Jenna.* She faced the camera. Her expression was glazed over, her focus drifting like she was lost. She wore only a bra and panties, and she sat on the bed, very still. Until somebody else walked into view.

Case gasped, his fingers tightening around the tablet. With each second, his eyes grew wider, and finally, he swiped the screen and slammed it back into the bag. He got a breath in, then a second, and ran for the curb in time to spew last night's burger into the hedges.

Bullet's hand appeared on his shoulder. "You okay?"

Case flinched. "Fucking no." He wiped his face and spat.

Bullet handed him a water. "What happened?"

Case tried to answer, but nothing came out. He didn't know the words. Or couldn't say them. Bullet stared at him and turned back toward the trailer. He got a couple of steps before Case stumbled up and grabbed his arm.

"Don't. Don't fucking touch that tablet. You got me? I'll break your fucking hands." There'd been other videos. Texts from before they'd left the festival. *He's been threatening them for a week, and they didn't breathe a single goddamn word.*

"I don't have to. I heard enough." Bullet's voice sounded strained. Case stared at him. "In the group home, I knew kids that had some things happen. Makes more sense now, how she and Jenna get, you know? They were like that. I wondered before, but..." He stuck a hand in his pocket and pulled out some gum. "Here. Get the nausea out before you get on a bike. I think you better be the one to call Joker."

He took the gum but spit into the grass a couple more times before he unwrapped the foil and stuck it in his mouth. "Thanks. And ... sorry."

"No problem." Bullet disappeared back into the trailer.

Case dug his phone out of his pocket with a shaky hand. The line was ringing before he could change his mind, and Joker answered on the first round.

"Wondered when you'd be calling," Joker said, his deep voice calm and steady. "You normally sleep this late?"

Case bit his lip, trying to say the words in his head. There was no way to get this right.

"Case? You there?"

"Y-yeah. I'm here. The girls—"

"I know. Ashlyn called."

"She did?"

"Yeah. Around four in the morning. She left a message."

"Joker, I—"

"Case. Listen. Right now, I don't give a shit about blame and fault. I sent you and Bullet 'cause I trusted you both."

Here it comes. He failed and now Joker would never trust them again.

"I still do. They're heading to Kansas City."

"How do you—"

"Really? Are you gonna ask me that?"

"Joker. It's Fitzgerald. That's where they're going. Kansas City. To him. He's got Carz, er, Carlos Reyes from the *Lobos Sangrientos*. And he's got blackmail on—"

"The fuck did you just say?"

"He wants two hundred thous—"

"No. About Reyes."

"Fitzgerald's got him. Holding him hostage unless the girls pay up."

"You got proof of that?"

"A proof-of-life picture. With videos. They're on Jenna's tablet."

"Send them to me," Joker said. "Send everything."

"No. Joker, the videos are… Listen, you don't need to—"

"I'm not asking." His voice was that of a commander. "The fucking Lobos think *we* took their guy. Whatever that asshole sent, I need it."

"Boss, it's not that simple. Some of the vids he sent ain't about that. I don't think you want them copied."

"Explain."

"Fitzgerald's blackmailing the girls. Two hundred k, plus Reyes now. He sent some screen caps and a couple videos that are … shit." He got a deep breath and forced himself to give a recap of what he'd seen. What he guessed the other files were.

Joker was silent, then exhaled. "Send it all to me. I'll figure it out."

"You don't want to see this shit, brother."

"World's full of shit I never wanted to see. Case, I need you to get your head on straight. I can't be there to call the shots. You ain't a Prospect anymore. Get your shit together, get on your bike, and figure out your next step."

Case nodded, forgetting Joker couldn't see.

After a beat, Joker spoke. "Can you do this, brother?"

"Yes, VP. I got it." His voice sounded more confident than he felt.

"Good. I'll call when they turn off I-80 or if anything changes."

He hung up, and Case shoved the phone back into his pocket. "You got everything you needed from the room?" he asked Bullet.

"Yep." Bullet straightened up from tying off the remaining strap on his saddlebag and pointed at the trailer. "That can't stay another night if we ain't here. And no telling what other devices or shit's in there."

"I know. Go check out. There's a chapter in Cheyenne. I'll call 'em to come get it." He'd have to text Joker to get the number to call, but that was still an easy fix. Even so, fuck the trailer. Everything in it could be replaced. Except one. He shook himself and grabbed the tablet out of Jenna's bag. "I'll lock it up. Hurry," he ordered, lifting the ramp so he could close the doors.

Joker replied, and Case made the call. The locals were sending a couple of their guys for the trailer. That done, he settled on his Electra, staring at the tablet. If he could see her history, then she'd see what he was doing, too...

He had no choice. Another nail in the coffin... *I'm sorry, gorgeous.*

He hit send, forwarding videos to Joker, then buried the tablet in his saddlebag. Bullet was already on his way out, and Case held his helmet, staring at his warped reflection. "She'll never forgive me."

"Bullshit." Bullet swung a leg over his own bike and strapped on his helmet. "Easiest way to get forgiven is to earn it. And considering the shit that girl's in, there's gotta be a few hundred possibilities."

"They're racing off to prevent that video from getting out, and I just let it out," he said, fumbling with the strap before getting his helmet straight.

"You ain't posting it on fuckin' Pornhub. And if it was about the videos, why wasn't she paying him off weeks ago?"

Case took a breath. *Maybe she was?* But that didn't feel right. The girls took off only after Bennett grabbed Carz. And Ash had said something, that last day at the Burn… Bennett letting people think a move was about one thing, when it was something else? "Just straight down I-80. If you need to stop, let me know. But let's try to limit stops to gas."

"I'm on full. Let's go." He revved his engine and grinned. "No fuckin' SUV is gonna stand a chance."

Case couldn't help but smile. He revved his engine in answer. "By the way," he shouted over the rumbling. "You've got my vote."

Before Bullet could respond, Case pulled in front to begin the first long stretch.

****

Jenna

She came awake to the peaceful hum of wind and growling engines. "How the hell did I fall asleep?" *It's only our entire lives on fire, and Carz may be dying. Totally sleep-able…* She blinked at the sun. The very-much-above-the-horizon sun.

"Ash?" She sat up. Her best friend cast a vague smile her way from the driver's seat. "What time is it?"

"Almost eight, I think?"

"What?" She grabbed her phone. "Why aren't we in Denver?" It was barely even two hours from Cheyenne. "We should be on a freaking plane by now! Fuck. We should be standing in KCI bitching about the driveshare lane!"

"I thought about it. But you were sleeping, and we both know you needed the rest. Anyway, we only have like four more hours. Five, max."

"Time we could have used to find Carz? Get cash?" Jenna sat all the way up, turning in the seat, ready to reach across and slap Ashlyn. "What if Ben moves up the timeline?"

"Chill. Ben won't move it up that much. I had this idea. And it wouldn't work the same if I had to fly."

Jenna sank down, trying to disappear into the leather seat. "I'm not going to like this."

"Probably." Ash's nose wrinkled. "Okay. So, let's say, theoretically, I had a gun that has no serial number and is probably untraceable. And like, let's say I got close to Ben and, you know, shot him? Then he's dead, or incapacitated. Either way. Then he can't let the vids loose, and you stay safe somewhere way far away from this whole meltdown."

"That's not a plan, that's a vague theoretical retelling of a *Lifetime* movie and I hate it. Hate. Full on, non-stop loathing. We are not doing that."

Ash glanced over. "I'm meeting Ben at the Caves. Alone. I mean, aside from Carz and Ivan probably. You fucking know that asshole's back to licking Ben's boots, 'cause who the fuck else could swipe Carz? But like, you know… shoot Ben. Ivan runs. Maybe shoot Ivan too."

"You cannot be serious. You've never shot anyone. You'll freak out. You'll freeze. Miss a shot. And Ben will straight up murder you." She scowled. "You think Carz might have a bomb somewhere that you can take with you, don't you?"

"Maybe?"

"In a mine?"

"Okay. So I'll take a knife as backup instead."

"What if they search you when you get there?"

Ash sniffed. "I'll ask Ben to do it and shoot him when he's trying to grab my boobs."

"You need someone for distraction." *Shit, when did I agree to this?* "I'll go. While he's busy trying to fuck with me, you shoot him." Jenna made a face, feeling her stomach trying to rebel against everything she'd eaten in the last six weeks. *Okay, think. Crazy girl has a gun. Who the fuck is getting between her and certain death?* "You have to pull over, I really need to pee."

"Fine. You're lucky we're almost in civilization. There's a town in a few miles."

Forty-five minutes later, Jenna fell against the door of a tiny, dingy restroom in Nowhere, Nebraska, and punched a contact she'd damn near deleted twenty-four hours before. No answer. But his voicemail came up. "Case? It's Jenna. I... I need help. Ash has a gun, and she's delusional about killing B, and I don't know what to do. We're meeting him in the Caves in Kansas City, at six. His parents store a boat in them. I can't remember the address. Call me? Please, I'm so sorry. I love—" the tone cut her off, and she sobbed until someone knocked on the door.

Jenna struggled to her feet and stumbled out of the restroom, much to the concern of an older woman waiting in the hall. Her knees buckled, and she struggled to swallow past the lump in her throat, half expecting to fall over with every step until she reached her Mercedes and opened the passenger door. The smell of gummy worms welcomed her back. Ash glanced at her, then held the bag out across the console. Taking a couple, she settled into the passenger seat and tied one in a knot instead of meeting her best friend's gaze.

Do I tell her? Not like she's told me everything lately. But...

"I called Case," she blurted before changing her mind.

Ash's brow quirked before she shifted the car into reverse. "What did you say?"

"As much as I could squeeze into a hysterical voicemail. Times. Places."

Ash sighed. "You realize you just invited a few

dozen armed mercenaries in leather, right?"

Jenna tied the next worm into a knot, then bit off its head. "We needed backup?" She took a drink of water. "I don't even know how we're going to get the extra money with only a couple hours' notice now he wants more for Carz. No bank's gonna fast track that shit. We honestly should have flown in!"

"Don't worry about the cash. That's covered."

"Covered how?" Jenna's head turned. "If you think I'm breaking into my stepdad's safe today, I hate to point out that I haven't been home. I don't know this week's code."

Ash laughed. "I meant I know where one of Carz's hidey-holes is. He's got plenty of cash there. I didn't want to use it, but I think he'll get over the inconvenience this time. Especially since we may have to slip in early to avoid Joker having the access roads blocked."

"And you know how to get into a safehouse?"

"Where do you think I crash when I'm in KC and you're not around?"

Jenna groaned and rubbed her forehead. "So he hasn't removed the cash lately or anything?"

"No. It's a permanent safehouse. I'm the only one who uses it." Ash's brow wrinkled. "Well. I think so. I haven't exactly asked. But I'm the only one how knows where the cash is."

"Okay. Assuming there's no crazed Lobo hiding there, we get the cash, then what?" Jenna trailed off. "Any weapons?" Outside, the endless flat horizon stretched into a cheerful blue void. *It could at least be pouring rain. But then we'd be going slower. Or crash on our way. There's an idea.*

"I'm not sure about weapons. I've got the one gun, but you're right. I don't think that's going to be enough." Ash's voice was flat as the landscape. Jenna turned from the window and her attention caught on the shiny gummy worm bag. She picked one up and bit its head off.

"I've got one idea. If we do it, we're going straight to hell."

"Does hell include living with Bennett?"

"Definitely not."

"Is it going to kill innocent bystanders?"

"No."

"Then what level of hell are we talking?" Ash glanced over. Jenna waved a gummy tail.

"Remember why we started getting these as snacks?"

"Not really."

"We used to get trail mixes. With peanuts." Jenna bit her lip, her stomach roiling as Ash's eyes met hers for a split second.

She sighed and said, "He usually has an epi-pen. Ivan might even have an extra."

"It's worth a shot? No pun intended."

Ashlyn laughed. "Guess it's better than nothing. And we've got a few miles to the city. Almost there. I picked up a couple burner phones. They're in that bag by your feet. Pick one and sign into your accounts, then turn yours off. I'm not sure how much tracking anyone's doing, but—"

"Shit. I didn't even think about that." Jenna pulled out a plastic package. "Do you think something like that's how Ben got Carz?"

"I have no idea how he got Carz, but I don't want to take any chances. No matter how paranoid."

Ash's nose wrinkled. "As best as I can figure, one of Carz's guys at the festival at least had to be a plant. No telling what he got access to."

Jenna tapped the new phone against her leg, calculating. *What would Jason Bourne do?* "We better ditch the car too. I think I know where to go."

****

Case

Another stop. Less than they normally took, but still more than he wanted. Couldn't change that the bikes ate gas, though. He motioned for Bullet to exit, following him down the ramp and turning into a Shell station. It was small, but there were a few cars on the lot. He pulled into the pump next to Bullet, killing the engine and taking the helmet off. They both checked their phones before reaching for the gas.

He had a few texts and a couple of missed calls. He swiped to see if they were important, expecting another voicemail from his mom. He'd deleted the last two without listening.

Jenna. He read her name twice before it seemed real. He almost fell scrambling off the bike and put his hand against the pump for support. The first message was the Cheyenne road captain, saying they had the trailer. He skipped to the next, heart in his throat as he cradled the phone to his ear, willing the background noise away.

Each word got harder to listen to. He could hear her tears coming, the fear and pain. She didn't even need to be in front of him, to finish the last sentence. *I got you, Jenna.*

"Bullet." He waved him over. "Call Joker. Tell him that the girls are meeting Bennett at the KC caves at six, and that Ash has a gun. I'm trying to call Jenna back."

He got the gas running while her phone rang. It went to voicemail. So he hung up and tried again. "Pick up," he begged. "Jenna, come on…"

No luck. *Fuck.* She had her own personalized voicemail. The message sounded so different. Cheery, singsong. A far cry from what he'd just heard. The tone pinged and the words tumbled out. "Jenna, I'm coming. We're not that far behind. Delay the meeting somehow. I don't know. But I'm coming as fast as I can. I promise. I—" *Beep.* End of message. *Fuck you too, phone.*

What if they were too late? What if Ash's plan got them both killed? Even if, in the end, Jenna walked away, out of his life, he needed to know she was going to be okay.

"Did you get him?" Case asked Bullet. "What did he say?"

"Psychic creepy shit like he already knew most of it. What fucking caves are they talking about? When did Kansas City turn into the Ozarks?" Bullet scowled and tucked his phone into an inner pocket.

"There's a whole bunch of 'em around there. Government uses some to keep shit in. I think there's one full of coffins or something."

"Huh. Fucking weird. We're supposed to haul ass, and he'll send us an address when we're at the turnpike. Sounds like we're about to meet the Kansas and Missouri crews. Whatever shit hit the fan this week, they're fixing to make a show of it."

He was replacing the pump when it hit him. "Wait... He knew? When the fuck was he going to tell us?"

Bullet's brows rose. "Was he supposed to?"

Case turned on the Prospect, ready for a fight. "Any time Ash breathes wrong, we owe him a message, but Jenna's heading into a fucking trap, and he doesn't have the goddamn time to call me—" He stopped himself, staring into Bullet's smirking face. "Fuck me. I'm turning into Joker."

Worse. I love Jenna.

"Nah, you ain't even close, bro. You ain't tracking her yet, for one."

"Nah, just reading her messages." He rubbed his temple and checked the pump again. "You knew, didn't you? That it was... Shit, Travis, why didn't you tell me to, I don't know. Stop?"

"Stop what? Falling for her?"

"Yeah. That."

Bullet's head fell back in a full-belly laugh. "You think telling you not to would'a done shit? Like you wasn't head over heels the first time she slapped you down."

Case's face turned red. "Fuck you. This shit's gonna be you someday. Now I gotta vote you in just to see it." Which only made Bullet laugh harder. "You done yet?"

Bullet's grin didn't dim. "No risk of me falling, boss, but I'll take the hit for the patch."

"I used to say that, too." *Now I got a solid three-hour ride to figure out how to keep Jenna from dying, killing me, or walking out. Should be simple, right?*

****

Jenna

Kansas City, KS

Their first move was checking in at the Argosy Casino hotel, maxing their ATM withdrawal limits on every single card, ditching the Mercedes, and swapping into a rental. Ben's people might know Jenna's car, but something picked randomly from the nearest rental service would be harder. *Especially this*, Jenna reflected bitterly as she slid behind the wheel of a silver Prius.

Ash navigated Jenna east along the Missouri River, then north into quiet, familiar territory.

"Briarcliff!" Jenna yelped as she turned off the interstate, along a patched and pitted access road she remembered from high school parties. "Carz has a hidey-hole in fucking Briarcliff?"

"Old Briarcliff," Ash snickered. "Who'd look here?"

"Can't argue that." The Prius trundled along the half-forgotten street, winding steeply upward between tall trees. Jenna shuddered on a hairpin turn with a near-blind intersection. "I'm glad we aren't doing this in winter."

"Small blessings." Ash pointed ahead. "Second road. Turn right." They pulled up in front of a gray house with pale stone trim. Not a sprawling mansion like those across the highway, it was spacious and pretty like those around it: a neighborhood that didn't shout its wealth but coughed discreetly and whispered as it slid an AmEx Black card across a polished marble countertop. Nothing about its neat lawn or paved walk proclaimed it hid a cartel fortune or illegal guns. "Does the neighborhood watch think it's an AirBnB?"

"Rental, probably." Ash hopped out, her attention more on her phone than the house. The front door had a keypad rather than a lock. Ash typed in the code, still staring at her phone while Jenna lugged the bag holding Ash's illicit gun over the threshold. Inside was all hardwood floors, oversize furniture, and slightly retro light fixtures.

"Tell me you didn't help decorate."

"Don't be silly. Carz hasn't had time for anything *that* involved. But if you volunteered, he might take you up on it?"

"Maybe I will. If we don't die today." Jenna dropped onto a wingback chair and pointed at Ash's phone. "Are you gonna tell me what's so interesting?"

"A million texts from Joker and Bullet. Some voicemail. I'm going to turn it back off and use the burner I grabbed in Nebraska, but…" She made a face. "What do I say? Don't show up with a full army?"

"That's a start. He won't listen, but you could at least put in the request."

"Ugh." The phone fell onto an ottoman. Ash pulled the burner from one of Jenna's bags. "So do I take this to mean you're trusting the Crows to show up?"

"I trust Joker isn't taking his wife going off the grid well. And when they track the SUV to a hotel room we aren't in, it's going to make him even happier."

"I'm not ducking *them*."

"And he's going to care about that minor detail?"

"Probably not." Ash settled onto the sofa. "I can't think of how to convince Ben to meet anywhere else, either."

"He won't move it unless it's his idea, so we might as well accept the caves." Jenna slumped sideways and put a hand over her face. "We're betting a lot on you getting close to Ben."

"We're both about to be coated in peanut dust and lotion. No way he won't get close to one of us. I mean, it may be as he's stabbing us. But…" Ash trailed off in a shrug.

"Leaving Ivan or whoever else he's got. I hope it's less than three goons."

"He'll have to come in in a pretty small vehicle. A van at most. That means unless he ships in dudes ahead, we can't be facing more than that."

"Any idea where Carz keeps the hand grenades? That might help." Jenna huffed and watched through one eye as Ash rose and walked over to the fireplace. She picked up a poker. "Ash?"

The poker crashed into the wall a couple of feet

left of the fireplace. "Shit!" Jenna yelped, scrambling upright. "What the hell?"

"You were expecting a safe?" Ash swung again. The drywall cracked, and a piece fell to the floor. Ash punched the wall with the metal a few more times, enlarging the hole. She reached in and dragged out a stack of bills, grinning. "It was this or the floorboards. This one's easier."

"Sure. Whatever you say. You keep doing, uh, that. I'm going to hunt for any stray guns." Jenna dragged herself from the chair and headed down the hallway, glancing over her shoulder.

"Carz usually sleeps in the blue room!" Ash called before another crash drowned out Jenna's answer.

Hopefully, he hasn't hidden it too well. Jenna stopped at the first bedroom, which was indeed a slightly garish shade just off the Royals blue. *Big four-poster bed, old-fashioned dresser. This place came furnished with somebody's grandma's stuff. I bet my trust fund. So, where to hide weaponry in a nice old lady's space?*

Groaning, she knelt and reached under the bed, tracing the frame, hoping for a handgun, not a rifle, and finding neither. She got up and flipped the duvet back down. "Next stop, the closet," she announced to no one. She kept moving. If she stopped, the scream building in her chest would come out. And the tears. She pictured Auggie standing in the doorway, smiling. He'd know where to find things. *The dresser drawer*, the ghost whispered. *Nowhere a maid would look. You know this.*

"I don't want to know. I liked not knowing. I liked influencing, and modeling, and not fucking thinking about this shit, Auggie." The words came out under her breath. And once they started, she couldn't stop them. Even as she dragged open the drawers and felt under clothes nobody would ever wear. "I wanted to be normal. I was normal."

Normal girls don't compare every man in the world to me. I'm hot, Jen, but I ain't perfect.

"You were for me. I don't want this."

You still talkin' about guns and gangsters? Or Case?

"Shut up. Dead fiancés don't get to comment."

Live girls hallucinating dead guys need all the help they can get.

Her hand closed on a snub-nosed barrel. She got hold of the handle and pulled out a semi-automatic pistol with less enthusiasm than she would a live cobra. "This isn't about Case." She swore she heard a chuckle under the next bang from the living room. When she turned back to the door, no one was there. She tilted the gun, checking the chamber. "But it might be tomorrow. If we get that far."

Jenna carried her prize back into the living room. Ash had a solid four-foot chunk of the wall destroyed and a stack of bills lined up by the duffel bag she'd brought from Wyoming. "Money covered," Ash chirped, kicking her legs up on a dusty chair. "I should shower. Then we pick up the peanuts and lotion and get super weird."

Jenna nodded. Exhaled. "If I get with Case, is it back to this kind of normal?"

"I doubt it?" Ash brushed the dust off her arm. "This isn't Case's fault. Or Joker's. This goes well, and our normal is going to be what we make it."

"Or what the Storm Crows make it. They're in the same world Ben's in."

"Adjacent to." Ash shrugged. "But it's your choice. If you can handle the club's world, and you get Case? Isn't that worth it?" She pointed at the gun. "Not like we aren't doing way weirder shit on our own."

"That's the problem. Maybe he needs to be with someone who isn't about to shoot an Albanian guerilla while her best friend poisons an ex. You and Joker? He's almost as scary as Carz. He's gonna run that whole damn club. So it kinda seems like it works if his wife's capable of doing this. But Case?"

"Case is Joker's pick, Jenna." Ash sat up, her expression serious. "He vouched for him, sponsored him as a prospect. Case is inner circle in the national charter. He's bodyguarding the VP's wife. You've been talking shit about how crap the Crows are this whole time, and you didn't put that detail together?"

"But he's so … sweet."

"So's Nathan."

"I can't believe you said that with a straight face."

Ash grinned. "Well, he is. To me. Ever notice how other people look at Case?"

"You think Case is sweet too. Don't pretend."

"You just pointed out that I think Joker's a cutesy-wootsy puppy dog. Ergo, if I think a guy's a cupcake…" She made an impatient motion with her hand, and the penny finally dropped. Jenna set the gun down and put her hands over her face.

"Shit."

"Don't worry about it. We might blow up in a cave in a couple of hours." Ash reached across, rubbing Jenna's shoulder. "Then it won't matter."

"I'm glad our imminent destruction is okay with you."

"Demolition clears my head."

"That's not at all upsetting. Any word from Joker?"

"He's pissy. And knows where we are going. So I figure I shouldn't vex him any further until after the bullets and death are all done with."

"You're too fucking chipper. Did you take an extra anxiety pill?"

Ash shook her head and pulled off her dust-flecked top before rifling through their discarded tote bags. "I ran out of panic. We are doing the best we can. If I die trying to stop Ben, at least I was doing something good."

"And if this fucks your marriage, but you live?" Jenna asked.

Ash sauntered away toward the master bedroom. "I'm choosing to trust Tomorrow-Me and Nathan to sort things out. I can't be her today." She paused at the door. "If I call him now, and we fall apart before this, I'll be an actual danger to you and me both. If we talked it out, made up, and then I walked into a disaster? That'll destroy him even more. Because there's no way I won't go in those caves tonight, and there's no way he's going to let me." She vanished through the archway. A few seconds later, the shower started. Jenna picked up her real phone, turning it in her hands.

****

Case

Almost ten hours' hard riding lay behind them. Case's legs cramped, his arms ached. Windburn lashed his cheeks and wrists despite the sunblock that he'd belatedly slapped on sometime this morning where the gloves and Under Armour gapped. At least it was a damn gorgeous day. If they'd come through rain, it would've been fucking hell itself. He glanced back at Bullet, making sure the kid was keeping up. Bullet's 2005 Sportser was older, and though lovingly rebuilt, they had the barest repair essentials and no backup trailer. But he'd held his shit together, and so had the bike.

They turned into a forgotten industrial area outside Independence, under a bright late-summer sky. Abandoned buildings lined the road, but a high fence blocked off their aim on a side lane: the Storm Crows KC clubhouse. Case slowed his bike as they neared the closed gate. A guard waved from inside the fence. *SCKC closed? Shit must've gotten neck deep in the last twenty-four hours.*

"State your name and business," the guard called.

"Name's Case. That's Bullet." He motioned with his thumb behind him. "Here to see Joker. He's expecting us. We're with PhaCo."

Satisfied, the guard opened the gate and waved them through.

Case nodded and rolled in, pulling his bike up behind a line of others by the main building. A few guys lounged around the yard on tables and a playground setup, but Case blew past them and headed in through the main doors. Inside, a metal and granite bar gleamed under gallery lights. A big table set up in the middle played host to half the National Charter, including Joker, Grim, and Grease, and four hard-ass strangers he guessed were the KC Crow officers. Maps, cups, and tablets covered the table, along with color file folders—some of them as beat to hell as Case felt. Joker sat at the head, circles under his eyes and a foreboding line between his brows. Case stopped, putting out an arm to keep Bullet back too, and waited.

The VP's dark gaze flicked up for half a second, and he gave the barest of nods, squeezed Grim's shoulder, and wordlessly walked around the table. Grim didn't appear to notice, swiping a laptop screen, totally fixated. Case watched carefully, moving when Joker's nod directed them to the bar. "Any word since last time?" He pulled his phone out of his pocket, thumb tapping a password. His frown deepened. "Ash ain't answering me."

"Any chance you can track her phone?" He paused. "Or, you know, the car?"

"It's Jenna's car. And not when the phone's off." He set the phone down on the chipped granite counter. "Guess that means Jenna ain't called you back?" He combed a hand through his hair, his balance teetering slightly.

"Not a whisper. Checked her Instagram at the last pit stop too." Case leaned against the bar, grateful to stretch his legs out. "Prospect, get some drinks."

Bullet gave a short grunt before limping toward an open cooler full of cans. *At least I'm not the only one cramped up.* He studied Joker next. The longer you watched, the worse the VP looked—like he'd been living rough and hadn't slept in a week. "You get any sleep, boss?"

"Not much." He let out a humorless laugh. "Of course, when I do, that's when Ash sends her goddamn text." He rubbed his face. "Shit hit the fan in more ways than one. Couple of Dusty's guys got jumped by Lobos. Fucking wolves biting at the bit to start a war."

"That's what they're good at." Case put out a hand for the soda Bullet offered upon his return. "But if Reyes shows back up alive, they'll have some back-pedaling to do, right?"

"Sure. Cartels are known to do that," Joker deadpanned.

"Well, what else they gonna do? Keep pushin' the war?"

"No. They'll just pretend it never happened."

Case sighed. "Shit. I hope Reyes is a tough motherfucker. If Fitzgerald's hooked up with another cartel? Do we fuckin' know what he's plugged into? I never got jack from Jenna about any of it."

"Yeah. I'm aware of the jack shit you got from her." Joker crossed his arms, glancing at the table. "Least she warned us about the Caves. Grim's narrowed it down to two places Fitzgerald could be keeping a boat. Lobos are gonna have two of their guys meet up with us there. Kinda wish they'd stay the fuck away, but gotta play nice or risk a two-front war."

Bullet stood back, awkward as hell, turning an unopened soda can between his hands. "I don't think it's another cartel," he said quietly. He darted a glance at Joker. "I know I got shit all too, VP, but when we were riding, it was clear, and I was thinkin' back... Ash mentioned somebody named Ivan once. She'd had a bad turn. Few weeks ago. Made me turn off *Eastern Promises*. Then those guys in Junction City? If that was this asshole after all?"

Case rubbed his forehead. "How the fuck'd he know where we were?" And even as he said it, he knew. "He was watching Jenna's house."

"All the fucking threads coming together." Joker exhaled loudly. "Fitzgerald's outplayed us since day one." Irritation gave way to anger, and Joker's dark gaze turned toward Grim. "Least I know how Reyes is caught up in all this now. Wondered why Ash and Jenna cared so damn much." He shuddered. "I take it you didn't see all the videos you sent me?"

"Fucking hell no." Case stared at him. "Why the fuck would anyone need to watch more than five seconds of the first one?"

"To find some answers Jenna wouldn't give you." His shoulders fell. "I gotta say, seeing Carlos Wolf-Bitch Reyes balls deep in my wife did answer some lingering questions I had about how the fuck the head of St. Louis Lobos was connected in all this."

Bullet looked sick. Case hoped his own twisting stomach didn't show on his face. "That ... doesn't make fuckin' sense at all, boss," he managed.

"He checked up on them at Burning Man," Bullet said after a blank-faced second. "Jenna said Ash stayed with him after the trial. They didn't act like—"

"Like he was one of the one's forcing them to fuck on video? Yeah, didn't figure. He looked drugged out of his goddamn brain, too." Something flashed across Joker's face. "Fuck, this all was five years or so back, wasn't it? Reyes took control the last couple years, when Suarez turned up missing. Dad always said the motherfucker was lucky to make it that long. Dad!" He yelled toward the sanctum. Apparently startled to hear that title, the Prez opened the door. His gray hair was in need of a comb, and he looked about a week past his last nerve.

"Son?"

"What do you remember about the old Lobos St Louis boss? Suarez, wasn't it? The one before Reyes. What was his deal?"

"Sick, twisted piece of shit." Tree actually spat on the floor. "Should've died years before."

"Yeah, but what was the actual—"

"You saw those videos." Tree's gaze cut toward Case and Bullet before he apparently decided they were safe enough to talk in front of. Which wasn't a good sign. Wronski didn't hide shit from his charter brethren. *But I guess he is discussing his daughter-in-law getting assaulted. Maybe a good time for extra discretion.* "He liked 'em young. Boys, girls, didn't matter. Not legal, and not sober, and I'm guessing a shit load of 'em not willing either. Used to have his goons trawling for the underage kids sneaking into the clubs. Griff even beat a few of 'em out of a theater parking lot once." The St.

Louis Crows' prez had been Tree's drinking buddy for decades, Case remembered. *Wonder how often they planned Suarez's end? If they helped disappear him?*

Then something else caught in in Case's brain. *Five years. Maybe six?* Case finally let himself do the math. *Jenna hadn't been eighteen yet, for damn sure.* How old did Carz look? *Hardened from a rough life on the streets, but...* "Bullet, get me a shot."

Carlos Reyes had come up under Suarez, with a younger brother to look out for. And at some point, their paths crossed with Jenna, Ash, and Fitzgerald. All of them fallen into the clutches of a cartel head with a taste for humiliation and underage sex. Bullet shoved a double shot of Crown into Case's hand. It didn't quite burn the bile out of the back of his throat, but it was a start.

"Please tell me Suarez suffered before he died," Joker said.

Tree shrugged. "You'd have to ask Reyes. But … I'm thinking yes."

Case rolled the plastic shot glass against the bar until the side cracked. "Prez, you know anything about Reyes's younger brother? Auggie? Reyes said he died. Was that Suarez's work too?"

"That's one secret nobody's spilled. Yet." Tree glanced at Joker again. "But Augustus Reyes was a goddamn genie in the ring. Watching that kid fight was a master class. There are still videos online if you know where to look. He could've been a legend in the right hands. And rumor was he was moving to those hands, and out of Suarez's claws. Official story is that he got hurt and retired to a nice place in the country with all the other pets that your daddy said went to a farm. I've never heard who that last bout was against, though. Not even where. But Carlos confirmed he's dead, huh?" He sighed, looking just about wistful. "Damn. That would explain how fast Carlos moved on Suarez." *And why Jenna loses her shit when I get into a fight.*

"Prez." A gruff voice sounded from the sanctum. Dragon lurked at the door. Without further exchange, Tree nodded to Joker and returned to the back room.

"Didn't think I could want to kill Fitzgerald more than I did five minutes ago. But fuck," Case hissed. "How the fuck did Jenna and Ash get caught up with a piece of shit like that?"

"Through Ash's mom." Joker made a sound that wasn't quite a laugh. "You've met Bella Tilden. Doesn't matter how black your fucking soul is if you got the right pedigree. I bet she still thinks he's better than me."

And Jenna's mom? The thought brought up a faceless *Real Housewife* silhouette, which was all the detail her daughter ever gave.

Starting to feel like nobody has good mothers anymore. And I thought I had it bad. When he left the service, he never paid attention to how Helen treated him. He'd been too angry, resentful, and then guilty for even feeling that way. Now, his head caught on the first nights back, sitting with her. The careful questions, the gentle presence. The patience. And the understanding when things did slip out—the rough edges of a story he wasn't going to tell, the hole where a buddy had been and still should've stood. She'd recognized his grief. Let him get it out. And he'd taken that for granted until this second, staring down the realization that the spoiled little girl he'd spent half the month cursing was carrying around a burden a hell of a lot like his own. And nobody had fucking let her grieve for … years? Had she seen Auggie die? And had to post the next smiling pic anyway? Did her parents even bother to notice?

Thinking of Jenna's spiky rages and endless

attitude, his heart broke. *I see you, babe. Fuck the rest of them.*

"Don't matter what Tilden thinks," Bullet said, snapping Case back to reality. "From what I seen, if she thinks you're bad for Ash, odds are you're the best fucking thing for her."

"Still worried you ain't getting that patch, huh?" Joker chuckled. Then he focused on Case, almost smirking. "You *were* going to tell me about Reyes being super BFF with my wife, right? 'Cause you left that part out in your call."

Case stared at the Prospect. "I had no idea they'd lived together, for one. And it's Ash, Joker. She was hugging half the camp. Only way I knew he was any different was that Jenna puts up with him too."

Joker snorted. "Bet you *loved* that. She decide to put up with you yet? Or you still telling yourself rescuing her is just another job?"

He swallowed and tried not to shuffle his feet. He felt his cheeks warm. "Fuck. I don't know. Probably is to her, don't matter what I think."

"If Ice wasn't so damn busy, I'd call him to come hit you." Instead, Joker's hand flashed up, leaving a stinging blow on the back of Case's skull before he could block. "Didn't know I sponsored a goddamn moron."

He winced, shooting a reproachful scowl at Joker, rubbing out the lingering pain. "Ow. What the fuck, man? Jenna's not givin' time of fuckin' day to a Crow. Not like that."

Joker wasn't impressed. "Then you're cool to chill here and field phone calls while we go out to the caves? Seems like you could use the rest. Bullet. Go take a leak. We leave in ten minutes."

"Fuck off, Joker," he said with a growl, all sense of decorum gone—or most of it. Not like it came out loud. "I'm going."

"That an order, Marine?" The VP clapped him on the shoulder. "Guess you should go take a leak, too."

****

Jenna

Jenna shivered under the zippered military jacket. She'd chosen it for Burning Man's cool nights, and it was heavier than she needed in the cave's near-constant sixty-five-degrees, but the chill had little to do with the temperature. Everything to do with the gun holstered at the small of her back. Ivan or anyone who searched her would find it. They might miss the very small, very sharp knife tucked in her ankle boot, though. Ash had a knife, too, and her gun. They'd taken time with hair and makeup, even wardrobe, to appear as harmless as possible. Ash wore a breezy, barely-hanging-on, white sundress with cowboy boots and girl-next-door makeup, so hopefully, nobody groped her thigh too much. The fact the store stocked a garter-style holster still spun Jenna's brain.

They smiled and waved their way through the guards at the storage entrance, then wound through dusty paths under bright white and yellow lights and several tons of stone. Boats, classic cars, and containers surrounded them, punctuated by thick stone pillars and big signs proclaiming rows and directions. On and on it went, until Jenna wondered if they were driving back to Cheyenne by underground.

At last, Ash stopped the car, her delicate features in a deep frown. "This is the spot he sent, but there's nothing here."

"Well, we figured it was a trap."

Ash sniffed and reapplied peanut-laced lip gloss. "Guess this is going to be a scavenger hunt. You stay. Be ready to climb over the console and scream out of here, okay?" She opened the door as Jenna reached for the wheel. Ash got out and circled the open parking space. She returned with a slip of paper. "He taped it to the column."

The next spot held another paper. This time, instructing them to park the car and walk. Through a wire fence. Jenna's frown matched Ash's. "This is crossing into someone else's territory, isn't it?"

"Probably." A former mine, the vast facility now held dozens of storage areas alongside other businesses, the boundaries marked by added walls, fences, or by yawning, empty darkness.

"Any chance Joker got people here ahead of us? Already reading clues?"

Ash's only answer was a shrug as Jenna stepped out of the car and glanced around before hoisting the bag full of money onto her shoulder. They already stood at the far end of the storage territory—a chain link fence barely six feet away kept the darkness and feral spelunkers at bay. A small access gate near the wall was open a few inches. Jenna shuddered. *Ben bribed an employee. Or cut the locks off?* Ash must have had the same thought because she started toward it. Jenna craned her neck, but silent, dusty objects and massive limestone pillars were only so interesting. No movement. No sign of a guard.

"You'd think they'd have a more impressive security system," Ash muttered. "There are some expensive things in here, and they aren't all boat-sized."

"Maybe this is employees only? Or they're working on an expansion." Jenna realized she'd reflexively pulled out her phone to search the news for any business information. But there was no signal, so she shoved it into the jacket pocket. "What's the note say?"

"Hope you have flashlights."

"Is he going to grab us as soon as we're on the other side?"

"That would be suitably cliche. But if you're right about an expansion, maybe we're about to have a construction accident."

"Fuck. I hate construction sites. And this one's under about eighty shit-tons of rock."

"That a scientific measurement?"

"An emotional one," Jenna snapped, adjusting the strap on her shoulder. "Be nice, or you're carrying this."

"Hand it over. You're better at kicking people in the balls anyway." Ash stopped on the other side of the gate, waiting with her arm outstretched. Jenna handed the money over and pulled her phone out again. It might be otherwise useless, but at least it had a light. The chain link had blocked off a wide area that narrowed down to two equally dark archways within a few yards. *From one mine section to another?* Jenna shivered again despite the jacket, checking both directions.

"Which way? I'll use my phone for ten minutes. Then we use yours. Switching off seems like a better idea than one going fully dead."

"Shouldn't take that long." Ash put the note in her hand. The bottom instruction read merely: *Left.* "At least he didn't expect us to know cardinal directions down here."

"Yeah. Asking us to walk into the darkness of an abandoned mine carrying a small fortune is enough." Finally, they reached the end of the storage facility's fluorescent haze. Jenna hung back. "Maybe you should've called Joker at the gate."

"Maybe if you hadn't told him the times. We were lucky enough he didn't already have someone set to grab us at the entrance." Ash toed a rock out of her way.

The sound echoed. Something skittered to the right, beyond the light. *Are cave rats scarier than normal rats?*

"So super lucky," Jenna grumbled. The back of her neck tingled, and she glanced over her shoulder. *No lights. No movement. Just rats?*

"There's something up ahead." Steady, electric light gleamed around a corner. *Another passage? How do mines even work? I should have Googled this. And cave rats. Should have Googled those.* Jenna reached down, checking the gun hidden at her back. She slowed, signaling Ash to keep a step behind, and peeked around the corner.

Heavy equipment, a few storage containers—probably with *more* equipment. *Or maybe products someone doesn't want on the main business books? Shit. That's the worst option. Breathe, Jenna. Panic later.* "I don't see any exits to the surface. They might be behind the columns?"

"Okay." Ash's exhale matched Jenna's. "No people?"

"Not out milling around anyway. Or waiting for us. You don't think Ben forgot to have us murdered before we got here? I mean, this isn't exactly construction. These could be old mining things people left? But the storage containers look new."

"Well, they had to get those down here. Must be an exit somewhere. Unless they came the way we did."

Jenna rested her shoulders against the cold limestone. She switched off the phone's light and checked the screen. No service. No new messages. "We're stalling."

"Yeah." Ash nodded and shifted the duffle bag. "So, walk past? Go in?"

"This seems like where we're supposed to be." She made a face at her phone and slid it into a pocket.

"The least he could've done was be on time to kill us."

"Maybe we'll get lucky, and Carz broke out and killed him first." Ash pushed her hair out of her face and squared her shoulders. "Come on." With that, she stepped around Jenna and marched into the light. They passed three rows of columns, two sealed, silent containers. Their steps sounded louder with each heartbeat.

"Jenna…?" Ash stopped short, spinning hard to the right. Jenna almost tripped, catching herself on Ash's shoulder as Ivan moved out of the shadows.

"Wondered if we'd have to go play hide-and-seek in the tunnels, ladies." His accent had thinned, along with his hairline. But the man's bulk remained as heavy and lethal as the tons of rock around them.

Jenna swallowed back the bile crawling up her throat and forced a smile. "Don't all the girls come running to you anymore, Ivan?" She'd always wondered why he picked that name. Ivan Abazi. It wasn't fooling anyone—the man's true identity was probably buried in a bloody mass grave in Kosovo or Bosnia. He claimed he was Albanian, but she trusted his stories as much as she did the warm laugh he deployed. As if he were welcoming them into his family dinner. Then again, maybe Ivan's family routinely killed each other over the garlic bread. It would explain his personality.

"They do. Come on. Mister Fitzgerald is waiting." He waved them over, indicating another container several yards past the next row of columns, with a wide-open door and a light inside. "Shall I take the bag, Ashlyn?"

"Not yet." Ash managed to sound calm, but Jenna's heart warred with her stomach about which could claw its way out of her body faster. "I want this all official. Unless you're about to tell me Carz isn't waiting with him?"

"Of course Carlos is here."

Trap. Trap trap trap... The word took over Jenna's entire brain.

Bennett appeared in the doorway, his laconic smile and dazzling, glittering blue eyes fit for any high-end ad campaign. He wore a suit shirt and impeccably tailored pants, one hand in the pocket. *Poised*, Jenna admitted, hating herself for the slight admiration she felt. *Why does sociopathy have to look so damn chill?*

"Hey, Ash." His smile widened. "Good to see you're not letting yourself go since the wedding. Then again, you've got another one coming up, right?"

"December. You got buff."

Did he? Jenna tried to breathe. She couldn't remember his size before, just those eyes. The way he smiled when he'd stood up, Ash's blood all over his arms. *Stop, stop. You can't freak out now.*

"Not much else to do in prison."

Jenna's mouth opened on its own. "I hear some people read. Get a degree or two." *Did that come out of my mouth?* Jenna tilted her chin as Ben's gaze flashed over her. *Shit, it did.*

"Maybe I did some of that too. Reading. I'll let Ivan do the math." He focused on Ash. "You want to hand over that money now, honey?"

"I do. Once I see Carz." Ash sighed. "You didn't have to do this the mean way, Ben. I could've figured out how to slide you some cash without you hurting him."

"But I wanted to hurt him. He cost me everything. He owed me a few ounces of blood." Those glacial eyes flicked over Jenna again. *Shit.*

They approached the doors, and Ben stepped to the side, revealing Carz a couple of yards within, tied to a chair, his face a swollen mess of bruises. He blinked owlishly with the one eyelid that still moved, without struggling against his bonds or the gag in his bloodied mouth.

"What did you do?" Ash asked softly, dropping the bag to the floor. "Ben, what did you give him?" She turned on her ex, her emerald gaze wide and shining. Ivan bumped Jenna aside to grab the money. "I trusted you."

"And I trusted you." Ben spat the words and grabbed Ash's arm, dragging her closer. "You took the cash and backed this fuckstick's play with Suarez!"

"After you almost killed me," she snapped, rearing back but reaching for him.

"I was high. I didn't mean—"

Her hand caught his cheek. He shook off the slap, gripping Ash's arm tighter until she yelped. "But you did, Ben."

"I'm sorry about that. I was so sorry, Ashy-baby. You should've listened to me. I know you wanted to. Until these two got in your head."

Jenna couldn't breathe. Didn't dare make a sound. Ivan didn't have the same interest. He knelt, opening the bag to check the cash. Jenna took a step back, out of the container. She frantically scanned the area, dreading what must be just beyond the lights. *There has to be other assholes with them.*

"Oh, no you don't." Ivan's giant hand closed on Jenna's wrist. He hadn't even stood up. His thin lips split in a vicious smile. "You run and I let my boys have their fun."

"I don't see anybody."

"They know their jobs better than that. Now stay still. Let me make sure a *suka* knows how to count."

Jenna flexed her right hand, keeping her back straight. No time to get bendy and show off the gun on accident. *What if I draw it right now?* "Your boys here to help us get Carlos to the car?"

"Something like that."

A few feet away, tears rolled down Ash's face. "You w-wanted me dead. You proved that. I c-couldn't..."

"I know. It got confusing. Not your fault." Ben put a hand on her hair, bent to kiss her forehead. Ash leaned back, surprising him with her lips on his. Ben froze, and Ash's arms wrapped around him.

"I missed you, I missed you..." she whispered.

Ben growled, and his tongue slid into Ash's mouth.

Jenna reached back, grabbed the Glock's hilt, and pulled.

"*Suka blyat!*" Ivan snarled, launching himself to his feet, straight at her. Jenna yelled a warning, stumbling back but not quite fast enough. He caught her, and they fell hard, the gun still in her hand, her throat in his fist. Something pinged to the right, metal on metal—a scuffling sound. Ivan's grip loosened. Jenna yanked her arm up and squeezed the trigger. Her ears rang with the blast, but Ivan's grip only tightened. Blood splattered. She squeezed again. More metallic crashes rang beneath the high-pitched echoes in her ears. She scrambled against Ivan's weight, the hot blood making her hand slide against his skin. Ivan's twisted face slackened, but his thick fingers cut into her neck.

"Jenna! Jenna!" Case's voice. That made no sense. He wasn't there.

The weight lifted, Ivan's face fell out of her view, and Case came into it. He was ridiculously flustered for a hallucination. His tanned cheeks were pale, aside from a streak of blood across his face, and his hair was a disaster. "Jenna!" he repeated, shaking her. "Snap out of it. Get up."

"Did he just kill me?"

"No." And then his arms got around her, pulling her until she was against his warm, oddly lumpy chest. Kevlar? The realization swam through her brain. He wore black and gray, and she was resting against body armor. *Huh.*

"Give me the gun, baby. Come on. Let go." He gently pried her fingers off the trigger. His lips grazed her temple. "We got this. You can let go."

"Ivan…?"

"Don't worry. Don't even look."

"Epi-pen!" Ash's voice pulled Jenna from the daze. A massive shadow crossed between her and the container. "Joker! I need that epi-pen!"

"Hey to you too, sweetheart. Here." Joker's face was a mess of black and green paint, his hair hidden beneath a helmet. If he hadn't spoken, Jenna wouldn't have known him.

Case stood up, helping Jenna to her feet and turning so she could see Ash. Her best friend's dress hung half off, the shoulder strap shredded, revealing her pink lace bralette. Her lower lip was split, but she didn't seem to notice. Instead, she knelt over a choking, groaning Ben.

Joker stopped, not quite letting Ash take the life-saving adrenaline. "He worth saving?"

"You need the information he's got. I didn't put up with his tongue in my mouth to let him die this easily."

Joker brushed Ash's hand away and got down beside her.

"You never have to touch him again, Ash." He jabbed the needle into Ben himself as Ash sprang to her feet and ran for Carlos. "Your ass should've died in prison, Fitzgerald. It would'a gone a hell of a lot easier for you." He didn't bother pulling the needle back out before he zip-tied Ben's wrists.

Other people slid into view—same gray and black, same near-silent tread. One of them got down to check Ben's pulse, and another pair joined Ash beside Carz. "What'd he give you? Carlos, answer me!" Ash tapped his cheeks, ignoring the oversized ghosts materializing around them. "Carz!" her voice broke, and she shoved someone's arm away. "Carz, don't you do this strong silent bullshit. Stay awake!"

"Tranq… 'sall…" Carz slurred, his busted lips turning up at one side. "*Duele … brazos…*"

Jenna sobbed, slumping against Case. "Hospital. We have to—"

"We're getting there." Case tightened his grip on her waist. "It's a hike to get the fuck out of here off the radar."

"Ivan said he had guys?"

"Had." Case grinned. "Told you we'd get here."

"But how?" Jenna glanced at Ash, who'd finally let other people start settling Carz onto a stretcher.

"You left the messages. So we started checking all the entrances."

"The epi-pens?"

"I did text Joker," Ash admitted, her expression rueful. "Just not a whole conversation."

"Once we knew the entrance you had to be using, finding the rats' nests in the vicinity got easier," Joker explained, coming up behind his wife. He draped a black jacket across her bare shoulders, his hands lingering on her arms.

Jenna frowned. "That wasn't rats in the tunnel, was it?"

"It … might have been?" Case laughed.

She elbowed him. "You followed us in here?"

"Not intentionally. We figured out coordinates based on the original space he told you. Some of that was our teams scrambling to catch up."

Jenna stared at him, then Joker, and the men carrying Ben. A hundred curses scrolled through her mind. Angry demands for answers. Solutions. She shook her head. "How do we get out of this?"

"We're taking Ben and Carz. You and Ash have to go back for the car. Ben already made sure the security cameras back there don't work."

"So we walk off like none of this happened? Like Ivan isn't..." She turned, but Case caught her shoulder and kept her facing him.

"We'll walk you back to the fence, gorgeous. And meet you on the other side of the guard shacks. A brother's gonna take the car from there. I got a cage waiting. We'll take you straight to the hospital. Tell them you got mugged."

"No. No hospital." She shuddered, and Case pulled her close again. "Did I...? Was it me? The shot—"

"One of them," Joker said, ignoring a look from Case. "But not the one that took off the back of his head. Hard telling which one killed him, though. You got him right in the chest."

"I should have shot him in the dick too."

"He ain't moving. Go on and empty the clip if you need to."

"Joker," Case hissed.

Jenna almost asked for the gun. But her hand wouldn't move. Ivan's black, empty stare felt too close already. She let the urge vanish. "I trust you guys. If you say he's dead, he's dead."

"I'll put another two in his head before we dump

him." Case kissed her hair.

"Thank you. And for, uh, this. Whole thing."

"She says thanks, she trusts us, she doesn't argue." Case's hand swept over her hair. "You hit anything when you fell, babe? Your head doing okay?"

"It's the shock. Enjoy it while it lasts." She meant to slap his hand off but somehow ended up holding it. Case squeezed her fingers.

"Then let's get going. Before you remember your usual reaction to being given instructions."

****

They made it back to the car. Ash drove them out, smiling at the guard, her torn dress hidden under a jacket from the backseat emergency-clothes stash, the lip momentarily camouflaged by makeup. Jenna hid behind sunglasses and a hoodie. Not all the blood had wiped off her arms, despite Case's best attempts, and some of it was in her hair, so she'd wrapped a scarf around her head, too, on the off chance anyone gave them a closer inspection.

"You're too normal," she snapped at Ash as the final guard motioned them through.

"I didn't shoot anyone. You're dealing with more trauma than I am."

"You poisoned your ex-fiancé."

"Yeah, but I planned to do that. You didn't plan to shoot Ivan's lungs up. Surprise violence is so much worse."

The words alone made Jenna's skull throb, and she banged her head back against the seat like it would jar the world into focus. "We're both insane."

Ash stopped the car. "Jen, if you need a hospital, we can go? Or, uh, do you need me to call Dr. Walters?" she added, quieter.

"I haven't seen her for a year."

"It's been a busy couple of months. Maybe you—"

"Not. Now." A massive Escalade rolled up beside them, disgorging a man in a Nautica polo that didn't hide the Storm Crow insignia on his right arm. Jenna flung her door open and rushed out. Anything to escape that conversation.

Anything except the next man out of the Escalade.

"Case?" she almost skidded to a stop, turning just in time for Nautica Biker to slide into the Prius's driver seat, grumbling about hippies. Ash walked around the front, giving a quick wave to the stranger taking their car. Their escape.

The Escalade's driver emerged then: too tall and too broad. Shaggy, sandy hair and cold, dark eyes. Joker. Both of them were free of greasepaint and fatigues, somehow. Jenna's thoughts evaporated into a dozen curses and panicked static. Ash didn't have that problem. She ran to her husband and hugged him. Like he was picking them up at a day spa.

"Where's Carz?" Ash asked the words, a little muffled against Joker's chest.

"Private clinic. They owe the KC crew some favors." Joker kissed her forehead and tightened his hold. Jenna slid back half a step, her gaze darting toward Case. He did not look like he wanted a hug. Truthfully, Joker didn't seem all that happy either. *But who can tell? Maybe that's his happy scowl.* "We gotta get going. Tree wants a debriefing at the clubhouse. He's in a sit-down with the Lobos right now."

"Shouldn't you be there too?" Ash asked.

"KC prez is in there, and it's more his concern than mine." Joker pulled Ash closer. "This needs some discussion before you're facing Dad and Dragon."

A familiar hand closed on Jenna's shoulder. "And don't even think about calling an Uber. Or running out into traffic right now." Case's voice rattled her out of the panic. She glanced up, meeting his calm gray stare. "I don't hit women, but if you take off right now, I swear to the gods, I'll tackle your ass. And not in a fun way."

"Still sounds a little fun," she answered weakly.

His full lips twitched, but he didn't smile. "Come on. In the car." He practically ushered her in, even fastened her seatbelt before closing the door and walking around the car. He got into the passenger seat, not the back. Joker drove. Ash crawled in behind the driver's side. *She didn't get buckled in or escorted. Case doesn't think she's a spoiled baby.* Jenna swallowed hard and reached for Ash's hand.

"Time to start talking," Case announced from the front seat, meeting Jenna's eyes again via the rearview mirror.

"Us first," Joker said before Jenna could protest. Ash's expression didn't change, but her hand tightened on Jenna's. "You got some questions?"

"How?" The word came out of her before she'd known she meant to speak. "I mean, how did you get here so fast? To the caves. How did you guess about Ben for sure?"

"Fitzgerald's been facilitating an uptick in trafficking through a couple bars. Working with some Russians. The KC charter called national for help getting the problem tracked down. When Tree realized Fitzgerald was one of the players, he figured this was part payback. Something we damn sure knew when that fucker sent two girls to the local clubhouse like some kinda fuckin' gift. We started tracking him. What we didn't anticipate was him roping in the Lobos by framing us for taking one of their regional heads. About that time, you two went rogue—"

"I can see how that timing sucked," Ash admitted. "Tell me you didn't kill any Lobos?"

Joker gave a careless half-shrug. "Nothing that can't be sorted out now Reyes is back in play."

"I did text you," Ash pointed out. "I said it was going to be fine."

"No, you said to trust *you*. Which I do. But we had a cartel up our ass and the fuckin' Russians scampering all over. And then you decide to walk into a trap."

"It's only a trap if you don't know it's a trap. And you don't call for backup. Jenna told Case! And I made sure you knew, too. "

Joker exhaled and took the next turn a little harder than necessary. "Where to be. When. That's not a fuckin' plan, baby."

"You wouldn't have liked the plan. You'd have yelled. We'd have wasted time, and you'd have been unnecessarily hostile when you showed up."

"No such thing as unnecessary hostility when it comes to that weasel-faced shit stain," Case snapped.

"I don't yell at you." Joker sounded offended.

"Lectured from the diaphragm. In an outside voice." Ash sighed. "We were doing the best we could."

"You could have fuckin' trusted us with a full story." Case again, his voice heavy.

"She couldn't." The words left Jenna's reluctant lips. She held Ash's hand like a lifeline. "We had a code. Nobody says anything unless we all agree. And I ... I didn't agree."

"All?" Joker's gaze flicked up to the rearview mirror. Jenna looked down.

"Jenna, me, and Carz," Ash clarified. "And don't give me that glare. Crows have a whole damn book of codes and secrecy. Just because the three of us didn't get matching jackets and tattoos doesn't invalidate the promises we made. I told you my story. I couldn't talk about the rest until Carz was back to give his thoughts anyway, and I figured I could convince Jenna before then. So I could tell you once we got back from the Burn. And Ben wasn't going to be out until May."

Joker winced at that. "Makes sense."

"But you weren't convinced, huh?" Case turned in his seat to face Jenna.

She stared at the smooth, black console. "I almost was. But then I got those messages. The videos. And…" She trailed off with a vague shrug. "The more people who know, the worse it feels."

"He forwarded it all to me," Joker said gently. "We had to get a tech on them. Figure out any data traces. See if it could track back anywhere. But since we have Fitzgerald now, I figure we can find out for certain if he's got anything else."

"How many teeth is he going to have left before you believe him?" she asked.

Case's eyes glinted. "Not that many." For a second, he was a stranger. Someone dangerous and hard, better suited to a combat zone than Burning Man. Then his fingers touched her knee, light and careful. "You did good today."

"I shot someone."

"He deserved it. And you only got his upper-right chest. It didn't kill him."

"But he died."

"That second bullet to the brain's hard to live through," Ash said with an almost-laugh. "Good shot, by the way."

"How'd you know it was me?" Case asked, looking at her.

Ash shrugged. "Bennett's face swelling up wasn't exactly worth watching."

Case's brow rose, and he smiled. "So how sure were you that he'd live?"

"Pretty sure. Unless you were slow. But then, if you were, he probably had one somewhere in the vicinity, and Jenna and I would've ended up in a gunfight. I'm just glad none of you got lost in the caves."

"You really ain't freaked out about this?"

Ash's expression darkened, and her fingers clung to Jenna's. "Every time he hurt me, he made it feel like it was my fault. When he hurt Jen... He even made it sound like it was Auggie's fault for getting killed. It *wasn't*." She wiped at her cheek with her free hand. "He made me feel like a monster. So if I had to be one to get rid of him? Fuck it."

"You weren't the monster," Jenna whispered. "The peanuts were my idea."

"Neither one of you is anything but fuckin' amazing. Shut it." Case settled back in his seat. "Leave the monsters to the real monsters, babe."

Joker cleared his throat. "So. Full story? You got all the votes together yet?"

"I'll tell it," Ash offered.

Jenna shook her head. "I was the one who held out. So I'll do it." She took a breath and watched the bright, green trees rolling past the window. "Auggie and Carz were street kids, working their way up Lobos ranks when someone noticed Auggie could fight. I don't know what they call it, but he *knew* what people would do sometimes. Like a natural gift, I guess. So their boss started putting him in bouts, and that's how we met them, 'cause Ben was hosting stuff at some of these big parties he threw on weekends."

"Professionally," Ash put in. "It started in high

school, finding vacant places for raves or whatever. Then snowballed because his dad cut him off when he found a bunch of drugs."

"And the fight nights kinda became a thing too," Jenna said, nodding. "But sometimes, their boss Suarez got, uh, creepy. So did some of the other people backing fighters. And one of Ben's partners brought in a guy who went up against Auggie. He got knocked out. Nobody expected it. And then we went down to celebrate, Auggie was..." Jenna couldn't finish the sentence. The word wouldn't come out.

"We had to hide his body," Ash said, her voice horribly even. "He and Carz weren't strictly fighting on their boss's orders that night. And a dead Lobo wouldn't have ended well either for any of us. So we did what we had to. But afterward, Ben had one more thing to hold over us. Especially when he figured out Carz was moving pieces to stop Suarez and his, uh, hobbies. Was going to stop a lot of Ben's income stream, too."

"That's when he tried to kill Ash. And me. So I testified at the trial, and Ash and Carz got Ben's partners paid off to dissolve the arrangements since he was going to prison."

"Let me guess: some of those partners can't be reached for questions." Case eyed them both.

"No comment at this time," Ash said with a sheepish glance at her husband's back. "I, um, I think most of them are ... probably available. Somewhere. Carz was trying to find all the vids that Ben made too, so he uh, may have gotten a bit intense."

"One of the vids was you and him," Joker said.

Ash bit her lower lip and cringed back into her seat. "Ben liked to watch. Don't hate Carz for it. He did what his boss made him."

"Suarez. He one of the partners who can't be

reached?" Joker asked, still quiet.

"Yeah, funny enough, he never came back from a meeting he took about a week before Ben tried to kill us," Jenna said to get some attention away from Ash.

Joker let out a long breath and made another turn, taking them into some kind of quasi-industrial area full of high fences and graffiti. "Tree and Dragon need to know why you met Fitzgerald, what you were planning, and they're going to ask why you dodged out of protection to do it. It's a private meeting, but they've got access to the tapes."

"So why'd you get us to tell everything now?" Jenna almost screamed in frustration. "We're going over all that again? What was this? Are you just fucking handlers?"

"You're watching too many movies," Case said, earning a glare.

"I wanted you to have an easier audience the first time." Joker cleared his throat. "If you convinced me, I figure you can handle Dad."

"Convinced you of what?" Jenna demanded, leaning forward. "That we were taking off to hook up with a Lobo? This was all an elaborate trap? Is this where your daddy decides if he should kill us both or not?"

Ash sighed. "Jenna, calm down. Tree mobilized a significant number of people so we wouldn't die killing Ben. Yeah, he has to justify that to himself, the local charter, and maybe a Lobo boss or two. And considering we got Carz to fly in, and that ended up being a trap, I don't think Tree is the one who we ought to worry about. Maybe he's in the top five, but definitely not the top two."

Jenna all but snarled. "Gangster shit. I'm so goddamn tired of gangster shit. Jesus. This is why we swore we'd do things right! Normal! This isn't fucking normal, Ash!"

"You were normal for the last three years. How'd that work out?" Ash countered as the car rolled to stop outside a towering metal gate. A guard in black leather nodded at Joker. The metal doors parted, revealing their destination: a tin-roofed clubhouse that almost passed for a hipster bar and grill, sitting in a small ocean of bikes and milling people in leather, denim, and Kevlar. Jenna's throat shut, and her stomach tightened. And her treacherous bitch heart slammed against her chest.

"A hell of a lot better than this." She bailed out of the car the second Joker stopped.

****

Case

"Don't." Ash's hand landed on his forearm, startling him into releasing the door handle. Steps away, Jenna stared up into a darkening sky, as distant as the moon. "Case. She has to stay together long enough to talk to Tree. If that takes her being an angry bitch for another two hours, please let her have it."

"Says the co—" He caught himself just in time and glanced warily at Joker.

"Cold bitch? Yeah. I do that in a crisis. She does angry. Everyone has their thing."

Joker snorted and got out, opening Ash's door for her. "We are going to talk after."

Ash took his hand before hopping out of the Escalade. "Yeah. I'll probably do a fuck ton of crying. Just a warning." She landed stiffly on the gravel, bobbling to the side before Joker caught her.

Case focused on Jenna as he got out. She wasn't moving any slower, despite what that bastard did. But now she stood in the light like a statue. He edged closer to her. "Babe? We gotta go in."

Her head whipped toward him at that. The blue scarf she'd wrapped around her hair only made her eyes stand out more, sharpening the color until it damn near stabbed him in the heart. He remembered the smears of drying blood still staining her skin under the borrowed jacket and turned to Joker and Ash. "Should we let them get cleaned up before this, man?"

"After." Joker held Ash's shoulders, glancing around like a house full of their brethren was about to become an ambush.

At least we could take them if it does.

Dusty probably had most of his guys out doing cleanup or staging. The charged atmosphere from the showdown with Fitzgerald still lingered because of what came next. Hopefully, dragging Reyes out of the caves meant no war with the Lobos, but who the fuck knew anymore? That question explained the mostly empty parking lot. He recognized about half the bikes, though, and doing a quick inspection of the rest accounted for what he guessed made up the KC officers.

"Slow night, huh?" Ashlyn looked up at Joker. "Half expected a big celebration."

"Day ain't over yet, babe," Joker explained. "Dad needs to get shit settled with the Lobos ASAP."

"What about our stuff?" Jenna spun on her heel suddenly, almost running into Case. He held his hands up to catch her arms, preventing the collision while ignoring the urge to pull her into a full embrace.

"Don't worry about it. Rig's gonna bring it in," Joker said.

Jenna leaned in, her gaze fixed on Case. "Whatever I said on that voicemail? I thought I was gonna die. So don't get weird about it." She backed away, breaking contact. "Where's the door?"

Oh, we are definitely talking about that later.

Case didn't say it out loud for once, but watched her follow Ash into the clubhouse, walking past Chains and Blaze like they weren't two hulking mountains guarding the entrance. When the door shut behind them, Blaze's shoulders shook as he chuckled and said something to Chains that Case couldn't hear.

Case didn't immediately follow after them. Instead, he slowly turned his eyes toward Joker, waiting for a cue. He could deal with Russian mobsters and homicidal ex-boyfriends in his sleep. Knowing they were also engaged in selling people made it easier. But this shit? Figuring out how to walk around Ash and Jenna when the fan was covered in shit and nobody knew how to clean it was a hell of a lot harder than putting a bullet in the back of Ivan's head.

Joker only hesitated a few more seconds before walking inside, and like the obedient puppy Jenna accused him of being, Case trailed behind him. He got about two steps in before a heavy arm fell on his shoulders and dragged him toward the bar where he was greeted by the familiar smell of good whiskey and cheap beer. His first instinct was to sit down in the empty seat beside one of the KC guys and throw back half a dozen bottles of Budweiser within the next hour. But he stopped and swatted Bullet's arm away.

"Ain't in the mood to drink," Case explained as he watched Joker vanish behind the door at the back of the room.

"Not really giving you the option." Bullet wisely took half a step back and quickly added, "Ice told me to make sure to get a shot into you. At least one."

Case sighed. "Next time, lead with that." He didn't fight when Bullet ushered him into the empty barstool he'd been eyeing seconds before, and when the shot of Jack appeared in front of him, he took it.

"There you go," the man next to him said. "Ain't no problem whiskey can't make better."

Case set the shot glass down, wiped his mouth with the back of his hand, and subtly glimpsed at the man's cut. *Mambo. Enforcer. Well, he's damn well built like one.* Sitting, Case guessed the guy didn't stand much taller than him, but in terms of muscle, he wagered he had him beat by twenty or thirty pounds. *Probably a scary motherfucker when pissed.* Right now, he seemed easygoing enough.

"What about alcoholism?"

"Never heard of it." He grinned and raised his glass.

Case almost laughed, but then the door to the back opened, and he froze, waiting. *Is it over? Damn, that was fast.*

A large shadow crossed the threshold, too big to belong to one of the girls, but maybe Joker? He saw the black boot first, dingy with mud and dirt, thudding hard on the wooden floor. A tall figure filled the door frame, dressed in all black, though his ink-covered arms were bare. Grim stopped, half turning to give his attention to someone Case couldn't see. *Has Grim always been that tall?* Maybe he missed it because next to Joker, everyone except Tree appeared short. That said, Ryan definitely hadn't been that built. *Must be hitting the gym more than usual now.*

"Yeah. I'll look into it," Grim said, and then reached back to close the door behind him. Like flipping a switch, his grave expression transformed into one of delight, and he grinned like a goddamn idiot as he approached the bar.

"Never thought I'd be so happy to see your mug," Grim said, slapping Case on the shoulder. "But shit, at this point, I'd probably be happy to see my ex-wife.

Homesickness is real, brother." Suddenly, he hit Bullet's back so hard that part of his drink sloshed onto the floor. "Glad you survived the Burn, Prospect. You gotta tell me all about it. I'd ask Case, but I'd rather hear from someone sane."

"It honestly felt like being trapped in a bad eighties movie," Bullet said.

"All eighties movies are bad," Six laughed.

Grim gasped dramatically. "I'll have you know, *The Empire Strikes Back* was made in 1980, and that is one of the greatest movies ever made."

Bullet bowed his head. "I've … never seen it."

Case rolled his eyes. He didn't have enough fingers to count how many times he heard Grim's *Star Wars* rant. He focused on the door again, trying to will it open with his mind, growing more and more impatient with each passing second. He cursed when a glass filled with tequila and not much else broke his concentration. He reared back, putting a hand up between him and the drink. "I don't want it," he grumbled.

Grim arched a single black brow. "What the hell, Case? Turning down a free drink? That ain't like you."

"Thinking now ain't a good time to get shitfaced is all." He nodded toward the door.

"Worried Tree's gonna drag you in?" Grim chuckled. "He knows how Ash can be. She'd have slipped away from any one of us."

Case's fingers tightened around the glass. *Shit. I hadn't...* Of all the things gnawing at his guts, somehow that escaped him until Grim opened his fucking mouth.

"You ain't helping," Bullet muttered.

Grim's brows cranked up another notch. "I'm missing something."

"Just leftover adrenaline."

"Brother, I've seen you after a fight. I know what

that looks like and this ain't it. You gonna tell me what's actually bothering you, or am I gonna have to beat it out of you?"

Six sniffed. "Best take it outside if you do. Prez don't seem in the mood for bullshit like that."

Case lifted the glass. "Fuck. I'd drink poison at this point if you'd shut up."

Grim's smile disappeared. "An asskicking it is, then."

Bullet jumped up to get between them. "Hey. It's been a long day for everyone. Let's just chill out."

Before Case could say anything, Grim grabbed Bullet's shoulder and moved him out of the way. Six cleared his throat, but Case didn't blink. He knew how this played out. He could fight his way out of most situations, but one-on-one against Grim? *Guess my winning streak ends tonight.*

"I'm not gonna actually fight him," Grim said. "Fucking idiot. Look, Case, one drink ain't gonna get you shitfaced. But you sure as shit need to calm the fuck down. Don't know what's got you all twisted, but sort it the fuck out before Joker or Tree sees you. They got enough on their plate, and trust me, it ain't a good idea to draw attention to yourself when Tree's in a fucking mood."

Case's shoulders sank. "Yeah. You're right." He tilted the glass to his lips. His hands stopped shaking after a few seconds, but the image of Jenna on the ground beneath that Russian bastard... *How close? If she didn't have the gun, she would've—* He held the glass higher, emptying half of it in seconds.

Grim watched him before he let out an exasperated sigh. "Just adrenaline? Has nothing to do with a pretty influencer?"

"Shut the fu—" Case froze when the door opened

again. The girls walked out—Jenna first, then Ash—but instead of joining the guys, they turned and headed straight down the hallway to the wash rooms. He put one foot on the floor before Ash's warning came back to him. *Time. Give her time. Fuck me.*

He drummed his fingers on the counter, watching the now-open sanctum. A few of the KC guys were filing out, and judging by their cuts, all of them fucking mattered. The VP, the Sergeant-at-Arms... Basically everyone but the president. A couple of them moved to the bar, the VP headed to the front door, a pack of cigarettes in his hand, and one made a beeline to the bathroom. Dragon came next. His green gaze swept over the bar, his penetrating stare landing on Case, and then he waved him over. *Shit.*

Sliding the glass back to Grim, he got to his feet, ignoring the nerves and nausea roiling in his gut. "What's up?"

"Tree wants to talk to you." He squinted at Case, crossing his log-like arms over his broad chest. "You don't look so hot. You ain't drunk already, are you?"

"No," he said honestly. "Just been a long fucking week."

"I hear that." Dragon extended his arm toward the sanctum. "Go on."

Is it too late to pick a goddamn lion's den?

Trapped in a room with Tree, Dusty, Dragon, and Joker... *Can think of worse places to be. But not many.* He stepped further into the room, hearing Dragon close the door, blocking the only escape. Joker stood in the corner, settled against the wall, his expression unreadable. On the opposite side of the room from Joker, Dusty half-sat on the ledge of a blacked-out window as he fiddled absently with a chain he wore around his neck.

"So, you gonna try explaining today?" Tree asked

from behind the KC charter table. It looked even older than the one back home, weathered and slightly smaller. A cup of pens sat at the corner, a stack of notebook paper beside it, but otherwise, it lacked for much else. Well ... except the Glock that lay dangerously close to Tree's hand. And the National Prez's expression had all the warmth of an arctic winter. "Starting with how two half-grown idiot girls got past a trained bodyguard and a Marine?"

How the fuck am I supposed to answer that?

"Because those idiot girls ain't exactly idiots," Joker answered from the corner of the room. "One of them is a goddamn Tilden. I know between us, we've had our fair share of trouble trying to keep one or two in our sights."

"Must be going senile. I could've sworn I warned you about Tildens before you stuck a ring on one..."

Case cleared his throat. Better to fall on the grenade than watch this devolve into a family feud. *Maybe.* "Jenna and Ash didn't spend their college years pledging Greek and hopping down to Miami Beach, either. They ain't no strangers to having to run or hide from people who know how to find them. I didn't know the full story, or I wouldn't have trusted them to stay put. No excuse. I should have kept a closer watch."

Tree's gaze swung from his son to Case. "But you didn't. So how the hell'd you get suckered?"

"Think that's the brunette's doing," Dragon put in, smirking.

"Am I going to have to put old, married motherfuckers on guard duty from now on? Jesus." Tree groaned, the picture of despair as he raked his gray hair off his face and slumped back in his seat. "I put the national charter on shit, they're supposed to get shit done. So it's a damn good thing you pulled this clusterfuck off at the end. Now, you." He pointed at Joker. "Better have a good fuckin' way to sell this shitshow to the Lobos."

"The way I see it, ring or no ring, we'd be right where we are anyway. Ain't no changing the fact that Fitzgerald had it out for the Lobos, and given the course he was on, we always would have wound up on his ass. Without Ash and Jenna, he'd have played us against them like a goddamn fiddle. They drew him out of his hidey-hole with five guys and minimal firepower, not to mention helping us take him alive."

"So your choice is 'tell the world you told your ol' lady to pull a hit.'" Tree chuckled. "It's original. I give you that."

"More like she volunteered. She's extremely loyal to the Crows, you know."

"Loyal to you at any rate." Tree almost smiled. "Girl's saved your ass twice now. Maybe I should make her the VP."

"You could try." Joker kicked back in an empty seat, attention leveled on his dad. "But she hates sewing. Not sure she can see over the handlebars either."

"A glimpse at your future, kid." Dragon's voice rumbled with a laugh. "If you don't let the brunette run. That one's a pistol."

"More like a Gatling gun." Tree snorted. "She's the one who winged the Russian. And came up with the method for their little hit scheme." His expression darkened enough that Case winced. "Dragon here says you're going to put your patch on her. That true?"

Case flushed, his gaze darting to Dragon like the man betrayed him. "I wish I had the crystal ball Dragon has." *Hell of a lot safer than saying Dragon talks too fucking much.* "I am figuring it out as I go, but ... I doubt she'll want to—"

"I'd wager we have a new Gatling gun in our arsenal," Joker cut in.

"Goddamn is youth wasted on the young these days." Tree leaned on his elbow, sizing Case up, tapping the table far too close to the Glock. "That girl's neck-deep in our shit. So, either you put your mark down, or I'll get another brother's on her. Call me a medieval bastard, but I don't think she's gonna do well in the wild 'til shit settles down."

Case felt his blood draining from his face. His fingers flexed against his thighs. "I agree," he said. "Besides, I've got a bit of a rule. Anybody who's met my mother and knows my real name ain't waltzing out and about to spread that shit. She'll wear my patch." *Just ... maybe not tonight. Or tomorrow. Or this month.*

"See how quickly he finds his spine." Tree laughed. "Just keep that thought right up front. You're gonna need it. Now, Joker, you want him here for the sit-down with Lobos? I—"

A frantic knock at the door cut him off a half-second before a pale KC Crow slid the door open barely wide enough for Ash to slide past.

"Sorry! He's super sorry, please don't kill him, Tree." The blonde's wet hair dripped down her half-bare shoulders, leaving droplets by her bare feet.

"Jesus, girl. Tell me you didn't walk out in the clubhouse like that," Tree said, his expression pained. Belatedly, Case realized she was wearing a giant Storm Crows t-shirt instead of a minidress.

"It was more like running. And you're the one who didn't keep a medic by the door, so don't yell at me. Can we please borrow Case?"

"We're not finished here."

Ash wrapped her arms around her waist, scowling. "I'm doing my best, Jacob. I couldn't find

Bullet. Jenna's melting down, and I can't get her out of the shower by myself, and you've got Case right here…"

Tree glowered but waved a hand. "Go, kid. And for fuck's sake, Joker, get your wife some damn clothes before the Lobos get here."

Dusty chuckled and said, "Tasha's on her way back up. I'll text her to bring some extra clothes."

"Does she have anything that'll fit them?" Dragon asked. "I know it's been a while since I last saw your wife, but those tits ain't easy to forget."

"We can make it work," Ashlyn said. "Thank you."

Case thanked Tree quietly and followed as Joker gently took Ashlyn by the elbow to escort her out of the room. Gods only knew where they were going to find pants for her. Nobody else in the clubhouse shopped in Juniors.

"If I didn't know better, I'd swear you have the biggest pair of anyone here, sweetheart," Joker muttered.

"Not big enough. I almost asked your dad about the Lobos… So, they're coming? Here? Is… Is Carz…?"

Joker frowned. "Carz ain't in a walking condition yet, baby. But they're coming with his blessing. And the fact that they're willing to meet us here? That's a good sign."

"Where's Jenna?" Case cut in. He glanced toward the main room, then ahead to the clubhouse's built-in apartments. They wouldn't have put the VP's wife in the Prospect dorm, but with so many guys in town, what was vacant?

"The back guestroom." Ash pointed down the hall to the right. "It has a bathroom, so they had us use it. She's not hurt just, you know, things hit at once. Like they do. I gave her a Xanax, but she needs like six tons of valium and a nap. And a therapist. But mostly, someone needs to get her out of the shower. Please." Her voice shook, and she leaned against Joker. "I can't pick her up, and she won't—"

Case didn't wait to hear the rest. He sprinted into the guest room, ignoring the scattered clothes but catching himself staring at an abandoned Glock lying on a chair. *Shit. That's gotta go.* He knocked on the bathroom door, fighting to keep his voice calm. Steady. "Jenna. It's Case. I'm coming in." He waited another second, then pushed the door open. Warm steam engulfed his face, temporarily obscuring the small room's contents. The gray tiled floor was slick, probably from Ashlyn, so he walked flat-footed to the shower, drawn by the soft sniffling just audible under the running water. Jenna sat under the stream, head bowed, knees up to her breasts.

"Jenna?" He crouched down to get closer to her level. "Come here, baby. Let me help you."

She lifted her head. Reddened eyes, her split lip bleeding again, all of it too bright against her pallid skin. "I-I'm a mess." She pushed her hands over her face, shrinking back against the wall. "I can't do this, Case. I can't. I want to go *home*."

He glanced up at the showerhead then down at the shiny vinyl and water circling the drain. *Fuck it.* Slipping out of his cut and shifting forward, he half-turned so he could slide into the shower beside her. Barely an inch separated them. He left his stiff legs out, but if he ignored the slight pinch at his side, he could get his arm around her shoulders. Her soft skin was clammy despite the heat.

"You're beautiful." He placed a kiss on her wet hair. "I know, Jenna. I'll take you home. But first, we gotta get out of the shower and get dressed."

"I can't." More tears, a strangled sob. "I can't go

home, Case. I don't work. I don't even feel bad about Ivan. Y-you're probably torturing Ben, and I … don't care." She coughed, shivering in the steam. "I don't know where to go."

"Jenna," he whispered, bending one knee, bringing it into the shower so he could face her fully. The dust and cave dirt from his shoe browned the water around his leg. He carefully grasped her wrist, tugging her hand away from her face. "Sweetheart, please." He stroked his thumb along her cheek. "You don't have to figure anything out right now. You don't gotta go anywhere. You can stay with … us. With me."

"You're just saying that because I said I love you." She finally looked up, her expression raw and somehow defiant. Like she wasn't the one naked and crying. "You don't want me to stay with you. You'd hate it."

"I'd hate it more if you left," he said softly. "Baby, I *want* you to stay with me. Never wanted anything more than that." He waited for her to meet his gaze. "I love you, Jenna. And maybe I shouldn't say that now or here, but it ain't us if it ain't weird. Stay."

Her face scrunched with another sob and then an odd, sharp laugh. "I hate when you're perfect. Stop it." But her arms circled his neck, and she put her head against his shoulder.

"Perfect, me? You did hit your head, didn't you?" He tried for a smile, but she only sighed and turned her face against his neck.

"I'm too tired to be sensible, Apollo. So if you don't mean any of it, stop. Before I can't ever leave."

He settled his cheek against her hair. A wet shirt, soaked denim, and quickly cooling water. He shouldn't be comfortable, but he felt right for the first time in days. Maybe longer. "That's the idea, baby. I know I ain't much, and I don't got much, but … I want to spend my life with you. And I will. If you'll let me."

"Now who hit their head?" Jenna wiped her cheek. "Let's turn off the water before anyone makes any full-on life choices. Well. Mostly you turn it off. I don't know if my legs work." She nuzzled his shoulder. "See if you can help me get dressed without getting into a fight."

He kissed her forehead and let himself hold her another five seconds before reaching up to the taps. "It's worth a shot." Getting up took longer than it should have with his stiff leg and twinging shoulder, but neither seemed to matter once he got Jenna back in his arms.

She might be right. This wasn't the time for making life-altering decisions. But wanting her? Loving her? Doing anything for her? All of that was already decided before they even left the fucking Burn. *But how the hell to clue* her *in on that?*

Epilogue
Jenna

September 12

The first, terrible night, she'd fallen asleep next to Case in a stranger's bed and woken up to Tree hustling her and Ash into an SUV. Dragon, Case, and two other Crows followed on bikes for the long trip back to Illinois. Jenna tried arguing, only to be reminded she'd helped take out an Albanian, and being anywhere near his network wasn't a great plan.

Luckily, Oak Grove was nowhere near anything or anyone. Not for a hundred years. Well, Case was there. So that was okay. Mostly.

Sort of.

Except he isn't *here.* He'd barely been present for the last week, continually vanishing to work or on errands Ash didn't actually need him to do. *Or maybe to see other girlfriends he'd said lovely things to in moments of extreme duress.*

That's all it was. Stress. Jenna kept repeating it in her head, pushing the memories from KC into the dark mental files she only peeked into every so often. If she acted like everything was the same as it was all summer, it would be. Screw the ache in her chest every time Case walked out the door. It was probably heartburn.

Joker and the others came back a few days later, spurring a new round of celebrations and plans for other bike runs and events. Ash asked for help with those, and Karli seemed happy to have extra hands, and with urgent wedding issues abounding, who could find time to think?

Until she found herself on Ash's new back deck, sipping a margarita and staring at the setting sun, phone forgotten on her lap mid-post, wishing Case was around to complain about the tequila. Footsteps at the patio door knocked her back to the present. She looked up, expecting Ice, but familiar brown eyes stared back at her instead. "Hey, Joker. Like the new deck furniture?" Or the new deck. It had materialized in the last few days. Ash was in a mood about home improvements, and the poor Crow Prospects didn't dare argue.

The corner of Joker's lips twitched. Like he almost wanted to smile but caught himself. Who knew with him? Lifting his bottle of Bud, he drank before shrugging and sitting down in one of the brand-new chairs. "I don't hate it." His long legs stretched out in front of him. If she ignored the boots and the gun at his hip, she'd almost call him relaxed. "I think the safe answer is if Ash likes them, then so do I."

"You're learning." Jenna laughed. "But if you didn't, I'm sure she'd return them. And drag you into the store to choose the replacements." She watched him easing into the cushions. *Okay, maybe he actually is relaxed.* There hadn't been any raging fights between him and Ash since he got back. Quite the reverse, if the sounds coming from their bedroom were any indication. Jenna took a drink to wash away the pang of jealousy.

This time, he did smile. "Oh, I'm aware. All I asked was no frills and lace, and she's respected that. Otherwise, this house is her canvas. Anything she needs to do to make it hers."

Jenna nodded slowly. "Any news from Kansas City? Like … should I be cleared to head home soon?"

He took another drink, his gaze floating back to her. She felt like a horse being judged for the derby.

"You talked to Reyes lately?"

"A few texts." Butterflies stirred in her stomach. "Why?" She'd assumed the sporadic replies were more related to his pain meds, but she found her attention focused on the gun Joker wore.

"Hm. I think, for now, it's best to stay clear."

"I don't like that *hmm* sound, Nathan. That sounds like 'classified information' in Biker."

"Yeah. Well." He made a vague motion that could've meant anything.

And yet no actual denial.

"You know, you're welcome here anytime, and for however long you want, Jenna. Though I get the feeling you'd rather be somewhere else?"

"I'd always rather be somewhere else." She shrugged. "Don't take it personally. It's why Ash and I always traveled so much. She had the same bug. 'Til lately. You've convinced her to try staying put." Jenna took a soothing sip of margarita.

"I never much liked leaving home," he admitted. "I give it a year or two before the bug comes crawling back. Then I guess I'll get to see more of the world." He set the bottle down on the table between them and sat up a little straighter. "I didn't mean it like that, though. So maybe this way is better: I get the feeling you'd rather be with someone else right now. Someone who could probably be here in a few minutes if I shot him a text."

She considered denying it, but what was the point? Ash knew, and somehow even if Ash didn't tell Joker, he figured it out. Being the spawn of Satan had perks. "If he has to be ordered somewhere, it doesn't count." She focused on her margarita, biting her cheek before she caved to the heavy, demonic-descended gaze fastened on her. "We got stupid and said stupid things in the heat of the moment. Don't make him wallow in it."

"Jenna." He managed to make her name sound like a mild, exasperated swear. "You think he ain't here 'cause he regrets it? Come on, you *know* better. You went through hell, and you ain't the comfort-with-cuddles type. Trust me. You call him, he'll come running. And if you don't do it soon, I'm gonna have to because I can't go through this shit again. Grim and Megan are enough fucking drama for the county."

Her jaw clenched. Throwing the margarita in his face would be a blasphemous misuse of tequila, but on the other hand, he deserved it. She kept her hand curled around the glass stem, in case he pushed her last remaining nerve. "I'm not calling. If he wanted to be here, he would be. You may be lord of the manor, Nathan, but you're not king. Your opinion on Case's love life isn't his. Obviously. And don't go presuming what I know. Just because you and Ash share some ESP wavelength doesn't mean it extends to me."

Joker grabbed his beer, his expression unchanged except for a slight upturn at the corner of his lips. "You're so determined to believe the worst. Easier to think he doesn't want to be with you than to accept that he does. Because then he could hurt you. Or worse, something could happen to him. You know how much it hurts. So, better to be alone, right?"

"Did Ice coach you for this?" Her voice came out flat and unfazed. "I'm impressed with the delivery. Keep going, and I'll make damn sure your wedding tux is trimmed in pink." Jenna drank the margarita instead of throwing it on his face. Barely. Her fingers twitched as she set it down. "If you want to relay that through the hivemind, add this. I know damn well if he wanted to push this, he'd be here doing it himself. So whatever punk bullshit you and the boys are running, fuck off with it."

Joker shrugged. "Maybe it ain't him, Jenna. Ain't no secret you hate it here. You ain't a fan of the club either. You made it clear you don't want any part of this world. What's the word you used? Normal? Yeah. Being with Case ain't that. It never can be. And it ain't like he can just pack up and walk outta here. Not with Helen. He's stuck here. But that don't mean you have to be. I know you ain't dumb, Jenna, but Jesus. Can't you see he's giving you an out? He wants to be with you, but from where everyone is sitting, it ain't so clear that you want the same thing."

Her knuckles went white on the glass. "I don't seem to be able to escape this world, so what does it matter? Club promoters, shady developers, dumbass party drugs. All leads back to the same place. So maybe it's time to accept and make the best of it. Like Ash."

Joker chuckled. "You sound so enthusiastic," he said, shaking his head. "Let me put it this way: I know what it's like to love someone you don't think you deserve. I would do anything for Ashlyn. But in the end, her staying here and being my wife had to be *her* choice. That's why I don't care what she does with this house. Because more than anything else, I want her to know that this is her home. That she will always have that here and that she will always have me. But she had to want the home first, Jenna."

"Did you swallow a self-help book in that beer?"

"Look, Case might not think it, but he deserves someone who wants him. Not someone who is just making the best of it. And it goes both ways. You deserve to be happy. Hell, you fucking earned it."

Jenna scowled, leaning back in her seat in case his head started spinning around. Her brain was already doing enough of that. "The truth is I don't hate it here, okay? But I'm not good at living in one place. And I like modeling. Traveling. And that's … not the sort of thing Case has in mind when he imagines settling down with a nice patch bunny who'll be waiting for him at the end of every long bike run."

"You met his mom and think he imagines a traditional relationship?" He swigged the last of his beer. "Case ain't the type to tie an anchor to your foot, Jenna. Asking you to give that up would be like you asking him to give up his patch. Don't think he's expecting some hundred-and-eighty-degree turn just 'cause you put his patch on."

"He hasn't asked me out yet, and you're leaping to patches." Her eyes rolled. "He wants the opposite of his mom. I'm more like a ninety-degree angle. And eventually, he's going to notice and start dreaming about girls who bake brownies and stay at home ironing jeans or whatever."

Joker smirked and settled into his seat, locking his hands behind his head. "You ain't like his mom. It ain't that Selene was moving around or not baking birthday cakes. It's that she dumped people left and right when it was convenient. Even her own kids. Family was just another word to her. Case ain't wired that way. Neither are you." He paused, but then added, "Also, you don't smell like patchouli or dance naked under the full moon. Least not as far as I can tell. Not that I think he'd mind."

Jenna's stomach fell. "You're giving me too much credit," she said softly, all too aware that she shouldn't. *Confessing to the prince of darkness can't end well. But what does anymore?* "There's a long trail of dumped friends and boyfriends stretching from here to Nepal who'd testify to what a flaky psycho I am. I came back because Ash was in trouble. I stayed because I trusted you Neanderthals even less than I do myself."

She turned the glass, watching the melting ice catch the fading light. "I only walked into that firestorm last week after I bailed out to Europe. You're getting to see my dodgy half-ass redemption arc, not the ugly screwing-up part."

He went quiet. Probably rethinking his words and judging her. Thinking *she* was the one not good enough for his friend. "Should have brought two beers," he said softly, hefting the empty bottle.

"You could go get another one." *And not come back, hopefully.*

"Shit." He stretched and let out an exhausted sigh. "I can't sit here and judge your past. We've all fucked up on other people. I got an ex-wife somewhere because I couldn't get my head out of my ass long enough to be a decent husband to her. I got plenty of regrets too. But I can't complain about how it turned out."

"That's because you got to be married to my best friend. Who is a perfect fairy princess."

"I'll agree on the princess part." He grinned. "I don't know where I'd be without Ashlyn. Technically, I guess I'd be dead, so there's that." His hand fell to his leg, fingers pressing into his thigh where she remembered Ash had said he had a shitload of surgery. "You and me ain't always gonna see eye-to-eye. But I love that you love Ashlyn. I don't give a shit that you hate me. You went through hell for her. I respect that."

"I don't hate you. I just don't like you very much all the time. But occasionally, you're acceptable." Jenna managed a smile. "Which is a miracle considering her track record with dudes." She narrowed her gaze. "If you ever tell anyone else I admitted to not hating you, I will deny it 'til the end of time and find your ex-wife for blackmail material."

"Your secret's safe with me." He released his leg and toyed with the empty beer. "My ex was—is—a good person. We didn't work anymore. People change." He grimaced. "Starting to sound like my shrink. Point is, from where I'm sitting, you have put yourself through all sorts of hell for your family when it'd have been way fucking easier to run and take care of yourself. That sets you apart from most people, Jenna, but especially Case's mom. And Case ain't some normal Society fuckface worried about his golf buddies' opinions. To be honest, I don't think you'd like him as much as you do if he was."

"He's one of the most normal guys I've hooked up with." She paused, considering that statement and winced. *God, it's even true.* "Assuming you consider biker gangs less weird than shamanistic activists living off the grid in an anarchic collective."

Joker laughed. "I'd say so, but I'm no judge. Might as well been born with the Crow ink. And compared to some of the shit you've lived through, this is vanilla as hell."

"So he's almost normal. I'm not." She made a face, but Joker laughed.

"Don't matter to him. But I guess it's up to the two of you to figure out if that's enough. Can't be done unless you're talking to each other." He pulled his phone out. "The offer's still standing. I can call him."

Jenna shook her head. "Thanks for the offer, but I'll handle it. I need to think first." She downed the rest of the margarita. "And get some more tequila."

Joker could talk about love so easily—but of course he could. He knew he had Ash's heart, and probably had known it since the first time he met her. Ash hadn't talked much about dating Joker. Like she'd woken up married to him and rolled with it. *Must be nice to have it be that easy.* "I gotta decide if I trust whatever crystal ball you're reading his intention with. Two more shots should do it."

"What is it with you two and crystal balls? As for the tequila, *that* I can help you with." He levered up to his feet and towered over her. "Just don't let Ash mix the drink for you if you're planning on doing any thinking tonight."

"And you hired her as a bartender?" Jenna snickered. "Admit it. You'd have fired her already if you weren't married to her."

"Oh, hell no." Joker smiled wide enough for a dimple to show. "No way am I saying shit when she's within ten miles. That woman's got the ears of a goddamn wolf." He grabbed the empty beer bottle and gestured with his arm for her to go ahead of him. "Besides, her drinks are great if you ain't planning to do much else after you drink them."

"Fair points." They made their way inside and Jenna hung back, letting Joker play bartender with the margarita mix, tuning out as Ash and Karli wandered in from the front discussing margarita machines. Then Ice and Blaze appeared, followed by Bullet and some other new Prospect Jenna hadn't heard a name for yet.

She managed to catch Bullet's elbow finally and dragged him into the hall. "Hey. You happen to know—"

"Where Case is?" His eyes rolled. "Checkin' on his stepmom. New home-care person interview or something."

"Don't suppose you're sober enough to give me a ride to his apartment?"

"Is this a going-to-his-place-to-drop-off-a-note situation, or do I need to stay sober for a return ride?"

"Nah. I'll call somebody else."

"Come on. Get a spare helmet in the garage, though."

****

Jenna waved Travis off at the curb and stared at the apartment block. She hadn't paid much attention to it before—an odd bit of recent architecture in the midst of

Oak Grove's Victorian postcard aesthetic. It was eight units, two stories, and someone in a fit of desperation to appease the city council pasted a front porch-slash-balcony on. It didn't help.

It's clean, though. And doesn't appear to be falling down. Things could be worse. She caught her lip, surveying it and the cracked asphalt parking area, the neon-bedecked gas station across the street, and the grocery store half a block up. A solid fifty percent of Oak Grove's business district, all in one handy area. She pulled her phone out and checked her notifications. Her apps. The countless bright images of other places beckoned. Beaches, mountaintop resorts, luxurious spas, savannahs and safaris. Then a handful of saved pics from the Burn: Case laughing at Bullet, Case hauling Ash over his shoulder after she'd eaten one too many edibles to remember how feet worked, Ash and Jenna making faces in fantasy costumes.

A motorcycle's roar summoned her out of the pixels. She watched Case's dark-blue Harley turn into the lot and roll toward her. She leaned against one of the columns, keeping her distance while he parked.

Jenna tugged the hem of her tank top down and hoped her mascara hadn't run. The sun was nearly set, the building's shadow stretching over them, but it wasn't dark enough to hide flawed makeup. Case pulled off his helmet, his dark gold hair shining. Whatever his mother's sins, she'd chosen the right name. Jenna swallowed hard. Case stood, swinging one long, jean-clad leg over the bike, staring at her as though trying to figure out if his brain was playing a trick on him.

"How was your day?" she called over the thunderous rattle of a passing coal truck.

"Looking better now." His expression relaxed, his lips forming a hesitant smile. He shoved his keys into his pocket and let out a long, over-dramatic sigh. "What are you doing here? Not that I'm not glad you're here, but how long have you been waiting?"

"Not long."

"That's a relief." He chuckled nervously, his hand rubbing the back of his head. "Want to come in?"

She glanced sidelong, hoping the few minutes in a helmet hadn't ruined her hair. "Do you want me to?"

He'd pivoted toward his door but stopped. He said something under his breath too soft to hear. By the time she opened her mouth to ask what, he closed the distance between them. Jenna froze as his callused hands cupped her face, tilting her lips up to meet his. He smelled like sunlight and grass, leather, *and* ... Case. He smelled like him. *Damn it. I want to pull all his clothes off and wear his t-shirt? I've gone insane.* Her body buzzed, blood rushing in her ears. As quickly as it started, it was over, his hands dropping to her shoulders. She almost cried.

"Fuck yes, I want you to come in," he whispered.

Her hand settled on his waist without meaning to, her breath catching. Jenna bit her lip and tried not to shiver under his touch. "What happens when I come in, Apollo? What do you want to happen?"

Case's fingers slowly slid down her arms until they threaded around hers. His lips lowered again, only this time they grazed her cheek and stopped at her ear. "I want to take you to bed and do all the things I've dreamt of doing with you. And keep doing them until I can figure out how to convince you to stay."

She touched his chest, just enough to keep herself from leaning up and trying to reunite their lips. "That's the problem," she whispered. "If you take me to bed, I'm not going to be able to leave. I'll stay here with you. Forever. Or until you throw me out." Jenna pulled his right hand from her shoulder, down to her heart. "Turns out I love you."

She heard his breath, felt the warmth over her ear, and the laugh that came next was airy, relieved. His arms went around her, squeezing and lifting her off the ground, bringing her lips to his. "Fucking finally!" He set her back down, taking her hand and walking her to his door. "We're going to bed, baby."

"The proper response is to say you love me too," she said, dragging her heels and laughing. "Before you go luring me into your sex dungeon."

He groaned, pushing the door open before his hands went to her hips, backing her over the threshold into the dark apartment. "Jenna, you know I love you. You didn't give me a choice." He kicked the door closed and blindly reached for the light switch. "You're so fucking brave. Smart. Beautiful. I'd be a goddamn fool to let you leave."

"Yes, but a fool with about a million fewer headaches. So I'd understand." The lights flickered on, and she took the moment to reach up for his stubbly cheek. "I wanted to say thank you for … everything. You may be an actual badass after all." Her smile returned. "And maybe I get why you do what you do, so we'll have to find something else to argue about." Jenna's hand slid downward, over his broad shoulders. She felt his fingers begin to trace over the waist of her pants, beneath the hem of her shirt, ghosting lightly over her skin. "I was waiting for you all week. Where've you been?"

"Waiting for you," he whispered. "I know exactly how I feel about you. I stopped running from it when I woke up and you were gone." He pulled her closer. "You scared the shit out of me, Jenna. I have never been that fucking terrified in my life. I wasn't sure…" He bowed his head to kiss her forehead. "Didn't know if you wanted what I wanted. I had to give you time."

"How much time?" She pouted despite her fingertips trailing along his t-shirt collar and the shivery effect of his hand on her abdomen.

"However long you needed."

"I almost convinced myself you got carried away and didn't want to admit it. I may have a tendency to overthink things when I'm left alone with them."

"Guess I gave you too much time," he said, clearly biting back a laugh. He lowered his lips to hers again, the kiss much sweeter. "I'm sorry, baby. It won't happen again." As the words left his mouth, his knees bent and he wrapped an arm around her legs, just below her ass, and seemed to lift her with no effort. "So let me remind you. I love you, Jenna."

She giggled, grabbing his shoulders for balance. Soft skin, rough stubble, and the weightless moment as he pinned her to the wall to deepen the kiss all combined to leave her moaning instead of answering. Jenna nipped at his lower lip, her dazed eyes opening finally to memorize his features: the angle of his jaw, the way his lips parted when she wriggled against him. "Tell me to stay, Apollo," she whispered, lips brushing his with each word, then drawing back again to meet his gaze. "I feel extremely accommodating. I might even wear one of those property patches if my badass biker told me he wanted me to." Her legs wrapped around his waist and squeezed so she could feel his erection through their clothes.

He grunted, his hips thrusting hard against her. He tugged at the front of her shorts, the snap ripping open. "Stay," he begged, his voice rough as the hands working up her sides, pushing her shirt higher. "Stay with me." He kissed her deeply and then trailed down the side of her throat.

"Yes." Her head fell against the wall. "I missed you so bad."

"Tell me you love me, Jenna." He turned, still holding her against him, making a quick walk to the bedroom as she nipped and teased his throat.

"I love you." The words came without hesitation, marked by kisses, ending on a moan as his grip tightened. He set her on the bed and dragged her shorts down. She hadn't bothered with panties. Judging by the way his jaw flexed, he appreciated the choice. Jenna watched him, spreading her legs and pulling her tank top down to bare her breasts. "I'm all yours, Apollo."

"Good." His gaze locked with hers, and she watched as he lifted his shirt up and off, tossing it aside. He unfastened his belt and quickly toed off his shoes. Then he crawled onto the bed, lowering his hips between her parted thighs, bracing his weight on his left arm while his other hand shoved his pants and boxer-briefs down to free his cock.

"I need you, gorgeous." He rubbed his tip against her clit until she moaned, then snapped his hips forward, filling her with a single, brutal thrust. Jenna arched up, almost screaming at the intrusion, the burning stretch. His girth was enough to hurt, even though he rained distracting kisses on her cheeks, and she dug her nails into his back. Somehow, the pain felt good. Addicting. Like she wanted more.

"Fuck! I'm sorry." He went still for a moment. "Sorry, baby. I'll make it up to you, I'm sorry—"

"Not objecting, Apollo." She tilted her hips again, flexing around him as her body adjusted. "More," she moaned. "If I can walk when you finish, you aren't forgiven." She bit his earlobe to emphasize the point.

The sound he made was almost a growl. His hand

shot up to the side of the headboard, the muscles in his arm rippling, matching the grip he used on her hip as he began thrusting. Hard. Fast. Relentless. He seized the back of her knee, lifting it higher until his cock slid a fraction deeper. "I ain't gonna be finished for a while," he promised as the bed hit the wall. Again. And again. "So good, Jenna. You feel like a goddamn dream."

She couldn't answer except to push her hips up and grab at the pillow, dragging one closer to cover her mouth as her body locked down on Case's cock in a frantic, screaming orgasm from weeks of desperate need.

"No." His voice was sharp. Commanding. He dropped her leg to pull the pillow away from her face, tossing it beyond her reach. "Let me hear you." He kept going, each rough thrust driving another cry from her. The heat in her body built again.

"Apollo, yes. Yes! More. Don't stop. Fuck..." She was screaming before the orgasm burst through her. His arm slid beneath her, angling her hips toward him as his own moved faster, frenzied. He cried out, his body shaking, and he pitched forward, filling her pussy. Jenna whimpered with his last thrusts, aftershocks shuddering through her. As he lowered her leg again, she moved to keep him inside her. "Your neighbors are definitely calling the cops if we do that again. They may already be on the line."

His chest was still heaving, but he managed to chuckle, putting his lips at the crux of her neck as he slowly rolled to his back, keeping her pressed against him. "Something tells me I'm gonna need a bigger place once the lease is up anyway."

"Are you asking me to move in with you while I've got your cum inside me? Neanderthal." She laughed, settling against his shoulder.

"Technically, I asked you before that, but I can

see how you mighta been distracted."

"You *hinted* before that." She managed a pout. "I wasn't distracted. It's just hard to think about anything except fucking you sometimes." She felt his cock stir at that and decided not to be too annoyed after all. "When's the lease up? Are there even any bigger apartments here? No offense, but I got the feeling there's about ten apartments in the county. Everything else is picket fences and farmhouse aesthetics."

His hand moved gently along her back, his breaths finally starting to even out. "October. There's a couple of options for bigger places that don't require a mortgage. Well … maybe *one*. It don't need to be *that* much bigger, right? We only need space for your clothes. And shoes. And makeup. Now that I think about it, might be easier to rent two apartments."

She traced a line around the wolf tattoo on his left arm, reveling in the freedom of simply being with him. Naked. No one to dodge, no angsty thoughts about leaving. No playa dust. "Is a mortgage a big deal? I mean, two cars and a bike, plus your furniture and my pieces in storage… Then I need a studio area, and you probably want a garage for all that mechanic stuff that is absolutely not living in our front room. A house would fit better. Mom might even buy it for me, she'll be so stoked I'm getting the hell out of her hair."

Case laughed. "Well, no. It's not. But I'm still figuring out how baby to make these steps we're doing. I'm sure it comes as a shock to you, but it's been a while since my last serious relationship. Wasn't sure if asking you to get a house with me was allowed yet. But shit, if your mom's gonna be offering, there's a nice place near where Tree lives…"

"How near?" Jenna pouted. "'Cause I do not want to look him in the eye wondering if he heard us having loud sex. He's scary enough without knowing he knows you've been fucking me all night long."

"Not *that* near!" He nuzzled her hair. "We got time. I ain't never been house hunting before, but I kinda like the idea of buying a lot and building on that. Might give Joker a break from contractors."

"Hm." Jenna bit her lip and tracked her fingers along Case's abs. "You know I travel a lot, right? Like I'm guessing you do too, sometimes. With club stuff. We might end up with a house Ash designed." She trailed off, remembering Joker's words about needing a home to feel like it fit. "I think I'd be okay with a white fence and cottagecore feel. It would fit here, and … and I think I like things that fit here. I just need you and your gorgeous smile, Apollo. Even this misidentified linen closet of an apartment would work. As long as you're here."

"That was *almost* romantic." He chuckled, lifting his palm to her cheek. "You're all I need, too." His mirth faded. "I guess my only request is we stay pretty close to my stepmom. I want you to meet her soon. She'll like you."

Jenna's orgasmic glow vanished. "Oh, God. That means you should meet my mom too, doesn't it?"

"Yeah." Case squeezed her ass, some of his playful expression returning. "I can't wait to meet your mom. Bet she'll love me. I'm totally the kind of guy parents love for their daughters."

"I'll tell her you're in real estate. It'll be fine." Jenna grimaced when his brows rose. "I'm kidding. Mostly."

"Mostly?"

"I, uh, know my parents are going to be rude. But if I'm happy, they'll be happy. Eventually." She cleared her throat. "I can't wait to meet Helen. She sounds lovely. I'm only sorry because, um, your family's all kind and weird and fun. And mine's... They're all the way in Kansas City, so you won't have to see them a lot?" Jenna touched his cheek. "They don't know much of what happened to me back with Ben and Auggie. I don't want them to. I saw the way Bella handled Ash after everything. I don't think I could endure it."

"They don't need to know," Case said. "So far as I see it, we got every reason to look ahead and not behind. But shit, if your mom's anything like Bella, we can go with I'm an engineer. Or an astronaut. Wait. Professional golfer... That's a thing people like, right?" He rolled so that they were on their sides facing one another, though his hand stayed on her hip, his lips brushing against hers. "I'm not gonna let anybody hurt you, Jenna. I don't give a shit who it is. You don't have to endure anything alone again."

"Neither do you." Jenna nuzzled his cheek, laughter banishing her fears. "I'll be right beside you every Thanksgiving when we pretend you're a mechanical engineering student working with Harley Davidson. And every bike run. When I suppose I'll be wearing some ridiculous patch. I hope you know you'll owe me a lot of sex every time that happens."

"Such a hardship," he said, his fingers gliding down to the inside of her thigh, inching higher. "Maybe I should start paying that debt now. Though, I gotta say, thinking of you in leather..." He stroked her, teased her, and then slid his long, perfect finger into her. "I'm sure you won't have to wear it long."

Jenna put her lips against his throat, moaning encouragement as his teasing strokes increased in pressure and speed. Her blood warmed, the ache in her body building with each touch. "I love the way you think."

"You love more than that." His chuckle cut off abruptly as her hand wrapped around his cock. "Jenna, careful."

"Hm?" She flicked a finger over his tip. "Why?"

"Because you keep that up, I'm gonna lose my mind. You okay for that?" he asked, his voice deeper. "I went a little rough on you—"

"I can take another round."

"There's gonna be a lot of rounds, sweetheart." He pushed her down, rolling on top of her with a wicked grin.

"I'm hoping for infinity." That made him laugh again and twitch his fingertips against her clit, sending Jenna's mind spinning.

"My girl gets what she wants," Case whispered as another orgasm claimed her.

The End

EVERNIGHT PUBLISHING ®

www.evernightpublishing.com